FROST AND FLAME

LIV OLSEN

BLACK SWAN
DIGITAL

First published in 2025
Concept created by Black Swan Digital. Developed by Mark Coleman.

1

THE RECKONING

The smell of blood filled the air long before the first scream. Astrid clung to her father's leg, her small fingers digging into the rough leather of his boots. Her breath frosted in the icy wind howling through the towering stones of Skarn's sacred circle. Around her, the crowd pressed close, bundled in thick cloaks of fur and wool, their faces ruddy from the biting cold. The snow beneath their feet was packed hard from the trampling of boots, its pristine white marred by dark streaks of blood that gleamed under the flickering firelight.

"Stay close," her father murmured, his voice a low rumble as he rested a calloused hand on her shoulder. His spear, its iron tip dulled with age, was clutched tightly in his other hand. Frost clung to his dark beard, and the heavy fur-lined cloak draped over his broad shoulders stirred in the wind, the wolf pelt atop it shifting like a living thing.

"I am, Papa," Astrid whispered, her voice trembling despite her best efforts to sound brave. The icy wind bit at her cheeks, turning them raw and red, and she tucked her chin into the high collar of her woolen tunic for warmth. At six years old, she was too young to fully understand The Reckoning, but she was old enough to feel the weight of it, pressing down like the sky itself had grown heavier.

Everywhere she looked, there were men, women, children, all wrapped in layers of coarse wool and patched leather, their cloaks clasped with brooches of iron or, for the wealthier clans, polished bronze. The warriors stood tallest, their chainmail glinting faintly in the firelight, their swords and axes hitched to their belts. But even they looked small beneath the sacred stones, which loomed high above, their jagged surfaces etched with runes that seemed to shift and flicker when Astrid stared too long.

"Mama, why do they have to fight?" Astrid asked, her voice small against the roar of the crowd. The combatants, a boy and girl barely older than her cousins, circled each other in the ring. Their breath pushing from them in harsh, visible bursts. The boy lunged, his blade slashing through the air, and forcing the girl to stumble back. Her boots slipped on the icy ground, but she managed to stay upright.

Astrid's mother, Thora, stood a few paces away, rocking her baby sister, Solveig, in her arms. Snow clung to the hem of her long, fur-trimmed cloak, and her leather boots were caked in mud and frost. Her pale braids, bound tightly against her head, glinted in the firelight, the only bright thing about her solemn, storm-gray features.

"Because the gods demand it, little one," Thora replied, her voice steady despite the wailing wind. Her gaze flicked to the fighters, then to the stone dais where the Jarls sat, draped in layers of fur and gold. Their cloaks, dyed in shades of crimson and deep green, stood out starkly against the muted grays and browns of the common folk.

"But why?" Astrid asked again, louder this time. She flinched as the girl in the ring cried out, her back slamming into the frozen ground. The boy hesitated, and in that moment, the girl's blade flashed upward. A spray of crimson arced across the snow, and the boy crumpled.

The crowd erupted in cheers, voices rising together like a crashing wave. Astrid's stomach turned as she watched two attendants drag the boy's body from the ring. His blood left a slick trail on the frosted ground.

Her father crouched down to her eye level. The wolf pelt of his cloak fell forward, brushing her cheek as he rested a gloved hand on her shoulder. The knuckles on his other hand were white where they gripped his spear.

"Life is harsh, Astrid. Cruel," he said, in his familiar low rumble. His dark eyes, shadowed by the lines of age and worry, searched hers. "The Reckoning teaches us what it takes to survive in a world where the weak are crushed beneath the strong."

Astrid blinked at him, her wide eyes reflecting the glow of the nearby torches. She wanted to believe him, wanted to make sense of the chaos around her, but something in his face stopped her. He didn't believe it. Not really.

"If life is so cruel," she whispered. "Why do we make it crueler?"

For a moment, her father didn't answer. Then he rose, letting his hand fall from her shoulder, and turned back to the circle as though he couldn't bear to meet her gaze.

Her mother's hand, rough but warm, replaced his on Astrid's shoulder. "What your father means..." Thora said quietly, leaning close. The wind caught the edge of her cloak, whipping it around her legs. "Is that the Reckoning isn't just about survival. It's about control."

"Control of what?" Astrid asked, her voice barely audible over the cheers of the crowd as the victorious girl raised her hands, her face a mask of exhaustion and hollow triumph.

"Everything," her mother said, nodding toward the dais

where the Jarls sat, their fur-lined cloaks and golden torcs gleaming like the trappings of gods. "The Jarls demand blood, yes. But only because they tell us the gods demand it."

Astrid shivered, though the cold wasn't the cause. Her small hands twisted in the coarse wool of her tunic as her mother's words settled like stones in her chest. The gods weren't watching, she realized. Not the way everyone claimed. It was the Jarls who sat on their high seats, their gazes cold and unfeeling as the fighters bled for their amusement.

The wind howled through the stones as the next pair of fighters stepped into the ring. Astrid watched as a gangly boy, barely older than the girl who'd just won, hesitated. She saw how his sword shook in his grip. She thought of the boy before him, the lifeless weight of his body as they dragged him away. She thought of her father's words and her mother's, their voices colliding in her mind.

One day, she thought, clenching her small fists, I'll be strong enough to fight. Not for the gods. Not for the Jarls. But for something worth fighting for.

2

THE EDGE OF THE WORLD

Bjornhold was a realm that thrived on the edge of despair, carved out of frost and fire, where every breath was a fight against the relentless cold and every step risked meeting the jaws of death. It was a land that tested its people constantly, shaping them into survivors, warriors, and, just occasionally, legends.

Astrid had heard the stories a thousand times. The history of Bjornhold was whispered around firelight, told at bedsides, heralded in song. It was woven into the fabric of their lives as much as the wool and fur cloaks they wore against the bitter cold. It was a harsh truth, as jagged and unyielding as the cliffs that lined the northern shores. Bjornhold was not meant for the weak. The Norns, those great weavers of fate, had spun this land from threads of suffering, hardship, and blood.

The archipelago stretched across the northern seas like a jagged scar, its islands battered by icy winds and lashed by frigid waves that rose higher than the longhouses of Frostfjord. The sea was a constant companion, both a source of life and a thief of it. On still days, its waters shimmered like liquid steel under the pale light of the sun. But when storms came, as they always did, it raged like an angry god, swallowing ships like candies, and leaving nothing but splintered wood and broken dreams.

The northernmost island of Bjornhold was Frostfjord. Astrid's home. Nestled among towering cliffs and blanketed in snow for most of the year, Frostfjord was a place of raw survival, not comfort. The village itself was a collection of sturdy wooden longhouses with steeply pitched roofs, their walls blackened by smoke from hearth fires that never truly went out. Seal pelts hung drying on racks, and the air carried the scent of salt and brine from the nearby fjord. Life here was hard. Fish, seals, and whatever game could be found in the frozen forests were all that sustained them. But the people of Frostfjord were harder. They had to be.

Astrid had grown up with her father's words etched into her mind: *The frost tests us, but it doesn't define us. We define ourselves.*

To the south, the lands grew warmer, but no kinder. Solfjord's wealth was born of its fertile fields and prosperous trade routes, which left its halls gilded with gold and arrogance. Its warriors were as sharp as their polished blades, their pride as cold as Frostfjord's winters. Solfjord might have seemed a haven to outsiders, but Astrid knew its beauty masked a rot of ambition and treachery. Besides, no clan in Bjornhold was safe from the harsh hand of the Norns, not even the richest.

To the east lay Ironcrag, a land of jagged mountains and unforgiving stone, where snow never fully melted and the air itself seemed to bite. Its people were as hard and unyielding as their land, their warriors raised on blood and bone. They spoke of honor and strength, but it was a brutal kind of honor that left no room for mercy.

And to the west, there was Seastone. The ocean was their lifeblood, their home, and their weapon. They were sailors and raiders, masters of the tides and storms. Their villages clung to the cliffs, and their sleek, deadly ships carried them far beyond

Bjornhold's unforgiving shores. They were clever, cunning, and as unpredictable as the sea they ruled.

These four clans had once been at war, their blood staining the snow and their hatred poisoning the land. But the Reckoning had changed everything.

It was said the gods had decreed the trials centuries ago, when Bjornhold was teetering on the brink of annihilation. The Jarls, who were the leaders of each of the clans, had come together to forge a fragile peace. To ensure the gods' favor and prevent the clans from destroying one another, they created The Reckoning. It was a brutal solution to a brutal problem. Every year, each clan would offer up one boy and one girl, chosen as oathsworns, to compete in the trials. They would fight, bleed, and die on the sacred island of Skarn, until a winner was proclaimed. And all for the promise of prosperity and survival for their people.

And thus it had been, year after year, generation after generation.

Skarn was a place of legend, its beauty hiding its danger. Its towering cliffs, their faces battered by waves and wind, rose like sentinels from the sea. Forests of ancient trees, gnarled and twisted, whispered in voices only the brave, or the desperate, dared to hear. Crumbling temples and weathered statues dotted the landscape, their runes unreadable, their purpose long forgotten. At the center of it all was Norn's Well, a sacred spring said to show glimpses of fate to those bold or foolish enough to drink from its waters.

The Reckoning wasn't just a trial of strength. It was a test of cunning, endurance, and will. Those who survived were hailed as heroes, and saw their families elevated in status. But those who didn't, those whose blood stained the stones of Skarn, were mourned quietly and forgotten quickly. Bjornhold couldn't afford to linger on the dead.

Astrid's mother had always said The Reckoning was a lie, a way for the Jarls to keep their power by convincing the clans they needed the gods' favor. Her father had never said as much, but Astrid had seen the way his jaw clenched when the trials were mentioned, the way his gaze darkened when the Jarls spoke of sacrifice and glory. They didn't believe in The Reckoning, not the way the Jarls did. But belief wasn't necessary. Duty was.

Every oathsworn knew what waited for them on Skarn. Death was all but guaranteed. And yet, year after year, the clans obeyed, their children marching off like lambs to the slaughter.

This was Bjornhold: a land of frost and fire, of gods and mortals, of survival and sacrifice. It was a place where even the strongest could fall, and where the weak never stood a chance. And Astrid Sigurdsdóttir, daughter of Thora, the shieldmaiden, and Sigurd, the fisherman, was about to learn what it meant to live at the edge of the world.

Astrid adjusted her grip on the fishing net, the icy wind tearing at her like a wild thing. Each gust stung her cheeks and sent her long braid whipping against her back. The bitter cold found its way into every gap in her woolen gloves, slicing through her fur-lined cloak and thick tunic as though the layers weren't even there.

She hauled harder on the net, her boots digging into the frost-slicked planks of the weathered boat. The sea fought her for its bounty, every pull of the net a battle against the weight of the catch and the icy waters threatening to tip her balance.

"Careful, girl," her father called from the stern. His voice was roughened by years of shouting into the wind and the wear of a life spent at sea, but it always had a softness for her. He leaned heavily against the tiller, his broad shoulders hunched beneath a cloak of wolf pelt, its grayed fur patchy and thinned with age.

"I've got it, Papa," Astrid replied, her voice muffled against the thick scarf she'd pulled over her mouth to keep the cold from biting her lips. She could feel the weight of his gaze on her as she tugged, his worry unspoken but ever-present. He'd always worried too much, even before her mother had died.

With a final heave, the net spilled onto the deck, releasing a cascade of silver fish that flopped and glinted in the pale light of the winter sun. Astrid staggered back, catching herself against the mast, and exhaled a long, frosty breath as the tension left her arms. She shook out her shoulders, pulling her scarf down to reveal her sharp, angular face with its high cheekbones flushed pink from the cold. Her gray eyes, as cold and stormy as the sea itself, swept over the catch.

"That'll keep us fed through the next storm," her father said, moving toward her with his heavy limp. His boots clunked unevenly on the deck. He peered down at the fish with a critical eye, then nodded in approval. It wasn't much, but it was enough.

Astrid straightened, brushing her gloved hands against her thighs. The thick woolen tunic beneath her cloak was worn and patched, its natural gray fibers rough against her skin. Over it, she wore a leather jerkin, cinched tightly at her waist to keep the wind out, and sturdy fur-lined boots that had been resoled so many times they barely resembled their original design. Her cloak was long and heavy, the edges stained and frayed from years of hard use. Everything about her spoke of practicality and survival. There was no room for vanity in Frostfjord.

Her father moved past her to adjust the net, his movements slow and stiff. Age had taken a toll on him, but grief had taken more. His face, once strong and proud, was weathered and lined, his beard streaked with silver that had appeared long before its time. He hadn't been the same since Thora died, and though he rarely spoke of her, Astrid could see the loss in every downward glance, every quiet sigh.

"You've done well today," he said gruffly, not meeting her eyes as he knelt to check the knots on the net. It was the closest he ever came to praise these days, but Astrid didn't need the words. She could see it in the way his shoulders relaxed, in the small nod of approval he gave her catch.

She turned her gaze toward the bow, where her younger sister, Solveig, sat bundled in layers of fur. Her long legs were stretched awkwardly in front of her, bent at odd angles where the fever had left them twisted and useless. She leaned heavily against the side of the boat, her face pale beneath the hood of her cloak, her breath visible in the icy air.

"You should be resting," Astrid called to her, her voice sharper than she intended. The sight of Solveig always stirred something deep and painful in her chest. A mix of guilt, protectiveness, and helpless anger. She loved her sister fiercely, but it killed her that she couldn't fix what the fever had taken from her.

Solveig glanced up, her lips quirking into a crooked smile. "And miss the show? You're a terrible fisher, Astrid. Someone has to make sure you don't fall in."

Her mouth twitched, fighting a smile. "I'll toss you in the fjord, cripple or not." It was a familiar exchange, one that had started when Solveig first began walking with her cane, her young pride bruised as much as her body was broken. Joking about it had been her way of taking the sting out of it, and Astrid had learned to follow her lead.

Solveig's legs hadn't worked right since the fever. The illness had stolen so much from her. Her strength, her balance, her ability to run and climb and fight. But not her sense of humor. She could walk with the help of a cane, but it was slow, painful work, and the village children who'd once played alongside her now looked at her with pity. That was what Solveig hated most. Not the pain, not the difficulty, but the pity.

Astrid had never pitied her sister. She didn't dare. If she had, it would only make her angrier. Instead, she carried her weight without complaint, helped her when she allowed it, and ignored the bruises on her heart when she refused.

Her father chuckled from the stern, a low, gravelly sound that was rare these days. It was a small thing, but it warmed Astrid more than the layers of wool and fur she wore. She glanced back at him, her heart lifting at the sight of the slight smile tugging at the corner of his mouth. He didn't smile often, not since her mother had died. Thora's death had left him hollow in a way that Astrid couldn't fix, no matter how hard she tried.

As they approached the narrow inlet where their longhouse perched on the cliffs, Astrid's shoulders loosened. The village of Frostfjord was spread across the rocky shoreline, its longhouses huddled against the cliffs like weary travelers sheltering from a storm. Smoke curled from their chimneys, mingling with the scent of salt and brine, but the fires inside could only do so much against the endless winter. Life here was a constant battle against the elements, and the longhouse Astrid shared with her father and sister bore the scars of that fight, with its cracked beams, a sagging roof patched with whatever straw and thatch they could find, and walls that groaned under the weight of snow and ice. It was brutal, but it was their home, and she loved it.

Her father guided the boat into the shallows, the keel scraping against the frozen rocks. Astrid jumped into the knee-deep water, her boots immediately soaking through, and hauled the boat onto the shore. The cold bit at her legs, but she ignored it, her focus on the task at hand.

"Come on, Solveig," she said, offering her arm as her sister struggled to her feet. Her weight was familiar and steady as she leaned against Astrid, and she braced herself, matching her slow, uneven pace as they made their way up the rocky path.

Her father followed behind them, his heavy boots crunching against the ice-crusted ground. The wind howled through the narrow pass, cutting through their cloaks like a blade, but they trudged on, heads down, steps steady. This was life in Frostfjord. Hard, relentless, and unforgiving. But they endured, because they had no choice.

When they reached the longhouse, Astrid paused with her hand resting on the worn wooden door. She glanced at her father, but he eased past her, his face etched with the same weariness she felt in her bones. Solveig leaned on her cane, her sharp eyes flicking to Astrid's.

"You're staring again," she said, softly.

"Am I?"

"You do that when you're thinking too much," she teased. "Try not thinking for a change. It might suit you."

Astrid shook her head, pushing the door open to reveal the familiar warmth of home. The hearth still held the faint glow of embers from the morning fire, and the room was cluttered with the tools of survival. Nets and spears, pots and furs. It wasn't much, but it was theirs. And Strid increasingly felt it was hers to protect.

3

THE CHOOSING FEAST

The wind had softened, but the air was no less biting as the village of Frostfjord swelled with strangers, their cloaks heavy with snow and their faces half-hidden behind scarves. The Choosing Feast had come again, and with it, the weight of the gods' demands pressed down on every soul in the village.

Astrid stood at the edge of the crowd that gathered in the center of Frostfjord's square, her arms crossed tightly over her chest to keep the cold from sinking in. The smell of smoke and pine hung heavy in the air, mingling with the faint, metallic tang of blood from the recent butchering of the feast's animals. Long wooden tables sagged beneath the weight of roasted fish, venison, and mead barrels, but no one dared eat yet. The food wasn't the purpose of this gathering.

The Choosing was.

The square was ringed by torches, their flames flickering weakly against the cold. Above the crowd, banners of the four clans swayed in the wind. Frostfjord's silver wolf, Solfjord's crimson falcon, Ironcrag's black bear, and Seastone's sapphire serpent. Each was a reminder of the fragile peace that bound them, and the blood that had been shed to achieve it.

Astrid could feel the tension in the air like a coiled rope, ready to snap. She glanced at her father, who stood just behind her. His wolf pelt cloak shifted as he folded his arms, his face as unreadable as the gray cliffs that loomed above them. Beside her, Solveig leaned on her cane, her pale features tense but determined.

"You should be home," Astrid murmured, her voice low enough that only Solveig could hear.

"And miss all the excitement?" she shot back, her lips quirking into a faint smile. "I wouldn't dream of it."

Astrid narrowed her eyes. "You shouldn't be standing this long. Your legs..."

"...are none of your concern," Solveig interrupted, though her tone was more weary than harsh. "I'm fine, Astrid. Please. Just let me feel part of it."

"You're not fine," she muttered, but she didn't push further. Solveig was stubborn, and Astrid had learned long ago when to pick her battles.

The crowd hushed as a figure ascended the raised platform at the center of the square. The Völva.

Astrid stiffened as the seeress stepped into view. Her dark robes billowed in the wind, and the intricate runes embroidered along the hems caught the torchlight as though alive. Her face was hidden beneath the shadow of her hood, but the greatness of her presence was undeniable. The staff she carried, crowned with the gnarled antlers of a stag, struck the wooden planks of the platform with every step, each strike sharp and deliberate.

"Bjornhold," the Völva began. Her voice was low and rasping, carrying across the square despite the wind. It was a voice that commanded attention, ancient and unwavering. "Once again, we gather to honor the Reckoning. The gods demand strength. They demand courage. They demand blood."

Astrid's stomach turned, the familiar words settling like

stones in her chest. Around her, the crowd stood silent, their faces a mix of reverence and fear.

The Völva raised her staff, and the light of the torches seemed to catch on the runes carved into its length, making them shimmer like frost on iron. "Tonight, we will choose the oathsworns," she continued. "Two from each clan. Those who will journey to Skarn and prove their worth to the gods. Those who will fight for the honor of their people."

Astrid felt the weight of her father's gaze on her. She didn't dare look at him. She kept her eyes fixed on the platform, her hands fidgeting beneath the folds of her cloak.

"Step forward," the Völva commanded, her gaze turning to the Ironcrag delegation.

Astrid hadn't caught the names, but two figures now emerged from the cluster of Ironcrag warriors. First, a boy with shoulders like a bear, followed by a girl whose braided hair gleamed like dark steel in the torchlight. They ascended the platform without hesitation, their faces set in grim determination.

Next came Seastone. A wiry boy with sharp, foxlike features was called forward first, followed by a girl with silver clasps on her cloak. She looked too gentle for this. Her pale face wary but watchful. Both shared the same fluid movements, almost casual, as if the Reckoning were just another stage in their developing lives.

Then the seeress moved on to the Solfjord clan. Their oathsworns were dressed in cloaks of deep crimson, their boots polished to a shine. Astrid watched as they climbed the platform with the confidence of those who had been preparing for this their entire lives.

Finally, the Völva turned to Frostfjord.

The air grew heavier, the silence deeper. Astrid felt her

father shift behind her, his hand brushing her shoulder as though to steady her. Or himself.

"First, the girl," the Völva said, her hooded gaze sweeping over the Frostfjord crowd.

Astrid's breath caught as the seeress's gaze lingered near her, then moved on. Relief flickered through her chest. Until the name was spoken.

"Solveig Sigurdsdóttir."

The world stopped. A cry of shock went up in the crowd.

Astrid's head snapped toward the square, her breath catching in her throat. The Völva's voice was calm, unyielding, as she stood once more on the platform, her staff raised.

"Solveig Sigurdsdóttir," she repeated.

Astrid's heart pounded in her ears as she turned to her closest friend and ally, Leif, who looked just as stunned as she felt. The crowd began to stir again, murmurs of confusion rippling through Frostfjord's people.

"No," Astrid whispered, her voice breaking.

Her legs moved before her mind could catch up. She pushed through the crowd, her cloak whipping behind her as she made her way back toward the square. Solveig was still standing where she'd left her, her cane trembling in her hand, her face pale and stricken.

"No," Astrid said again, louder this time, as she reached her sister. She grabbed Solveig's arm, her grip firm despite the panic clawing at her chest. "This isn't right. There's been a mistake."

The Völva's hooded gaze turned toward her, and for a moment, Astrid thought she saw something flicker beneath the shadow of her hood. Was that pity?

"The gods make no mistakes," the Völva said.

The square had fallen into silence, but Astrid's pulse roared like the storm-churned sea in her ears. The cold was a distant thing now, fading beneath the heat of her blood as her sister's words echoed over and over in her mind: *"Let me be part of this."*

But she couldn't.

Astrid stepped forward, planting herself between Solveig and the platform, her hands trembling at her sides. The torches flickered in the wind, their light catching on the Völva's staff as she turned her hooded gaze toward Astrid.

"No," Astrid said, her voice rising above the whispers that rippled through the crowd. "You can't take her."

The seeress tilted her head, the shadow of her hood obscuring her expression. The runes carved into her staff seemed to glimmer faintly, catching the firelight.

"The gods have spoken, Astrid Sigurdsdóttir," she said, her voice calm but implacable, carrying the weight of inevitability.

"The gods are wrong," Astrid shot back, her words sharp and desperate. Her heart was hammering in her chest, each beat a painful reminder of what would happen if she stayed silent.

Behind her, she heard the faint click of Solveig's cane against the frozen ground. "Astrid..."

"No," she said again, her voice cracking as she turned to face him. The sight of her sister's trembling hand broke something inside Astrid. Her face was pale, her sharp features drawn with exhaustion and tension, and the way she leaned on her cane, knuckles white against the wood, made her stomach twist. She wanted to reach out, to steady her, but her hands felt frozen at her sides.

"You can't go," Astrid said, her voice softening, though the desperation in it was unmistakable. "You won't survive, Solveig. You know that."

For a moment, her eyes flashed with anger. "Of course I know that," she hissed. "Do you think I don't know exactly what this means?"

She couldn't find the words to respond, so she just shook her head.

Solveig leaned forward, her own voice softening. "If I don't go, they'll take someone else, Astrid. Someone who doesn't deserve it." Her eyes searched Astrid's, pleading for her to understand. "This is the only thing I can do. Let me do it."

"No," Astrid said, her voice firmer now. She stepped closer, lowering her voice so only she could hear. "You don't have to prove anything to anyone, Solveig. Not to them, not to the gods, and certainly not to me. You've battled enough." Her voice cracked slightly, and she swallowed hard, forcing herself to keep her composure. "I won't let them take you."

Solveig's mouth opened as though to argue, but Astrid didn't give her the chance. She turned back to the Völva, her shoulders squared, her chin lifting as she stepped forward.

"I'll take her place," she said, her voice ringing out across the square.

The murmurs swelled instantly, rising like a tide. Astrid could feel the weight of the crowd's stares, the shock and disbelief radiating from every direction. Her father's hand gripped her shoulder for a brief moment, but then it fell away, leaving her alone in the cold.

The Völva tilted her head again, her staff striking the wooden platform with a deliberate, echoing *thud*. "You would defy the gods' will?"

"I would protect my sister," Astrid said, her voice steady now, though her chest felt as though it might collapse under the pressure. She lifted her chin higher, meeting the shadowed gaze of the seeress. "I volunteer. Take me instead."

The whispers grew louder, and Astrid caught fragments of their words. "Madness", "honorable", "reckless". She didn't care. She stood her ground, her gray eyes fixed on the Völva.

Behind her, Solveig's cane thudded against the ground as she moved toward her. "Astrid, stop," she said, her voice raw with desperation. "Please don't. You don't have to do this..."

"I do," she interrupted, her voice firm. She turned to Solveig, her expression softening as she reached out to grip her shoulders. "You know I do."

Solveig's lips pressed tight, holding in her protests. Her eyes glistened with unshed tears. "Astrid..."

"Enough," she said, shaking her head. "It's done."

The Völva's staff struck the platform again, silencing the crowd. "So be it," she intoned, her voice resonating with finality. "Let it be known that Astrid Sigurdsdóttir has taken her sister's place. The gods have accepted her offering."

Astrid exhaled slowly, the tension in her chest loosening for the briefest of moments before it was replaced by the weight of her choice. She released Solveig's shoulders and turned back to the platform, ignoring the burning stares of the crowd.

"And now, the male oathsworn of Frostfjord," the Völva announced.

Astrid's heart sank as the seeress's gaze swept over the crowd again. She barely registered the murmurs until the name rang out.

"Thorwulf Haldorsson."

The crowd parted as Thorwulf stepped forward, his fur-lined cloak billowing behind him like a banner. He moved with a confidence that bordered on arrogance, his broad shoulders and tall frame impossible to miss. His dark hair, tied back with a leather cord, caught the torchlight, and his sharp features held a smirk that only deepened as he climbed the platform.

Astrid watched him. He was everything she wasn't. He oozed confidence and charisma, and he seemed untouchable. She had seen him occasionally in the village, but she barely knew him. There was something about his family that kept them on the outskirts, as though they were too good for the rest of them.

"Well, this is shaping up to be an interesting Reckoning," he said, his voice carrying easily over the murmurs. He glanced toward Astrid, his dark eyes locking onto hers. "Isn't it, Sigurdsdóttir?"

She didn't respond. She couldn't. The weight of her decision was pressing too heavily on her chest.

As the Völva struck her staff one final time, silencing the crowd, Thorwulf's smirk softened into something unreadable.

"Don't worry," he said softly, his voice low enough that only she could hear. "That was brave of you. But bravery only goes so far. I'll watch your back. If you can keep up."

Astrid turned away, scanning the crowd from the high platform. Finally, she found Solveig in the chaos, her pale face drawn with worry and anger. A single tear slid down her cheek.

Astrid felt the weight of Thorwulf's gaze on her, but she didn't turn around. She couldn't afford to. There was no room for regret now.

Instead, she let the Völva's voice wash over her as the ceremony continued, though she barely registered the words. Her thoughts were elsewhere, swirling with the reality of what she'd done.

The Reckoning. Skarn. Death.

When the final names were sworn in as the oathsworns and the Völva descended from the platform, the crowd began to disperse. Frostfjord's delegation moved in a slow, somber procession toward the long tables where the feast awaited, but Astrid didn't follow. She slipped through the edges of the crowd, her footsteps silent against the snow-packed ground.

She wasn't sure where she was going until she saw him.

Leif stood near the edge of the square, leaning against one of the towering wooden pillars that framed the main entrance to the village. His arms were crossed over his chest, his hood pushed back to reveal dark blond hair that was tousled by the wind. His expression was grim, though it softened slightly when he saw her.

"You're a fool," he said, his voice low as she approached.

Astrid rolled her eyes, though her lips twitched into something close to a smile. "Good evening to you too, Leif."

"I mean it," he said, stepping forward. "What were you thinking, Astrid? Volunteering? You know what happens to the oathsworns."

"I know exactly what happens," she shot back, her tone sharper than she intended. She pulled her cloak tighter around her shoulders, the cold finding its way into the cracks of her resolve. "But what was I supposed to do, Leif? Stand there while my sister's name was called?"

"That's not the point," Leif said, his voice dropping into something softer, something that hurt more than his anger. "You're not responsible for fixing every mistake, Astrid. You don't have to carry this alone."

"Don't I?" she said, turning to face him fully. The torchlight caught in her gray eyes, making them glint like steel. "My mother is gone. My father can barely hold himself together most days. And Solveig..." She stopped, and looked away.

Leif hesitated, his expression caught between frustration and something gentler. He stepped closer and lowered his voice. "You think I don't know what you've taken on? I see it, Astrid. Every day. You've done more than anyone should have to, and still..." He trailed off, running a hand through his hair. "But this? The Reckoning? You're throwing yourself into the fire."

She flinched at the word, but she didn't deny it. Instead, she shook her head. "It doesn't matter now, does it? I made my choice."

Leif exhaled slowly, his breath fogging in the icy air. For a moment, neither of them spoke. The silence stretched between them like a chasm.

"I'm going with you," he said finally, breaking the stillness.

Astrid blinked, startled. "What?"

"I'll find a way," he said, his tone resolute. "I'll make sure you're not alone out there."

She stared at him, her heart lurching in her chest. For a moment, she didn't see the boy who used to race her across the cliffs or the young man who had always seemed to find her in the village no matter where she was. She saw someone who would break himself for her if she let him.

"You can't," she said, her voice barely above a whisper.

"Why not?"

"Because I need you here," she said, meeting his gaze. "For Solveig. For my father. Someone has to keep them safe. You're the closest thing to family they'll have."

Leif's jaw tightened, and she could see the protest rising in his throat. But before he could speak, a voice cut through the cold air like a knife.

"Astrid Sigurdsdóttir," the Völva called. "Your feast awaits."

4

ASTRID'S DECISION

The square had deepened into silence, but the whispers of Frostfjord's winds carried with them the weight of centuries, of sacrifice and unspoken grief. The torches burned low, their flames barely flickering as if even they understood the gravity of what had unfolded. Astrid stood alone at the edge of the longhouse, her breath rising in slow, clouded plumes before vanishing into the biting air. Her nails dug into her palms as if anchoring her to the moment.

The Choosing Feast was over, but the consequences of her choice were only just beginning. She couldn't stop replaying the scene in her mind: Solveig's pale, drawn face, the murmurs of the crowd, the Völva's final words ringing with an inevitability she couldn't escape. The frost beneath her boots felt steadier than her resolve, and yet, there was no turning back.

The creak of the longhouse door behind her pulled her from her thoughts. Heavy boots thudded against the frozen ground, and the uneven rhythm was unmistakable. Astrid didn't need to look to know it was her father. His steps had always carried the weight of grief, each one heavier than the last since her mother's death.

He stopped beside her, his silhouette sharp against the pale glow of the moonlight reflecting off the cliffs. Sigurd hadn't been the same in years. The broad, strong man she remembered from her childhood had been eroded by loss, his shoulders stooped beneath the weight of a burden he never spoke of. His once-thick beard, streaked with silver now, was unkempt, and his hands were always busy repairing nets, sharpening tools, anything to keep from stillness.

"You've barely said a word," Astrid said, her voice quiet but sharp, the tremor in it betraying her anger. She turned to face him, the cold stinging her cheeks. "Not when Solveig was called. Not when I volunteered. Nothing."

Sigurd didn't meet her eyes. Instead, he stared out toward the cliffs, his face shadowed and unreadable. "What do you want me to say?" he asked, his voice low and tired.

Astrid clenched her jaw, the tension radiating through her body. "I don't know. Maybe that I'm not just another offering for the gods to take. Maybe that it matters to you whether I come back or not."

Her father's shoulders stiffened as he exhaled a long, slow breath. "You think it doesn't matter to me?" he said finally, his voice rough. "You think I haven't already lost enough?"

"I'm not her," Astrid snapped, her voice breaking. "I'm not Mama. You can't just shut yourself off because it hurts too much to care."

Sigurd's gaze snapped to hers, and for the first time in years, she saw the fire that had once made him the strongest man in Frostfjord. "You think I don't care?" he said, his voice trembling with restrained anger. "Every day I look at you and Solveig, and all I can see is what I couldn't save. I cared too much, Astrid. And it cost me everything."

The words hit her like a blow, stealing the breath from her

lungs. For a moment, she could only stare at him, her chest tight with a thousand unspoken arguments.

"It didn't cost you everything," she said softly, her voice trembling. "You still have us. But you..." she shook her head, tears burning in her eyes. "You won't even fight for us."

Her father's face crumpled, the anger draining from his expression to leave him hollow and broken.

"What do you want me to do?" he asked, his voice barely above a whisper. "Fight the gods? Fight the clans? You made your choice, Astrid. Just like your mother made hers."

The mention of her mother felt like a knife twisting in her chest, but she didn't let it show. Instead, she turned away, her voice quiet but firm.

"Goodbye, Papa. Take care of Solveig for me."

He didn't stop her as she walked away, and that hurt more than his words ever could.

Astrid didn't know how far she walked before she found herself at the edge of the cliffs, the sound of the waves crashing far below echoing in the stillness of the night. The air here was sharper, cleaner, and the stars above seemed closer, though their cold light offered no comfort.

"You always come here when you're brooding," a voice said softly behind her.

She turned to find Leif standing a few paces away, his hands tucked into the folds of his thick wool cloak. His broad frame was silhouetted against the torchlight, and his blond hair hung loose and wind-tousled around his sharp, angular face. His jawline was strong, his nose slightly crooked from a fight he never talked about, and his pale blue eyes held a depth that spoke of years of hardship. He looked like he belonged in an epic tale, like a warrior of legend. But the truth was far more complicated.

Leif had been her closest friend for as long as she could remember. He had grown up in a family of hunters, scraping by on whatever pelts and meat they could trade. His mother had died when he was young, leaving his father bitter and cold, and Leif had carried the weight of his family's survival on his shoulders ever since. He'd always been resourceful, clever, but there was a sadness in him that Astrid couldn't ignore. It was a sadness and loss that mirrored her own.

"I needed to breathe," Astrid said, her voice hollow.

Leif stepped closer, his boots crunching softly on the frost-covered ground. His movements were deliberate, and his presence solid in a way that steadied her even when she didn't know she needed it to. "I brought you something."

She frowned as he pulled a small leather cord from his pocket, a rune-carved pendant dangling from it. The wood was dark and polished, the runes etched deep into its surface.

"What is it?" she asked, taking the necklace as he held it out to her.

"A ward," he said simply. "For protection. My mother used to carve them." His voice softened, his gaze dropping to the pendant. "She said they kept the bad spirits away."

Astrid ran her thumb over the runes. "Leif..."

"You don't have to say anything," he interrupted, his voice steady but soft. "I just... I couldn't let you leave without something to remind you that you're not alone. That you have people who care about you. No matter what happens."

His words were like a knife to her resolve, cutting through the armor she'd built around herself. She looked up at him, her throat tight, and for a moment, she saw past the stoic facade he always wore. He was scared for her, for Solveig, for what would come next. There was something in his that made her heart ache.

"You can't make promises like that," she said, her voice cracking. "Not with what's coming."

Leif's gaze didn't waver. "Then I'll make this one instead: I'll look after Solveig. If you don't come back, I'll take care of her. I swear it."

Her breath hitched, and she had to look away, the tears threatening to spill over. "That's not fair," she whispered.

"I don't care if it's fair," he said, his voice rough with emotion. "It's the truth. You don't have to carry everything, Astrid. Let me carry this."

She closed her eyes, clutching the pendant tightly in her hand. The ache in her chest was almost unbearable, but she forced herself to breathe, to push it down. When she opened her eyes, she met his gaze, her lips trembling with the words she couldn't say.

"Thank you," she said instead.

Leif nodded, stepping back as the wind whipped between them. For a moment, it felt as though the distance between them was more than just physical, as though the choices they had made had placed them on opposite sides of a chasm neither could cross.

"Goodbye, Leif," she said softly, her voice carrying on the wind.

His expression broke for the briefest of moments, and then he nodded again. "Goodbye, Astrid."

As she turned and walked away, the pendant clutched tightly in her hand, she didn't look back. She couldn't.

The weight of the world was waiting for her, and she had no room left for regret.

5

THE LONGSHIP TO SKARN

The longship groaned as it carved through the churning waves, the sea stretching out like an endless sheet of cold iron. The air grew sharper with every passing league, the salt carried on the wind biting against Astrid's face until her skin felt raw. The prow of the ship was shaped like a snarling wolf, its red-painted eyes glaring forward. Its gaze seemed to taunt her, as if daring her to face what lay ahead.

Astrid clutched the ship's rail. Her gloved hands gripped the frost-slick wood as though it might keep her grounded. Behind her, Frostfjord's jagged cliffs had shrunk to little more than a distant smudge on the horizon, swallowed by the endless expanse of the sea. The realization struck her with the force of a storm: there was no going back.

She told herself she didn't regret her choice. Solveig would live. That was all that mattered. But as the icy wind howled around her and the longship creaked beneath her feet, the reality of what she'd done began to settle over her like the weight of the sea itself. She wasn't going home. Not to her father's worn and smoky longhouse. Not to Solveig's quiet, determined presence. She had volunteered to face the gods' test, and deep down, she didn't know if she was strong enough to survive it.

"Second thoughts already?"

Astrid turned her head sharply, finding Thorwulf leaning against one of the ship's mast supports, his ever-present smirk curling his lips. The wind tousled his dark hair, strands escaping the leather cord that tied it back, and his broad shoulders seemed immune to the cold. Even his fur-lined cloak barely moved in the breeze. He looked, as always, infuriatingly confident. Like a man who had never questioned his place in the world or his right to be there.

"I have nothing to say to you," Astrid replied, her tone sharper than the wind.

Thorwulf raised an eyebrow, his smirk deepening. "You're awfully touchy for someone who just signed up to become a living sacrifice."

"Is there a point to this, or are you just here to be insufferable?"

Thorwulf chuckled, the sound low and easy, as if her anger amused him. He stepped closer, resting his forearms on the rail beside her. "You can pretend all you want, Sigurdsdóttir, but you're scared. I can see it."

Astrid stiffened. "Of course I'm scared," she snapped. "Only an idiot wouldn't be."

"Good," he said simply, his grin softening into something less mocking. "Fear means you're paying attention."

She turned to him, her gray eyes narrowing. "What about you? Are you paying attention? Or do you think you can swagger your way through the Reckoning like you do everything else?"

Thorwulf's smirk didn't falter, but a flicker of something darker and sharper crossed his eyes.

"You think I don't know what's waiting for us on Skarn?" he asked, his tone quieter now. "I've spent my whole life fighting, Astrid. This isn't any different. You survive, or you don't."

His words sent a chill down her spine, not because they surprised her, but because she knew he was right. She turned back to the horizon, her gaze locking on the distant shape of Skarn.

The island loomed ahead, its jagged cliffs rising like broken teeth from the sea. Mist clung to its edges, swirling in eerie patterns that seemed to shift and writhe as the ship drew closer. The landscape was both beautiful and bleak. It was a stark reminder of the gods' indifference. Patches of snow and ice clung stubbornly to the rocky outcroppings, while twisted, ancient pines dotted the higher peaks. The shoreline was jagged and unwelcoming, the kind of place where even the most skilled sailors would think twice about landing.

The sea around them had grown darker, its once-steely surface now almost black. Astrid could see the reflections of the gray sky rippling on the water, distorted by the wind and the movement of the ship. The air felt heavier here, as though the island itself carried the weight of centuries of blood and sacrifice.

"I see why they call it the gods' crucible," Thorwulf said, his voice cutting through the wind.

Astrid didn't reply. Her mind was racing, her thoughts spiraling as she imagined what awaited them on that forsaken island. She had grown up hearing stories of Skarn. They had listened to tales of the Trials, of the oathsworns who had never returned, of the way the island seemed alive, as though it were testing them just as much as the gods were.

The sound of boots on the deck drew her attention, and she turned to see Jorunn approaching. The Rite of Passage Guide moved with purpose, her lean frame cutting through the wind like an arrow. Her dark hair, braided tightly against her head, gleamed faintly in the dim light, and her piercing blue eyes swept over Astrid and Thorwulf with a mixture of scrutiny and disdain.

"Getting acquainted, are we?" Jorunn asked, her voice sharp.

Thorwulf straightened, his smirk returning. "Just exchanging strategies," he said. "You know, bonding as teammates."

Jorunn's gaze flicked to him, unimpressed. "Save the charm, Haldorsson. It won't help you where you're going."

Thorwulf chuckled, leaning back against the rail. "You keep saying that. Starting to think you don't like me, Jorunn."

"And I'm starting to think you're as insufferable as you look," Jorunn shot back without missing a beat. Her gaze shifted to Astrid, and her expression hardened. "Sigurdsdóttir, is it? The one who volunteered?"

Astrid nodded, bracing herself.

Jorunn studied her for a long moment, her sharp eyes narrowing. "What exactly do you bring to the Trials? What skills do you have that'll keep you alive?"

The question hit Astrid like a blow. She hadn't thought about it in those terms. She had been so focused on protecting Solveig, on sparing her from this fate, that she hadn't stopped to consider her own survival. What did she bring to the table?

"I'm resourceful," she said finally, though the words felt weak even as she spoke them.

Jorunn's expression didn't change. "Resourceful," she repeated flatly. "Let's hope that's enough."

Thorwulf snorted, and Astrid shot him a glare.

"And you, Haldorsson?" Jorunn asked, turning her sharp gaze on him.

Thorwulf's grin widened, and he spread his arms. "Strength, charm, good looks… take your pick."

Jorunn rolled her eyes. "Strength, maybe. The rest won't matter on Skarn."

Astrid barely heard them. Her gaze was fixed on the island ahead, the ache in the pit of her stomach growing with every passing moment. The wind howled around them, and the sea churned beneath the ship, but all she could think about was the stories she had heard of Skarn. They were all stories of betrayal, of blood, of trials designed to break even the strongest.

She didn't regret her choice. But she wasn't ready to die.

The longship rocked as the sea grew rougher. Its prow slicing through the swelling waves and the carved wolf head at the bow seemed to glare at the horizon, its red eyes glinting faintly in the light of the rising sun. The boat smelled of damp wood, salt, and the faint metallic tang of rusted nails. Its deck was crowded but organized, with every crate of provisions, every coil of rope, and every weapon stored with precision, as though someone had prepared for every eventuality.

Astrid had claimed a spot near the stern, keeping her back to the mast and her eyes on the horizon. The icy wind whipped around her, tugging at her fur-lined cloak, but she barely noticed the cold. Her thoughts churned as violently as the sea, a tangle of fear, doubt, and the heavy realization of what she had agreed to face.

Thorwulf, of course, seemed oblivious to any sense of tension. He leaned casually against the rail a few feet away, his dark eyes watching her with a mixture of amusement and curiosity.

"You know," his voice carried easily over the sound of the waves. "You might feel better if you actually said something. Or are you planning to brood your way through the entire journey?"

Astrid shot him a glare. "So what if I am?"

Thorwulf grinned, pushing away from the rail and taking a

step closer. "Brooding suits you, Sigurdsdóttir. Very dramatic. But I think you'd look better smiling."

"Do you ever stop talking?" she snapped, her patience already worn thin by the constant rocking of the boat and the weight of her own thoughts.

"Not when there's someone worth talking to," he said with a wink, leaning against the mast beside her.

Astrid let out an exasperated sigh, turning her gaze back to the horizon. The cliffs of Skarn loomed closer now, their jagged edges catching the pale light. The island seemed almost alive, with its peaks shrouded in mist that swirled and shifted like restless spirits.

"You're wasting your time," she said flatly.

"Am I?" Thorwulf asked, his tone still annoyingly light.

"Yes." She glanced at him, her gray eyes cold and unyielding. "I didn't come here to make friends."

Thorwulf's grin faltered for a moment, and she caught a flicker of a frown. It was gone almost as quickly as it had appeared, replaced by his usual smirk.

"Good," he said, his voice softer now. "Because neither did I. I came to win."

For a moment, the air between them was heavy with unspoken tension. Astrid could see the cracks in his bravado, the faint shadows beneath his eyes, the way his grin didn't quite reach the corners of his mouth. He was hiding something, though she couldn't begin to guess what it was.

"You're annoying," she said finally, turning back to the horizon.

"I know," Thorwulf replied, his grin returning. "But admit it, you'd miss me if I wasn't here."

She snorted, shaking her head. "Don't count on it."

But deep down, though she would never admit it, she was grateful for the distraction. Thorwulf's constant chatter and teasing kept her from sinking too deeply into her own thoughts, and from dwelling on the terrifying reality of what lay ahead.

Jorunn approached from the center of the boat, her sharp eyes scanning the horizon before landing on the two of them. "Enjoying yourselves?" she asked, her tone dry.

Thorwulf straightened, throwing her a lazy grin. "Always, Jorunn. Care to join us?"

The Guide's expression didn't change. "You might want to save your energy, Haldorsson. You'll need it."

Thorwulf shrugged, leaning back against the mast. "I've got plenty to spare."

Jorunn ignored him, her gaze shifting to Astrid. "And you, Sigurdsdóttir? Are you ready for what's coming?"

Astrid met her gaze. "I'll survive."

Jorunn raised an eyebrow, as if unconvinced. "We'll see."

She moved past them, barking orders to the oarsmen as the ship began to crest another wave.

The landscape around them had changed as they neared Skarn. The once-open sea had narrowed, the waves growing choppier as the wind funneled through rocky outcroppings that jutted from the water like the ribs of some ancient, sunken beast. Beneath the islands cliffs with their jagged edges capped with frost and snow, ancient pine trees clung stubbornly to the rock, their twisted branches swaying in the wind.

In the distance, Astrid could see the remnants of what must have been a long-abandoned settlement. Crumbling stone walls and broken towers rose from the cliffs. Dark shapes that were barely distinguishable through the swirling mist. The sight sent a shiver down her spine.

"This place has some stories," Thorwulf said, his voice softer now as he followed her gaze.

"Stories?" Astrid asked, glancing at him.

He nodded, his grin gone, replaced by a more serious

expression. "Skarn isn't just a testing ground. It's cursed. They say the island itself is alive, that it knows what you fear, what you're hiding, and it uses that against you."

Astrid swallowed hard, her grip tightening on the rail. "Do you believe that?"

Thorwulf hesitated, his dark eyes distant. "I believe there's more to this place than we're told."

His words hung in the air between them, heavy and unsettling. Astrid looked away, her gaze returning to the island. The cliffs were closer now, the waves crashing against their base with a ferocity that seemed almost unnatural.

The longship lurched suddenly, the impact of a wave sending Astrid stumbling. Thorwulf caught her arm, steadying her before she could fall.

"Careful," he said, his grin returning, though it didn't quite reach his eyes. "Wouldn't want you falling overboard before the fun even starts."

Astrid pulled her arm free, her cheeks flushing. "I'm fine."

"Of course you are," Thorwulf said, stepping back with a mock bow.

The boat began to slow as they approached a narrow inlet, the oarsmen working in unison to guide them through the jagged rocks. The tension on the ship was palpable now, the air heavy with the weight of what was to come. Astrid could feel it in the way the crew moved, their usually steady rhythm less uncertain.

She took a deep breath, forcing herself to focus. She had made her choice. She would have to find a way to survive.

But as the cliffs of Skarn towered above them, their jagged edges disappearing into the mist, she couldn't shake the feeling that she was stepping into the jaws of a beast that was already waiting to devour her.

6

SKARN'S WELCOME

The longship scraped against the jagged rocks of Skarn's shore, the sound sharp and grating, cutting through the already tense air. The oarsmen worked quickly, securing the boat against the pull of the restless sea. Every movement was precise and practiced, as if they had done this many times before. They probably had. These oathsworns were not the first to step onto this cursed island, and they would not be the last.

Astrid lingered at the edge of the ship, her hands gripping the rail. The island loomed before her, bleak and unwelcoming. Mist clung to the shoreline like a living thing, twisting around the jagged rocks and ancient ruins that jutted from the earth like broken teeth. The cliffs rose high into the sky, their jagged peaks crowned with frost and snow, casting long shadows over the narrow inlet where the ship had landed.

The air was heavy here, thick with the scent of salt and something metallic and bitter that made Astrid's stomach twist. The gods were watching; she could feel it in the weight of the wind, the way it seemed to carry whispers that she couldn't quite hear.

Thorwulf jumped down onto the rocky shore, his boots

crunching against the frost-coated stones. He turned back to her, his dark eyes glinting with amusement. "What's the matter, Sigurdsdóttir? Second thoughts already?"

Astrid shot him a glare. "I'm fine."

"Sure you are," he said, his tone laced with sarcasm.

She ignored him, hoisting her pack over her shoulder before climbing down after him. The rocks shifted beneath her boots, slick with ice and seawater. Around her, the other oathsworns were gathering, their faces paler and more drawn than she'd seen any of them look so far. No one spoke; the only sounds were the crash of waves against the cliffs and the low, mournful wail of the wind.

Jorunn stood near the edge of the group, her sharp eyes scanning the oathsworns as they arrived. "Move quickly," she barked. "The Jarls are waiting."

Astrid adjusted her cloak, pulling it tighter against the biting wind as she followed Thorwulf and the others up the rocky incline. The path was narrow and uneven, winding through a landscape that seemed torn straight from an old skald's tale.

The ruins of Skarn rose around them, ancient and foreboding. Massive stone statues lined the path, their faces weathered and cracked but still imposing. Astrid recognized some of them as figures from the old stories her mother used to tell. There was Odin, with his single eye carved with a watchful intensity. Freyja, fierce and unyielding, her stone features softened only by the faint traces of what might have once been a smile. Loki, his grin sly and mocking, as though he were laughing at all of them.

But there were other statues too, ones Astrid didn't recognize. Their faces were strange, alien, their features twisted into expressions of pain or rage. She shivered, pulling her cloak tighter as the group pressed on.

The temple came into view at the top of the incline, its

crumbling pillars reaching toward the sky like skeletal fingers. The building was massive, carved from dark stone that seemed to absorb the light rather than reflect it. Its roof was partially collapsed, and the jagged edges that remained were dusted with snow. Its walls were etched with runes so ancient that their meanings had been lost to time.

Inside, the air was even colder than it had been outside, and Astrid felt the chill seep into her bones as she stepped onto the stone floor. Torches lined the walls, their flames flickering weakly against the gloom.

At the far end of the room stood the Jarls and the Völva.

The Jarls were a formidable presence, each one representing a different clan. Jarl Ingvar of Frostfjord was a tall, broad-shouldered man with a silver-streaked beard and piercing gray eyes. His cloak was made from the pelt of a massive wolf, its head resting on his shoulder, its glassy eyes staring out at the room. Beside him stood Jarl Sigrid of Solfjord, her crimson cloak shimmering faintly in the torchlight. Her golden hair was braided into a crown, and her expression was sharp and calculating. Jarl Bjorn of Ironcrag was a hulking figure, his arms crossed over his chest. His bear-pelt cloak looked as though it had been freshly skinned, the claws still attached. Finally, there was Jarl Ingrid of Seastone, her dark blue cloak embroidered with silver waves. Her hair was tied back in a simple braid, and her face was calm and impassive, though her eyes missed nothing.

The Völva stood at the center of the group, her dark robes billowing as though caught in a wind no one else could feel. Her staff, crowned with those gnarled antlers, struck the stone floor with a soft *thud* as she stepped forward. The runes carved into its length shimmered faintly in the torchlight, their meanings just out of reach.

"Welcome to Skarn," the Völva said, her voice low and

resonant. It echoed off the stone walls, filling the room as though it carried the weight of the gods themselves.

Astrid forced herself to stand tall, though the chill in the air seemed to wrap around her like a vice.

"The Reckoning awaits. This is not merely a test of strength," the Völva continued, her gaze sweeping over the oathsworns. "It is a sacrifice. The gods demand proof of your worth, of your courage, of your willingness to bleed for the survival of your clans."

One of the Jarls, Ingvar of Frostfjord, stepped forward. When he spoke, his voice was rough and commanding. "The Reckoning exists because we exist. The gods are not kind. They are not forgiving. They are powerful and wild, and they demand balance. If we do not offer them this trial, they will take their anger out on us in ways you cannot imagine."

Jarl Bjorn grunted, his deep voice rumbling like distant thunder. "The storms. The famine. The plagues. They all come when the gods are displeased."

Jarl Sigrid's lips curved into a faint, bland smile. "This is not just a trial for you. It is a shield for us. A bargain struck with the divine to keep their wrath at bay."

Astrid's heart skipped as she listened. She had heard the stories before, of course. Every child in Bjornhold had. But hearing it here, on Skarn, with the weight of the gods pressing down on her, it felt different. Real.

"There are no rules in the Reckoning," the Völva said, her voice cutting through the heavy silence. "You will face trials that will test every part of you. Your body, your mind, your soul will all be called upon. The gods will decide who of you survives. If any."

The words settled over the room like a shroud, heavy and suffocating. Astrid glanced at Thorwulf out of the corner of her eye. His usual smirk had been replaced by a grim set to his jaw.

"Survive," the Völva said simply. "That is all the gods ask of you. Each of you must prove yourselves in their eyes, for they each seek something different from you. To triumph, you must embody the traits they value most."

Astrid's stomach tightened as the Völva gestured to the towering statues that lined the temple walls, their features worn but still commanding. Each god seemed larger than life, their forms carved from dark stone that seemed to drink in the torchlight.

"Odin, the Allfather," the Völva began, gesturing toward the first statue. The figure loomed over the room, his single, watchful eye carved with intricate detail. His beard flowed like a frozen river, his giant stone hand resting on the hilt of a massive sword. "He values wisdom above all else. To him, cunning is a greater weapon than any blade. Those who win his favor will outwit their enemies, for the sharpness of their mind will guide them through even the darkest trials."

Astrid's gaze lingered on Odin's statue. Wisdom. Cunning. She could only hope that she had enough of both.

The Völva turned to the next statue, a figure with a gleaming hammer raised high above his head. His stance was powerful, unyielding, his expression one of fierce determination. "Thor, the Thunderer. He values strength and bravery. He seeks warriors who can stand unflinching in the face of danger, who will meet their foes with unrelenting ferocity."

Thor's gaze seemed to bore into Astrid, and she shifted uncomfortably. She had always known she wasn't the strongest, but she had always fought for those she loved. Would that be enough?

"Freyja," the Völva continued, her voice softening slightly as she gestured to a statue carved with graceful lines. Freyja's form was clad in flowing robes, her hair cascading like waves down her back. A falcon sat perched on her arm, its wings spread wide. "She values resilience and beauty, not only of the body but of the spirit. To her, true strength is the ability to endure, to rise again no matter how many times the world seeks to break you."

Astrid's heart twisted at the words. Resilience was something she understood, though it had often felt more like a burden than a virtue.

The next statue was of Loki, his grin sly and knowing. He was depicted holding a serpent in one hand and a dagger in the other, his pose one of perpetual motion. "Loki," the Völva said, her tone wary. "He values guile and unpredictability. He seeks those who can think beyond rules and limitations, who can use the chaos around them to their advantage."

Thorwulf let out a soft chuckle beside her. "Sounds like my kind of god," he murmured.

Astrid shot him a sharp look but said nothing.

The Völva moved to the final statue, one that seemed to radiate an almost tangible aura of authority. The figure was Hel, half her face beautiful and whole, the other half a grinning skull. She held a scale in one hand and a blade in the other, her presence cold and unyielding. "And Hel," the Völva said, her voice lowering. "She values justice and sacrifice. She seeks those who will do what must be done, no matter the cost."

Astrid shivered, her gaze locked on Hel's chilling form. Justice and sacrifice. The words felt heavy, almost personal, as if they were meant for her alone.

"These are the gods you must prove yourselves to," the Völva concluded, and her gaze swept over the gathered oathsworns once more. "Each trial will test you in ways you cannot yet imagine. If you wish to survive, you must learn to embody what they seek."

The silence that followed was broken only by the soft rustle of cloaks and the distant howl of the wind.

Astrid's attention shifted to the other oathsworns, her gaze lingering on each of them in turn. Ragnar of Ironcrag stood apart from the others, his massive frame wrapped in a bear-pelt cloak. His dark eyes were sharp, calculating, and his hands rested on the hilt of the broad axe strapped to his back. There was a hardness to him, an edge that spoke of a life lived in constant battle. There was no connection between him and the hard face Ironcrag girl. No love lost. No loyalty.

Freya of Seastone was smaller, her slender frame draped in a dark blue cloak embroidered with silver waves. Her expression was calm, almost serene, but her eyes held a sharpness that made Astrid uneasy. She looked at the world as though she saw more than was there. And she moved with a quiet grace, like a predator stalking unseen through the mist.

Astrid felt a flicker of tension as she glanced at Thorwulf, who stood beside her with his usual easy confidence. His dark eyes were unreadable now, his smirk gone as he studied the gods' statues. There was a weight to him that she hadn't noticed before, a quiet intensity beneath the bravado.

"You're awfully quiet, Sigurdsdóttir," Thorwulf said, his voice low and secretive.

"I'm thinking," she replied.

"About what?"

"About how much I'm already regretting this," she muttered, though the words lacked heat.

Thorwulf chuckled softly. "Too late for that."

Astrid ignored him, her attention returning to the statues. The gods were watching, waiting, and she was horribly aware that every step she took on this island would be weighed and judged.

As the group began to disperse, Astrid lingered for a moment, her gaze on Hel's statue. Justice and sacrifice. She had already made her choice to protect Solveig, but standing here, she couldn't help but wonder if the gods had more in store for her than she could handle.

The oathsworns were formally dismissed, and their footsteps echoed through the temple as they filed out into the cold, misty air. Astrid stopped near the entrance, her gaze drawn to the ruins that stretched out toward the horizon.

"You look like you're ready to run," Thorwulf said, coming to stand beside her.

"I'm not running anywhere," she replied, her voice somehow steadier than she felt.

He nodded, and fixed his gaze on the ancient ruins. "Good. Because we can't outrun this."

She glanced at him, studying the tension in his shoulders, the faint shadows beneath his eyes. Beneath his bravado, he was just as scared as she was.

But neither of them said it.

"Don't overthink it. What will come, will come," Thorwulf said. "You'll drive yourself mad before the trials even start."

Astrid shot him a withering glare but said nothing. Deep down, she knew he was right.

As the mist closed in around them, Astrid took a deep breath, steeling herself. Skarn was waiting, and the gods were watching.

The Reckoning had begun, and there was no turning back.

7

TRAINING BEGINS

The morning broke over Skarn with a grim, cold light that seemed to sap the warmth from the earth. The mist clung to the frosted ground in stubborn patches, twisting and curling around the jagged ruins that dotted the clearing. Pines loomed at the edges of the training grounds, their gnarled branches swaying under the biting wind that carried the faint scent of salt and decay from the cliffs.

Astrid stood in the clearing, her boots crunching against the frozen ground as she shifted her weight. The wide space had been crudely marked with trampled grass and frost, its natural boundaries formed by the ruins of broken statues and half-buried stones carved with runes long forgotten. It wasn't an arena meant to inspire. This place was meant to test and break.

The Jarls watched from a raised wooden platform at the edge of the clearing, their fur-lined cloaks heavy with frost. Jarl Ingvar of Frostfjord loomed like a wolf on a ridge, his silver-streaked beard glinting in the weak sunlight. His gray eyes were sharp, dissecting the oathsworns with a practiced gaze that made Astrid's skin prickle. Jarl Sigrid stood beside him. Her golden hair caught the light like a blade. Her crimson cloak shimmered faintly as she leaned forward, and her calculating expression betrayed nothing but expectation.

Thorwulf stood a few feet away from Astrid, his dark hair tousled by the wind. He looked every bit the warrior. His broad, solid frame was wrapped in a fur-lined cloak, a leather jerkin beneath fitted with steel rivets that gleamed faintly in the dim light. His axe rested casually on his shoulder, its edge nicked and worn from years of use. He exuded confidence, though his grin was the kind that could inspire both trust and irritation in equal measure.

Jorunn stepped into the center of the clearing, her sharp eyes narrowing as she surveyed the oathsworns. "We'll start with weapons training," she barked, her voice carrying over the low hum of the wind. "Choose your weapon and pair up with your clansmen. Show us what you can do."

Astrid swallowed hard, the weight of the Völva's earlier words pressing down on her shoulders. The gods were watching, their judgment hanging over every step she took. She moved to the weapons rack at the edge of the clearing, her fingers hovering over the handles of axes, spears, and swords. She reached for a simple sword, its leather-wrapped hilt familiar and steady in her grasp.

"Sigurdsdóttir," Jorunn called, her tone brisk. "You're up first."

The clearing fell silent, the murmurs of the oathsworns fading as all eyes turned to her. Astrid clenched her jaw, her heart pounding as she stepped forward. She tightened her grip on the sword, and found the weight of it both comforting and daunting.

"Guess that makes me your partner," Thorwulf said, stepping into the circle with an easy confidence that set her teeth on edge. His dark eyes gleamed with amusement as he unslung his axe from his shoulder, twirling it once before settling into a relaxed stance.

"Try not to embarrass yourself," he added with a smirk.

Astrid glared at him. "I should be saying that to you," she shot back, her voice steady despite the nerves coiling in her stomach.

The Jarls leaned forward slightly, their eyes gleaming with interest. Jarl Bjorn of Ironcrag cracked a faint smile, and crossed his massive arms over his chest. His bear-pelt cloak draped over his shoulders like a second skin, the claws still attached and gleaming faintly. Jarl Ingrid of Seastone stood silent, her dark blue cloak rippling in the wind as her sharp, aquiline features remained impassive.

"Begin," Jorunn commanded, stepping back.

Thorwulf moved first, his axe cutting through the air in a wide, heavy arc. The sound was sharp, a whistle that ended with a *crack* as it met the frost-hardened earth where Astrid had stood a moment earlier. She sidestepped the blow, her sword flashing as she brought it up to block his follow-up swing.

The clash of metal rang out, sharp and jarring. Astrid gritted her teeth as the force of his strike reverberated through her arms. Thorwulf was stronger than she had expected, each swing of his axe calculated to overwhelm rather than outmaneuver.

He pressed forward, his movements fluid despite the heavy weapon he wielded. His strikes were relentless, forcing Astrid to retreat step by step as she blocked and dodged, the frosted ground crunching beneath her boots.

"Come on, Sigurdsdóttir," Thorwulf taunted, his grin widening. "I thought you said not to hold back."

"I did," she snapped, her voice tight with exertion.

She feinted to the left, her blade darting toward his side. Thorwulf twisted at the last moment, his axe coming down in a heavy arc that she barely managed to deflect. The impact sent a jolt up her arms, but she refused to falter.

The onlookers murmured softly, their whispers carrying just enough to sting. Astrid could feel their judgment, the weight of their expectations pressing down on her.

From the corner of her eye, she caught a glimpse of Ragnar, the oathsworn from Ironcrag, watching her. His massive frame was tense, his dark eyes sharp as he assessed every move she made. His bear-pelt cloak shifted as he leaned forward slightly, with an expression unreadable but intense. Beside him, Freya of Seastone stood with her arms crossed, her spear resting lightly against her shoulder. Her piercing blue eyes were calm, her posture elegant and poised, but there was a sharpness to her that reminded Astrid of the edge of a blade.

"Focus," Thorwulf said, his voice breaking her concentration.

Astrid's gaze snapped back to him just as his axe came swinging toward her again. She ducked low, her sword slicing upward in a desperate attempt to regain the offensive. The blade caught the edge of his axe, sparks flying as metal grated against metal.

Thorwulf chuckled, the sound low and almost impressed. "Not bad," he said, stepping back slightly. "You've got fight in you, Sigurdsdóttir. I'll give you that."

She didn't respond. Her breath came in quick, shallow gasps as she straightened, her grip on the sword firm despite the ache in her arms.

"Enough," Jorunn barked, stepping forward to end the match.

Astrid lowered her sword, her chest rising and falling as she struggled to catch her breath. Thorwulf slung his axe back over his shoulder, his grin returning.

"You'll do fine," he said, his tone softer now. "Just don't get in my way."

Astrid glared at him, but before she could respond, Ragnar stepped into the circle. His massive axe gleamed in the pale light, its blade almost as intimidating as the man who wielded it. His first strike sent his opponent sprawling, the force of it reverberating through the clearing like a thunderclap.

Astrid watched the other matches in tense silence. She couldn't match Ragnar's strength, and Freya's deadly precision would be equally out of reach. But she couldn't think about them now. She had to focus on herself. On surviving.

As the sun climbed higher, casting long shadows over the clearing, Astrid hefted her sword. She wasn't the strongest. She wasn't the fastest. But she wouldn't let them break her. Not yet.

The morning sun hung low and pale in the sky, casting a weak glow over the clearing that did little to warm the frost-covered ground. The air was sharp, every breath biting against Astrid's lungs as she stood with the other oathsworns. The ruins of Skarn rose around them like the ghosts of a forgotten age, their jagged edges casting long shadows over the makeshift training grounds. The pine trees that bordered the clearing groaned softly in the wind, and their twisted branches reached skyward as though pleading with the gods themselves for release from this place.

Astrid shifted her grip on the hilt of her sword, her gloved fingers tightening against the leather. The weight of it was familiar, grounding her in the chaos of the morning. Around her, the other oathsworns were already pairing off, their movements tense and sharp.

When it came to the second round of matches, Ragnar of Ironcrag was the first to step forward. His massive frame was an imposing presence as he hefted his axe onto his shoulder.

The first clash of weapons rang out. It was a sharp, brutal

sound that echoed across the clearing. Ragnar's opponent this time was a wiry boy from Solfjord. He was already struggling, his movements frantic as he tried to dodge the sheer force of Ragnar's strikes. The Ironcrag warrior didn't just swing his axe, he wielded it with frightening precision and strength, each blow calculated to overwhelm.

Astrid tried not to watch, but it was impossible to look away. Every time Ragnar's axe connected, the sound was like thunder, reverberating through her bones. The boy barely managed to stay on his feet, his face pale with exertion and fear.

"Brute strength," Freya of Seastone muttered, her voice soft but cutting as she stood beside Astrid, leaning casually on her spear. "It's effective, but it's not everything."

Astrid glanced at her. Freya's pale blue eyes were sharp, her expression unreadable as she watched Ragnar's match. She was smaller than most of the other oathsworns. Her frame was lithe and wiry, but there was a quiet confidence in the way she held herself. Her dark blue cloak was embroidered with intricate silver waves, a testament to her Seastone heritage.

"And what about you?" Astrid asked, her voice low. "What do you rely on?"

Freya smiled faintly, her gaze never leaving the fight. "Precision. A single well-placed strike is worth more than a dozen wild ones. And observation."

Astrid nodded, her stomach twisting. Precision. Strength. Resilience. Everyone here had something to prove, something to protect. And they all knew what they had to do to win.

"Sigurdsdóttir!" Jorunn's voice cut through the air, sharp and commanding.

Astrid snapped her head around to see Jorunn standing at the edge of the clearing, her piercing gaze fixed on her. "You're up."

Astrid swallowed hard, her heart pounding as she stepped

forward. The other oathsworns parted to let her through, their eyes heavy with curiosity and judgment. Thorwulf was already waiting for her in the center of the clearing, his axe resting casually against his shoulder.

"Well, well," he said, his smirk as infuriating as ever. "Ready for round two?"

Astrid glared at him, gripping her sword tightly. "I thought we already settled this."

"Not quite," Thorwulf replied, stepping into a ready stance. The sunlight caught on the edge of his axe, the blade gleaming like a predator's smile. "It seems the gods want a rematch. Let's see if you've got more fight in you."

Jorunn stepped forward, her voice cutting through the tension. "This is not about winning. It's about showing what you're capable of. Prove to us, and to the gods, that you belong here."

Astrid took a deep breath, forcing herself to focus. The clearing felt smaller now, the weight of the Jarls' gazes pressing down on her. Jarl Ingvar stood at the edge of the platform, his expression impassive but his sharp eyes missing nothing. Jarl Sigrid leaned slightly forward, her golden hair catching the sunlight as she studied Astrid with cool calculation.

"Begin," Jorunn said.

Thorwulf moved first, his axe slicing through the air with a deadly whistle. Astrid barely had time to react, her sword flashing up to block the strike. The force of the blow jarred her arms, the impact reverberating through her bones.

"Not bad," Thorwulf said, his voice light as he stepped back, spinning the axe in his hands. "But you'll have to do better than that."

Astrid didn't respond. She darted forward, her movements quick and precise as she aimed a strike at his side. Thorwulf twisted at the last moment, his axe coming up to deflect her blade. Sparks flew as metal met metal, the sound sharp and grating.

Their movements were a blur of motion. Strike, block, dodge, repeat. Thorwulf's attacks were relentless, each swing of his axe carrying enough force to split her blade in two if she faltered for even a moment. But Astrid was fast. Her smaller frame allowed her to slip past his strikes and land glancing blows that forced him to stay on his toes.

"You're quick," Thorwulf said, his breath coming in short bursts as they circled each other. "But speed won't save you forever."

"And brute strength won't win every fight," Astrid shot back, her voice steady despite the burning in her arms.

Thorwulf grinned, his dark eyes gleaming with amusement. "Good point."

He lunged at her again, his axe arcing toward her shoulder. Astrid ducked, and sliced her sword upward in a desperate counterattack. The blade caught the edge of his cloak, tearing through the fabric before he twisted away.

"Careful," he said, his tone teasing. "I only have one of these."

"Then maybe you should stop showing off," Astrid snapped.

The onlookers murmured softly, their whispers carrying just enough to sting. Astrid felt their judgment like a physical weight, but she refused to let it distract her.

Finally, Jorunn stepped forward, raising her hand. "Enough."

Astrid lowered her sword. Her chest heaving as she struggled to catch her breath. Thorwulf slung his axe over his shoulder, and she saw his smirk soften into something closer to respect.

"You're better than I thought you'd be," he said, his voice quieter now.

Astrid glared at him, though the heat in her chest wasn't entirely from anger. "I don't need your approval."

Thorwulf chuckled, shaking his head. "You might not, but you'll need my help if we're going to get through this alive."

As he turned and walked away, Astrid felt a flicker of unease settle in her chest. Thorwulf was skilled, there was no denying that, but he was also dangerously confident. As much as she hated to admit it, he was right about one thing: surviving Skarn would take more than just skill.

It would take trust.

And that was something Astrid wasn't sure she could afford to give.

8

THE TRIAL OF ICE

The howling wind was relentless, a deafening roar that seemed determined to drown out every rational thought. Snow stung Astrid's face like shards of glass, seeping through her hood and biting into her skin. The blizzard had turned the world into a swirling void of white, where the land blurred into the sky, and the air felt thick with icy menace. She had never seen a storm like this, not even in Frostfjord. It felt alive, as though the gods themselves had summoned it to weed out the weak.

Astrid pushed forward, her boots crunching through the knee-deep snow, every step an agonizing battle against the elements. The landscape was treacherous. It was an endless maze of jagged cliffs and shadowy pine trees that loomed like silent sentinels. Ice-coated boulders jutted from the ground, their surfaces slick and glinting like fractured mirrors. Each breath burned in her lungs, visible in short, panicked bursts as she fought to keep moving.

They had been sent out into the wilderness, each with a task, something to recover. It was part of their training, but Jorunn had warned them that, even in training, they could kill or be killed.

Ahead, a shadow moved through the storm. Freya of Seastone. Her dark blue cloak trailed behind her like a wisp of smoke. She was nimble, leaping over patches of ice with the grace of a falcon in flight. Astrid envied her poise, but knew that grace alone wouldn't guarantee survival here. The gods demanded more than agility.

A sharp *crack* split the air, and Astrid froze. Her eyes darted to the source of the sound just as Freya stepped onto a snow-covered patch of ground that suddenly gave way beneath her. A hidden pit opened up, its jagged spikes glinting faintly in the storm's dim light. Freya stumbled, her arms flailing as she teetered on the edge.

Thorwulf appeared out of the storm like a force of nature, his hand shooting out to grab Freya's cloak. With a sharp tug, he yanked her back from the brink, the two of them collapsing into the snow together.

"Careful, Seastone," Thorwulf said, his voice cutting through the storm. "You're no use to anyone if you fall before the fun even starts."

Freya glared at him, brushing snow from her cloak with trembling hands. "Don't think this makes us allies," she snapped, her voice sharp with embarrassment. But there was a flicker of unease in her eyes, as if she, too, had felt the gods' judgment in that moment.

Astrid clenched her jaw and turned away, forcing herself to keep moving. She had no time to worry about Freya or Thorwulf. Every second spent standing still was a second closer to failure, or possibly worse. The altar of Ægir was out there, somewhere beyond this frozen nightmare, and she had to find it before anyone else.

The storm grew even fiercer the higher she climbed into the cliffs. The wind howled through the narrow paths like a banshee. The ground beneath her boots was slick with ice, forcing her to move with agonizing caution. Her sword hung heavy in her hand, its weight was a constant reminder of what was at stake.

A sudden movement caught her eye, and she turned to see the oathsworn boy from Solfjord standing frozen in the middle of the path. His spear dangled loosely from his hand, his wide eyes staring blankly ahead. He looked like a statue, his body rigid with fear. The ground around him was cracking, tearing apart like paper.

"Move!" Astrid shouted.

The boy didn't respond. He was paralyzed, his chest rising and falling in shallow, rapid breaths. Astrid hesitated, her heart twisting as she took a step toward him. But before she could reach him, the ice beneath his feet cracked with a deafening *snap*. The boy cried out, his arms flailing as he plummeted into the darkness below.

Astrid stopped, her breath catching in her throat. The pit yawned open before her, its jagged edges glistening with frost. For a moment, she couldn't move, her mind replaying the boy's fall in excruciating detail. She didn't even know his name.

Her stomach twisted, but she forced herself to turn away. There was no time for hesitation. Only one could win. The gods had made their rules clear. She pushed on, skirted the crack.

The path narrowed even further as she climbed higher, the jagged cliffs pressing close on either side. The snow whipped around her in violent spirals, blinding her to everything but the faint glow in the distance. The altar. It was close.

Astrid's foot caught on something beneath the snow, and she stumbled, her sword slipping from her grasp. She hit the ground hard, the impact jolting through her body as the wind howled around her. She scrambled to her knees, her hands clawing at the snow in search of her weapon.

A shadow loomed over her, and she looked up to see

Thorwulf standing above her, his axe resting on his shoulder. His dark eyes gleamed with amusement, but there was something else there, too. She couldn't quite place his expression.

"Need a hand?" he asked, extending his free hand toward her.

Astrid glared at him, her pride warring with the cold, hard reality of her situation. She didn't want his help. She didn't want to owe him anything. But the storm was unforgiving, and she couldn't afford to let her pride get her killed.

She grabbed his hand reluctantly, allowing him to pull her to her feet. "I didn't ask for your help," she muttered, brushing snow from her cloak.

Thorwulf chuckled, his grin widening. "No, but you needed it."

Astrid didn't respond. She bent to retrieve her sword, and felt the steel cold and reassuring in her hand. She hated that he was right, that she probably did need him, even if she would never admit it out loud.

"Come on," Thorwulf said, his tone softer now. "The altar's close."

The glow grew brighter as they pushed forward with the wind screaming in their ears and the ice biting their cheeks. Suddenly, the path opened into a wide clearing, and there it was. The altar of Ægir.

It was a massive stone structure, with a surface etched in glowing blue runes that pulsed faintly in the storm's dim light. A single medallion rested on a pedestal at its center, shimmering like ice.

Astrid's heart pounded as she stepped into the clearing, her eyes scanning for traps. She knew the gods wouldn't make this easy.

Her heart sank to see Ragnar on the opposite side of the

clearing. He'd found the altar at the same time. But still, Astrid didn't go for the medallion. She could feel something in the air around it. It was charged. She sensed a trap.

Sure enough, the ground beneath Ragnar shifted as he lunged for the medallion, triggering a burst of freezing water that hurled him backward into the snow. Astrid darted forward, her instincts screaming at her to seize the opportunity. But as she reached for the medallion, her foot caught on another hidden tripwire, and the ice beneath her began to crack.

She braced for the fall, but a strong hand caught her arm and yanked her back just in time. Thorwulf again.

"You've really got to watch where you step, Sigurdsdóttir," he said, his tone teasing but his grip firm. "I can't keep saving you."

Astrid wrenched her arm free, her cheeks burning with a mixture of frustration and something else she couldn't quite name. "Again, I didn't ask you to."

Thorwulf shrugged, his grin returning. "Maybe not. But it's starting to feel like a habit."

As the storm raged around them, Astrid turned her attention back to the altar. The medallion gleamed like a shard of frozen light. The gods were watching, and the trial wasn't over yet.

Thorwulf looked to his side as Freya of Seastone slipped on a patch of ice, her spear clattering against the rocks as she caught herself on one knee. She let out a hiss of frustration but was quick to recover, her sharp blue eyes darting around for threats. Ragnar pulled himself up again, lumbered toward the medallion once again.

His massive axe was gripped tightly in one hand, his breath coming in heavy bursts as he pressed forward with sheer determination.

"We're running out of time," Thorwulf muttered beside Astrid. "One of us needs to get that medallion before he does."

Astrid didn't respond. Her eyes were fixed on the faint glow rising from the altar.

"Careful," Thorwulf said, his hand brushing against her arm as she stepped cautiously forward. His tone wasn't teasing now, it was serious, almost protective.

Astrid glanced at him but didn't pull away. She couldn't deny that his presence was a comfort, even if she refused to admit it out loud.

Another trap revealed itself as Ragnar's foot caught on something hidden beneath the snow. A sharp *snap* echoed through the storm as a hidden mechanism triggered, sending a cascade of rocks tumbling down from above.

"Move!" Astrid shouted, her voice cutting through the howling wind. She lunged forward, toward the glowing medallion, seeing Thorwulf dive to the side just in time, the rocks crashing down where he had stood only moments before. He scrambled to his feet, his eyes narrowing as he scanned the cliffs above.

"They're really testing us," he growled, his voice rough and angry.

Astrid nodded, smiling, as she held the medallion aloft in her hand.

Thorwulf's face broke into a wide grin. "Well play, Sigurdsdóttir," he said, laughing. "Well played."

Suddenly, the storm stopped, as though the wind had been sucked into a vacuum. All was still for the briefest moment. Ragnar wrestled himself out from beneath the rockpile and dusted his shoulders down, scowling at the medallion in Astrid's hand.

Jorunn's voice echoed from somewhere in the skies above them. "Frostfjord's Sigurdsdóttir wins. Return to camp."

Ragnar let out a howl of frustration, but Astrid saw a nod of approval from Freya. Alliances, fragile as they were, were beginning to form. But so were enmities.

As suddenly as it had stopped, the wind whipped up again, bringing snow and ice in drifting waves.

"Come on," Thorwulf said, setting off. "This isn't just a storm."

Astrid could feel it too. The gods were present in every gust of wind, every shift in the snow beneath her boots. They were watching, waiting to see who would rise and who would fall.

The group pressed on, their movements slower now as the storm seemed to grow more malicious. The snow whipped around them in violent spirals, blinding them to anything more than a few feet ahead. The cold bit into Astrid's fingers, even through her gloves, and her legs ached with the effort of pushing through the drifts.

Thorwulf fell into step beside her again, his voice low. "You need to pace yourself," he said. "We won't make it back to camp if you try to keep up this speed."

Astrid shot him a glare, though her exhaustion made it less effective. "I'm fine."

"You're stubborn," Thorwulf said with a faint grin. "But stubbornness is dangerous out here. We need to work together."

Astrid clenched her jaw, forcing herself to focus on the path ahead. She hated that he was right, again. Her body was screaming for rest, her muscles trembling with every step, but she couldn't afford to stop.

"This way," Thorwulf said, his voice tight.

"Gently," Astrid muttered. "Slow down." Her instincts prickled with unease, and she held her sword tighter as they entered the canyon. The snow here was deeper, nearly to her thighs, and every step felt like wading through quicksand.

Suddenly, a piercing scream cut through the storm. Astrid

whipped her head around to see one of the oathsworns, the girl from Solfjord, caught in a snare that had yanked her into the air. She dangled helplessly from a tree, her spear lost in the snow below her.

"Help me!" the girl cried, her voice shrill with panic.

Astrid hesitated, her heart lurching at the sight. But before she could move, Freya grabbed her arm, her expression cold and unyielding. "Leave her," Freya said. "She's already lost."

She pointed into the canopy of the tree, where strange shadows were already shifting. Unseen creatures closing in on the helpless girl.

Astrid's chest heaved, a wave of guilt crashing over her. The girl's cries grew fainter as the group pressed on, her silhouette fading into the storm. Astrid forced herself to keep moving. She couldn't afford to make sacrifices for others. Not here.

The canyon opened up into a wide clearing, and there it was. The camp. Snow had piled high around its walls. In her hand, the medallion glowed bright and hot, and then faded to a dull slate gray. The challenge was over. The task complete. But only six of the eight oathsworns had made it back to camp.

Astrid's breath caught in her throat as she stepped into the clearing. The storm seemed to ease finally inside the camp walls, the wind dying down to a low whisper. The air was still heavy with the weight of the gods' presence, making every shadow feel like another trap.

"Stay close," Thorwulf said, his voice low.

Astrid nodded, her heart pounding. They were back in the safety of camp, but the trial hadn't even begun. The gods weren't done with them.

9

NORN'S WELL

When they woke in the morning, the storm had faded, but the silence that followed was worse. The air hung thick and heavy, as though the gods themselves were holding their breath.

They'd woken to find themselves in a remote clearing, just Astrid and Thorwulf. With no sign of the camp, or the other oathsworns. They'd been huddled together in their sleep, the warmth of their bodies feeding each other. Astrid had pushed him away harshly as she came round, only to yearn for his closeness again when she saw how isolated they were.

The clearing was flanked by jagged cliffs that seemed to lean inward, looming over them like ancient guardians. The air was sharper here, colder, and each breath felt like it froze before it even reached her lungs. The sun was a pale, distant disk in the sky, its light smothered by a layer of thick gray clouds. This place was cold, lifeless, abandoned. As if even time dared not linger.

"What is this place?" Thorwulf muttered, his voice barely above a whisper. His tone was lighter than the fear in his eyes suggested, his hand gripping the handle of his axe like a lifeline.

Astrid didn't answer, her focus locked on a faint trail that twisted away through the landscape. She felt it too. There was a shift in the air, a creeping dread that prickled along her skin like frostbite. The land itself felt wrong, as though it had been twisted by something ancient and powerful. It wasn't just the cold that bit at her, it was the presence of the gods.

"We should move," Astrid said. "We're not safe here."

Thorwulf nodded. "So. The Reckoning has begun in earnest."

Astrid didn't reply. She didn't need to. Each step she took away from the clearing was a reminder of the weight pressing on her shoulders. Her boots crunched against the brittle snow, a lonely sound that echoed faintly in the oppressive stillness.

The ravine grew steeper as they descended, the icy walls glistening in the weak light. The twisted branches of the pine trees arched over them, forming a canopy that blocked out most of the sky. Shadows danced along the frost-rimmed edges of the path, flickering just out of sight, and Astrid felt her pulse quicken as her imagination conjured shapes and figures that couldn't possibly be there.

And then they saw it.

An ancient stone well appeared suddenly as they rounded a bend in the trail, nestled in the center of a clearing that seemed carved out of the earth itself. The well was older than time, its stone walls blackened by moss and slick with a thin layer of frost. A ring of runes surrounded it, carved deep into the frozen ground. The runes glowed faintly, their eerie blue light pulsing in rhythm with Astrid's racing heartbeat.

The clearing itself was unnaturally still. The trees formed a perfect circle around the well, their gnarled branches clawing at the sky as if reaching for something unseen. The snow here was untouched, pristine, as though even the wind didn't dare disturb it. The silence was absolute, broken only by the faint sound of whispers that seemed to rise from the well itself.

Astrid froze, her breath catching in her throat. The whispers grew louder as she stepped closer, their tones shifting and weaving together like a mournful song. It was impossible to make out the words, but the meaning was clear enough. This place was calling them in.

"This is Norn's Well," Thorwulf said, his voice low, almost reverent.

Astrid nodded, her gaze fixed on the shimmering water within the well. It wasn't like any water she had ever seen. It glowed with a silvery light, the surface smooth and still despite the faint breeze that stirred the edges of her cloak. The reflections shimmered and shifted, twisting into shapes that dissolved before she could fully grasp them.

"They say the Norns wove the threads of fate here," Thorwulf continued, his tone tinged with something close to reverence. "That anyone who looks into the water can see their future."

"Or their end," Astrid said quietly, her voice trembling slightly despite herself.

Thorwulf glanced at her, his dark eyes sharp. "My mother once told me that the gods don't show us what we want to see. They show us what we need to face."

Astrid's stomach twisted at his words, but she didn't respond. She could feel the weight of the gods' judgment in the air around her, their presence so thick it was suffocating. The well wasn't just another ancient place. It was alive, humming with the power of the divine, and it terrified her.

"Go on," Thorwulf said, gesturing toward the well with a faint smirk. "Take a look. Let's see what the gods think of you."

Astrid glared at him, but the ache in her chest was stronger than her irritation. She had to see. Slowly, she stepped toward the well, the whispers growing louder with every step. They seemed to coil around her, their voices overlapping in a chaotic, haunting melody. She could feel their pull, an almost physical force drawing her closer to the shimmering water.

Leaning over the edge, she gazed into the depths.

The vision hit her like a blade.

She saw herself standing victorious at the end of the Reckoning, the medallion of frost clutched tightly in her hand. The other oathsworns were gone, their faces and names lost to the wind. She stood alone on a barren cliff, the wind howling around her, her cloak tattered and her hair streaked with frost. The medallion gleamed in her hand, but her face was hollow, her eyes shadowed with a grief so deep it stole her breath.

The whispers grew louder, their tones mocking now, and Astrid staggered back from the well, her heart pounding. She felt like she couldn't breathe, the cold pressing in on her like a vice.

"What did you see?" Thorwulf's voice broke through the haze, sharp and insistent.

"Nothing," she said quickly, her voice cracking. She turned away from the well, avoiding his gaze. "It's just a trick. The gods are trying to rattle us."

Thorwulf frowned, his expression skeptical. "You're lying."

Astrid forced herself to stand tall. "It doesn't matter," she snapped. "We need to keep moving."

He didn't press her, though she could feel his eyes lingering on her as they left the clearing. The oppressive air of the well faded as they climbed back onto the trail, but the vision lingered in Astrid's mind, its weight pressing down on her chest like a stone.

Thorwulf fell into step beside her, his tone softer now. "Whatever you saw back there, it doesn't define you," he said.

Astrid glanced at him, her expression guarded. "You don't know that."

"I know the gods test us in ways we don't understand," he

replied. "But that doesn't mean they've already decided our fate. You still have a choice, Sigurdsdóttir."

Astrid didn't respond. The path ahead twisted and narrowed, the storm beginning to stir again in the distance. The gods were watching, and the well's vision was a warning she couldn't ignore. But she was determined she would prove them wrong.

The snow crunched beneath their boots as Astrid and Thorwulf left the clearing behind. The whispers of the well followed them out, only to be replaced by the distant howl of the wind as the storm began to stir again. The silence between them was heavy, though whether it was born of exhaustion, unease, or something else entirely, Astrid couldn't say.

She kept her gaze fixed on the path ahead, her thoughts swirling like the snowflakes that clung to her cloak. The vision from the well was seared into her mind, the haunting image of herself standing alone, victorious but hollow. No matter how hard she tried, she couldn't shake the weight of it.

"You're quieter than usual," Thorwulf said, breaking the silence. His tone was casual, but there was a trace of concern there.

"Just thinking."

"Dangerous habit," he said with a faint smirk.

She rolled her eyes, pulling her cloak tighter against the cold. "Not all of us can rely on brute strength and casual charm to get through the Reckoning."

Thorwulf chuckled softly, the sound oddly warm against the biting chill of the air. "Fair enough," he said. "But you did just admit you find me charming."

She tutted, smiling, but said no more.

He fell quiet for a moment, his gaze distant as they continued down the narrow trail. Then, without looking at her, he said, "Do you ever wonder if the gods are laughing at us?"

Astrid frowned, her steps faltering slightly. "What do you mean?"

He shrugged, his shoulders tense beneath his fur-lined cloak. "Think about it. They set us against each other, make us fight and bleed and die, all for their amusement. They dangle power and glory in front of us like a prize, but in the end, we're just pawns in their game."

Astrid studied him, surprised by the bitterness in his voice. For all his bravado, there was a sharp edge to his words that hinted at something deeper. "You sound like you've thought about this a lot."

Thorwulf laughed, but it was a hollow sound. "You could say that." He was quiet for a moment, his gaze fixed on the snow-covered path ahead. Then he sighed, his breath fogging in the cold air. "Do you know why I'm here, Sigurdsdóttir?"

Astrid raised an eyebrow, curious despite herself. "To win the Reckoning, like the rest of us."

He shook his head, a bitter smile tugging at his lips. "Not quite. I'm here because I have to be. Because my family's name is worth less than the dirt beneath your boots."

Astrid blinked, caught off guard by his candor. "What are you talking about?"

Thorwulf hesitated, as if he was debating whether to continue. Then, with a deep breath, he said, "My father was Jarl Haldor. He was once a respected leader in Seastone. He was strong, clever, everything a leader should be. But he made a mistake. Trusted the wrong allies, took risks he shouldn't have. And when it all fell apart, he was the one left to take the blame."

"What happened?" Astrid asked, her voice quieter now.

Thorwulf gripped the hilt of his axe. "A deal with the Ironcrag clan went bad. Supplies were lost, warriors were killed, and my father's honor was called into question. The other Jarls stripped him of his position, and my family was cast out, branded as traitors. My father... he didn't take it well."

Astrid felt a pang of sympathy despite herself. "I'm sorry."

Thorwulf shrugged, though his expression was strained. "It was a long time ago. My father drank himself into an early grave, and my mother... She tried to hold us together, but it wasn't enough. The name Haldorsson became a curse in Seastone. People spit when they say it. So, we fled to Frostfjord. And we've been on the outside there ever since."

Astrid glanced at him, noting the tension in his jaw and the way his shoulders hunched slightly, as if he were carrying the weight of his family's shame on his back. For all his confidence and charm, there was a vulnerability in him that she hadn't seen before.

"So you're here to restore your family's honor?" she asked.

Thorwulf nodded, his gaze fixed on the ground. "If I win the Reckoning, perhaps the gods will bless my name. No one will dare question my loyalty or my strength. My family will be remembered as more than failures. Even if it's by a different clan."

Astrid was silent for a moment, her mind turning over his words. She understood the weight of expectations, the pressure to prove yourself worthy. But hearing it from Thorwulf, someone she had dismissed as little more than an arrogant warrior, gave her pause.

"And what about you?" Thorwulf asked, his tone lighter now. "Why are you here, Sigurdsdóttir? What are you fighting for?"

Astrid hesitated. "That's none of your business."

Thorwulf raised an eyebrow, a faint smile tugging at his lips. "Fair enough. But you should know, whatever it is you're carrying, you don't have to do it alone."

She shot him a sharp look. His words a harrowing echo of the last thing Lief had said to her before she left.

"I don't need your help."

"Maybe not," he said, his voice softening. "But it's there if you want it."

Astrid didn't respond. She turned her attention back to the path, her thoughts swirling like the snowflakes around them. Thorwulf's words lingered in her mind, his vulnerability a stark contrast to the confidence he usually exuded. Not for the first time, she wondered if there was more to him than she had given him credit for.

Thorwulf's voice broke the silence again, this time lighter but no less thoughtful. "It's strange, isn't it? That we've lived in the same clan most of our lives and never crossed paths until now."

Astrid frowned, her curiosity piqued. "Where exactly do you live?"

"Far north," Thorwulf said, gesturing ahead as if the landscape beyond the mountains might hold his village. "Past the cliffs of Skold. A fishing village by the sea. Small, cold, isolated. Just like my family. But we made it our home."

Astrid's brow furrowed. "That's days away from where I grew up."

Thorwulf nodded. "Frostfjord may be one clan, but it's a world of its own. My family's disgrace kept us isolated. Even before that, the distance between villages made our lives separate. No trade routes, no reason for us to travel south. My mother used to say Frostfjord is bound together by the gods but broken apart by the land."

Astrid considered this, her mind turning over the divide that seemed to exist even within her own clan. "It's strange to think about how many lives we'll never know, even within our own people."

"Maybe the gods knew what they were doing," Thorwulf

said with a faint grin. "Maybe they were saving this meeting for the Reckoning."

Astrid's gaze flicked to him, but his expression was unreadable. She wasn't sure if she believed in fate or the gods' grand design, but as the storm began to pick up again and the path ahead twisted into the unknown, she couldn't shake the feeling that their paths had crossed for a reason. Whether she liked it or not.

10

FORMING ALLIANCES

The storm had settled into an uneasy lull, the kind that felt more like a predator waiting to pounce than any sort of reprieve. The landscape around them was stark and unforgiving, with jagged cliffs rising like teeth from the snow-covered ground. The trees thinned the higher they climbed, their twisted branches casting long shadows in the faint light of the overcast sky. Every crunch of their boots on the frost-laden earth echoed in the stillness, a reminder of how alone they were. Or rather, how surrounded they might be by hidden enemies.

Astrid's gaze flicked toward Thorwulf. He was walking slightly ahead, his axe slung over one shoulder as if he were unconcerned about the dangers lurking in the shadows. But she knew better. The way his eyes scanned the horizon, the subtle shift in his stance when they passed through an open stretch of terrain gave him away. Thorwulf might act like he was invincible, but he was as tense as she felt.

"Do you think they're close?" Astrid asked, her voice barely louder than a whisper. She didn't have to specify who she meant.

Thorwulf glanced over his shoulder, a faint smirk tugging at his lips. "If you're asking about Ragnar, I'd bet he's not far. He's too stubborn to let us get ahead without a fight."

Astrid frowned, her stomach twisting. Ragnar of Ironcrag wasn't just strong, he was relentless. She'd seen it during the training trials, the way he powered through the traps and obstacles with sheer brute force. There was something almost inhuman about the way he moved, like nothing could touch him.

"Then we shouldn't be standing out here in the open," she muttered, glancing around at the exposed ridgeline they were crossing.

Thorwulf nodded, his smirk fading. "Agreed. Let's find some cover and regroup."

They descended into a narrow ravine, the rocky walls rising high on either side. The wind died down as they entered the shelter of the cliffs, but the tension in the air only seemed to thicken. Astrid's senses were on high alert, every crack of a twig or distant rustle of snow making her muscles tighten.

They rounded a bend in the ravine, and that's when they saw her.

Freya of Seastone was crouched near a shallow stream that had frozen over, her spear resting against her shoulder as she scanned the trail behind her. Her dark blue cloak was dusted with snow, the edges tattered from the trials they'd already faced. She looked up as they approached, her sharp blue eyes narrowing.

"Sigurdsdóttir. Haldorsson," she said, her tone clipped. "I was wondering when you'd show up."

Thorwulf raised an eyebrow, his smirk returning. "Missing us already, Freya?"

She rolled her eyes, rising to her feet. "Hardly. I figured you'd be smart enough to keep moving, but then again, I suppose even you need to rest sometime."

Astrid stepped forward, her gaze steady. "What are you doing out here alone?"

Freya hesitated. "Watching. Waiting. Ragnar's not far behind, and he's gathering anyone he can convince to join him."

Thorwulf frowned. "Ragnar? Leading an alliance? That doesn't seem like his style."

Freya's expression darkened. "It's not an alliance. It's intimidation. He's picking off the weaker oathsworns and forcing the rest to follow him. If they don't, well..." She trailed off, her meaning clear.

Astrid's stomach sank. She'd seen what Ragnar was capable of, but the idea of him building a following through fear and brute strength was worse than she'd imagined. If he kept this up, he wouldn't just be a rival, he'd be an army unto himself.

"Then we need to stop him," Astrid said, her voice firm.

Freya let out a harsh laugh. "Stop him? You don't stop Ragnar. You survive him. And if you're smart, you stay out of his way. Ragnar is end game material. It's why the gods chose him."

Thorwulf crossed his arms, his expression thoughtful. "And what about you? Are you planning to survive him on your own?"

Freya hesitated, her sharp features softening just slightly. "I'm not stupid. I know I can't take him on alone. That's why I've been watching you two. You're not as reckless as the others." Her gaze flicked to Astrid. "And you've got more fight in you than most."

Astrid raised an eyebrow. "Are you saying you want to join forces?"

Freya straightened, her expression unreadable. "I'm saying we might have a better chance together than apart. But let's be clear, this isn't a partnership. It's just about survival. If you slow me down, I'll leave you behind."

Thorwulf laughed, the sound echoing off the ravine walls. "Fair enough. But let's not pretend you're doing us any favors,

Freya. If anything, you're lucky we haven't left you behind already."

Freya's eyes narrowed, but she didn't rise to the bait. Instead, she turned her attention to Astrid. "What about you, Sigurdsdóttir? Can you handle the idea of working together? Can you trust me? Or would you rather be alone with Thorwulf here?"

Astrid clenched her jaw, her mind racing. Trust wasn't something she gave freely, and especially not here, where the stakes were this high. But the alternative was going it alone, and she knew how that would end. She thought of the vision from Norn's Well, the image of herself standing alone, victorious but haunted. Maybe this was the gods' way of telling her she needed to make a choice. Maybe Thorwulf was right. Maybe she could still decide her own fate.

"Fine," she said finally. "But if you betray us, I'll make sure you regret it."

Freya smirked, but there was a glimmer of respect in her eyes. "Fair enough."

Thorwulf clapped his hands together, his grin wide. "Well then, looks like we've got ourselves a team. Let's see how long this lasts."

Astrid shot him a glare, but she couldn't deny the faint sense of relief that came with the uneasy alliance. The three of them were stronger together than apart, and if Ragnar was as ruthless as Freya claimed, they'd need every advantage they could get.

As they moved deeper into the ravine, the tension between them eased slightly, though the weight of the Reckoning hung heavy in the air. The storm was stirring again, and the gods were still watching.

Astrid fixed her eyes on the path ahead. She didn't fully trust Freya yet, and she wasn't sure she trusted Thorwulf either. But for now, she'd take what she could get. Survival came first, and the gods wouldn't make it easy.

The ravine stretched ahead of them like a gash in the earth, its jagged walls rising high on either side. The snow had thinned here, leaving patches of bare, frozen ground exposed beneath their boots. Astrid's senses were sharp, her gaze flicking to every shadow and corner as they moved. The uneasy alliance with Freya was fresh, and while the Seastone warrior was proving her resourcefulness, trust was still a distant prospect.

Freya walked ahead, her spear resting lightly on her shoulder, her movements fluid despite the uneven terrain. Thorwulf stayed closer to Astrid, his axe slung across his back, though his hand hovered near the handle as if expecting trouble. He glanced at her occasionally, his brow furrowed with something that looked uncomfortably like concern.

"Do you have to hover?" Astrid muttered, keeping her eyes on the path.

Thorwulf's lips curved into a faint smile. "Just making sure you don't get yourself killed."

"I can take care of myself," she snapped, quickening her pace.

"I don't doubt it," Thorwulf said, his tone light. "But this isn't a fight you win alone, Sigurdsdóttir."

Astrid didn't respond, but his words stung. She hated the idea of relying on anyone, especially here, where alliances could crumble as quickly as frost under the sun. Still, she couldn't ignore the subtle ways Thorwulf seemed to position himself between her and potential threats, his eyes constantly scanning their surroundings. It wasn't just strategy either. There was something personal in the way he watched her.

Up ahead, Freya raised a hand, signaling for them to stop. She crouched low, her sharp eyes narrowing as she scanned the terrain. Astrid followed her gaze, her heart sinking as she saw what had caught Freya's attention.

There were fresh tracks in the snow. But someone had tried to cover them.

"Ragnar's group?" Thorwulf asked, his voice low.

Freya crouched to inspect the tracks. "Four, maybe five. They're close."

The Reckoning had started with eight participants, two from each of the four clans. Two had fallen already, as far as Astrid knew. She'd seen them herself. But that still left a dangerous number of rivals out there, each one as desperate as they were to survive. And if they were all working together, too, they'd be harder to evade.

"We need to move," Freya said, rising to her feet. "If they're ahead of us, they're either heading for the frost medallion, or waiting to ambush anyone else who is."

Thorwulf nodded, his expression grim. "Then let's not give them the chance."

They pressed on, their movements quieter now, each step deliberate as they navigated the narrowing ravine. The tension in the air was palpable, the kind that made the hairs on the back of Astrid's neck stand on end. She couldn't shake the feeling that they were being watched, that eyes were tracking their every move.

Her instincts were right.

The attack came suddenly, a blur of motion and violence that shattered the stillness. A spear hurtled through the air, narrowly missing Freya as it embedded itself in the rocky wall beside her. She spun, her own spear snapping into position as a group of figures emerged from the shadows.

Three oathsworns, their faces hardened by the cold and desperation, rushed toward them with weapons drawn. Two carried axes, their blades chipped but deadly, while the other wielded a crude sword. Their cloaks were torn and bloodstained, their eyes glinting with a ruthless determination that sent a chill down Astrid's spine.

"Run!" Freya barked, but there was no time.

One of the attackers lunged at Astrid, his axe swinging in a wide arc. She ducked, the blade whistling past her ear, and drove her sword forward. The tip of the blade caught his shoulder, drawing a grunt of pain as he stumbled back.

Thorwulf was already in motion, his axe flashing as he met another attacker head-on. The clash of metal rang out, sharp and jarring, as Thorwulf's strength sent the man reeling. "Stick together!" he shouted, his voice cutting through the chaos.

Freya spun her spear in a blur of movement, her strikes precise and deadly. She drove one attacker back with a series of quick jabs, her expression calm and focused despite the blood that spattered her cloak.

Astrid's heart pounded as another rival charged her, sword lunging. He was fast, his strikes aggressive and relentless, but Astrid matched him blow for blow. Her muscles burned with the effort, her breath coming in short, sharp gasps as she parried his attacks.

A scream tore through the air, and Astrid's gaze flicked toward the source. One of the oathsworns, a girl no older than sixteen, had fallen. Her blood stained the snow as she struggled to rise. But one of her compatriots, sensing her weakness, turned on her, not giving her the chance. His axe came down in a brutal arc, and the girl's body went still.

Astrid's stomach turned, but there was no time to grieve. The fight raged on, each moment a blur of motion and sound.

Thorwulf fought like a force of nature, his axe cleaving through the air with terrifying precision. He blocked a spear thrust with the flat of the blade, spinning to deliver a crushing blow to his attacker's ribs. The man crumpled to the ground, gasping for air as Thorwulf turned to face Freya.

She had cleared the attackers and was already on the path ahead, turning slowly to scan for more assaults.

Astrid's opponent faltered, his movements slowing as exhaustion and fear took hold. She saw the opening and didn't hesitate. Her sword sliced through the air, catching him across the chest. A thin line of red bloomed. Wounded, he staggered back, his eyes wide with shock, before turning and running into the trees.

"Go!" Freya shouted. "Now!"

They didn't need to be told twice. Thorwulf grabbed Astrid's arm, pulling her on. The three of them sprinted down the ravine, their breaths coming in ragged gasps.

When they finally stopped, their bodies aching and their lungs burning, Astrid leaned against the rocky wall, her sword still clutched tightly in her hand. Her gaze flicked to Thorwulf, who was watching her with an intensity that made her heart skip.

"You alright?" he asked, his voice low.

"I'm fine," she said quickly, though her hands trembled.

Thorwulf didn't press her. Instead, he turned to Freya, who was catching her breath beside them.

"That was close," Freya said, her tone grim. "Too close. We need to move faster if we're going to stay ahead of them."

Astrid nodded, her mind still reeling from the attack. The Reckoning wasn't just a trial, it was a battlefield, and every step they took was a step closer to death.

11

BLOOD ON THE SNOW

The forest was eerily silent, its towering trees standing like sentinels against the pale gray sky. Their gnarled branches reached toward the heavens, heavy with snow that fell in soft, steady flurries. The air was sharp and cold, each breath biting against Astrid's lungs as she crouched low. Her eyes scanned the clearing ahead, where a faint trail of animal tracks disappeared into the dense undergrowth.

Freya knelt beside her, her spear balanced lightly in her hand as her sharp blue eyes followed the same trail. Thorwulf stood a few paces back, his axe resting against his shoulder, his gaze sweeping the trees for any sign of movement. They hadn't eaten in hours, and the hollow ache in Astrid's stomach was a constant reminder of how high the stakes were. Food was a necessity for their survival, but every second spent hunting was a gamble against their rivals.

"Rabbit," Freya murmured. She pointed toward the tracks, her expression tense. "Looks fresh. Might be close."

"Let's hope so," Thorwulf muttered. "I'm not keen on starving to death out here."

Astrid shot him a glare but said nothing. The three of them

had fallen into a tenuous rhythm over the past day, each of them contributing to their survival in their own way. But the weight of the Reckoning hung heavy in the air, a constant reminder that alliances were fragile and temporary.

They moved silently through the trees, their footsteps muffled by the snow. Astrid's senses were sharp, her ears straining for any sound that didn't belong. The rustle of leaves, the crack of a branch, the whisper of movement. Every sense was heightened.

The rabbit appeared suddenly, darting into view from behind a cluster of bushes. Freya was the first to react, her spear flashing as she hurled it through the air. The weapon struck true, pinning the animal to the ground with a sickening thud. Freya strode forward to retrieve it, but before she could reach the kill, the air was shattered by a sharp, mocking laugh.

"Well, well," a voice called out, dripping with malice. "Look what we have here."

Astrid's heart jumped into her throat as three figures stepped out from the shadows of the trees, their weapons drawn and their expressions predatory. The leader, a wiry man with a crooked smile and a jagged scar across his cheek, held a long knife in one hand, its blade glinting in the faint light. The others, a stocky girl wielding a mace and a lanky boy clutching a bow, fanned out to surround them.

Freya straightened, her grip tightening on her spear as she faced them. "You don't want to do this," she said evenly, her voice calm but firm. "Walk away, and no one gets hurt."

The scarred man laughed again, his knife spinning lazily in his hand. "Oh, I think we do want to do this. See, we're hungry too. And that rabbit looks mighty fine." His gaze flicked to Astrid and Thorwulf, his smile widening. "Besides, this is our island now. And three on three? Seems fair to me."

Thorwulf stepped forward, his expression hardening. "Walk

away now, and you might live to see another day. You are not part of the Reckoning."

The stocky girl smirked, hefting her mace in her hand. "What if we *are* the Reckoning?" she said, menacingly.

"You don't belong here," Astrid shouted.

The man's smile faltered, but he quickly recovered, his knife shifting into a ready position. "We'll see about that."

The fight erupted like a thunderclap. The girl charged at Freya, her mace swinging in a wide arc. Freya ducked under the blow, her spear flashing as she countered with a sharp jab that forced the girl back. Thorwulf moved to intercept the boy with the bow, closing the distance before the rival could nock an arrow. The clash of metal on metal rang out as Thorwulf's axe met the boy's dagger, the force of the blow sending sparks flying.

Astrid barely had time to react as the scarred man lunged at her, his knife aiming for her throat. She sidestepped instinctively, her sword flashing up to block the strike. The blades met with a sharp clang, the force of the impact reverberating up her arm. The man was fast, his movements aggressive and unrelenting as he pressed the attack.

Her breath came in short, ragged bursts as she parried his strikes, her muscles screaming with effort. He was stronger than she'd expected, his strikes wild but powerful, and she struggled to keep up. Her foot slipped on a patch of ice, and she stumbled, her heart lurching as his knife arced toward her.

Time seemed to slow as her instincts took over. She twisted her body, her sword slicing upward in a desperate counterattack. The blade caught him across the chest, tearing through his cloak and biting deep into his flesh. He staggered back, his eyes wide with shock as blood seeped into the snow beneath him.

Astrid froze, her chest heaving as she stared at him. He clutched at the wound, his knife falling from his hand as he collapsed to his knees. For a moment, their eyes met, and she saw the fear and pain in his gaze. He opened his mouth as if to speak, but no words came. Then he slumped forward, his body still.

The world seemed to go silent. The sounds of the fight faded into the background, leaving only the sight of blood staining the snow and the weight of her sword in her hand. Her stomach twisted, bile rising in her throat as the reality of what she'd done hit her.

"Sigurdsdóttir!" Thorwulf's voice snapped her out of her daze.

She turned to see him standing over the fallen archer, his axe dripping with blood. Freya had dispatched the girl with the mace, her spear embedded in the rival's chest. The fight was over.

Thorwulf stepped toward her, his expression unreadable. "Are you hurt?" he asked, his voice softer than she expected.

Astrid shook her head. "I'm fine."

He studied her for a moment, his dark eyes searching hers. "You fought well."

"I don't need your approval," she said sharply, her voice trembling despite her best efforts. "And I still don't need your help."

Thorwulf's lips quirked into a sad smile. "I'm starting to believe that."

Freya turned, pulling her spear free from the fallen girl. "We need to keep moving. Ragnar's clearly not the only one we have to worry about." She glanced at Astrid, her gaze lingering. "First human kill?"

Astrid didn't answer. She turned away, forcing herself to focus on the path ahead. The blood on her sword felt heavier than the weapon itself, and the memory of the man's eyes as he fell burned in her mind.

As they moved deeper into the forest, Thorwulf fell into step beside her, his expression thoughtful. He didn't say anything, but Astrid could feel his gaze on her, as though he was trying to understand her. She hated the way it made her feel so exposed, so vulnerable.

She didn't need his protection. She didn't need anyone.

But as the snow began to fall again, soft and relentless, she couldn't shake the image of her sister's face from her mind. She had stepped into the Reckoning to save her, to give her a chance at life. Now, she wondered if she had truly understood what that choice would cost her.

The forest had grown darker as the day waned, the sky overhead a bruised shade of gray. Snow continued to fall in soft, relentless waves, blanketing the landscape in a silence so profound it was oppressive. The trees loomed tall and twisted around them, their branches reaching like skeletal fingers toward the heavens. Every step Astrid took felt heavier than the last, her boots crunching softly against the frozen ground as she trailed behind Thorwulf and Freya.

Her fingers still gripped the hilt of her sword, though the blade was clean now. She had wiped it on the snow before they'd moved away from the fight. Still, it felt heavier now, as if it carried the blood of the man she'd killed. Her first kill. The thought churned in her stomach, leaving her light-headed and raw.

"Keep your head up," Freya called over her shoulder, her voice sharp but not unkind. "The forest isn't as empty as it looks."

Astrid didn't answer, her gaze fixed on the path ahead. She knew Freya was right. Out here, danger could come from anywhere, at any time. But her mind was elsewhere, replaying the kill over and over again: the look in the man's eyes as he fell, the sound of his body hitting the snow, the way his blood had stained the pristine white like spilled ink.

Thorwulf slowed his pace until he was walking beside her again, his expression unusually subdued. He said nothing at first, his gaze flicking between her face and the trail ahead. It wasn't like him to stay quiet, and Astrid wasn't sure whether she found the silence comforting or unnerving.

"You're shaking," he said finally, his voice low.

Astrid flinched at his words. "I'm fine."

Thorwulf raised an eyebrow, his tone softening. "You don't look fine."

She shot him a glare, but it lacked her usual fire. "I said I'm fine."

"Sigurdsdóttir," he said, his voice gentler now. "You just killed a man for the first time. You don't have to pretend it didn't matter."

Astrid stopped walking and turned to face him. "Do you think I'm weak?" she demanded, her voice sharper than she intended.

Thorwulf's brow furrowed, his expression serious. "No. I think you're human."

The words struck her harder than she expected, and for a moment, she didn't know how to respond. Her chest ached with the weight of emotions she couldn't name, a chaotic swirl of anger, guilt, and something dangerously close to relief.

"I didn't want to kill him," she said finally, her voice barely above a whisper.

Thorwulf nodded, his gaze steady. "I know."

"I didn't have a choice," she continued, her words tumbling out before she could stop them. "It was him or me. I..." She broke off.

Thorwulf stepped closer, his voice calm and even. "You did what you had to do to protect us all. That doesn't make it easy, but it's the truth. Out here, it's survival. There's no right or wrong. You just have to do what keeps you alive."

Astrid's hands trembled, and she hated herself for it. "Is that how you see it? Just survival?"

Thorwulf hesitated, his dark eyes searching hers. "It's not about what I see, Astrid. It's about what you can live with."

The use of her first name caught her off guard, and for a moment, she couldn't look away from him. There was something raw and unguarded in his gaze that made her heart skip. She wanted to argue, to push him away and tell him she didn't need his comfort. But the truth was, she actually did. She wasn't sure she could face this alone.

"You volunteered for this," Thorwulf said quietly, his tone softer now. "To save your sister. That's the kind of person you are. You protect the people you care about, even if it means sacrificing yourself."

The mention of Solveig stirred a fresh wave of emotion in her. "She wouldn't have survived this," she said, her voice breaking. "Not with her legs. She wouldn't have made it past the first trial."

Thorwulf nodded, his expression serious. "And you couldn't stand by and let that happen. That's what makes you stronger than anyone else out here."

Astrid looked away, her gaze falling to the snow at her feet. "I don't feel strong," she admitted.

"That's because strength doesn't feel like strength when you're carrying it," Thorwulf said, his voice steady. "It feels heavy. But it's what keeps you moving, even when everything else is telling you to stop."

Freya's voice cut through the moment, her tone laced with impatience. "If you two are done bonding, we need to keep moving. This trail isn't going to stay quiet for long."

Astrid straightened, her walls snapping back into place. She adjusted her grip on her sword, her expression hardening.

"I'm fine," she said again, though this time it felt like she would be.

Thorwulf didn't press her, but as they resumed their journey, she could feel his gaze on her, watchful and steady. He didn't hover, but he stayed close enough that she could feel his presence. And it was a quiet reassurance she wasn't fully ready to acknowledge.

Freya, walking slightly ahead, cast a glance over her shoulder. Her sharp blue eyes lingered on Astrid and Thorwulf, a flicker of something unreadable crossing her face. She didn't say anything, but the tension in her shoulders seemed to ease slightly, as if she'd decided their alliance might be worth more than she'd initially thought.

The forest thinned as they climbed higher, the snow falling harder now, the wind biting against their faces. The path ahead was treacherous, lined with jagged rocks and patches of ice that made every step a risk. But for the first time since the Reckoning began, Astrid felt a glimmer of hope. She wasn't entirely alone.

As they pressed on, the whispers of the gods followed them, weaving through the trees like shadows. The Reckoning was far from over, and the medallion was still waiting. But for now, Astrid took a steadying breath, her sword heavy in her hand but her resolve stronger than ever.

12

THE FEAST OF THE JARLS

The clearing should have felt like a sanctuary after days of blood, ice, and exhaustion. Instead, it felt like another trap. The towering trees that bordered the space seemed to lean closer, their shadows stretching toward the tables as the sun dipped lower in the gray sky. A bonfire roared in the center, sending spirals of smoke and sparks into the air, but its heat didn't reach Astrid. The cold felt sharper here, biting through her cloak, the kind of chill that seeped into your bones and refused to leave.

Astrid's fingers brushed the hilt of her sword as she scanned the clearing again. The oathsworns weren't just competitors, they were predators, too. There were too many glances darting her way, too many conversations that stopped abruptly when she turned her head. Each person here had blood on their hands, and each of them was calculating whether the risk of striking now was worth the reward. But tonight, here at the feast, there was supposed to be a truce. Though no one trusted it.

Beside her, Thorwulf was a picture of ease. He leaned back slightly on the bench, his axe propped against the table, one hand resting casually on the handle. But Astrid wasn't fooled. His eyes moved constantly, taking in every detail, every movement, his body coiled like a wolf ready to strike. His calm was the kind that hid teeth.

Freya, across from them, was less subtle. She ate her stew in deliberate, unhurried bites, her sharp blue eyes watching the other tables like a hawk. She didn't bother with small talk or feigned ease. Her face was guarded. Her spear leaned against her shoulder as ever, its polished tip catching the firelight. If anyone came too close, they'd regret it.

Astrid forced herself to take a bite of bread, the dense crust cracking beneath her teeth. It tasted better than anything she'd had in days, but her stomach churned with nerves. Every instinct told her this feast was a test designed to weed out the weak. The gods didn't hand out kindness, or feasts, without demanding a price.

Across the clearing, Ragnar stood from his table, drawing the attention of everyone present. The firelight caught on his scar, the jagged line running down his face like a brand. His fur cloak seemed untouched by the trials, its pristine white a sharp contrast to the blood and dirt that clung to everyone else. He looked less like a survivor and more like a conqueror.

"Ah, look at us," Ragnar said, spreading his arms wide. His voice boomed over the crackle of the fire, its tone laced with mockery. "The best of the clans. Or what's left of us. Gathered here like wolves circling a carcass. What a sight."

A ripple of uneasy laughter spread through the crowd. A couple of the oathsworns looked away, unwilling to draw his attention, while Freya watched him with unveiled hostility. Astrid kept her gaze steady, defiantly refusing to look away when his eyes found hers.

Ragnar's smile widened. "And here we have the heroes of Frostfjord," he said, his voice dripping with false warmth. "Astrid Sigurdsdóttir and Thorwulf Haldorsson. Tell me, how does it feel to carry the weight of your clan's expectations on such weak shoulders? Must be exhausting."

Thorwulf leaned forward slightly. "Better than carrying the weight of your arrogance," he said, his tone calm but edged with steel.

A few of the oathsworns snickered, but Ragnar's smile didn't falter. If anything, it sharpened. "Oh, I admire your confidence," he said. "It's almost endearing. But let me offer you some advice. Confidence won't save you when the gods decide it's your time."

The tension in the clearing was thick enough to cut with a blade. Freya set her bowl down carefully, her gaze flicking between Ragnar and Thorwulf. "He's trying to get a rise out of you," she murmured, her voice low enough that only Astrid and Thorwulf could hear. "Don't give him the satisfaction."

Thorwulf didn't look away from Ragnar, but his grip on his axe relaxed slightly. "The gods may decide a lot of things," he said evenly. "But my fate isn't one of them."

Ragnar chuckled, the sound low and menacing. "Maybe it'll be up to me to decide for them."

Astrid couldn't stop herself. "Bold words from a man who hides behind a gang of lackeys," she said, her voice cold. "Or do you only feel strong when you've got someone to bully?"

The silence that followed was haunting. Ragnar's smile vanished, his eyes narrowing as he stepped around the table, closing the distance between them. The firelight made his scar seem deeper, darker, as he loomed over her.

"You've got fire, Sigurdsdóttir," he said, his voice soft but dangerous. "I'll give you that. But fire burns out. Strength... strength is all that lasts."

Astrid didn't flinch, though her pulse pounded in her ears. "Maybe. But I'd rather burn out than rot in a stinking carcass like yours."

For a moment, she thought he might strike her. His hand

twitched toward the axe at his hip, and the air seemed to hold its breath. But then he stepped back, a slow, mocking smile spreading across his face.

"Enjoy the feast while you can," he said, his tone light but laced with menace. "The gods won't be this kind again."

As he turned and walked back to his table, Astrid exhaled slowly, her shoulders still tense. Thorwulf leaned closer, his voice low. "That was reckless."

"He started it," she muttered, tearing another piece of bread, though her appetite was gone.

Freya snorted softly. "You've got guts, I'll give you that. But you're playing a dangerous game, Sigurdsdóttir."

Astrid didn't respond. She stared into the fire, and found its flickering flames mirrored in her thoughts. Ragnar's threats had shaken her more than she wanted to admit, but she wouldn't let him see it. She couldn't afford to.

The feast continued, the tension never fully lifting. Laughter and conversation were subdued, the shadow of the trials looming over every word. As the flames burned lower, Astrid's resolve hardened. The gods might be watching, but so was she. And she wouldn't falter.

The low hum of conversation returned to the clearing, but the tension lingered like smoke after a fire. Ragnar had settled back at his table, his expression unreadable, but Astrid could feel his gaze burning into her. She forced herself to keep her chin high, though her pulse still thudded in her ears.

Thorwulf, however, was calm again. He leaned back on the bench, one arm draped casually across the edge of the table, a faint smile playing on his lips. His relaxed demeanor was deliberate, calculated. It was his way of telling Ragnar that he wasn't intimidated.

As if sensing Thorwulf's quiet challenge, Ragnar's eyes flicked toward him. The air between them felt taut, charged with the unspoken promise of violence. Thorwulf, unfazed, raised his cup of mead in a mock toast.

"Well done, Ragnar," Thorwulf said, his voice carrying easily across the clearing. "You've got that whole brooding, menacing thing down to an art. Truly, it's impressive. But I have to ask..." He tilted his head, his smirk widening. "Do you still have to practice in front of a mirror, or does it just come naturally now?"

A few oathsworns laughed, their nervous chuckles breaking the tension like cracks in ice. Freya stiffened beside Astrid, her eyes darting between Thorwulf and Ragnar.

Ragnar snarled, his hand curling around the handle of his goblet. "Careful, Haldorsson," he said, his voice low and cold. "You're not as clever as you think."

Thorwulf shrugged, his smirk never wavering. "Maybe not. But I don't need to be clever to see through your act." He leaned forward slightly, his tone sharpening. "You talk a big game, Ragnar, but we both know what this is really about. You're scared of us."

The laughter died instantly, the clearing falling into a heavy silence. Ragnar's allies, a group of oathsworns who hovered near his table like vultures, shifted uncomfortably. The largest of them, a broad-shouldered man with a patchy beard, muttered something under his breath, but Ragnar silenced him with a sharp gesture.

"Scared?" Ragnar repeated, his voice a dangerous growl.

Thorwulf nodded, his expression calm but his eyes gleaming with challenge. "Scared of anyone who doesn't bow to you. Scared of losing control. Scared that maybe, just maybe, you're not as untouchable as you want us to believe."

The clearing felt frozen in time, every eye fixed on the two of them. Ragnar's fingers tightened around his goblet, the veins in his hand standing out starkly against his skin. For a moment,

Astrid thought he might throw the cup. Or worse, reach for his axe.

But then he laughed, the sound sharp and humorless. "You've got guts, I'll give you that," Ragnar said, his smile returning but not reaching his eyes. "Too bad it won't save you when the time comes."

Thorwulf raised his goblet in another mock toast, his smirk widening. "We'll see."

Ragnar didn't respond. He turned his attention back to his table, his allies leaning in close as he muttered something to them. Whatever he said, it made the man glance toward Astrid and Thorwulf, his expression darkening.

Freya exhaled slowly. "That was reckless, too," she muttered, her voice low enough that only Astrid and Thorwulf could hear.

Thorwulf grinned, leaning back on the bench. "Reckless? Maybe. Satisfying? Definitely."

Freya shot him a sharp look. "You just put a target on both of your backs."

Astrid frowned, her gaze flicking toward Ragnar's table. "You think we didn't already have one?"

Freya hesitated, her expression grim. "Ragnar's not just targeting you because you're from Frostfjord. It's more than that. You two are both making waves here, and he doesn't like competition."

Astrid's stomach twisted. "What kind of waves?"

Freya glanced around the clearing, her voice dropping even lower. "People are talking about you. About the way you've handled the trials so far. You've got a reputation now. And it's one that Ragnar doesn't want you to have. He sees you as a threat, and he's not going to wait for the gods to decide your fate. He'll try to take you out first."

Thorwulf's grin faded, his expression hardening. "Let him try."

Freya rolled her eyes. "You're missing the point. Ragnar doesn't fight fair. He won't come at you when you're ready. He'll wait until you're vulnerable, until you think you're safe. That's when he'll strike."

Astrid clenched her jaw, her mind racing. She knew Freya was right. Ragnar's gaze had been too calculating, his words too deliberate. He wasn't the kind of man to leave things to chance.

"Let him watch," Astrid said quietly, her voice cold. "If he wants a fight, we'll give him one."

Freya sighed, leaning back on the bench. "You're both insane. But maybe that's why you've made it this far."

Thorwulf chuckled, though the sound lacked its usual warmth. "Insanity's just another word for survival out here."

As the feast continued, the tension in the clearing never fully dissipated. Conversations were hushed, and the firelight cast long, flickering shadows that seemed to stretch toward Astrid and Thorwulf like grasping hands. Ragnar's laughter occasionally broke the quiet, sharp and grating, a reminder that he was still watching.

Astrid's fingers brushed the hilt of her sword, her resolve hardening with every passing moment. The gods might have set this trial in motion, but they weren't the only ones pulling the strings. If Ragnar wanted to test her, she would be ready.

13

THE VALKYRIE'S WARNING

The night's cold was sharper than any blade Astrid had ever wielded. It sank deep into her skin, burrowing into her bones no matter how tightly she wrapped her fur-lined cloak around herself. Their small fire crackled weakly, its embers glowing faintly as Thorwulf coaxed the flames to life with the wood he'd gathered. Around them, the wilderness of Skarn stretched into the shadows, an endless maze of jagged rocks and skeletal trees that seemed to lean closer with every gust of icy wind.

Astrid pressed her gloved hands to her face, willing warmth back into her cheeks. The snow beneath her felt like stone, unyielding and bitterly cold, and every breath she exhaled formed a pale mist that vanished as quickly as it appeared. Freya shifted beside her, adding a few branches to the fire. Her sharp blue eyes scanned the darkness, ever watchful, even as her face betrayed the weariness etched into her bones.

"We need to build a better windbreak," Freya muttered, her voice low. She pulled her hood tighter around her face, her breath curling into the air. "This clearing is too exposed. If the wind picks up again, we'll freeze before morning."

Thorwulf straightened, brushing snow off his broad

shoulders. His cloak, worn and tattered from the trials, barely seemed enough to protect him from the relentless cold, yet he carried himself with the same unyielding strength as always. "There are enough rocks nearby. We'll stack them higher and block the wind."

Freya shot him a look but didn't argue. Together, they moved quickly, gathering loose stones from the edge of the clearing and piling them around the fire. Astrid helped where she could, though her fingers felt stiff and clumsy in the biting cold. The wind howled through the trees, a mournful, eerie sound that made the hairs on the back of her neck stand on end.

Somewhere in the distance, a wolf howled, its cry echoing through the mountains like a ghost's lament. The sound sent a shiver down Astrid's spine, a reminder of the predators lurking in the shadows, both animal and human. She glanced toward Thorwulf, who paused mid-motion, his dark eyes narrowing as he listened. He didn't speak, but the tension in his posture told her he'd heard it too.

"The wolves are watching us," Freya said quietly. "They always watch. They're patient and they're wait for weakness."

Astrid swallowed hard, her gaze flicking toward the darkness beyond the firelight. She could almost feel the weight of unseen eyes, the shadows pressing closer, but she forced herself to focus on the task at hand.

The fire burned brighter now. Its warmth was a fragile barrier against the icy grip of the night. They sat close together, their breath mingling with the smoke as they ate what little food they had left. Freya gnawed on a strip of dried venison, her sharp features half-hidden in the flickering light. Thorwulf leaned back against the windbreak, his axe resting across his knees, his dark gaze fixed on the flames.

"You were reckless today," Freya said abruptly, breaking the silence. Her tone wasn't accusatory, but it carried an edge of frustration.

Thorwulf smirked, tilting his head toward Astrid. "Which one of us are you blaming? I seem to remember both of us handling Ragnar just fine."

Freya rolled her eyes. "You provoked him. And you," she pointed her spear at Astrid. "You let him see exactly how much he gets under your skin. Ragnar thrives on that. You think he'll let today slide? He'll wait for the right moment and strike when you least expect it."

Astrid frowned, the memory of Ragnar's mocking smile flashing in her mind. "Let him try," she said quietly, though her voice lacked its usual conviction. "We'll be ready."

Freya shook her head, her expression grim. "You don't understand. Ragnar doesn't fight fair. And he's not the only one you have to worry about."

Astrid exchanged a glance with Thorwulf, who seemed unusually subdued. The firelight cast shadows across his face, making him look older, wearier. "Then we stay one step ahead," he said finally. "That's all we can do."

The conversation died after that, the three of them retreating into their own thoughts. The fire crackled softly, its warmth barely enough to stave off the bitter cold. Astrid leaned against the windbreak, exhaustion tugging at her eyelids as the howling wind and distant cries of wolves faded into a dull hum.

~

In her dream, the world was a vast expanse of white, stretching endlessly in every direction. The snow beneath her feet was untouched, pristine, yet it felt impossibly cold, as if the very ground was leeching the warmth from her body. The sky above was a shifting, ethereal gray, heavy with the promise of a storm.

She turned slowly, her breath visible in the frozen air. There was nothing. No trees, no mountains, no sign of the fire or her companions. Just snow and silence.

And then, she appeared.

The Valkyrie.

She emerged from the shadows as if born of the wind itself, her form shimmering like sunlight on ice. She was taller than any mortal, her wings vast and glimmering with hues of silver and frost. Her hair flowed like a river of light, and her eyes burned with an intensity that made Astrid hold her breath.

"Astrid Sigurdsdóttir," the Valkyrie said, her voice a haunting melody that resonated in the emptiness. "The gods have turned their eyes upon you."

Astrid's throat felt dry, her voice trembling as she spoke. "Why me?"

The Valkyrie's gaze softened, but her presence remained as imposing as the mountains of Frostfjord. "Because you carry the burden of choice. Because your heart beats for more than just survival or honor."

Astrid's breath came in shallow bursts. "What do you want from me?"

The Valkyrie tilted her head, her wings shifting slightly. "It is not what I want, Sigurdsdóttir. It is what the gods demand. Betrayal will test your resolve. Shadows will rise to challenge your light. And in the end, you must decide what you are willing to lose to protect what you love."

Astrid stepped forward, desperation clawing at her chest. "Who will betray me? Who can I trust?"

The Valkyrie's expression was unreadable, her voice quiet but firm. "Trust is both your strength and your weakness. Guard your heart, Astrid. For the trials ahead will not only test your body but your soul."

Before Astrid could ask more, the Valkyrie reached out, her

icy fingers brushing Astrid's forehead. The touch sent a shock through her, a burst of light and cold that consumed everything.

Astrid jolted awake, her chest heaving as she sat up. The fire had burned low, its embers glowing faintly in the darkness. Thorwulf and Freya were still asleep, their breaths steady in the cold air. The wind had quieted, but the chill remained, wrapping around her like a second skin.

She touched her forehead, the Valkyrie's words echoing in her mind. Betrayal would test her. Shadows would rise. And the gods… they were still watching. Still judging.

Astrid pulled her cloak tighter, her gaze flicking toward the fire. The dream had felt too real, and far too vivid to dismiss. The gods weren't just watching, they were pulling the strings, shaping their fates with every choice they made.

And Astrid couldn't shake the feeling that her next choice would cost her more than she was ready to give.

~

As the dawn broke reluctantly over the mountains, the pale light struggled to pierce the thick veil of gray clouds. Snow still fell in sporadic flurries, dusting the jagged rocks and frozen earth with a fresh layer of white. Astrid woke to the sound of Freya stirring beside the dwindling fire, her breath a visible cloud in the frigid air. Thorwulf sat a few paces away, sharpening his axe in deliberate, measured strokes, as his dark eyes scanned the horizon.

Astrid pushed herself upright, her muscles stiff and aching from the cold. The dream lingered in her mind like a shadow, its weight heavy on her chest. She glanced toward Thorwulf, but his face was unreadable, his focus fixed on his weapon. Freya caught her gaze and nodded toward the fire.

"Eat something," Freya said briskly, handing Astrid a strip of dried venison. "We'll need the energy if we're going to make it through the pass before nightfall."

Astrid nodded, chewing on the tough meat as she surveyed the landscape ahead. The trees had thinned significantly, their gnarled branches giving way to vast stretches of open ground. The mountains rose like jagged teeth in the distance, their peaks shrouded in mist. The path ahead was steep and treacherous, the kind of terrain that could break even the strongest warrior if they weren't careful.

By the time they broke camp, the sun was a faint disc behind the clouds, offering little warmth. They moved in silence at first, their boots crunching over the snow and ice as they navigated the uneven ground. The wind had softened, but its chill remained, biting at their exposed skin and tugging at their cloaks. The air felt thinner here, sharper, as if even the gods had abandoned this desolate stretch of land.

It was Freya who broke the silence as they ascended a narrow ridge, her voice carrying over the sound of their footsteps. "Do you ever wonder if this is all just... pointless?"

Astrid frowned, glancing at her. "What do you mean?"

Freya adjusted the strap of her spear, her sharp blue eyes fixed on the trail ahead. "The Reckoning. The trials. Everything we're putting ourselves through. Do you ever think the gods are just... toying with us? That none of this actually matters?"

Astrid hesitated, the question catching her off guard. She had always believed in the gods, in their power and their will, but the events of the past few days had shaken her faith. The Valkyrie's warning echoed in her mind, a reminder of the shadows that loomed over them.

"I don't think it's pointless," Astrid said finally, her voice quieter than she intended. "The gods may be cruel, but they're not indifferent. They're watching us, and testing us. If we prove ourselves worthy, they'll reward us."

Freya snorted, her expression darkening. "And what kind of reward will that be? More blood? More trials? The gods don't care about us, Astrid. They want a show, nothing more. We're just entertainment for them."

Astrid's steps faltered, her gaze snapping to Freya. "That's not true. The gods have guided us for generations. Without them, we'd have nothing. Without them we have no purpose, no unity. The Reckoning isn't just a trial; it's a way to prove we're strong enough to survive. For our clans."

Freya stopped walking, turning to face Astrid fully. Her face was hard, her jaw tight with suppressed emotion. "Do you really believe that?" she demanded. "That strength is all that matters? That the gods decide our worth based on how many people we can kill?"

Astrid opened her mouth to respond, but Freya didn't give her the chance. "I've seen what the Reckoning does to people," Freya continued, her voice rising. "I've seen families torn apart, children sacrificed for the sake of tradition. And for what? So that the gods can have their bloodsport? That's not justice. That's cruelty."

The words hit Astrid like a blow, stirring something deep and uncomfortable within her. She thought of her sister, of the sacrifices she'd already made to protect her. She thought of the man she'd killed, his blood staining the snow, and the hollow feeling that had lingered in her chest ever since.

"You don't understand," Astrid said quietly, her voice trembling. "The Reckoning isn't about more than survival, it's about honor. It's about proving that we're worthy of the gods' favor. Without the Reckoning, we'd fall apart. The clans would go to war, and everything we've built would be destroyed."

Freya laughed bitterly, shaking her head. "You think this is unity? You think the clans are stronger because of this madness? Look around, Astrid. We're all here because we're disposable.

The Reckoning is only ever about control. The gods use it to keep us divided, to make sure we never realize how much stronger we'd be if we stood together."

Astrid stared at her, the weight of her words sinking in. For a moment, she didn't know what to say. She wanted to defend the gods, to argue that Freya was wrong, but the doubt gnawed at her like a wolf at a carcass.

Thorwulf, who had been silent until now, cleared his throat softly. Both women turned to look at him, their gazes questioning.

"What about you?" Freya asked, her tone challenging. "Do you think the gods are watching us with benevolence? Or are we just their pawns?"

Thorwulf's dark eyes flicked between them, his expression unreadable. He shrugged, the movement slow and deliberate. "I think the gods are... complicated entities," he said finally, his voice quiet but firm. "They don't owe us understanding. And we don't owe them blind faith. What matters is what we do here and now. And that might not be what they expect from us."

Freya arched an eyebrow, clearly unsatisfied with his answer, but she didn't press further. Astrid, however, found herself turning Thorwulf's words over in her mind. They carried a weight that lingered, a subtle challenge to everything she thought she believed.

As the day wore on, the landscape grew harsher, the ground beneath their boots turning from snow to jagged, frost-covered rock. The trees all but disappeared, leaving them exposed to the elements as they climbed higher into the mountains. The wind picked up again, carrying with it the faint howl of wolves that seemed to echo endlessly through the peaks.

Astrid pulled her cloak tighter, her thoughts churning as they pressed on. Freya's words lingered in her mind, stirring a doubt she couldn't quite shake. The gods were watching. Of that much, she was sure. But whether they were just or cruel, benevolent or indifferent, she no longer knew.

Thorwulf walked slightly ahead, his axe in hand, his steps steady despite the treacherous terrain. Freya followed close behind, her spear ready, her sharp eyes scanning for danger. And Astrid, caught between her faith and her doubt, kept moving, her heart heavy with questions she wasn't sure she wanted answered.

14

THE LABYRINTH OF THE LOST

The entrance to the labyrinth loomed ahead. It was a jagged stone archway carved with runes so old they were barely legible. Vines wound through the cracks, their brittle leaves dusted with frost, and the air smelled of earth and decay. Astrid's heart was pounding in her chest as she stared into the darkness beyond the threshold. Like the whole island, the labyrinth seemed to breathe, exhaling a faint mist that coiled around her boots like ghostly fingers.

"Looks inviting," Thorwulf muttered, his voice low but laced with tension. He stood at her side, his axe slung across his back, his eyes scanning the shadows for movement.

Freya stepped forward, her spear tapping the ground as she tested the first stone. "It's meant to unsettle us," she said, her voice steady. "The gods thrive on fear. They want us to hesitate."

Astrid swallowed hard, her gaze flicking to the runes above the archway. She couldn't read them, but their jagged lines felt ominous, like the whisper of a warning just out of reach.

"Then let's not give them the satisfaction," she said, stepping through the archway before she could second-guess herself.

The air inside the labyrinth was colder. It had sharp edges, as if it carried the weight of centuries. The narrow passage was lined with ancient stone walls, whose surfaces were etched with runes and images of warriors long forgotten. The ceiling arched high above, disappearing into shadow, and the faint sound of dripping water echoed through the corridor.

Freya followed close behind her, Thorwulf bringing up the rear. The tension between them was palpable, each of them hyper-aware of the potential for traps, or worse, ambushes.

The corridor opened into a vast chamber, the floor a mosaic of broken tiles that glinted faintly in the dim light. At its center stood a massive stone pedestal, its surface carved with intricate patterns. Three smaller pedestals surrounded it, each holding a stone disc engraved with different symbols: a serpent, a sun, and a wolf.

"A puzzle," Freya said, stepping closer to examine the carvings. Her sharp eyes darted over the symbols, and her brow furrowed. "The gods love their riddles."

Astrid approached cautiously, feeling her pulse quicken. The carvings on the central pedestal formed a circle, their patterns intertwining like the threads of fate. She reached out, tracing one of the lines with her gloved finger, and felt a faint hum beneath her touch.

"What do you think it means?" Thorwulf asked, standing at her shoulder.

Astrid stared at the discs, her mind racing. The symbols seemed to shimmer in the faint light, their meanings just out of reach. "It's just another way to test us," she said finally, her voice steady despite the knot of anxiety in her chest. "The gods want us to prove we're worthy to move forward. We have to place the discs in the right order."

Freya frowned, her fingers brushing the edge of the serpent disc. "And what happens if we're wrong?"

The silence that followed was answer enough.

Astrid closed her eyes, focusing on the runes she'd seen above the entrance. They'd been faded, but one word had stood out. It was a word her mother had taught her long ago, back when stories of the gods had been woven into her bedtime tales.

"Wolf first," she said, opening her eyes. She reached for the disc, her hand steady despite the tremor in her gut. "The wolf is the watcher, the one who guards the path."

Thorwulf exchanged a glance with Freya but said nothing as Astrid placed the disc on the central pedestal. It slid into place with a faint click, the hum beneath her fingers growing stronger.

"Sun next," Astrid continued, her voice more certain now. "The sun is the guide, lighting the way through darkness."

Freya handed her the sun disc, her expression skeptical but willing to trust her judgment. Astrid placed it beside the wolf, the hum shifting to a low, steady thrum that vibrated through the chamber.

"And the serpent," she said finally, taking the last disc. "The serpent is the end, the keeper of secrets."

The moment the third disc clicked into place, the mosaic beneath their feet lit up, the broken tiles glowing with a golden light that spread outward in rippling waves. The air vibrated with energy, and the walls of the chamber seemed to shift, the runes glowing faintly as the central pedestal sank into the floor, revealing a hidden staircase.

Astrid exhaled slowly, the tension in her chest easing slightly. "That wasn't so bad," she said, her voice tinged with relief.

A sharp laugh echoed through the chamber, cutting through the air like a blade.

"Maybe not for you," Ragnar said, stepping out of the shadows at the far end of the chamber. His axe gleamed in the golden light, and his smile was as sharp as the edge of a blade. "But let's see how you handle this."

Astrid's heart lurched as Ragnar's allies emerged behind him, their weapons drawn. There were three of them, each one as ruthless and bloodied as their leader.

Thorwulf stepped in front of her, his axe raised, his posture defensive. "Ragnar," he said, his voice calm but edged with steel. "I was wondering when you'd show up."

Ragnar's smile widened, his gaze flicking to Astrid. "You've been making quite the impression, Sigurdsdóttir. Solving puzzles, defying the odds... it's almost like the gods favor you."

"They don't," Astrid said coldly, her sword in hand. "And neither do they favor you."

Ragnar chuckled, his allies fanning out to surround them. "You're clever, I'll give you that. But cleverness won't save you now."

The tension snapped like a bowstring as Ragnar lunged, his axe swinging in a brutal arc. Thorwulf met him head-on, their weapons clashing with a deafening crash that echoed through the chamber. Freya darted to the side, her spear flashing as she engaged one of Ragnar's allies.

Astrid found herself face-to-face with a wiry boy wielding twin daggers. His movements were quick and unpredictable. He feinted left, then struck from the right, forcing her to pivot and block with her sword. The impact jarred her arm, but she held her ground, her movements sharp and precise.

The chamber became a blur of motion and sound, the golden glow of the tiles casting strange, flickering shadows as the fight raged on. Astrid ducked beneath a wild swing, her blade slicing through the air to catch her opponent across the shoulder. He cried out, stumbling back, and she pressed the advantage, her strikes relentless.

Thorwulf roared as he drove Ragnar back, their weapons a blur of steel and fury. Freya fought with precision, her spear darting like a serpent's fang as she kept two of Ragnar's allies at bay.

The air was thick with the clash of metal and the grunts of exertion, but Astrid's focus remained razor-sharp. She couldn't afford to falter. Not with Ragnar watching.

The labyrinth hadn't just been a test of wit. It was a crucible of war, and the gods were waiting to see who would emerge unbroken.

The clash of weapons rang out, sharp and jarring in the confined chamber. The glow of the golden tiles bathed everything in an otherworldly light, illuminating the chaos as Astrid ducked and weaved through the fight. Her opponent came at her again, his twin daggers flashing in the dim glow. She blocked one blade with her sword and twisted just in time to avoid the other, the edge grazing her cloak.

Sweat slicked her palms despite the cold, and her muscles burned with effort. The man was fast, his movements fluid and calculated, but Astrid refused to back down. She feinted left, then swung upward, her blade catching the edge of his sleeve and drawing a thin line of blood.

He hissed, staggering back, and she pressed her advantage. Her movements were quick and precise, every step deliberate as she forced him toward the edge of the room. But before she could deliver the final blow, a roar cut through the air, and she turned just in time to see Ragnar charging toward her.

Ragnar's axe gleamed, the blade swinging toward her with terrifying speed. She barely had time to react, her sword rising instinctively to block the blow, but she knew it wouldn't be enough. The force behind his attack would shatter her defenses, and possibly her arm.

Before the axe could connect, Thorwulf stepped between them like a shield. His own axe met Ragnar's with a resounding crash, the impact reverberating through the room.

"Get back!" Thorwulf barked, in a voice sharp with authority. He didn't wait for her to respond as he parried Ragnar's next strike.

Astrid stumbled back, her heart pounding as she watched Thorwulf and Ragnar clash. Their weapons sang as they collided, each strike fiercer than the last. Thorwulf's expression was grim, his jaw tight as he met Ragnar's brute strength with his own.

"You're protecting her now?" Ragnar sneered, his voice dripping with mockery. "How noble. Do you think she'll thank you for it?"

Thorwulf didn't answer, his focus unyielding as he deflected another blow. His movements were calculated, his strikes precise, but Ragnar's attacks were relentless. The two men were evenly matched, their strength and skill pushing each other to the limit.

Astrid's heart raced as she watched, torn between the instinct to help and the knowledge that she would only be a liability in this fight. She turned her attention back to her own opponent, who was recovering from her earlier strike.

The man lunged at her, his daggers aiming for her throat. She sidestepped, her blade flashing as she caught him across the ribs. He cried out, staggering, and she followed with a quick, decisive strike that sent him sprawling to the ground.

Freya, on the other side of the room, dispatched one of Ragnar's allies with a brutal jab of her spear. She spun toward Astrid, her sharp eyes narrowing as she took in the scene. "Help Thorwulf!" she shouted, her voice cutting through the chaos.

Astrid didn't hesitate. She sprinted toward the center of the room, where Thorwulf and Ragnar were locked in a deadly dance. Ragnar's axe came down in a powerful arc, and Thorwulf barely managed to dodge, the blade slicing through the air inches from his shoulder.

"You can't protect her forever," Ragnar growled, his eyes blazing with fury. "She's weak. She'll fall, just like the rest of them."

Thorwulf's lips curled into a grim smile. "You don't know her at all."

With a surge of strength, Thorwulf forced Ragnar back, his axe striking with a ferocity that sent sparks flying. For a moment, Ragnar faltered, his footing unsteady, and Astrid saw her chance.

She darted forward, her sword aimed for Ragnar's exposed side. He turned just in time to deflect her strike, his eyes narrowing as he realized she wasn't retreating.

"Clever girl," he said, his tone mocking. "But not clever enough."

He swung his axe, and Astrid braced herself for the impact. But Thorwulf was faster. He stepped between them again, his axe blocking the strike with a deafening crash.

"Stay behind me," Thorwulf growled, his voice low and fierce.

Astrid clenched her jaw, feeling her frustration warring with her gratitude. She hated being shielded, hated feeling like a burden, but the intensity in Thorwulf's voice left no room for argument.

Ragnar sneered. "This isn't over," he snarled, his gaze shifting between them. With a sharp whistle, he signaled his remaining allies to retreat.

A sound whispered in the shadows behind Astrid that chilled her heart. A sharp intake of breath. Wet, gurgling, agonized.

Astrid turned to see Freya standing frozen, her spear slipping from her grasp. A blade jutted from her side, and her blue cloak was drenched with blood.

One of Ragnar's allies grinned as he pulled back from her.

His face was smeared with blood and triumph, and he let out a low chuckle before vanishing into the shadows.

"Freya?" Astrid whispered.

Freya stumbled, her hand reaching for the hilt of the dagger as if to pull it free, but her knees gave out. She collapsed against the base of a broken pillar, her blood already pooling dark and fast.

Thorwulf swore, rushing to her side, but one look at the wound stole the breath from his lungs. Astrid dropped beside her, fingers shaking as she pressed them to Freya's wound. "No. Freya. No, stay with us..."

Freya's gaze locked on hers. Her eyes were still fierce, but the light was already fading.

"You found the path," she murmured. Her voice was hoarse but steady. "Now follow it."

"Don't..." Astrid started, but Freya shook her head, just once.

"There's no time," she whispered. Her eyes flicked to the glowing staircase now revealed by the shifting tiles. "The Reckoning waits. You will win it together."

And then, the fire left her eyes. Astrid didn't move. Couldn't breathe. Thorwulf reached out and gently closed Freya's eyes, jaw clenched, grief carved deep into his face. For a moment, they said nothing, crouching beside their fallen friend. Astrid leaned against his shoulder, allowing the weight and warmth of him to support her, just for a moment.

Thorwulf rose first.

"We can't stay," he said, his voice low and tight. "We will finish this. For her."

Astrid stood too. The glow of the golden tiles had dimmed, the energy in the room shifting as the staircase loomed ahead. They were still alive, reduced to just the two of them, and the gods weren't finished with them yet.

As they descended into the darkness, Astrid couldn't shake

the weight of Thorwulf's loyalty, or the warning in Ragnar's parting words.

15

AN OATHSWORN SACRIFICE

The echo of falling stone still reverberated through the chamber, a grim reminder of what had just happened. The air was heavy with dust and the sharp tang of scorched stone, but all Astrid could focus on was the silence. The absence of Freya's voice, her sharp wit, her steady presence pushed down on her thoughts. It didn't seem real.

Thorwulf stood at the edge of the chasm, his broad shoulders hunched as he stared into the shadows below. His axe lay forgotten at his feet, his fists clenched so tightly that his knuckles were white. Astrid had never seen him like this before. He looked so still, so vulnerable. It was as if the weight of Freya's loss had stripped away his usual bravado, leaving only raw, unfiltered emotion.

"She didn't deserve to die," Thorwulf said, his voice low and strained. There was a tremor in his tone that Astrid had never heard before. "Not like this."

Astrid swallowed hard, the lump in her throat making it difficult to speak. "None of us deserve this," she said quietly, stepping closer to him. "But she knew the risks. We all do."

Thorwulf shook his head. "She was better than any of us.

Smarter, stronger. She helped keep us alive out here. And I..." He trailed off, his voice breaking.

Astrid hesitated, unsure of what to say. She wanted to comfort him, to tell him that they would get through this, but the words felt hollow. Freya was gone, and nothing she could say would change that.

Thorwulf's gaze dropped to the ground, his shoulders slumping. "I should have stopped it," he muttered. "I should have saved her."

"You couldn't save both of us," Astrid said gently, her hand hovering near his arm before she finally placed it there. His cloak was rough beneath her touch, but the warmth of his skin beneath it grounded her. "Thorwulf, this isn't your fault. Ragnar attacked us. He's the one to blame, not you."

Thorwulf turned to look at her, his dark eyes shimmering with unshed tears. It was the first time Astrid had seen him so exposed, so utterly unguarded. The sight of it tugged at something deep within her, tweaking a part of her that had been locked away since the Reckoning began.

"She trusted me," he said, his voice rough. "And I couldn't protect her."

Astrid's chest ached at the anguish in his words. She stepped closer, her fingers tightening on his arm. "She trusted you because you earned it," she said firmly. "Because she knew you would do everything you could to keep us alive. And you have. Freya knew the risks, and she made her choice. Don't let Ragnar take more from us than he already has."

Thorwulf's gaze lingered on hers, his expression softening as he took in her words. For a moment, the weight of his grief seemed to lessen, replaced by something quieter and more vulnerable.

"I don't want to lose anyone else," he admitted, his voice barely above a whisper.

Astrid felt her breath catch in her throat. She wanted to tell him that he wouldn't lose her, that she would fight tooth and nail to survive. But she couldn't make that promise. Not here, not in this cursed labyrinth where the gods watched and waited for their next move.

Instead, she said, "We won't let Ragnar win. For Freya. For all of us."

Thorwulf nodded slowly, his hand brushing against hers as he turned back toward the path ahead. The brief contact sent a jolt through her, a warmth that contrasted sharply with the cold around them. She didn't pull away, and neither did he.

For a moment, they stood there together, their grief and determination binding them in a way that words couldn't. The silence between them was steady, like the quiet rhythm of a heartbeat.

As they moved silently away from the chasm, Astrid found herself watching Thorwulf more closely. The way his shoulders remained tense, as though he carried the weight of Freya's death on them. The way his gaze darted to every shadow, every corner, as if searching for the traps he now expected at every turn. He had always been strong, unyielding, but there was a tenderness beneath the surface that she hadn't seen before.

Her own grief lingered, a dull ache in her chest that refused to fade. Freya had been a reluctant ally, sharp-tongued and guarded, but Astrid had come to respect her. Losing her felt like losing a part of their group's foundation, and the emptiness it left behind was palpable.

"Freya would have hated this," Thorwulf said suddenly, breaking the silence. His voice was still rough, but there was a faint note of humor in it. "All this mourning. She'd tell us to stop sulking and get on with it."

Astrid smiled faintly, the image of Freya rolling her eyes at their grief bringing a bittersweet warmth to her chest. "She would," Astrid agreed. "And then she'd probably insult us for being too sentimental and wasting time."

Thorwulf chuckled softly, the sound low and warm. "She'd have a few choice words for me, that's for sure."

Astrid glanced at him, the corners of her lips lifting despite the weight in her heart. "She respected you, you know. She might not have said it, but she did."

Thorwulf's expression softened, his dark eyes meeting hers. "And you?" he asked quietly. "Do you?"

Astrid hesitated, her heart pounding at the unexpected question. She searched his gaze, finding no mockery there, only a quiet vulnerability that made her heart soar.

"I do," she said finally, her voice steady. "You've proven yourself time and time again, Thorwulf. You're someone I can trust."

The words hung between them, heavy with unspoken meaning. Thorwulf's gaze lingered on hers, his expression unreadable, but the faintest flicker of warmth touched his lips.

"Good," he said softly. "Because I trust you too."

Astrid felt her cheeks flush, the cold doing little to hide the warmth that spread through her. She looked away, her gaze fixing on the path ahead as they continued their journey. The labyrinth still stretched before them, its dangers lurking in every shadow, but for the first time, she felt a flicker of something she hadn't expected.

The labyrinth seemed alive with malice, its cold stone walls pressing closer with every step. The faint light of the runes flickered erratically, casting jagged shadows across the uneven ground as Astrid and Thorwulf pushed deeper into the twisting maze. The silence was heavier now, a suffocating reminder of Freya's absence, and each step forward felt like a betrayal to the woman who'd kept them alive for so long.

The air here carried a biting chill, sharper than any Astrid had felt in Frostfjord's harsh winters. She pulled her cloak tighter around her shoulders, but the cold wasn't just in the air, it was in her bones, her chest, even her soul. The weight of Freya's death pressed down on her, and with each moment that passed, the realization sank deeper: Freya was gone, and it was Ragnar's doing.

Astrid glanced at Thorwulf, his profile hardened by the flickering light. He was silent, his jaw tight and his grip on his axe tighter. He walked slightly ahead of her with his shoulders squared as if bracing against the crushing weight of his own grief. But she could sense a quiet storm brewing beneath the surface, a rage he hadn't yet unleashed.

When he spoke, his voice was low, roughened by the tension that had been building between them since Freya had fallen. "We can't keep going like this," he said, his tone flat but filled with unspoken emotion.

Astrid slowed her pace, her brow furrowing. "What do you mean?"

Thorwulf turned his head slightly, his dark eyes flicking to hers before returning to the path ahead. "Just wandering blind. Ragnar knows we're weaker now. Freya was the tactician, the one who always saw the traps before we stepped into them. Without her..." He trailed off, the words hanging in the air like frost on a blade.

"We're vulnerable," Astrid finished, the truth of it settling like a stone in her stomach.

Thorwulf's lips tightened, and he nodded. "If we're going to make it out of here, we can't rely on just surviving the gods' tests. We need to outthink Ragnar. Outsmart him."

Astrid's gaze flicked to the faint runes glowing on the walls, their meanings elusive and yet tantalizingly close. "The medallion," she murmured, her voice steadier than she felt.

"That's the key. If we can find it first, we can force Ragnar into a position where he can't win."

Thorwulf tilted his head, his lips twitching into the faintest of smiles. "Always planning," he said softly. "It's one of the things I admire most about you, Astrid."

Her heart gave an unexpected lurch, and she quickly looked away, focusing on the walls instead of the warmth in his voice. She couldn't afford to think about admiration or whatever else might be stirring between them. Not now. Not here.

"The runes," she said, changing the subject and gesturing toward the carvings on the walls. "The gods have been using them to guide us. Or maybe to test us. If we can figure out what they're saying, it might give us an edge."

Thorwulf stepped closer to one of the walls, his fingers brushing over the weathered stone. His movements were slow, almost reverent, and the flickering light caught on the angles of his face, making him look younger, softer somehow. "Do you really think the gods are helping us?" he asked, his voice quiet.

Astrid hesitated, her fingers closing around the hilt of her sword. "I don't know," she admitted. "But I think the clues are all here, if we can just find them. I can feel them watching. Always. That much is certain."

Thorwulf didn't respond immediately. He traced the edge of a rune with his gloved hand, his brow furrowed as if trying to read its secrets. "If they're watching," he said finally, "I hope they see what Ragnar did to Freya. And I hope they care."

Astrid stepped closer, her hand brushing his arm before she could think better of it. "The gods may be cruel, but Ragnar is the one who set that ambush," she said, her voice steady. "He's the one who chose to spill her blood. And he's the one we'll stop."

Thorwulf turned to her, his dark eyes locking onto hers. For a moment, the weight of his grief and anger was laid bare, unguarded, and it was almost too much to bear. But then he nodded, resolute. "We will," he said, the words a promise.

They pressed on, the labyrinth growing darker and colder with each step. The air seemed heavier now, thick with the weight of unseen eyes. Astrid's thoughts churned, the silence between her and Thorwulf filled with all the things she couldn't bring herself to say.

"Back there," Thorwulf said suddenly, his voice breaking the quiet. "When Ragnar came for you..."

Astrid glanced at him, her brow furrowing. "What about it?"

He hesitated. "Why didn't you run?"

The question caught her off guard, and she blinked at him. "What?"

Thorwulf stopped walking, turning to face her fully. The flickering light from the runes cast shadows across his face, but his eyes were steady, piercing. "You could have run. You should have. But you stayed."

Astrid's heart thudded painfully in her chest. She opened her mouth, then closed it again, unsure of what to say. Finally, she found her voice. "Because I couldn't leave you behind. We're in this together, Thorwulf. I'm not running. Not from Ragnar, not from this."

Thorwulf's expression softened, the hardness in his gaze giving way to something warmer, something vulnerable. "You're braver than anyone I've ever known," he said quietly.

Her breath caught as she stared at him. The weight of his words settled over her, heavier than the chill in the air. She wanted to look away, to focus on the path ahead, but she couldn't tear her eyes from his.

"Thorwulf..." she began, but the words faltered on her tongue.

He stepped closer, his presence solid and steady, grounding her in a way she hadn't expected. "I couldn't let him hurt you back there, Astrid," he said, his voice low. "I couldn't lose you."

The confession hung between them, heavy with unspoken emotion. Astrid felt a warmth rise in her chest, cutting through the cold and the fear, and for a moment, the weight of the Reckoning didn't seem so crushing.

"We'll make it through this," she said softly, her voice steady despite the storm inside her. "Together. That's what Freya said."

Thorwulf nodded, his gaze lingering on hers for a heartbeat longer before he turned back to the path ahead. "Together," he echoed.

As they moved deeper into the labyrinth, the air grew colder, the shadows darker. But for the first time, Astrid felt something she hadn't allowed herself to feel since the Reckoning began: hope.

And though she couldn't bring herself to say it aloud, she realized something else, too. Thorwulf wasn't just an ally. He was something more. Something she wasn't ready to name yet, but something she couldn't ignore.

16

THE HUNT

The forest was a maze of jagged trees and shadows, their twisted branches clawing at the slate-gray sky. Snow fell steadily now, blanketing the ground in a thick, sound-muffling layer, and the air was so cold that Astrid's breath froze in faint puffs before disappearing into the icy wind. Her boots crunched softly against the snow as she crept forward, her sword held low but ready, and her senses sharp and humming with tension.

Beside her, Thorwulf moved like a shadow. His axe was a constant weight in hand and his dark eyes scanning the dense forest ahead. His usual charm and easy confidence were gone, replaced by a quiet intensity that made Astrid's pulse quicken. Every movement he made was deliberate, every step calculated.

"Do you think Ragnar's allies are as clever as him?" Astrid whispered.

Thorwulf glanced at her, his lips twitching into a faint, humorless smile. "No," he said softly, his breath visible in the cold air. "But dumb enough to follow his orders. That makes them even more dangerous."

Astrid nodded. The memory of Freya's death was still fresh, a sharp ache in her chest that refused to fade. Ragnar might have been the one to set the trap, but one of his allies had driven the blade into her side. And they would pay for it.

Ahead, the trees began to thin, revealing a frozen river cutting through the forest like a jagged scar. The ice was cracked in places, jagged fissures radiating out from the edges where the current churned beneath the surface. Astrid crouched low, her eyes scanning the riverbank for any sign of movement.

"There," Thorwulf murmured, his voice so quiet she almost didn't hear him. He pointed to a set of tracks in the snow, faint but fresh.

Astrid followed his gaze, her heart quickening as she saw the trail leading toward a cluster of boulders near the edge of the river. The tracks were uneven, as if whoever made them had been limping.

"Split up?" she asked, glancing at Thorwulf.

He hesitated. "No. Not yet. Let's see what we're dealing with first."

She nodded, her stomach twisting with a mix of anticipation and dread as they moved toward the boulders. Every step felt like an eternity, the silence around them broken only by the distant creak of ice and the faint rustle of the wind.

As they neared the rocks, Thorwulf held up a hand, signaling for her to stop. He crouched low, his gaze fixed on the ground ahead. Astrid followed his line of sight and saw a faint glint of metal buried beneath the snow, a trap waiting to be sprung.

"They're setting snares," Thorwulf muttered, his tone grim. "Ragnar's getting desperate."

Astrid frowned, her mind racing. If Ragnar's allies were laying traps, it meant they were nearby. Watching. Waiting. She scanned the forest, her breath coming in shallow bursts.

"We can use this," she said quietly, her gaze flicking to Thorwulf.

He raised an eyebrow, his expression cautious but intrigued. "How?"

A slow smile spread across her lips, though there was no humor in it. "We turn their trap against them."

~

The plan came together quickly, born of necessity and a growing sense of urgency. Astrid worked swiftly, her fingers numb from the cold as she dismantled the snare and reassembled it just a few paces away, hidden beneath a fresh layer of snow. Thorwulf stood guard, his broad frame a reassuring presence as his eyes scanned the treeline.

"They'll come back to check on it," Astrid whispered, straightening and brushing the snow from her gloves. "When they do, we'll be ready."

Thorwulf nodded, his expression grim. "If they don't see through it first."

"They won't," Astrid said with more confidence than she felt. "Ragnar's too focused on us. He's expecting us to run, not fight back."

Thorwulf's lips twitched into a faint smile. "I like this side of you, Sigurdsdóttir. Fierce and determined as ever, but with a touch of dark cunning."

Astrid felt her cheeks warm, though she quickly blamed it on the cold. "Focus, Haldorsson," she said, though her tone lacked its usual sharpness.

They didn't have to wait long. The sound of crunching snow reached their ears, faint but unmistakable. Astrid's pulse quickened as she crouched low behind a boulder, her sword in hand. Thorwulf was beside her, his axe resting across his knees, his gaze fixed on the approaching figures.

Two of Ragnar's allies emerged from the trees, their cloaks

pulled tight against the cold. One of them, the one who'd stabbed Freya, was muttering under his breath, which was steaming in the frigid air. The other, a girl with a bow slung across her back, moved more cautiously, her sharp eyes scanning the ground ahead.

Astrid held her breath as they approached the trap, her heart pounding in her chest. The man reached out with his foot, prodding the snow-covered snare.

The trap sprung with a sharp snap, the metal teeth clamping around his leg. He screamed, the sound sharp and piercing, and Astrid surged forward before the woman could react.

Her sword caught the bow-wielder across the arm, forcing her to drop her weapon with a cry of pain. Astrid didn't hesitate, her movements quick and precise as she disarmed her opponent and forced her to the ground.

Thorwulf was already on the wiry man, his axe flashing in the dim light as he struck with brutal efficiency. The man's screams were cut short, and the forest fell silent once more, save for the sound of Thorwulf's labored breathing.

Astrid turned to the woman, who was clutching her bleeding arm, her eyes wide with fear. "Where's Ragnar?" Astrid demanded, her voice sharp.

The woman glared at her, blood trickling from the corner of her mouth. "You'll never make it to him," she spat. "He'll kill you both."

Astrid kept her grip on her sword steady. "Where is he?"

The woman's lips curled into a defiant smile, but she didn't answer. Thorwulf stepped closer, his presence looming, and for the first time, the woman's resolve seemed to waver.

"North," she said finally, her voice trembling. "He's heading north. To the caves. That's where he will win this."

Astrid exchanged a glance with Thorwulf, her eyes narrowing. The caves were dangerous, a maze of tunnels that few ever returned from. But if Ragnar was there, it was where they had to go.

With a cold brutality she didn't know she had, but fueled by what they'd done to Freya, Astrid slid her sword into the woman's chest, dispatching her quickly, as Thorwulf silenced the man in the trap.

"Let's move," Thorwulf said, his voice steady.

Astrid nodded, her resolve hardening as they disappeared into the forest, leaving the bodies behind.

The hunt for Ragnar had only just begun.

The wind clawed at Astrid's face as she and Thorwulf moved deeper into the forest. The trees grew denser, their twisted branches forming a skeletal canopy above that blocked out what little light the gray sky provided. Each step forward felt heavier, as if the forest itself wanted to swallow them whole.

Astrid's thoughts churned with the weight of the woman's words. North. To the caves. The very mention of the caves sent a shiver down her spine, not just from the cold, but from the stories she'd heard as a child. The caves were a place of shadows, where the gods were said to whisper their most terrible secrets. Few who ventured there ever returned, and those who did were rarely the same.

"Are you sure this is a good idea?" Astrid asked, breaking the silence. Her voice sounded small in the vast emptiness of the forest, and she hated how uncertain it made her feel.

Thorwulf didn't slow his pace. His axe was slung across his back now, his broad shoulders hunched against the wind. "No," he admitted, his tone blunt. "But it's the only idea we've got."

Astrid frowned, quickening her steps to match his. "You realize Ragnar is probably setting another trap for us, right? He's leading us straight to him because he thinks we'll be desperate enough to follow."

Thorwulf glanced at her, his expression unreadable. "We are

desperate. But so is he. He's running out of allies, and he knows it. He's hoping he can end this before we get the upper hand."

"And what if he does?" she pressed. "What if we're walking into something we can't fight our way out of?"

Thorwulf stopped abruptly, turning to face her. His dark eyes locked onto hers, and for a moment, the cold seemed to fade, replaced by the heat of his intensity. "Then I'll make sure you walk out of it, even if I don't."

The words hit her like a blow, stealing the breath from her lungs. She stared at him as his meaning sank in. "What are you talking about?" she demanded, her voice sharper than she intended.

"You know exactly what I'm talking about," he said, his tone steady but quiet. "I'm not letting Ragnar take you, Astrid. Not after Freya. Not after everything we've been through."

Astrid shook her head, her pulse quickening. "You can't just decide that, Thorwulf. We're in this together. If one of us falls, the other..."

"...keeps going," he interrupted, his voice firm. "You're the one who's meant to survive this, Astrid. Not me."

The raw honesty in his voice left her momentarily speechless. She wanted to argue, to tell him he was wrong, but the look in his eyes stopped her. There was no bravado there, no hint of the charming arrogance he so often used to deflect. This was something deeper and it terrified her.

"Why?" she asked finally, her voice barely more than a whisper.

Thorwulf's gaze softened, and for a moment, she thought he might look away. But he didn't. "Because I've seen what you're willing to fight for," he said quietly. "You didn't enter the Reckoning to save yourself. You did it to save your sister. To protect someone who couldn't protect herself. That kind of strength... it's rare. And it's worth fighting for."

Astrid's chest ached with a mix of emotions she couldn't name. She wanted to tell him he was wrong, that she wasn't as strong as he thought, but the words wouldn't come. Instead, she looked away, focusing on the snow-covered ground beneath her boots.

"This isn't just about me," she said after a long moment. "If we're going to survive this, we need to fight for each other. Not just one of us. Both of us."

Thorwulf's lips curved into a faint smile, though it was tinged with sadness. "You don't understand, Astrid. If it comes down to you or me, the choice has already been made."

She clenched her fists, frustration and something deeper bubbling beneath the surface. "Don't say that," she said sharply. "Don't you dare say that."

His smile faded, and he stepped closer, his voice low and steady. "I mean it, Astrid. I'll fight for you. Until my last breath, if I have to."

The intensity of his words left her reeling, her heart pounding in her chest. She wanted to push him away, to tell him she didn't need his protection, but the truth was, she did. And that terrified her more than anything.

As they reached the edge of a small clearing the wind began to pick up, carrying with it the faint scent of smoke. Thorwulf held up a hand, signaling for her to stop, and she crouched low beside him, her breath coming in shallow bursts.

"There," he murmured, nodding toward a faint plume of smoke rising from the trees ahead. "They've made camp."

Astrid followed his gaze, her eyes narrowing as she spotted the flicker of firelight through the trees. Ragnar and his remaining two allies were there, huddled around the flames, their voices low.

"There's just two of them," Thorwulf said, his tone calm and measured. "One with a sword, one with a bow. The archer's the biggest threat."

Astrid nodded, her mind already racing. "We'll need to separate them," she said, her voice steady. "Draw the swordsman away from the camp and take him out first. Then we deal with the archer."

Thorwulf's lips twitched into a faint smile. "You've got a devious side, Sigurdsdóttir. I like it."

"Focus," she muttered, though she couldn't help the faint warmth that crept into her cheeks.

Together, they moved into position, their footsteps muffled by the snow. The plan was simple but dangerous, relying on timing and precision to succeed. Astrid's pulse quickened as they crept closer, her heart pounding in her chest as she gripped her sword tightly.

Thorwulf gave her a quick nod, and she returned it, her resolve hardening. They might be outnumbered, but they weren't outmatched. And the odds were swinging in their favor. And as they prepared to strike, Astrid couldn't shake the feeling that no matter what happened, Thorwulf would keep his word. He would fight for her, even to his own death.

And that scared her more than Ragnar ever could.

17

THE FROZEN LAKE

As they'd dispatched the last of Ragnar's allies, the coward had slipped away. Now, Astrid and Thorwulf were following a trail of quickly disappearing footprints in the ice, which had led them to the edge of a frozen lake.

The icy wind howled across the expanse of the lake, carrying with it a bone-deep chill that cut through even the thickest furs. The surface stretched out before them, a vast, shimmering sheet of thick ice that reflected the pale gray sky above. Cracks spidered across the surface, faint and ominous, as if the lake itself were warning them to turn back.

Astrid stood at the edge of the ice, her breath curling in the frigid air as she stared at the treacherous path ahead. The rules of the next trial were painfully simple: cross the lake, reach the marker on the far side, and survive. But the simplicity of the task only made it more dangerous. The gods never intended for this to be easy and, by the look of the prints, Ragnar was already on his way.

Thorwulf stepped up beside her, his axe slung across his back and his dark eyes scanning the lake. His expression was unreadable, but Astrid could see the tension in his shoulders, the way his jaw tightened as he studied the cracks in the ice.

"Well," he said, in a low and steady voice. "This looks like a bad idea."

Astrid snorted, though there was no humor in the sound. "When has that stopped us before?"

Thorwulf's lips twitched into a faint smile, but it disappeared as quickly as it came. "Stay close to the edge," he said, his tone serious. "The ice will be thicker there. If we spread out our weight and move slowly, we might make it across."

"Might," Astrid echoed, her stomach twisting.

Thorwulf glanced at her, his gaze steady. "We've made it this far, haven't we?"

Astrid nodded, forcing herself to take a deep breath. She adjusted her cloak, her fingers brushing the hilt of her sword for reassurance, and stepped onto the ice. It groaned beneath her weight, a low, ominous sound that sent a shiver down her spine.

Thorwulf followed, his movements slow and deliberate. Together, they began their trek across the lake, the cold biting at their faces and the wind tugging at their cloaks.

The first stretch of the journey was uneventful, though every step felt like a gamble. The ice cracked and shifted beneath their boots, faint popping sounds echoing across the frozen expanse. Astrid kept her gaze fixed on the far shore, where the marker stood. It was a simple wooden post adorned with runes that glowed faintly in the distance.

But the farther they went, the more the cracks in the ice deepened, and the groaning beneath their feet grew louder.

"Watch your step," Thorwulf said, his voice tight. He

gestured to a dark patch ahead, where the ice was thinner and the water beneath it churned ominously. "Go around."

Astrid nodded, her heart pounding as she skirted the edge of the weak spot. The wind whipped at her face, making her eyes water, and she glanced back to make sure Thorwulf was following.

He was a few paces behind her, his steps slow and careful. But as he reached the center of the lake, the ice beneath him let out a sharp, splintering crack.

"Thorwulf!" Astrid shouted, her voice carrying across the lake.

He froze, his gaze snapping to the ice beneath him as it began to give way. "Don't move!" he barked, his tone commanding.

But it was too late. The ice shattered with a deafening crack, and Thorwulf plunged into the freezing water below.

Astrid's heart stopped as she watched him disappear, the icy water swallowing him whole. For a moment, she stood frozen, panic clawing at her chest. Then she forced herself to move, her boots slipping on the ice as she scrambled toward the hole.

"Thorwulf!" she screamed, dropping to her knees at the edge of the broken ice.

The water churned violently, and for a terrifying moment, there was nothing. Then Thorwulf's head broke the surface, his face pale and his breaths ragged as he clawed at the ice.

"Astrid!" he gasped, his voice hoarse. His hands scrabbled for purchase, but the ice around the hole was too slick, too fragile to hold his weight.

Astrid dropped her sword and reached for him, her fingers closing around his arm. "I've got you," she said, her voice steady despite the terror pounding in her chest.

Thorwulf's dark eyes locked onto hers, a mix of fear and

determination in his gaze. "The ice. It's too thin," he choked out. "You can't..."

"Shut up," Astrid snapped. "I'm not leaving you."

She braced her knees against the ice, leaning back to counter his weight as she pulled with everything she had. The ice groaned beneath her, cracks spreading outward like spiderwebs, but she didn't stop.

Thorwulf's other hand reached for her, his fingers cold and trembling as he found purchase on her forearm. With a final, desperate heave, Astrid hauled him out of the water, the two of them collapsing onto the ice in a heap.

Thorwulf lay gasping beside her, his clothes soaked and his body shivering violently. Astrid sat up, her chest heaving as she stared at him, her heart pounding in her ears.

"You're an idiot," she said breathlessly, her voice wavering.

Thorwulf let out a weak laugh, his lips turning blue from the cold. "Takes one to know one."

Astrid felt the mix of relief and anger flooding through her. She grabbed his arm, hauling him upright despite his protests. "We need to move," she said, her voice firm. "You'll freeze if we don't get you warm."

Thorwulf nodded weakly, leaning heavily on her as they began to shuffle toward the far shore. The marker was closer now, its faint glow a beacon of hope in the icy wasteland.

As they moved, Astrid couldn't help but glance at him, her thoughts racing. He'd almost died. If she hadn't been there, he would have. The realization hit her like a blow, and she gripped his arm tighter, as if anchoring him to her would keep him safe.

"Thank you," Thorwulf murmured.

Astrid's heart twisted, but she forced herself to keep her tone steady. "Don't thank me yet. We're not out of this mess yet."

But as they reached the far shore and the ice groaned its final warning beneath their feet, Astrid realized something she wasn't ready to admit. Thorwulf wasn't just an ally anymore. He was a part of her now and losing him was just not an option.

~

The fire crackled weakly, its flames struggling against the biting wind that whipped through the small hollow Astrid had chosen for shelter. She crouched beside it, feeding the blaze with twigs and scraps of bark she'd scavenged from the forest floor. The warmth was barely enough to fight off the cold, but it was all they had.

Thorwulf sat a few feet away, his sodden clothing steaming as the fire's heat began to dry him. His skin was pale, his lips tinged with blue, and his hands trembled as he held them out to the flames. Astrid had stripped away his outer cloak and laid it near the fire to dry, but the cold had already seeped deep into his bones.

"Are you trying to die?" she muttered, her tone sharper than she intended. Her hands worked quickly to adjust the fire, piling more wood onto the flames in the hope of coaxing more heat from it.

Thorwulf managed a faint smile, though it didn't quite reach his eyes. "Not today," he said, his voice hoarse.

Astrid shot him a glare, but the knot of worry in her chest refused to loosen. She hated how fragile he looked, how his usual strength and confidence seemed to have been leeched away by the icy water.

She grabbed her own cloak and moved to sit beside him, draping the thick fabric over his shoulders. "You're freezing," she said, her voice softening.

Thorwulf chuckled weakly, the sound barely more than a rasp. "I noticed."

Astrid frowned, her frustration bubbling to the surface.

"You're impossible," she muttered, sliding closer until their sides were pressed together. Her arms wrapped around him, pulling him against her as she tried to share her body heat.

Thorwulf stiffened for a moment, clearly caught off guard, but then he relaxed, his weight leaning into her. "Astrid…" he murmured, his voice trailing off.

"Shut up," she said, her cheeks burning despite the cold. "Just sit still and warm up."

The firelight danced across their faces, casting flickering shadows on the snow-covered ground. For a while, neither of them spoke, the only sound the crackle of the flames and the distant howl of the wind.

"You saved me," Thorwulf said finally, his voice quiet.

Astrid tightened her grip on him, her jaw clenching. "You're an idiot for falling through the ice in the first place."

"I mean it," he said, his dark eyes locking onto hers. "You could've let me go. But you didn't."

Astrid looked away. "I couldn't just let you die," she said, her voice barely above a whisper. "We're in this together, remember?"

Thorwulf's lips curved into a faint smile, and he reached up to brush a strand of hair from her face. His fingers were still cold, but his touch sent a warmth through her that had nothing to do with the fire.

"Astrid," he said softly, his gaze intense. "I…"

Before he could finish, she leaned forward, her lips brushing against his in a tentative kiss. It was brief, hesitant, but it sent a jolt through her that made her heart pound. She pulled back quickly, her cheeks flaming as she avoided his gaze.

"I… sorry," she stammered.

Thorwulf reached for her hand. His grip was firm despite the lingering tremor in his fingers. "Don't apologize," he said.

"Astrid, I..." He hesitated, swallowing before continuing. "I care about you. More than I probably should."

Astrid's breath caught, her chest aching at the raw honesty in his words. She wanted to say something, to tell him she felt the same, but the words wouldn't come. Instead, she looked away, her cheeks flushing.

"We can't do this," she said finally, her voice barely more than a whisper.

Thorwulf frowned, his gaze searching hers. "Why not?"

"Because this isn't real," she said, forcing the words out even as they cut her. "It's the Reckoning. We're just trying to survive, and this... this will only make it harder."

Thorwulf's expression darkened, and he leaned closer, his gaze burning into hers. "You're wrong," he said quietly. "This is the only thing that's real. Out here, in this madness, it's the only thing that matters."

Astrid swallowed hard, and struggled to hold his gaze. The firelight danced in his dark eyes, and for a moment, she felt as though the world had narrowed to just the two of them.

But then she looked away, the weight of her responsibilities crashing down on her. "We can't," she said again, her voice trembling. "Not now."

Thorwulf sighed, his shoulders slumping. "Fine," he said, his tone resigned. "But just so you know, I'm not giving up on you, Astrid. Not now. Not ever."

Her throat constricted, and she forced herself to meet his gaze, her chest aching with a mix of emotions she couldn't name. "Don't make promises you can't keep," she said softly.

Thorwulf smiled faintly, his gaze unwavering. "This is one promise I fully intend to keep."

Astrid didn't respond, her heart pounding as she turned her attention back to the fire. But as the flames crackled and the wind howled outside their small haven, she couldn't help but feel the warmth of his presence, the steady comfort of his words.

18

THE TEST OF THE GODS

The air shifted the moment they stepped into the clearing. It was subtle at first. Just a faint hum in the distance, almost imperceptible over the whispering wind. But as Astrid and Thorwulf moved deeper into the strange, open space, the hum grew louder, vibrating in their bones, in a low, menacing note that made the hair on the back of Astrid's neck stand on end.

The clearing itself was unnervingly perfect, a circle of scorched earth surrounded by ancient, towering pines. Their dark branches stretched skyward like skeletal fingers, blocking out the weak sunlight and casting long, jagged shadows across the ground. In the center of the clearing stood an altar. A jagged slab of black stone, slick with frost and etched with runes that glowed faintly in the dim light.

Astrid's grip tightened on her sword as she approached, her boots crunching against the icy ground. The air felt heavier here, charged with something ancient and angry. It pressed against her chest, making it hard to breathe, and every instinct she had screamed at her to turn back.

Thorwulf stepped beside her, his axe in hand and his gaze fixed on the altar. His face was pale, his jaw tight, but his movements were steady. If he felt the same crushing weight that she did, he didn't show it.

"What is this place?" Astrid whispered, her voice lifting over the hum.

"Another game," Thorwulf muttered, his tone grim. "The gods' way of reminding us who's in charge."

Astrid swallowed hard. She'd faced many trials since the Reckoning began, but this place felt different. It wasn't just a test of strength or cunning. This felt far more dangerous.

The hum grew louder, shifting into a low, guttural chant that seemed to echo from the shadows themselves. Astrid's heart pounded as the runes on the altar flared to life, their glow pulsing in time with the chant.

"This doesn't feel right," she said, her voice trembling.

Thorwulf didn't respond. His gaze remained fixed on the altar, his dark eyes narrowing as a figure began to take shape in the center of the clearing.

It was a woman. Or at least, something that resembled one. Her form was shadow and light, flickering like a flame as she stepped forward. Her face was obscured, but her presence was undeniable, a towering force that seemed to radiate power and malice.

"Astrid Sigurdsdóttir," the figure said, her voice echoing in the still air. "Thorwulf Haldorsson. You have come to face the Test of the Gods."

"What do you want from us?" Astrid demanded.

The figure tilted her head, as if amused. "The gods demand loyalty. Faith. Sacrifice. You will prove your worth. Or you will fall."

The shadows around them began to shift, curling and twisting like living things. The clearing grew darker, the hum rising to a deafening crescendo that made Astrid's head pound.

"What kind of test?" Thorwulf asked, his voice steady despite the tension in his jaw.

The figure turned her gaze to him, and though her face was hidden, Astrid felt the weight of her attention like a blade against her skin.

"You will choose," the figure said simply.

Astrid's stomach dropped as the shadows coalesced into two shapes. They were perfect replicas of herself and Thorwulf. The doppelgängers stood motionless, their faces blank and expressionless, but there was something deeply unsettling about them.

"The gods demand a sacrifice," the figure said, her voice cold and unyielding. "One of you will cross the threshold alone. The other will remain behind."

Astrid's blood ran cold as the meaning of the words sank in. "You want us to abandon each other?" she asked, her voice barely more than a whisper.

The figure didn't respond, her shadowy form dissolving into the air as the chanting grew louder. The runes on the altar flared brighter, their light casting jagged shadows across the clearing.

Thorwulf stepped forward, his axe glinting in the eerie light. "No," he said firmly, his voice cutting through the noise. "We're not playing your game."

The chanting faltered, and the shadows seemed to pause, as if startled by his defiance. Astrid stared at him, her heart pounding.

"Thorwulf," she began, but he shook his head, cutting her off.

"We're not leaving each other," he said, his gaze locking onto hers. "Not now. Not ever."

Astrid's heart ached at the raw intensity in his voice, and for a moment, she couldn't find the words to respond.

The shadows surged forward, their movements jagged and

unnatural, and the doppelgängers stepped closer, their faces twisted into eerie, mocking smiles. The air grew colder, the chanting louder, and the weight of the gods' anger pressed down on them like a physical force.

Thorwulf stepped in front of her, his axe raised. "If they want a fight, we'll give them one," he said, his voice steady.

"Together," she said, her voice firm.

The doppelgängers lunged, their movements unnervingly fast, and the clearing erupted into chaos. Astrid's sword clashed against the shadowy figure of herself, the sound ringing out like a bell in the heavy air. The fight was unlike anything she'd ever faced. Her opponent moved like her, fought like her, and every strike felt like she was fighting her own reflection.

Thorwulf battled his own double, his axe flashing as he blocked and countered each strike. His movements were fierce and unrelenting, his determination burning brighter than the oppressive darkness around them.

As the battle raged on, Astrid caught a glimpse of Thorwulf's face. His jaw was set, his eyes blazing with a fire that refused to be extinguished. And in that moment, she knew he wasn't just fighting for himself. He was fighting for her.

The gods' test was meant to break them, to force them to abandon each other in the name of survival. But as Astrid and Thorwulf stood side by side, their weapons flashing and their hearts pounding, they defied the gods' expectations.

They would not yield. And if the gods demanded a sacrifice, they would have to come for it themselves.

Astrid's breath came in sharp, shallow bursts as she swung her sword against her shadowy doppelgänger. Each strike felt heavier than the last, as if the shadows themselves were feeding off her strength.

Thorwulf's grunts of exertion punctuated the chaos. His axe gleamed in the dim, flickering light, cutting through the oppressive dark as he fought his own reflection. Blood trickled from a shallow cut on his temple, but he didn't falter. He moved with unrelenting force, his focus unshakable.

Astrid felt the weight of the gods' gaze pressing down on her, a suffocating reminder of what was at stake. The chanting of the unseen voices reached a fever pitch, the shadows swirling wildly around the clearing as if enraged by their defiance. But through the chaos, Astrid's resolve only hardened.

She caught a glimpse of Thorwulf's double lunging for his exposed side. Without hesitation, Astrid spun, her blade slicing through the shadowy figure before it could reach him. It dissolved into wisps of darkness, its shriek echoing like the cry of a wounded animal.

Thorwulf staggered back, his dark eyes meeting hers, wide with a mix of gratitude and shock. "I had it," he said, but there was no bite in his tone.

Astrid raised an eyebrow, her chest heaving. "You're welcome."

Before he could reply, the chanting abruptly stopped. The silence that followed was heavy and oppressive, as if the world itself had paused to hold its breath. The shadows receded, retreating into the corners of the clearing, and the remaining doppelgänger faded like smoke on the wind.

The altar pulsed once, a deep, resonant thrum that vibrated through Astrid's chest, and then it went still. The oppressive weight of the gods' presence lifted, leaving behind an eerie stillness.

Astrid straightened, her sword still clenched in her trembling hand, and turned to face the center of the clearing. The shadowy figure of the Valkyrie had reappeared, her flickering form standing tall and imposing against the backdrop of the dark forest. This time, there was something different about her. Her presence, though still menacing, held a note of curiosity.

"You defied the will of the gods," the Valkyrie said, her voice echoing like the clash of steel. "You were given a choice, and you refused to choose."

Astrid stepped forward, her chin lifted despite the pounding of her heart. "I won't abandon him," she said, her voice steady. "Not for your tests. Not for anything."

The Valkyrie tilted her head, her form flickering as if she were made of embers caught in the wind. "Such loyalty is rare among mortals," she said, her tone contemplative. "But beware. Betrayal will test your resolve."

Astrid felt the weight of the Valkyrie's gaze, though her face remained obscured. "What do you mean? Whose betrayal? The gods?" she asked, her voice quieter now.

The Valkyrie didn't answer immediately. Instead, she stepped closer, her flickering form towering over Astrid. "Perhaps you will prove to be more than a pawn in their games," she said at last. "The gods may test you, but it is I who will watch you."

With that, the Valkyrie dissolved into the air, her presence fading like a dying flame. The silence that followed was heavy, but it carried with it a sense of finality.

Thorwulf moved to Astrid's side, his breathing still labored. "What just happened?" he asked, his voice low.

Astrid shook her head. "I think..." she began, but the words faltered on her tongue. "I think we passed the gods' test."

But the relief that had begun to settle over her quickly dissipated as the sound of boots crunching on snow reached her ears. Astrid turned sharply, her heart sinking as a group of figures emerged from the shadows at the edge of the clearing.

The Jarls.

Their cloaks billowed in the icy wind, their faces hidden

beneath heavy hoods, but their presence was unmistakable. They radiated authority and disdain, their postures rigid as they approached. Jarl Ingvar of Frostfjord stepped forward, his gaze locking onto Astrid.

"You defied the will of the gods," he said in a voice as cold and sharp as the winter air. "Such insolence cannot go unanswered."

Astrid's stomach churned, but she forced herself to stand tall. "I did what I had to do," she said firmly. "If that angers the gods, so be it."

The Jarl's eyes narrowed, his expression hardening. "You think yourself above their judgment?" he demanded. "Do you think your defiance makes you more worthy?"

"I think loyalty is its own strength," Astrid shot back, her voice steady despite the tension in her chest. "And if the gods can't see that, then maybe they're not as wise as you think."

A murmur rippled through the other Jarls, their faces shadowed by their hoods. Jarl Ingvar's lips curled into a sneer, his hands clenching at his sides. "You are reckless," he said, his tone laced with contempt. "And you will pay the price for your arrogance."

Thorwulf stepped forward, his axe held loosely at his side but his stance radiating quiet menace. "If you have a problem with her, you'll have to go through me," he said, his voice low and dangerous.

The Jarl's gaze flicked to Thorwulf, and for a moment, the tension in the clearing was palpable. But then the leader's sneer deepened, and he turned away, his cloak billowing behind him.

"The gods may tolerate your insolence for now," he said over his shoulder. "But they will not forget it. Neither will we."

As the Jarls disappeared into the shadows, Astrid let out a shaky breath, her heart pounding in her chest. Thorwulf turned to her, his expression hard but his eyes filled with concern.

"We've made some pretty powerful enemies," he said quietly.

Astrid nodded, her gaze fixed on the spot where the Jarls had stood. "Let them come," she said, her voice firm despite the weight of her words. "I'm not afraid of them."

But as the cold wind howled through the clearing, carrying with it the faint echo of the Valkyrie's warning, Astrid couldn't shake the feeling that her defiance had set something dangerous in motion.

19

SHADOWS OF BETRAYAL

The campfire crackled softly in the clearing, its warm glow casting flickering shadows on the surrounding trees. The night sky was a tapestry of stars, but the beauty of it was lost on Astrid. She sat near the fire, her sword resting on her knees, her gaze fixed on the flames as if their dance held the answers to the doubts that churned in her mind.

The Valkyrie's warning echoed in her mind, a cold whisper that sent a shiver down her spine despite the warmth of the fire. *Betrayal will test your resolve.* The words lingered like a shadow, and she couldn't shake the feeling that the real danger wasn't Ragnar or the trials. It was closer to home. There was only one person here that could betray her. Only one person she trusted. And yet...

Thorwulf leaned closer, his voice low. "You're quiet. What's on your mind?"

Astrid hesitated, her gaze fixed on the fire. "The Valkyrie," she admitted after a moment. "She warned me about betrayal. About how it would test me."

Thorwulf frowned, his expression darkening. "Do you think she meant Ragnar?"

"Maybe," Astrid said softly. "Or maybe she meant you. Ragnar doesn't have to kill us himself if we tear each other apart first."

Thorwulf's eyes darkened and a frown knitted his brow. "That will never happen. You have my word."

Astrid saw the intensity in his dark eyes. "We need to be careful, Thorwulf. Even with each other."

The words hung in the air, heavier than the tension in the clearing. Thorwulf didn't flinch, but his expression betrayed the faint trace of hurt flickering across his face before he masked it.

"I understand," he said quietly. "But for what it's worth, Astrid, you don't need to doubt me. I'm not here to betray you."

Astrid wanted to believe him, but the Valkyrie's warning loomed like a shadow in her mind. Maybe trust was a luxury she couldn't afford. Not when every step they took brought them closer to the end.

The uneasy quiet of the clearing was shattered by the distant sound of a howl, low and mournful, echoing through the night like a warning. Astrid tensed, her hand reaching for her sword as the shadows around them seemed to deepen.

"We need to move," Thorwulf said. "Ragnar's out there, and if we sit here any longer, we're as good as dead."

Astrid nodded, rising to her feet and sheathing her sword and kicking dirt into the embers of the fire. "Let's go."

20

THE BATTLE AT DAWN

The first faint streaks of dawn clawed their way across the horizon, bathing the forest in a pale, ghostly light. The air was brittle with cold, every breath Astrid took curling into visible tendrils before vanishing into the ether. She crouched low in the underbrush, her heart pounding in her chest as Ragnar's voice drifted through the trees, low and sinister.

"Tonight, we finish this," Ragnar growled, his tone carrying the promise of violence. "Astrid and Thorwulf think they're clever, but they've overplayed their hand. When the sun rises, they'll be dead, and the Reckoning will be ours to control."

Astrid's felt the weight of her sword biting into her palm. Beside her, Thorwulf lay still, his broad shoulders barely rising with each shallow breath as he listened. His axe rested on the ground between them, the edge sharpened to a lethal gleam in preparation for the fight they both knew was coming.

"It'll be two-on-two," another voice said, the last of Ragnar's allies. "And they're powerful fighters. We'll need to be quick."

Astrid's jaw clenched, anger flaring hot in her chest. Ragnar's arrogance burned brighter than the firelight flickering through the trees where he camped. She glanced at Thorwulf, his face shadowed but his dark eyes sharp and focused.

"Quick?" Thorwulf murmured under his breath, the faintest hint of a smirk tugging at his lips. "That's optimistic of him."

Astrid suppressed a snort, her pulse steadying at his quiet humor. "We'll see how quick they think it is when we're standing over them," she whispered back, her voice fierce.

Thorwulf's smirk faded, replaced by a seriousness that chilled her. "Stick close to me," he said, his tone low. "They'll try to separate us. Don't let them."

Astrid nodded, her fingers brushing his arm briefly before she pulled away. "You're not the only one with tricks, Haldorsson."

~

As the first rays of sunlight broke over the treetops, the stillness of the forest shattered. Ragnar and his ally were on the move, their weapons glinting as they stomped through the clearing, their eyes scanning for any sign of Astrid and Thorwulf.

Astrid moved like a shadow, her steps silent as she circled around their camp. She could feel the weight of her sword in her hand, the familiar heft a comfort against the storm of nerves churning in her stomach. Thorwulf was a few paces behind her, his movements equally stealthy despite his size.

When Ragnar's back was turned, Astrid struck.

Her blade sang as it sliced through the air, clashing against Ragnar's sword with a force that sent shockwaves up her arm. He spun to face her, his expression twisting into a snarl as he parried her next strike.

"Well, well," Ragnar sneered, his voice dripping with mockery. "The little Frostfjord girl thinks she can take me?"

Astrid didn't waste words. She drove forward, her sword a blur of silver as she forced him back step by step. The clang of steel against steel rang out, sharp and violent, as they fought in the center of the clearing.

Behind them, chaos erupted as Thorwulf met Ragnar's ally head-on, his axe cleaving through the air with brutal precision. The man was no match for Thorwulf, and caught off guard by their attack fell back immediately, gathering himself for the fight.

Thorwulf moved like a force of nature, his strength and speed unmatched as he ran at the man. But his foe had already composed himself, and lifted two broadswords to parry Thorwulf's attack, their blades flashing as they whirled around him.

"Thorwulf!" Astrid shouted, her voice sharp with fear as she saw the man lunge for his exposed side.

Thorwulf moved just in time, his axe coming up to block the strike, but the distraction cost him. The second blade sliced across his arm, drawing a line of crimson against his pale skin. He gritted his teeth, his movements faltering as blood dripped onto the snow.

Astrid forced herself to focus. Ragnar was still in front of her, his strikes growing more erratic as she pressed him harder. She saw the opening before he did, a slight misstep that left his side exposed, and she didn't hesitate.

Her blade plunged into his side, the force of the strike sending him to his knees. He gasped, his hand clutching at the wound as blood spilled onto the snow, staining it red.

"You think this is over?" Ragnar rasped, his eyes blazing with hatred even as his strength faded. "The gods will never let you win."

Astrid's chest heaved as she stepped closer, her sword still poised, her voice icy and firm. "The gods don't choose who wins the Reckoning. I do."

With one swift, decisive motion, she drove her sword through his chest. His eyes widened in shock, his final breath escaping in a gurgle as blood bubbled up from his lips. Astrid felt the blade sink deep, cutting through flesh and bone, and she forced herself to meet his gaze as life fled his eyes.

When she pulled her sword free, Ragnar's body slumped forward into the blood-soaked snow, his lifeless form a grim reminder of the Reckoning's brutal reality.

She turned away, her gaze immediately searching for Thorwulf. Her heart dropped as she saw him staggering, blood soaking through his tunic as he fought off Ragnar's friend.

"Thorwulf!" she screamed, rushing to his side. Her sword flashed as she drove it through the man who had wounded him, her movements fueled by desperation and fury.

Thorwulf swayed, his axe slipping from his hand as he fell to his knees. Astrid caught him before he hit the ground, her arms wrapping around him as she lowered him gently into the snow.

The snow beneath him turned crimson, the stark contrast of the blood against the pristine white sending a shiver down her spine. The metallic tang of it filled the air, sharp and unrelenting.

"Stay with me," she whispered, her voice trembling as she pressed her hand against the wound in his side. "You're going to be fine."

Thorwulf's lips curved into a faint, pained smile. "I've had worse," he said, his voice weak but laced with that familiar humor that made her heart ache.

"Don't you dare joke right now," she snapped, her eyes burning as she fought to keep her hands steady. "I need you, Thorwulf."

His gaze softened, his dark eyes locking onto hers. "Astrid," he murmured. "I'm not going anywhere. We're the last one standing. We've done it. I'm not going to leave you now."

She held his gaze as she fought back the fear threatening to consume her. Around them, the clearing fell silent, the echoes of the battle fading into the stillness of the forest.

Astrid pressed her forehead against his, her voice breaking as she whispered, "You'd better not."

But as the first rays of sunlight bathed the clearing in golden light, Astrid knew that the fight was far from over.

~

The faint streaks of dawn stretched across the horizon, spilling light over the barren mountainside. Jagged peaks loomed around them, their icy faces glinting like fractured glass in the cold morning sun. The air was thin and sharp, cutting at Astrid's lungs with every breath. The wind howled down the slopes, carrying with it a biting chill that sank deep into her bones.

Astrid crouched beside Thorwulf, her knees digging into the frost-coated ground as she cradled him against her. His weight was heavy in her arms, his breath shallow and quiet. His tunic was still stained with his blood, but she'd packed the wound, and bound it in cloth from one of the fallen oathsworns' cloak.

Around them, the remnants of the final battle lay scattered. Ragnar's lifeless body slumped against a jagged rock, his ally sprawled across the snow, sword still clutched in lifeless hands.

She pressed her hand gently against Thorwulf's cheek, watching his chest rise and fall.

"Stay with me," she whispered, her voice trembling. "Thorwulf, do you hear me? I need you to stay with me."

His dark eyes fluttered open and he looked up at her. "Astrid," he murmured. "You're too stubborn to need anyone."

She smiled, but a wash of fear still lingered. "Don't joke," she said, her tone laced with quiet sadness. "I could have lost you."

His lips quirked into the faintest of smiles, though it didn't reach his eyes. "I'm fine," he said, though the weakness in his voice betrayed him.

"No, you're not," she said fiercely, her grip on him tightening. "And I can't. I can't lose you, Thorwulf."

Her words hung in the air, raw and unguarded. She couldn't imagine moving forward without him. Not after everything they had endured, not after everything they had fought for.

Thorwulf's hand lifted, his cold fingers brushing against her cheek. "You're stronger than you think," he said softly. "Strong enough to finish this, with or without me."

"No," she said sharply, her voice breaking. "That's not an option."

His hand dropped back to his side, his chest rising and falling in shallow breaths. "You've always been so damn stubborn," he murmured, a faint trace of humor flickering in his gaze. "Let me sleep, and stay with me. I'll be fine in a little while."

Astrid forced a shaky laugh. As he drifted off in her arms, she looked out over the mountainside, the treeless expanse stretching out before them. Sharp ridges and craggy slopes carved their way down into shadowy valleys, the snow glistening like fractured diamonds in the pale morning light. The wind howled around them, carrying with it the faint cries of scavenger birds circling high above.

And then, like a flicker of warmth in the cold storm of her thoughts, a memory surfaced. A rule whispered in hushed tones, a glimmer of hope buried in the lore of the Reckoning.

There could be more than one winner, if the gods allowed it.

Astrid's heart pounded as the thought took root, spreading through her like fire. They could both win. They'd already overcome the other oathsworns. If they could just endure, if they could survive the remaining trials, they could both make it out alive.

"Thorwulf," she said softly, her voice steadier now.

He blinked up at her, his dark eyes clouded with exhaustion. "What?"

"There can be more than one winner," she said, her words carrying a fierce determination. "They said so at the start. We can do this, Thorwulf. We just have to make it to the end."

His brow furrowed, and for a moment, she saw the faintest flicker of hope in his gaze. "You really believe that?" he asked, his voice hoarse.

"I do," she said firmly, her hand tightening on his. "But only if you stop bleeding all over the place and start pulling your weight again."

Despite the pain etched into his features, Thorwulf let out a weak chuckle. "You're impossible," he murmured, his lips twitching into a faint smile.

Astrid allowed herself a small smile, though her chest ached with worry. "You're just figuring that out now?"

His gaze softened, and he squeezed her hand weakly. "If anyone can make it to the end, it's you, Astrid."

She forced herself to meet his gaze with steady resolve. "No," she said quietly. "If we're going to make it to the end, we're going to do it together. Do you hear me, Thorwulf? We're in this together."

He nodded slowly, his eyes drifting shut as his breathing evened out. Astrid stayed by his side, her hand never leaving his as she looked out over the barren mountainside. The dawn light bathed the rugged peaks in hues of gold and crimson, the snow glittering like broken glass.

For the first time since the Reckoning began, Astrid could see an end in sight. If they could endure the trials, if they could prove their worth to the gods, they could both stand victorious.

And as the wind howled around them, carrying with it the promise of more trials to come, Astrid made a silent vow: she would fight for Thorwulf. They would fight for each other.

And together, they would see the Reckoning to its end.

21

THE JARLS' VERDICT

The wind howled through the valley below, carrying with it the echoes of the past battles fought on this unforgiving land. Astrid stood stiffly on the jagged plateau, the cold biting at her cheeks as she stared at the council of Jarls assembled before her. Their cloaks billowed in the wind, heavy furs lined with silver clasps that reflected the pale morning sun. Behind them, the jagged peaks of the mountains loomed, casting long shadows over the makeshift arena.

Thorwulf stood beside her, his breathing steady. The crimson stain on his tunic had darkened, but he'd refused to let her help him further. She had fought so hard to get them this far, to keep him alive, and now it all felt like it could just slip through her fingers.

The leader of the Jarls, a man with a thick beard streaked with gray and eyes like shards of ice, stepped forward. His presence was commanding, his voice cutting through the wind like a blade. "The gods have spoken," he said, his tone sharp and unyielding. "You request has been denied. The Reckoning must end with only one winner."

Astrid's pulse hammering in her ears as the words sank in.

"What?" she whispered. She glanced at Thorwulf, her heart clenching at the grim expression on his face.

The Jarl ignored her, his gaze sweeping over the gathered oathsworn. "This trial is a test of the gods' favor, and they demand a single champion. Only one of you will leave this island alive."

Astrid stepped forward. "You can't do this," she said, her voice rising with desperation. "You promised. We just had to survive. We've done that. That's the rule."

The Jarl's cold eyes fixed on her, his expression unyielding. "The gods' will is not bound by promises made to mortals," he said. "They have seen your actions, your defiance, and they have demanded a change. The Reckoning must have a singular winner to restore balance for your actions."

Her stomach twisted, her mind racing. This wasn't balance. This was punishment. She could feel it in the way the Jarl's gaze lingered on her, in the disapproving stares of the council. Her defiance at Norn's Well, her refusal to abandon Thorwulf, had not gone unnoticed.

"They're punishing us," Astrid said, her voice trembling with fury as she turned to Thorwulf. "For what we did. For surviving together."

Thorwulf's dark eyes narrowed as he looked at the Jarls. "This isn't about the gods," he said, his voice low and dangerous. "This is about you trying to control us."

The leader of the Jarls bristled, his expression hardening. "Watch your tongue, Haldorsson," he growled. "You are here because we allow it. Do not test our patience."

Astrid's nails dug into her palms, her body trembling with suppressed rage. She turned back to the Jarls, her voice breaking as she said, "We've fought for this. We've bled for this. You can't just change the rules now."

The Jarl's expression didn't falter. "The gods have decreed it," he said coldly. "And you will obey."

The finality of his words struck Astrid like a blow, her breath catching in her throat. She looked at Thorwulf, her heart aching as she met his gaze. She could see the pain in his eyes, the same mix of fear and anguish that mirrored her own.

For a moment, neither of them spoke. The wind howled around them, carrying with it the distant cries of birds circling high above.

Thorwulf broke the silence first, his voice quiet but steady. "We'll find a way," he said, his dark eyes locking onto hers. "No matter what, we'll figure this out."

Astrid shook her head. "How, Thorwulf? How do we figure this out when they've made it impossible?"

His hand reached for hers, his fingers cold but steady as they entwined with hers. "We've made it this far together," he said. "We'll finish it together."

Her vision blurred, tears stinging her eyes as she fought to keep her composure. She wanted to believe him, and cling to the hope that they could somehow defy the odds once again. But the weight of the Jarls' decree was crushing, suffocating in its finality.

The Jarl Ingvar stepped forward once more, his cold gaze fixed on them. "You have until sundown tomorrow to prove your worth," he said. "You decide who survives. The gods will have their winner."

Astrid's chest ached as the Jarls turned and walked away, their cloaks billowing in the wind as they disappeared into the shadows of the mountain. She felt Thorwulf's hand squeeze hers, anchoring her as the world seemed to spin out of control.

"I won't fight you," she said quietly, her voice trembling.

Thorwulf's gaze softened, his expression filled with a quiet determination. "And I won't fight you," he said.

She closed her eyes, the tears slipping free as the wind howled around them. "Then what do we do, Thorwulf? How do we survive this?"

He didn't answer immediately, his silence stretching between them like a chasm. When he finally spoke, his voice was quiet but resolute.

"We do it the same way we've survived everything else," he said. "Together."

Astrid opened her eyes, her gaze locking onto his. In that moment, she made a silent vow to herself. She wouldn't let the Jarls, the gods, or anyone else tear them apart. They would find a way to endure, to defy the odds once again.

Because she refused to accept a world where Thorwulf wasn't by her side.

The wind screamed across the barren mountainside, whipping Astrid's hair into her face as she stood frozen, her hand still clasped in Thorwulf's. The chill bit into her skin, but it was nothing compared to the cold dread that had taken root in her chest, spreading like ice through her veins.

Thorwulf's grip tightened around hers, grounding her, but it wasn't enough to stop the flood of emotions threatening to drown her. She had never felt so helpless, so utterly consumed by the weight of the moment. The Jarls had stripped away the last fragile hope she'd clung to, the belief that they could both survive, and replaced it with an impossible choice.

She turned to Thorwulf, her vision blurred by the tears she refused to let fall. His dark eyes, usually so steady and filled with humor, were clouded with pain and exhaustion. The blood soaking through his tunic had turned black in the cold air, a stark reminder of how much he had already endured.

He looked at her with a quiet intensity that stole her breath. "Astrid," he said softly, his voice low and hoarse. "You're thinking too much again."

The lump in her throat made it hard to breathe. "What am I supposed to do, Thorwulf?" she whispered. "They've made it impossible."

He released her hand and cupped her face, his rough, calloused fingers warming her chilled skin. "It's not impossible," he said, his tone steady despite the storm in his eyes. "We'll figure it out. We always do."

She shook her head, her tears spilling over as her hands came up to grip his wrists. "You don't get it," she said, her voice breaking. "I can't do this without you. I won't."

His brows drew together, his expression softening as he leaned his forehead against hers. "Yes, you can," he murmured. "You're stronger than you know, Astrid."

A sob tore from her chest, and she closed her eyes, her tears freezing on her cheeks as they fell. "Stop saying that," she whispered. "Stop acting like this is okay, like this doesn't mean one of us has to..."

"Stop." His voice was firm, cutting through her spiraling thoughts. He pulled back just enough to meet her gaze, his dark eyes locking onto hers. "We don't know how this will end yet. But what I do know is that I would rather die on this mountain than let them turn us against each other."

Her breath hitched, her chest heaving as his words settled over her. The thought of losing him, of watching him fall and knowing she couldn't stop it, was unbearable. She couldn't let that happen.

"Thorwulf," she said, her voice trembling. "I can't let you die."

"You're not letting me do anything," he interrupted, his tone softer now. "We're in this together. No matter what."

She shook her head, her tears blurring her vision again. "It's not fair," she whispered. "None of this is fair."

He let out a humorless laugh, his lips twitching into a faint smile. "Fairness doesn't exist in the Reckoning," he said. "But you know what does? Us. You and me. We've made it this far together, Astrid, and I'm not giving up on that now."

Her heart ached, the weight of her feelings for him crashing over her like a wave. She had fought so hard to keep her walls up, to protect herself from the pain of losing someone she cared about, but Thorwulf had broken through them all the same. And now, standing here on this godforsaken mountain with the wind screaming around them and the blood of their enemies staining the ground, she couldn't deny it anymore.

"I can't lose you," she whispered.

He smiled faintly, his thumb brushing away a tear from her cheek. "You won't," he said. "Even if this is the end, I'm not going anywhere, Astrid. Not really."

The thought only made the ache in her chest worse. She closed her eyes, her hands trembling as she gripped his wrists tighter. "There has to be another way," she said desperately. "There has to be something we can do."

Thorwulf was quiet for a long moment, his gaze searching hers. "We survive," he said finally, his voice steady and resolute. "That's all we can do. Survive."

Her breath hitched, and she opened her eyes to meet his. The fire in his gaze, the unshakable determination that had carried them this far, gave her a flicker of hope. Maybe he was right. Maybe they could find a way to defy the Jarls, to defy the gods themselves, and survive together.

She nodded slowly and whispered, "Okay. We survive."

He smiled, a faint but genuine smile that sent warmth through her frozen limbs. "That's my girl," he murmured.

The words sent a rush of heat to her cheeks, and she quickly looked away, her emotions threatening to overwhelm her again. She couldn't afford to lose control, not now. They didn't have time for doubt or hesitation.

Astrid straightened, her grip on his wrists loosening as she stepped back. The wind howled around them, biting at her skin, but she barely felt it. She looked out over the mountains, her resolve hardening like steel.

The Jarls wanted to break them, to force them into an impossible choice, but Astrid refused to play their game. She would fight for Thorwulf, just as he had fought for her, and together they would defy the gods themselves if they had to.

She wasn't just fighting for her survival anymore. She was fighting for *them.*

22

THE DROWNING

The cold gnawed at Astrid's fingers as she stood at the edge of the jagged cliff, staring down into the furious waters below. The icy ocean churned violently against the rocks, its waves cresting with white foam before crashing into the cliffside with an unrelenting roar. The sheer power of it was mesmerizing and terrifying at the same time.

Astrid's heart thundered in her chest, her breath coming in sharp bursts as the salt-laden wind whipped around her. Her cloak snapped behind her like a banner, but she didn't flinch. Beside her, Thorwulf stood just as still, his broad frame outlined against the pale gray sky. His face was pale, his wound still fresh beneath his tunic, but his dark eyes burned with defiance.

"This is madness," Thorwulf said, his voice swirling above the roaring waves.

Astrid glanced at him, her lips trembling, though not from the cold. "It's the only way," she said, her voice steady despite the storm raging inside her.

Thorwulf's hand gripped the hilt of his axe so tightly that his knuckles turned white. "You think they'll let us walk away from this? That they'll just... relent?"

"No," Astrid admitted, turning her gaze back to the ocean. "But they'll have no choice. If we die here, the Reckoning dies with us. The gods lose their champion, the Jarls lose their spectacle, and the clans lose their truce." She swallowed hard, the weight of her words pressing down on her chest. "They won't risk it."

Thorwulf let out a bitter laugh, the sound carried away by the wind. "You're betting everything on their pride, Astrid."

"I'm betting on their fear," she corrected, her voice sharp. She stepped closer to the edge, the rocks slick beneath her boots. "They're not as powerful as they want us to believe. The gods thrive on worship, but the Jarls thrive on control, and if we take both away from them..."

"They crumble," Thorwulf finished, his tone softer now.

Astrid nodded, looking back at him. "But we have to be willing to do it. If they're going to believe it, we have to commit."

Thorwulf's dark eyes searched hers, and for a moment, she thought he might argue. But then he nodded, a flicker of admiration crossing his face. "You're braver than I gave you credit for," he said, a faint smile tugging at the corner of his lips.

"Save the compliments for when we survive," she shot back, though her voice wavered just slightly.

He held her gaze for a long moment, then stepped forward to stand beside her at the edge. The ocean roared below them, the spray misting their faces as the wind howled around them. Thorwulf reached for her hand, his grip firm and warm despite the cold.

"Together," he said simply.

Astrid nodded. "Together."

She lifted her voice, letting it carry across the winds to where the Jarls stood on the far ridge, their silhouettes stark against the gray sky.

"Jarls! Gods! Do you hear us?" she shouted, her voice strong and unwavering. "You want a winner? Then watch us take your Reckoning to the grave!"

The Jarls didn't answer, but she could feel their eyes on her, their judgment like a physical weight pressing down on her shoulders.

Astrid turned to Thorwulf, her heart hammering as she squeezed his hand. "On three," she said, her voice trembling now.

He nodded, his gaze steady. "One."

"Two," she whispered, her breath catching.

And then, before she could say three, the sky seemed to split open.

The wind surged, the ocean's roar growing deafening as the world seemed to hold its breath. The voices of the Jarls rang out across the cliffs, sharp and panicked.

"Stop!"

Astrid froze, her pulse pounding as she turned her head toward the ridge. The Jarl Ingvar stepped forward, his cloak billowing in the wind, his voice booming with authority.

"Enough!"

Thorwulf's grip on her hand tightened, his body tense as they waited. The silence that followed was heavy, broken only by the crash of waves below.

"The gods have spoken," the Jarl declared, his voice ringing out like a judgment. "Your defiance has earned their favor, Astrid of Frostfjord. Thorwulf of Frostfjord. You are no longer oathsworn."

Astrid's breath hitched, her knees nearly buckling as the words sank in.

"You have won," the Jarl continued, his tone grudging but final. "Joint champions of the Reckoning."

Thorwulf let out a shaky laugh, his grip on her hand never

loosening. "I knew you'd figure it out," he said, his voice low and filled with awe.

Astrid turned to him, her chest tight with emotion. "I didn't think they'd actually..."

He grinned, his dark eyes shining despite the exhaustion etched into his features. "Maybe they were just scared of defying you."

She let out a breathless laugh, tears streaming down her cheeks as she stepped back from the edge. Her legs felt weak, her body trembling as the adrenaline began to fade. Thorwulf pulled her close, his arms wrapping around her as the wind faded around them and a bright, warm sun lit the sky.

"We did it," he murmured, his voice soft in her ear.

Astrid buried her face in his chest, her hands clutching at his tunic. "We did it," she whispered back, her voice thick with relief. She let herself believe, for the first time, that they had truly won.

The wind had dropped completely, as if the world itself had exhaled in the wake of the Jarls' declaration. But the sea beneath the cliffs churned on, restless and wild, its fury untempered by the momentary reprieve. Astrid let herself collapse to her knees, her breath hitching as her body trembled with exhaustion, relief, and the lingering edge of fear.

Thorwulf knelt beside her, his hands bracing against the frozen earth as he fought to steady himself. His dark hair clung to his damp face, and the faintest smile played on his lips as his gaze met hers. "Well," he said, his voice hoarse but laced with a familiar humor, "that was one way to win."

Astrid let out a breathless laugh, though it was tinged with disbelief. Her chest still felt tight, her pulse thrumming in her ears. "You call this winning?" she asked, her voice breaking slightly. "We've bled for this. Killed for this. We will never be the same again."

Thorwulf reached out, his rough, calloused fingers brushing against hers. "We're alive," he said softly. "And together. That's enough for me."

She couldn't help the way her hand curled into his, holding on as if he were the only thing tethering her to solid ground. For so long, she had fought to keep herself guarded, to hold back the feelings that had steadily grown for him. But now, after standing on the brink of death together, she couldn't deny it any longer.

Thorwulf's thumb brushed over her knuckles, and she looked up to find him watching her, his expression uncharacteristically vulnerable. "Astrid," he murmured, his voice low and steady, "I meant what I said before. I'd rather die than let them tear us apart."

Her heart twisted painfully, and she felt the words rising in her throat before she could stop them. "And I'd rather fight the gods themselves than lose you," she whispered, her voice trembling with the weight of her emotions.

For a moment, neither of them moved, the air between them heavy with unspoken feelings. Then Thorwulf leaned in, his hand coming up to cradle her cheek as his lips found hers. The kiss was slow and deep, filled with a quiet desperation that made her heart race. It wasn't just a kiss. It was a promise, a vow made without words, that they would face whatever came next together.

When they finally pulled apart, Astrid rested her forehead against his, her breath mingling with his in the cold air. "What now?" she asked softly.

Thorwulf's brow furrowed, and his hand slid from her cheek to cup the back of her neck. "Now," he said, his voice heavy. "We go home."

Astrid pulled back slightly, her gaze searching his. "Do you think we've angered them?"

"The gods?"

She nodded, her fingers tightening around his hand. "We defied them. We didn't play by their rules. What if this isn't truly over?"

Thorwulf's expression darkened, and for a moment, the humor that so often softened the edges of his demeanor was gone. "It's always been about survival," he said. "The gods don't give their favor lightly, and they don't forget when it's challenged. But we've made it this far, Astrid. Whatever they throw at us, we'll face it together."

His words brought her a measure of comfort, but the unease in her chest didn't fully fade. She glanced toward the distant ridge where the Jarls still stood, their figures silhouetted against the stormy sky. They were watching, waiting, their faces grim with something that looked suspiciously like disapproval.

"They don't look pleased," Astrid said, her voice bitter.

Thorwulf followed her gaze, his lips twisting into a faint smirk. "They wanted a champion to kneel before them," he said. "Instead, they got us."

She couldn't help but smile at that, though the worry lingered in the back of her mind. The gods were not known for their forgiveness, and neither were the Jarls. Defying them had bought her and Thorwulf their lives, but at what cost?

"We should move," she said finally, pushing herself to her feet. Her legs felt unsteady beneath her, but she forced herself to stand tall. "The Reckoning might be over, but I don't trust them not to change the rules again."

Thorwulf grunted as he rose beside her, his hand brushing against his side where his tunic was still stained with blood. "You're not wrong," he said, his tone light but his expression serious.

They turned together, their backs to the cliff's edge as they began the long trek down the mountain. The wind howled around them, and the path ahead was treacherous, but Astrid felt steadier with Thorwulf at her side.

The gods might be watching. The Jarls might be plotting. But for now, they had each other. And that was enough.

23

SHADOWS IN FROSTFJORD

The longship cut through the icy waters like a dagger, its hull creaking with each rise and fall of the waves. Astrid stood at the prow, her hands gripping the carved wooden railing as the familiar silhouette of Frostfjord's jagged cliffs came into view. The biting wind carried the scent of salt and pine, mingling with the faint metallic tang of snow. It should have felt like a homecoming, but something was wrong.

Behind her, Thorwulf sat near the mast, his tunic still darkened with blood from the Reckoning. His dark eyes were fixed on the horizon, his expression unreadable. The crew gave them a wide berth, their hushed whispers barely audible over the crash of waves against the ship. Astrid didn't need to hear the words to know what they were saying.

"They're afraid of us," she said quietly, her breath curling in the cold air.

Thorwulf's gaze shifted to her, and a faint smile tugged at the corner of his lips. "Good," he said. "Let them be afraid. It's better than them trying to test us."

Astrid's stomach churned. The Reckoning was over, but it

felt like the real battle was only beginning. The Jarls had declared them joint winners, but their fury had been palpable, their reluctant concession laced with barely veiled malice. They might have survived the trials, but Astrid doubted the Jarls would let their defiance go unpunished for long.

As the ship drew closer to the harbor, the familiar sight of Frostfjord's village came into focus. Wooden longhouses with thatched roofs clustered together at the base of the cliffs, their walls darkened by soot and time. Smoke curled from chimneys, mingling with the gray sky, and figures moved along the docks, their shapes growing sharper as the ship approached.

But the usual bustle of the harbor was subdued. The villagers stood in clusters, their faces turned toward the incoming ship, their expressions guarded. Astrid's heart lurched as she caught sight of her father among them, his shoulders hunched and his face pale. Beside him stood her younger sister, her crutch digging into the snow as she leaned heavily on it, and her wide eyes filled with both relief and unease.

"They're here for us," Astrid said, her voice quiet.

Thorwulf rose to his feet, his movements deliberate as he adjusted the axe slung across his back. "Then let's not keep them waiting."

The longship slid into the harbor, its hull scraping against the wooden dock as the crew leapt into action, securing the ropes and lowering the gangplank. Astrid stepped forward, her boots crunching against the snow-dusted wood as she disembarked. The murmurs of the crowd swelled as she and Thorwulf stepped onto the dock, their presence like a ripple through the tense silence.

"Astrid!" Her sister's voice broke through the murmurs, high and desperate. She hobbled forward, her crutch slipping on the icy dock, but Astrid caught her before she fell.

"Solveig," she said, her voice breaking as she pulled her into a tight embrace. Solveig's small frame trembled against her, and she closed her eyes in relief.

"I thought... I thought you wouldn't come back," she whispered, her voice muffled against Astrid's shoulder.

"I'm here," Astrid said softly, her hand stroking her hair. "I'm here, and I'm not going anywhere."

Her father approached slowly, his face lined with worry. "Astrid," he said, his voice low and strained. "You... you survived."

The words felt heavier than they should have, and Astrid pulled back from Solveig to meet her father's gaze. "We did," she said, her tone steady despite the unease coiling in her chest.

Her father's eyes flicked to Thorwulf, who stood a few paces behind her, his expression guarded. "And they... they let you both live?"

Astrid frowned. "The Jarls didn't have a choice."

The murmurs around them grew louder, the villagers exchanging glances and whispers that prickled at the back of her neck. She turned to face the crowd, her voice cutting through the noise.

"We fought," she said, her tone firm. "We survived. And we did it together."

For a moment, the crowd was silent. Then a voice called out, sharp and accusatory. "You defied the gods!"

Astrid's stomach twisted as she scanned the faces in the crowd, trying to find the source of the voice. The speaker stepped forward. It was a man she recognized as one of Frostfjord's fishermen, his weathered face twisted with fear and anger.

"You broke the rules of this Reckoning," he said, his voice rising. "The gods demanded a single champion, not two."

"We were declared joint winners," Thorwulf said, his voice calm but carrying an edge of warning. "If the gods were that displeased, we wouldn't be standing here."

The man faltered, but the unease in the crowd didn't dissipate. Astrid could feel their eyes on her, heavy with suspicion and doubt.

"They're afraid," Thorwulf said quietly, stepping closer to her. "Not of us, but of what we represent. Change."

Astrid's gaze swept over the crowd. She saw the fear etched into their faces. She had fought to protect them, to bring honor to her clan, but now it felt like she had brought something darker with her, that threatened to unravel everything they had once believed in.

"We need to talk to the Jarls," she said softly, her voice meant only for Thorwulf.

He nodded, with a grim expression. "And find out what they're planning. Because they're not done with us yet."

As the crowd began to disperse, their whispers carried on the cold wind, Astrid couldn't shake the feeling that their victory had come at a cost they had yet to fully understand. The gods' favor was fickle, and the Jarls' fury was far from spent.

For now, they were heroes of a sort. But shadows were already gathering in Frostfjord, and Astrid could feel the weight of them pressing down on her like a storm waiting to break.

The Frostfjord Clan was a world of ice and iron, shaped by the relentless winds and unforgiving winters of the north. It was a place where survival was earned, not given, and strength was measured not just in battle but in resilience. The clan's hierarchy mirrored its harsh environment. It was rigid, cold, and steeped in tradition. At the top were the Jarls, their authority absolute and backed by the gods' supposed favor. Beneath them were the chieftains, who governed the village and enforced the Jarls' decrees. Below them were the clansfolk, the hunters, fishermen, craftsmen, all bound by loyalty and duty.

Astrid and Thorwulf walked through the village under a flurry of watchful eyes. The air was thick with tension, the usual bustling sounds of life muted by whispers that clung to the wind like frost. Some villagers looked at them with awe, their expressions a mix of admiration and fear. Others scowled openly, their disapproval cutting through the crowd like knives.

A group of women tending to nets paused as Astrid passed, their chatter falling silent. One of them, a tall, broad-shouldered woman Astrid recognized as Hilda, the head net-weaver, gave her a curt nod.

"You fought well," Hilda said, her voice grudging. "But defiance has a cost, girl. Don't forget that."

Astrid didn't respond, her jaw set as she forced herself to keep walking. She could feel Thorwulf's presence at her side, solid and steady, but the weight of the villagers' stares pressed heavily on her shoulders.

At the center of the village, the central longhouse loomed. It was a massive structure of weathered timber and stone, its roof steep and dusted with snow. This was the seat of Frostfjord's leadership, where the chieftains convened to deliberate and where the clan gathered for feasts and ceremonies. It was a place of power, and now, it felt like the eye of a storm.

As Astrid and Thorwulf approached, the doors swung open, and a figure stepped out.

"Leif," Astrid said, her voice softening as her childhood friend strode toward her.

He looked the same as ever, his golden hair tousled by the wind and his expression sharp with intensity. But there was something in his eyes. A flicker of tension, of something unspoken clouded his gaze as he saw her. Astrid's stomach twisted at the sight of it.

"Astrid," Leif said, his gaze flicking briefly to Thorwulf before settling back on her. "You're back."

"Clearly," Thorwulf said, his tone light but edged with something sharper.

Leif's jaw clenched, but he ignored Thorwulf, his attention focused solely on Astrid. "We need to talk," he said, his voice low.

Astrid hesitated, glancing at Thorwulf. He gave her a small nod, though his eyes remained wary. "I'll wait," he said, stepping back.

Leif led Astrid to the edge of the village, where the trees thinned and the wind carried the faint scent of pine. He stopped, turning to face her, and for a moment, neither of them spoke.

"I heard the Jarls' decree," Leif said finally, in a heavy tone. "And the whispers it's stirred."

Astrid crossed her arms, her brow furrowing. "What whispers?"

Leif's expression darkened. "That the Jarls are furious. That they see your victory as a challenge to their authority. And worse, there are rumors that some of Frostfjord's leadership agrees with them."

Astrid's stomach clenched, her mind racing. "What are you saying, Leif? That the clan would turn on us?"

"Not the clan," he said carefully. "But the chieftains... they're divided. Some see you and Thorwulf as heroes, proof of Frostfjord's strength. Others think you've endangered us all by angering the gods and the Jarls. They think the gods will punish the entire clan for your defiance."

She felt the weight of the Reckoning's aftermath pressing down on her. "They declared us winners," she said, her voice shaking slightly. "If the gods were truly angered, wouldn't they have stopped us? Or let us die?"

Leif sighed, running a hand through his hair. "Astrid, you know as well as I do that the gods' will is as unpredictable as the sea. People are afraid, and fear breeds division."

Astrid wanted to argue, to shout that they had earned their victory, but the truth was, she felt the same fear gnawing at her.

Leif stepped closer, his voice softening. "I don't trust Thorwulf," he said bluntly. "He's dangerous, Astrid. And now that the Jarls have named him your soulmate..."

Astrid's breath caught, her gaze snapping to his. "That wasn't our choice," she said sharply. "It was their decree."

"And yet, you seem content with it," Leif said. "Do you even know who he is? What he's capable of?"

Her anger flared, hot and unyielding. "Thorwulf fought beside me," she said, her voice low and fierce. "He saved my life more times than I can count. Don't you dare question his loyalty."

Leif's eyes narrowed, his jealousy evident in the sharpness of his tone. "You've changed, Astrid," he said quietly. "Since the Reckoning... you're not the same girl I grew up with."

"Of course, I've changed," she snapped. "I had to. We both did."

The silence between them was heavy, the wind whipping through the sparse trees around them. Finally, Leif sighed, his shoulders slumping. "Just be careful," he said. "The world isn't as simple as it used to be."

Astrid watched him walk away, her chest aching with a mix of frustration and sadness. When she returned to Thorwulf, his dark eyes met hers, and she saw the unspoken question in his gaze.

"What did he want?" Thorwulf asked, his voice calm but laced with tension.

Astrid hesitated, her gaze drifting toward the longhouse. "To warn me," she said quietly. "About the whispers. About the chieftains."

Thorwulf's expression hardened. "Let them whisper," he said. "We'll deal with them if they come for us."

Astrid nodded, but her heart was heavy. The shadows in Frostfjord were growing, and she wasn't sure if even the gods could save them from what was coming.

24

THE GODS DEMAND BLOOD

The hall of the Frostfjord longhouse was dark, the flickering light of torches casting jagged shadows against the smoke-stained timber walls. The air was thick with tension, heavy with the unspoken threat that hung between the Jarls seated at the raised dais and the two figures standing before them. Astrid stood rigid, her chin lifted in defiance, while Thorwulf stood at her side, his presence as steady and unyielding as the mountains outside.

The Jarls were draped in furs and adorned with intricate braids and heavy gold pendants that gleamed in the firelight. Their expressions were carved from ice, their eyes cold and unforgiving as they regarded the two oathsworn-turned-champions. At the center of the dais sat Jarl Eirik, the eldest and most imposing of the council, his gray beard braided with silver strands and his piercing blue eyes fixed on Astrid with an intensity that made her skin crawl.

"You stand here today," Eirik began, his voice deep and resonant, "not as champions, but as offenders to the gods. Your actions in the Reckoning have not gone unnoticed, and neither has your defiance."

"We survived," Astrid said, her voice steady despite the storm raging inside her. "We fought, we bled, and we proved ourselves worthy. How is that an offense?"

Eirik's gaze hardened. "You threatened to take your own lives, to deprive the gods of their chosen champion. That act alone is sacrilege. It's a direct challenge to their will."

Thorwulf stepped forward, his dark eyes blazing with defiance. "The gods didn't stop us," he said, his voice calm but laced with steel. "If they were displeased, they would have struck us down. Instead, they allowed us to stand victorious. What does that tell you?"

The murmur of the gathered clansfolk rippled through the hall like the distant roar of an avalanche. Eirik's hand shot up, silencing them instantly. "Do not presume to speak for the gods," he said sharply. "Your survival is no proof of their favor. It is a test. A chance for you to atone for your arrogance."

Astrid's heart pounded with the weight of the accusations. She could feel the eyes of the crowd on her, their judgment pressing down on her like a physical force. "What do you want from us?" she asked, her voice low and trembling with suppressed anger. "We fought with honor. We followed the rules."

"You bent the rules to your will," Eirik interrupted, his voice cutting through hers like a blade. "And now the gods demand restitution."

Astrid's stomach dropped, her mind racing. Restitution. The word hung in the air like a noose, and she could see the dark satisfaction in Eirik's eyes as he let it sink in.

"The gods demand blood," he said, his tone almost reverent. "An offering to balance the scales and restore their favor."

Astrid's breath caught in her throat, her pulse thundering in her ears. She glanced at Thorwulf, seeing flicker of worry in his expression. For all his strength and bravado, even he couldn't hide the unease that now shadowed his features.

"Whose blood?" Thorwulf asked, his voice low and dangerous.

Eirik's gaze swept over the two of them, his expression inscrutable. "That is for the gods to decide."

A murmur of agreement rippled through the other Jarls, their faces impassive as they watched the scene unfold. Astrid's anger flared.

"This isn't about the gods," she said, her voice rising. "This is about control. You're afraid of us. You're afraid of what we represent. You think you can use this tribunal to put us back in our place."

Eirik's eyes narrowed, his expression hardening. "Careful, Astrid," he said, his voice low and menacing. "You walk a fine line between defiance and heresy."

Astrid took a step forward, her heart pounding. "I'm not afraid of you," she said, her voice steady despite the tremor in her chest. "And I won't let you use the gods as an excuse to punish us for surviving."

The tension in the hall was suffocating, the silence stretching like a blade poised to strike. Thorwulf stepped closer to Astrid, his presence a steadying force beside her.

"What's the real reason we're here?" Thorwulf asked, his voice cutting through the heavy air. "What do you gain by turning the clan against us?"

Eirik's expression darkened, and for a moment, the mask of authority slipped. There was something raw and furious in his eyes, a flicker of fear that he couldn't quite hide.

"The gods demand blood," Eirik repeated, his voice tight. "And if you refuse to give it, they will simply take it."

Astrid's breath caught, her pulse thundering as the full weight of his words settled over her. She felt Thorwulf's hand brush against hers, a subtle gesture that grounded her even as the storm inside her threatened to consume her.

"We've given enough blood," Astrid said, her voice trembling with fury. "More than enough. If the gods want more, they can come for it themselves."

A gasp rippled through the crowd, and Eirik's eyes blazed with fury. "You dare—" he began, but Astrid cut him off.

"I dare," she said, her voice steady now. "Because I've stood on the edge of death and come back stronger. I've faced the gods' trials and survived. And I will not be broken by you or anyone else."

The hall erupted into chaos, the murmurs and gasps rising to a roar as the clansfolk reacted to her words. Eirik's face was a mask of rage, his hands clenching the arms of his chair as he leaned forward.

"Enough!" he bellowed, his voice silencing the crowd. He pointed a gnarled finger at Astrid and Thorwulf, his expression cold and deadly. "You have until the next full moon to provide the gods with their blood offering. Fail, and the gods' wrath will fall not just on you, but on all of Frostfjord."

Astrid's heart pounded, but she refused to flinch. She met Eirik's gaze head-on, her chin lifting in defiance. "We'll see what the gods truly demand," she said, her voice steady and resolute. "And we'll prove that we're stronger than their fear."

As the Jarls rose from their seats and the hall began to empty, Astrid felt Thorwulf's hand on her shoulder. She turned to him with a mix of fear and determination.

"What now?" he asked, his voice quiet but firm.

Astrid's gaze swept over the longhouse and the faces of their clan. "Now," she said in a low and fierce voice. "We fight back."

The hall seemed to close in around them, the air thick with tension and the oppressive weight of the Jarls' judgment. The firelight flickered against the dark wood, throwing shadows across the walls that seemed to dance with menace. Astrid felt every eye on her, every whisper crawling over her skin like a thousand icy needles. But she refused to back down.

Astrid stepped forward, her shoulders squared, her voice steady. "You speak of the gods' wrath, but you forget: we are standing here because we passed their trials. We bled, we fought, and we proved ourselves worthy. If you think the gods demand blood from us, then perhaps it is you who misunderstand their will."

A ripple of gasps and murmurs spread through the gathered crowd as the Jarls stopped in their tracks. Even Thorwulf stiffened beside her, his hand twitching toward the hilt of his axe as if ready to defend her from the storm her words might unleash. But Astrid didn't falter.

Jarl Eirik turned back, striding angrily towards her. She held his gaze, her blue eyes as sharp and unyielding as the frost-rimmed peaks beyond Frostfjord.

Eirik's face darkened, his icy eyes narrowing to slits. "You tread dangerously close to heresy, Astrid," he said, his voice low and venomous. "Defiance may have served you in the Reckoning, but here, it will be your undoing."

Thorwulf stepped forward then, his calm, measured voice cutting through the growing uproar. "With all respect, Jarl Eirik," he began, bowing his head slightly but keeping his tone firm, "Astrid speaks from a place of truth. We did not win by chance or trickery. The gods allowed us to stand together as winners. They saw our bond and deemed it strong enough to endure their trials. Surely that is not defiance, but proof of their favor."

Eirik leaned back in his seat, his fingers drumming against the armrest of his carved chair. "You claim favor, yet you threatened to take your lives. That is not strength. That is weakness. Cowardice."

Astrid bristled, but Thorwulf placed a steadying hand on

her arm, his touch grounding her. He turned back to the Jarls, his tone softening. "It was not cowardice," he said. "It was resolve. We would rather die as one than allow ourselves to be pawns in a game of division. If that angers the gods, then so be it. But we will not apologize for surviving."

The room fell into a heavy silence, the crackle of the fire the only sound. The Jarls exchanged glances, their expressions inscrutable, and for a moment, Astrid thought they might issue their final judgment. Her hand instinctively moved to the hilt of her sword, her pulse quickening as she prepared for the worst.

But then Jarl Sigrun, the only woman among them, leaned forward. Her silver hair shimmered in the firelight, and her voice was low and measured. "There is wisdom in their words, Eirik," she said, her tone carrying a weight of authority that stilled even the most restless murmurs in the hall. "The gods have not struck them down. They have not sent omens of their displeasure. Perhaps we are too quick to judge."

Eirik scowled but did not interrupt as Sigrun continued, her gaze piercing as she looked at Astrid and Thorwulf. "But," she added, her voice dropping to a dangerous hush, "the gods do not forget. You may have survived their trials, but your defiance has not gone unnoticed. There will be consequences."

Astrid's heart sank, but she refused to let the fear show on her face. "If the gods have a quarrel with us, we will face it," she said boldly. "We've faced everything else they've thrown at us."

Sigrun's lips curved into a faint smile, though it held no warmth. "You are brave, Astrid of Frostfjord. Perhaps too brave for your own good."

Eirik straightened his shoulders, his fur-lined cloak sweeping behind him as he towered over the hall. "Very well," he said, his voice booming. "The gods will decide your fate, but for now, we grant you a reprieve. You are free to return to your homes, but know this: the gods demand balance. Blood will be spilled. Whether it is yours or another's remains to be seen."

Astrid's stomach churned, but she kept her expression steady, refusing to show any sign of weakness. She felt Thorwulf's presence beside her, solid and unwavering, and it gave her the strength to hold her head high.

"Thank you, Jarl Eirik," Thorwulf said, his voice calm but edged with tension. "We will honor the gods' will, whatever it may be."

Eirik's gaze bore into him, and for a moment, it seemed as though he might say more. But then he nodded curtly, signaling the end of the tribunal. The other Jarls rose, their cloaks brushing against the floor as they filed out, leaving Astrid and Thorwulf alone in the center of the hall.

As the doors slammed shut behind them, Astrid let out a shaky breath, her shoulders slumping under the weight of the confrontation. Thorwulf turned to her, his dark eyes searching hers. "That could have gone worse," he said wryly.

Astrid let out a humorless laugh. "Could it? Because it feels like we just traded one death sentence for another."

Thorwulf stepped closer, his hand brushing against hers in a subtle gesture of reassurance. "We've faced worse, Astrid. And we'll face this, too. Together."

She met his gaze with a small smile. For all their bravado in the hall, she could feel the uncertainty lingering between them, the unspoken fear of what the gods, or the Jarls, might do next.

"We need to be ready," she said, her voice low. "For whatever comes."

Thorwulf nodded. "We will be."

As they stepped out of the longhouse and into the biting wind, Astrid couldn't shake the feeling that their reprieve was nothing more than a pause in the storm. The gods demanded blood, and the shadows gathering over Frostfjord promised that the worst was yet to come.

25

RIFTS AMONG THE CLANS

The bitter chill of the Frostfjord winds swept through the village, tugging at cloaks and rattling the wooden shutters of the longhouses. Astrid stood at the center of the village square, her breath curling in the icy air as she stared at the crowd gathered before her. The tension rippled through the crowd in whispers of discontent and anger, swirling like the snowflakes that dusted the ground.

Frostfjord had always been a place of resilience, a clan forged in the crucible of ice and hardship. But now, cracks were forming in the unity that had kept them strong. The Reckoning was supposed to bring honor and balance, yet it had only deepened the divides.

"Have you heard?" A man in the crowd spoke up, his voice sharp with frustration. "Solfjord has closed their borders to us. They're withholding their grain shipments."

A murmur of outrage spread through the villagers, their expressions darkening. Frostfjord relied on Solfjord's surplus during the harsh winters, trading sealskins and iron for the grain that kept their stores full. Without it, hunger would stalk the village like a wolf.

Astrid turned to face the speaker. "And why would they do that?" she asked, her voice steady but edged with fury.

The man hesitated, glancing nervously at the others before answering. "They say it's punishment," he said. "For your defiance. For what happened in the Reckoning."

The crowd erupted into a cacophony of anger and fear, the noise rising as they argued among themselves. Astrid felt the weight of their accusations, their fear, pressing down on her like a physical force.

"Enough!" Thorwulf's voice cut through the noise like a blade, silencing the crowd. He stepped forward, his broad frame casting a long shadow over the snow-covered square. "Solfjord may think they can starve us into submission, but Frostfjord has endured worse. We don't need their charity."

A murmur of agreement rippled through the crowd, though it was tinged with uncertainty. Astrid could see the fear lingering in their eyes, the doubt that Thorwulf's bravado couldn't erase.

"They're testing us," Astrid said, her voice rising above the whispers. "Solfjord thinks they can break us, but they've forgotten who we are. Frostfjord doesn't bend. We don't bow. We survive."

Her words sparked a flicker of hope in the crowd, their postures straightening as they nodded in agreement. But she knew it wouldn't be enough. Solfjord's actions were only the beginning.

As the villagers began to disperse, muttering among themselves, Astrid felt a hand on her arm. She turned to see Leif, his expression grim.

"They're afraid, Astrid," he said quietly. "And fear makes people desperate. You need to be careful."

Astrid sighed, her shoulders slumping as she glanced toward the horizon, where the mountains loomed like silent sentinels.

"What would you have me do, Leif? Apologize to the Jarls? Beg Solfjord for mercy?"

Leif's frown was barely noticeable, his golden hair catching the weak sunlight. "No," he said. "But you need to be smart. There are those who admire you, Astrid. Other clans who see your defiance as a symbol of strength. If you can rally them..."

"Rally them for what?" she interrupted, her voice sharp. "A war? More bloodshed? That's exactly what the Jarls want."

Thorwulf stepped up beside her, his dark eyes glinting with determination. "He's not wrong," he said. "The clans are watching, Astrid. They're looking for someone to lead them. If we don't take control of this, someone else will."

Astrid turned to him, not wanting to hear it. She had fought so hard to survive the Reckoning, to protect Frostfjord, but now it felt like she was being pulled into something far bigger than herself.

"Thorwulf," she said softly, her voice trembling, "I'm not a leader. I didn't ask for this."

He placed a hand on her shoulder, his touch warm despite the cold. "You didn't ask for it," he said, his voice steady. "But it's yours all the same. The clans see you as a symbol, Astrid. A reminder that even the gods can be defied. You have a choice: either step into that role, or let someone else decide what happens next."

Her chest ached with the weight of his words, the enormity of the decision before her. She glanced back at Leif, who nodded silently, his expression unreadable.

"I'll think about it," she said finally.

As they turned to leave the square, Astrid knew that the ground beneath her feet was shifting, that the fragile peace between the clans was crumbling into something far more dangerous.

The long shadows of the late afternoon stretched across the village, casting an eerie stillness over Frostfjord. Astrid sat at the edge of the frozen river that snaked through the valley, the jagged mountains towering in the distance. Her breath curled in the frigid air, but she barely noticed the cold. Her mind was a whirlwind, pressed down by a weight she didn't know how to carry.

Behind her, she heard the crunch of boots on snow, the sound drawing closer until Leif dropped down beside her. He didn't speak at first, simply watching the slow current of the ice-laden water. The silence stretched between them, comfortable and familiar, but Astrid could feel his hesitation.

"Say what's on your mind, Leif," she said finally, her voice soft but edged with weariness.

He sighed, running a hand through his golden hair. "You've changed, Astrid," he said. "The girl who used to chase me through these woods, who climbed the cliffs without fear... she's still in there somewhere. But now, you carry so much on your shoulders. Too much."

Astrid glanced at him, her brow furrowing. "And what would you have me do? Abandon the people who look to me for strength? Walk away from the role the Reckoning forced on me?"

Leif shook his head. "That's not what I'm saying. But I see the toll it's taking on you. You're questioning everything, your place here, your choices. I can see it in your eyes."

She looked away, her gaze fixed on the river. "I don't know who I am anymore, Leif," she admitted, her voice barely above a whisper. "Before the Reckoning, I knew my place. I had a family to protect, a life that made sense. But now... everything feels different. The village looks at me like I'm some kind of savior, but I don't feel like one. And the Jarls..."

"Are waiting for you to fail," Leif finished, his tone dark. "You've shaken the balance, Astrid. And they don't forgive that easily."

She wrapped her arms around her knees, the icy wind tugging at her hair. "What if I can't do this?" she asked softly. "What if I'm not strong enough?"

"You're stronger than you think," Leif said, his voice firm. "But you don't have to carry this alone. You have people who care about you. People who want to help."

She turned to him, her gaze searching his. "Like you?"

"Always," he said, the word heavy with meaning. "But I can't be the only one. You trust Thorwulf, don't you?"

Astrid hesitated, her thoughts drifting to the man who had become her partner in every sense of the word. Thorwulf's steady presence, his unwavering loyalty, had been her anchor through the Reckoning and its aftermath. But with that trust came a vulnerability she wasn't sure how to handle.

"I trust him," she said finally. "But that doesn't mean I'm ready to rely on him completely. What happens if I do and he... leaves? Or changes his mind?"

Leif's frustration flickered across his face. "Thorwulf isn't going anywhere," he said, his tone clipped. "You're the one holding back, Astrid. Maybe it's time you stopped running from what you feel."

Before she could respond, the sound of approaching footsteps made her turn. Thorwulf emerged from the trees, his dark eyes scanning the scene before he stepped closer. His presence was like a storm rolling in, both commanding and impossible to ignore.

"Am I interrupting?" he asked, his voice calm but laced with curiosity.

Leif stood, brushing snow from his cloak. "Not at all," he said, his tone cooler now. "We were just... catching up."

Thorwulf's gaze flicked between them, his expression unreadable. "Good," he said, his attention settling on Astrid. "Because we need to talk."

Leif hesitated, his eyes lingering on Astrid for a moment longer before he turned and walked away, his shoulders stiff. Thorwulf watched him go, but he said nothing. Instead, he lowered himself to sit beside Astrid, his gaze softening as it met hers.

"You've been quiet," he said, his voice low. "Since the meeting. What's on your mind?"

Astrid let out a heavy breath, and brushed her fingers against the frost-covered grass. "Everything," she admitted. "The clan, the Jarls, Solfjord's blockade... I feel like I'm being pulled in a thousand different directions, and I don't know which way to go."

Thorwulf leaned back on his hands, his dark hair catching the light of the fading sun. "You don't have to have all the answers right now," he said. "But you do need to decide what matters most to you. The clan? The gods? Yourself?"

His words struck a chord, and Astrid turned to him, her brow furrowed. "What do you mean?"

"I mean," he said, his gaze steady, "that you can't lead if you don't know where you stand. The Jarls will try to manipulate you. The other clans will push for their own agendas. If you don't figure out what you're fighting for, they'll tear you apart."

Astrid nodded. "I don't want to be a leader, Thorwulf," she said softly. "I just want to protect the people I care about."

"Then start there," he said simply. "Lead for them, not for the Jarls or the gods. For your family. For Frostfjord. For the people who believe in you."

His words settled over her like a blanket, warm and grounding. She met his gaze, her heart aching with gratitude for the way he seemed to understand her, even when she didn't understand herself.

"Thank you," she said quietly.

Thorwulf smiled faintly, his hand taking hers. "You don't have to thank me," he said. "We're in this together, Astrid. Always."

For the first time in days, Astrid felt a flicker of hope. The road ahead was uncertain, the challenges daunting, but with Thorwulf and Leif by her side, she knew she wouldn't face them alone.

As the sun dipped below the horizon, casting the village in shadows, Astrid made a silent vow. She would find her place in Frostfjord. She would fight for the people she loved. And she would prove to the gods and the Jarls alike that she was stronger than they had ever imagined.

26

THE RAID

The first scream pierced the night like a blade. Astrid sat bolt upright in her cot, her breath catching in her throat as the sound of shouts and clashing steel reached her ears. The faint glow of firelight flickered through the cracks in the wooden walls of her family's longhouse, casting eerie shadows that danced like demons.

"Raiders!" someone bellowed from outside, the panic in their voice unmistakable.

Astrid didn't waste a second. She threw off the furs and grabbed her sword, the weight of it familiar in her grip as she rushed to the door. Her father, Sigurd, was already up, his face pale but determined as he tightened the straps of his leather armor. Solveig huddled near the hearth, her crutch clutched in trembling hands.

"Stay inside," Astrid told her, her voice firm despite the pounding of her heart. "Don't open this door unless it's me."

Solveig nodded, with wide eyes filled with fear. Sigurd stepped forward, his hand gripping Astrid's shoulder. "Be careful," he said, his voice rough with worry.

Astrid nodded, swallowing hard before pushing the door open and stepping into the chaos.

The village was ablaze.

Flames consumed the thatched roofs of longhouses, their heat scorching the frigid night air. Shadows danced across the snow, illuminated by the glow of the inferno, and the screams of the villagers mingled with the clash of weapons. Masked raiders surged through the streets, their faces obscured by iron helms etched with the snarling wolf sigil of Ironcrag.

Astrid's stomach twisted as she recognized the brutality of their movements. These weren't opportunistic bandits or desperate men seeking food. This was an orchestrated attack, a calculated strike meant to cripple Frostfjord.

Her gaze locked onto a figure in the center of the chaos. A towering man clad in dark furs, his axe dripping with blood as he strode through the carnage. Hakon. Ragnar's brother. His presence radiated menace, his eyes gleaming with cold fury even through the slit of his helm.

Astrid gritted her teeth, the weight of her sword grounding her as she stepped into the fray. The first raider who charged her didn't even get the chance to swing. She sidestepped his clumsy attack, her blade finding the gap between his shoulder and neck. Blood sprayed across the snow, and he crumpled to the ground, lifeless.

Another came at her, this one wielding a spear. He was faster, more skilled, but Astrid's reflexes were sharper. She ducked under his thrust, her sword slashing across his abdomen. He staggered, clutching his stomach as he fell to his knees.

The sounds of battle filled her ears. The screams, the cries for help, the clash of steel. Frostfjord's warriors fought valiantly, but the raiders were relentless, their numbers overwhelming.

Astrid's chest heaved as she fought her way through the chaos, her blade slick with blood.

"Astrid!" Thorwulf's voice rang out, and she turned to see him cutting down a raider with brutal efficiency. His face was smeared with soot and blood, his dark eyes blazing as he made his way to her.

"Thorwulf," she gasped, relief flooding her chest at the sight of him.

"They're everywhere," he said grimly, his axe resting on his shoulder as he scanned the battlefield. "We need to push them back."

Before Astrid could respond, a deep, booming voice cut through the night.

"Astrid!" Hakon's shout was like thunder, silencing the chaos for a brief moment. He stood on a raised platform of crates near the center of the village, his massive frame illuminated by the firelight. In his hand, he held the limp body of a Frostfjord warrior, blood dripping from the man's lifeless form.

Astrid's heart clenched, fury burning in her veins as Hakon's gaze locked onto hers. "Come out and face me, you coward!" he bellowed, his voice echoing through the village. "Or I'll burn this place to the ground and kill every last one of your people!"

Thorwulf stepped forward, his hand tightening on his axe. "We can take him," he muttered, his voice low.

Astrid's mind was racing. Hakon wasn't just here for blood, he was here for revenge. For Ragnar. And he wouldn't stop until he got it.

"We can't fight him like this," she said, her voice steady despite the fear clawing at her chest. "Not with the village in chaos."

Thorwulf hesitated, his expression torn. "Then what do we do?"

Astrid's gaze swept over the carnage, her heart heavy as she saw the bodies of village men, women, even children strewn across the snow. She felt the weight of their lives pressing down on her, the responsibility she had taken on when she stepped into the Reckoning.

"We push them back," she said firmly. "And then we deal with Hakon."

Thorwulf nodded, his trust in her unwavering. Together, they rallied the remaining warriors, their shouts cutting through the chaos as they pushed against the raiders. The fight was brutal, the snow stained red with blood, but slowly, they began to gain ground.

As the last of the raiders retreated, dragging their wounded back into the shadows, Hakon remained on his perch, his dark eyes fixed on Astrid. He raised his axe, pointing it at her like a challenge.

"This isn't over, girl," he snarled, his voice carrying across the square. "Frostfjord will burn. And you will pay for my brother."

With that, he disappeared into the night, leaving the stragglers of his raiding party to their work amid the smoldering ruins of the village and the chilling promise of his return.

The clash of steel and the cries of the wounded rang in Astrid's ears, a deafening symphony of chaos that seemed to drown out the very world around her. The heat of the fires mixed with the biting cold of the Frostfjord wind, and her breath clouded the air as she parried another blow. Her sword felt like an extension of her arm now, an instinct, not a tool.

"Behind you!" Thorwulf's warning was sharp and immediate.

Astrid spun, slashing her blade upward just as a raider lunged at her with a dagger. Her sword caught the edge of his weapon, sending it spinning into the snow before she drove her knee into his gut and her blade into his chest. He crumpled at her feet, his blood seeping into the icy ground.

Thorwulf was moving through the remaining raiders, pushing them back, his axe cleaving through the air with deadly precision. He fought like a force of nature, every swing calculated, every strike brutal. His dark eyes darted to Astrid constantly, ensuring she was still standing, still fighting.

"Stay close!" he shouted over the chaos, cutting down another raider who had dared to approach him.

Astrid nodded, her heart pounding as she stepped closer to him. The two of them moved in unison, a lethal partnership that carved a path through the battlefield. But for every raider they cut down, it seemed three more took their place.

A sudden cry drew Astrid's attention, and she turned to see a young village boy, barely old enough to hold a blade, cornered by two masked raiders. His wooden shield was splintered, his face pale with terror.

"Thorwulf!" she called, already moving toward the boy.

Thorwulf followed without hesitation, his axe swinging wide to take out one of the raiders before they even saw him coming. Astrid ducked under the other's strike, her blade finding its mark in his side. The boy stumbled back, his eyes wide with shock as he looked between them.

"Go!" Astrid barked, pointing toward the relative safety of a nearby longhouse. "Find shelter and stay there!"

The boy nodded, his legs shaky as he bolted away. Astrid turned back to Thorwulf, her chest heaving. "We can't save everyone," she said, the weight of the truth bitter on her tongue.

"No," Thorwulf agreed grimly. "But we'll save as many as we can."

The battle raged on, the village square a hellscape of fire and blood. Astrid found herself fighting back-to-back with Thorwulf, their movements perfectly synchronized as they protected each other from the endless onslaught. She felt his presence like a shield, his strength bolstering hers in a way she hadn't realized she needed.

At one point, a raider broke through their line, his blade arcing toward Astrid's unprotected side. She saw it too late and raised her sword, but not fast enough.

"Watch it!" Thorwulf's shout was accompanied by his body slamming into hers, knocking her to the ground just as the raider's blade sliced through the air where she had been standing. Thorwulf's axe swung in a deadly arc, and the raider fell, his body hitting the ground with a sickening thud.

Astrid scrambled to her feet, her heart pounding as she stared at Thorwulf. "You could've been killed," she said, her voice trembling with a mix of anger and fear.

Thorwulf grinned, though there was a tension in his expression that betrayed his weariness. "And yet, here I am," he said. "You're welcome, by the way."

Astrid's glare softened, and she nodded. "Thank you," she said quietly.

The fight finally began to wane as the remaining raiders, seeing their comrades fall, started to retreat. Their movements were chaotic, desperate, but Astrid and Thorwulf didn't relent until the last of them disappeared into the shadows beyond the village.

The silence that followed was eerie and ominous.

Astrid stood in the center of the carnage, her chest heaving as she took in the devastation. Bodies littered the snow, both raiders and villagers, their blood painting the ground in dark crimson streaks. The fires still burned, the heat from the flames a cruel contrast to the icy wind that cut through the village.

"We did it," Thorwulf said, his voice low and hoarse. He wiped the blood from his axe and turned to her, his dark eyes filled with both relief and exhaustion.

Astrid nodded, but the victory felt hollow. She looked

around at the shattered remains of her home, at the faces of the survivors. Some were grieving, others staring blankly at the destruction. The weight of their loss threatened to suffocate her.

"This is my fault," she said, her voice barely above a whisper. "They came because of me."

Thorwulf frowned, stepping closer. "Hakon came because he's a coward who can't accept his brother's defeat," he said firmly. "This isn't on you, Astrid."

She shook her head, tears stinging her eyes. "If I hadn't killed Ragnar, if I hadn't defied the Jarls..."

"You'd be dead," Thorwulf interrupted, his voice sharp. "And so would I. We did what we had to do to survive. Don't let Hakon make you doubt that."

Astrid met his gaze. She wanted to believe him, to take comfort in his certainty, but the guilt gnawed at her like a ravenous beast.

Thorwulf reached out, his hand resting on her shoulder. "Astrid," he said softly, his tone gentler now. "Frostfjord is still standing because of you. These people, they're alive because of you. Don't let the weight of what's happened crush you. You're stronger than that."

Her breath hitched, and she nodded, the tears spilling over as she leaned into him. His arms wrapped around her, solid and reassuring, and for a moment, she allowed herself to find solace in his presence.

But even as she stood there, held by the man who had become her partner in every way, Hakon's warning echoed in her mind, a chilling reminder that Frostfjord's trials, and her own, were far from over.

27

A FRACTURED COUNCIL

The great hall of Frostfjord was colder than usual, its stone walls amplifying the icy wind that seeped through every crack. Astrid stood near the hearth, the weak flames barely taking the edge off the chill that settled in her bones. Around her, the council members gathered in a semicircle, their faces weathered and grim, illuminated by the dim light of iron sconces lining the walls.

It had been days since the raid, and the tension in Frostfjord had only thickened. Whispers of treachery and fear coiled through the village like smoke, and Astrid had felt every accusing glance, every murmured word directed her way. She could handle the villagers' mistrust, but the thought of betrayal within the council itself churned her stomach.

Sigurd, her father, sat near the end of the table, his once-proud posture hunched under the weight of grief and exhaustion. Across from him, her uncle, Jorik, leaned back in his chair, his fur-lined cloak giving him an air of authority that set Astrid on edge. Jorik had always been an imposing figure, his deep voice and piercing gaze commanding respect among the clan. But lately, there had been something off about him. There had been a subtle shift in his demeanor that made Astrid's skin prickle.

The council meeting began as expected, with talk of rebuilding the village, rationing food, and preparing for the next inevitable hardship. But Astrid barely heard the words. Her focus was on Jorik, on the way his eyes flicked toward her and Thorwulf when he thought no one was looking, on the faint smirk that tugged at the corners of his mouth when Sigurd spoke of unity and resilience.

Something was wrong.

As the meeting dragged on, Astrid's unease grew. She glanced at Thorwulf, who stood by the wall with his arms crossed, his sharp gaze scanning the room like a hawk. He caught her eye, and she saw the same suspicion reflected in his expression. He gave her a subtle nod, a silent confirmation that he, too, felt the undercurrent of deceit.

Finally, Astrid couldn't take it any longer. "Enough," she said, her voice cutting through the low murmur of conversation. The council members turned to her, their expressions ranging from surprise to annoyance.

"What is it, Astrid?" Jorik asked, his tone dripping with condescension. "Do you have something to add?"

Astrid ignored the bite in his words. "We're sitting here talking about rationing and repairs while Ironcrag is out there plotting our destruction. Hakon won't stop until Frostfjord is ash. If we don't act, we'll be left defenseless."

Jorik raised an eyebrow, his smirk widening. "And what would you have us do? March to Ironcrag and demand their surrender? You've already angered the gods, girl. Perhaps it's time you stopped pretending to have all the answers."

Thorwulf stepped forward then, his voice calm but laced with steel. "Astrid's right. Hakon's raid was a warning of more to come. He won't stop until he gets what he wants. We need to strengthen our defenses and rally the other clans, not sit here bickering."

The room fell into an uneasy silence, the council members exchanging glances. But Jorik only laughed, the sound low and menacing. "Rally the clans? And who would follow us? Frostfjord is already on the brink of collapse, thanks to your Reckoning. The other clans see us as weak and tainted by your defiance."

Astrid's blood boiled, but before she could respond, the doors to the hall creaked open. A young messenger stepped inside, his face pale and his breath ragged. He hesitated, glancing nervously at the council before speaking.

"Lady Astrid," he said, his voice trembling. "I have a message... from Ironcrag."

The room erupted into chaos, council members shouting over each other as the boy held out a rolled parchment. Astrid stepped forward, snatching it from his hands and breaking the seal. Her heart pounded as she read the words, her stomach twisting with each line.

Hakon's demand was clear: surrender Astrid to Ironcrag, or Frostfjord would burn.

She passed the parchment to Thorwulf. His expression darkened as he read it, and he handed it to Sigurd, whose face went pale.

"This is a ploy," Astrid said, her voice steady despite the storm raging inside her. "Hakon knows I won't surrender. He's trying to divide us."

"Perhaps it's a division we need," Jorik interrupted, sounding cold and calculated. The room fell silent as everyone turned to him. He leaned forward, his hands clasped on the table, his gaze locked on Astrid. "You've brought nothing but trouble to Frostfjord since the Reckoning. Maybe the gods would be appeased if we gave them what they want."

Astrid's breath caught as the weight of his words settled over her. "You can't be serious," she said, her voice low and dangerous.

Jorik shrugged, his smirk returning. "I'm thinking of the clan, Astrid. The lives we could save. Sometimes sacrifices must be made."

Thorwulf stepped between them, his towering presence a shield. "If you think you can hand her over without a fight, you're a fool," he said, his voice like thunder. "Astrid's worth ten of you."

Jorik's smirk faltered, his eyes narrowing. "Careful, Thorwulf," he said. "You're not true Frostfjord blood. Your loyalty is to her, not the clan. Perhaps you're the one who doesn't belong here."

Astrid's hand flew to her sword, but Sigurd's voice cut through the tension. "Enough!" he shouted, slamming his hand on the table. He turned to Jorik, his eyes blazing. "You would betray your own blood to save your own skin? Have you forgotten who we are?"

Jorik's expression hardened, and for a moment, Astrid thought he might argue. But then he stood, his cloak billowing as he turned to leave. "Think what you will," he said. "But when Hakon returns, don't say I didn't warn you."

The doors slammed shut behind him, leaving the hall in silence. Astrid's chest heaved, her heart pounding as she looked at Sigurd, then Thorwulf. The weight of Jorik's betrayal settled over her like a shroud, and she knew Frostfjord's troubles were far from over.

The longhouse emptied slowly, the murmurs of the council fading into the bitter night air as Astrid remained rooted to the spot. Her hand gripped the hilt of her sword so tightly her knuckles burned, but it was the ache in her chest that overwhelmed her. Jorik's words echoed in her mind, cutting deeper than any blade. He was her uncle, her family, and he had all but condemned her to Ironcrag's mercy to save himself.

Thorwulf touched her shoulder, his voice low. "Astrid, you can't take his words to heart. He's scared. People do reckless things when fear consumes them."

"Reckless?" she whispered, her voice trembling. "He's willing to hand me over to Hakon like a lamb to slaughter. That's not fear, Thorwulf. That's treachery."

Thorwulf sighed, his dark eyes searching hers. "Then you need to make sure the rest of Frostfjord doesn't follow his lead."

Astrid nodded stiffly, her jaw tight as she turned toward the doors. "I'll deal with him," she said. "But first... I need to see what's left of our home."

The village lay in ruins, its streets littered with broken timbers and scorched earth. The smell of smoke lingered, mingling with the sharp tang of iron and blood. Villagers moved like shadows through the wreckage, their faces pale and gaunt as they salvaged what they could. Children clung to their mothers' skirts, their wide eyes reflecting the devastation.

Astrid stepped through the debris, her heart sinking further with every step. One longhouse had been reduced to charred skeleton beams, its roof collapsed inward. The forge lay in ruins, its tools scattered like forgotten relics. Even the communal barn, which had once housed their precious stores of grain, was a smoldering husk.

She stopped near the center of the square, where a group of villagers worked to rebuild a wooden palisade. The stakes had been torn down during the raid, leaving the village exposed. A man grunted as he hefted a beam into place, his face streaked with soot and sweat.

"This is what we're left with," Astrid muttered to Thorwulf, who stood beside her. "A shattered village, and a people who are too exhausted to fight."

"They're still fighting," Thorwulf said quietly, nodding toward the villagers. "They're here. They're rebuilding. That's resilience, Astrid. And it's because of you."

Astrid wanted to believe him, but the guilt weighed heavily on her. Every ruined home, every lost life, felt like a mark against her leadership. She spotted a woman kneeling beside the remains of her longhouse, cradling a small, charred trinket. A toy, perhaps. Astrid turned away, her chest tight.

The door to Jorik's private longhouse creaked open, the dim firelight inside casting his shadow against the wall. He sat at a heavy wooden table, a mug of ale in hand and a fur-lined cloak draped over his shoulders. He didn't look up as Astrid entered, but she saw the faint smirk tug at his lips.

"You've come to lecture me, I assume," he said, taking a slow sip from his mug.

Astrid's temper flared, and she slammed the door shut behind her. "You betrayed us," she said, her voice low but trembling with anger. "You betrayed me."

Jorik leaned back in his chair, his expression cold. "I did what I had to do to protect this clan," he said. "You've brought nothing but trouble to Frostfjord since the Reckoning, Astrid. Your defiance has painted a target on all our backs."

Astrid stepped closer. "I did what I had to do to survive," she said. "And because of that, Frostfjord still has its oathsworn. Its people still have hope. If you think sacrificing me to Hakon will save the clan, then you're a fool."

Jorik's eyes narrowed, and he set his mug down with a heavy thud. "You think this is about Hakon? This is about the gods, Astrid. You defied their will. You turned the other clans against us. Solfjord has cut us off. Ironcrag is at our throats. You've made us pariahs."

"And what would you have done?" Astrid snapped. "Grovel before the Jarls? Hand over your own kin to a murderer?"

Jorik stood abruptly, his chair scraping against the floor. "You think leadership is about standing tall and swinging a sword? It's about sacrifice. About making hard choices for the good of the many. You don't understand that."

Astrid's breath caught, the weight of his words pressing down on her. She turned away, her gaze falling to the floor as she fought to steady herself. "I never asked to lead," she said quietly. "But that doesn't mean I'll abandon Frostfjord."

Jorik scoffed, shaking his head. "You're too young, too stubborn to see the truth. You're not leading, Astrid. You're dragging this clan into ruin."

Her head snapped up, her blue eyes blazing. "I'm trying to save it," she said fiercely. "And if you can't see that, then you're the one who's blind."

The tension between them was suffocating, the crackle of the fire the only sound. Jorik's lip curled, but he said nothing more. Astrid turned on her heel, pushing the door open and stepping out into the cold night.

The wind bit at her cheeks as she stood outside, her chest heaving with suppressed emotion. Thorwulf waited nearby, his dark eyes watching her closely. He didn't say anything, but the question in his gaze was clear.

"I'm fine," Astrid said, though the words felt hollow. She looked out over the ruined village, her heart heavy. "But I don't know if Frostfjord is."

Thorwulf stepped closer, his presence a quiet reassurance. "You'll find a way," he said simply. "You always do."

Astrid didn't answer. She stared out at the village, the weight of her choices pressing down on her. Leadership, she realized, wasn't just about strength. It was about sacrifice, about bearing the burden of every failure and every loss. And it was a burden she wasn't sure she could carry.

28

SECRETS OF THE NORN'S WELL

The journey to the Norn's Well was silent, the only sounds the crunch of snow beneath their boots and the whisper of the wind through the barren trees. The air was colder here, sharper, as if the gods themselves were watching. Astrid pulled her cloak tighter around her shoulders, glancing at Thorwulf as he walked beside her, his face set in grim determination.

The Norn's Well sat atop its jagged hill, its dark waters shimmering even in the pale winter light. The path up was treacherous, the snow masking uneven ground and slick stones, but Astrid barely noticed. Her mind churned with unanswered questions, her heart heavy with the weight of the clan's plight and her uncle's betrayal.

As they reached the summit, the sacred spring came into view. It was smaller than Astrid remembered, a pool of impossibly still water ringed by weathered stones etched with ancient runes. The well seemed to hum with an otherworldly energy, its surface reflecting not the sky above but something deeper, darker.

Thorwulf stepped closer to her, his breath visible in the cold.

"Are you sure about this?" he asked, his voice low. "The well doesn't just show visions. It tests you. Challenges you."

Astrid nodded, though her stomach twisted with unease. "We need answers," she said. "The gods have left us with riddles and wrath. If they want me to lead, then they need to show me the way."

Thorwulf's gaze softened, his hand brushing against hers briefly. "I'm with you," he said, the simple words grounding her.

Astrid stepped to the edge of the well, her reflection rippling as she peered into its depths. The runes around the stones seemed to pulse faintly, the air humming with an almost imperceptible vibration. Taking a deep breath, she knelt and touched the water.

It was freezing, so cold it burned, and the world around her seemed to dissolve into darkness.

She was no longer on the hill. Instead, she stood in the center of a burning Bjornhold. The flames roared around her, consuming longhouses and engulfing the forests in an unholy blaze. Screams echoed in the distance, and the acrid stench of smoke filled her lungs. She spun in place, her heart pounding as she tried to make sense of the chaos.

"Astrid."

The voice was soft but commanding, and she turned to see a figure standing amidst the inferno. It was the Valkyrie, her raven-black hair and golden armor untouched by the flames. Her piercing gaze pinned Astrid in place.

"This is the price of defiance," the Valkyrie said, her voice resonating like a thunderclap. "Bjornhold burns because of the choices you have made. But the gods are merciful, Astrid. They will grant you a choice."

The flames seemed to part, revealing two paths. On one, she saw Thorwulf, his body broken and bloodied, reaching for her with pleading eyes. On the other, she saw the people of

Frostfjord, along with her father, her sister, Lief, cowering as the flames closed in around them.

"One must fall for the other to rise," the Valkyrie said, her expression unreadable. "The gods demand balance. Choose, Astrid. Your soulmate or your people."

Astrid's breath came in short gasps. The weight of the choice crushed her, the impossibility of it suffocating. She took a step toward Thorwulf, then hesitated, her gaze shifting to her family. How could she choose between them?

"Why?" she demanded, her voice shaking. "Why must I choose? I've sacrificed everything for Frostfjord. Isn't that enough?"

The Valkyrie's gaze didn't waver. "The gods' will is not for mortals to question. It is for you to obey."

The vision began to blur, the flames closing in as Astrid fell to her knees. Her heart felt like it was being torn in two, the pull toward Thorwulf and her people equally strong.

"No," she whispered. "I won't choose. I'll find another way."

The Valkyrie's expression darkened, her eyes narrowing. "Defiance will not continue to go unpunished, Astrid. The gods' patience is not infinite."

The vision shattered, and Astrid gasped as she was thrown back into the present. The cold wind bit at her cheeks, and she realized she was lying on the ground near the well. Thorwulf was kneeling beside her, his hands gripping her shoulders.

"Astrid!" he said, his voice filled with worry. "What happened? What did you see?"

She sat up slowly, her head pounding and her body trembling. The images of the burning village and Thorwulf's broken form still lingered in her mind, vivid and haunting.

"They're testing me," she said, her voice hoarse. "The gods... they want me to choose. You or Frostfjord."

Thorwulf's expression hardened as he helped her to her feet.

"Then they're crueler than I thought," he said, his voice low. "Because I won't let you make that choice. We'll find a way to save them both."

Astrid looked at him, her chest aching with the weight of his words. She wanted to believe him, to cling to the hope in his voice, but the Valkyrie's warning rang in her ears.

"The gods don't make empty threats, Thorwulf," she said softly. "If I defy them again, there will be consequences."

"Then we'll face them together," he said firmly, his dark eyes meeting hers with unshakable resolve. "You don't have to bear this alone, Astrid."

The sincerity in his voice, the unwavering support in his gaze, was almost too much. She nodded, swallowing hard as she looked back at the well. The runes still glowed faintly, a reminder of the power that had brought her here.

As they began the descent back to the village, the wind howled around them, carrying with it the faint echo of the Valkyrie's voice. One must fall for the other to rise.

The wind screamed as Astrid and Thorwulf descended the jagged hill from the Norn's Well, the biting cold clawing at their exposed skin. The silence between them was heavy, the memory of the Valkyrie's vision pressing on Astrid's chest like a stone. She hadn't told Thorwulf the full detail yet. The choice she'd been given, the flames licking at Bjornhold, the impossible weight of saving him or her people. How could she?

Thorwulf walked beside her, his steps deliberate as if he sensed the storm in her mind. His dark eyes flicked to her every few moments, watching, waiting. The sky above them was a slate of gray, the clouds thick and pregnant with the promise of snow. The sparse trees dotting the rocky landscape groaned under the weight of the wind, their bare branches clawing at the sky like skeletal hands.

As they neared a narrow outcropping, Thorwulf finally

broke the silence. "I saw the look on your face up there," he said, his voice low but firm. "Whatever the gods showed you, it's tearing you apart."

Astrid stopped in her tracks, the icy wind whipping her hair into her face. She didn't look at him, her gaze fixed on the path ahead. "I told you," she said quietly. "They're testing me."

Thorwulf stepped in front of her, blocking her path. His broad shoulders cast a shadow over her, his expression a mix of concern and determination. "Testing you how?" he pressed. "Astrid, if we're going to get through this, I need to know what you saw."

She hesitated. Part of her wanted to tell him everything, to unburden herself of the terrible choice the Valkyrie had presented her. But the stubborn, cautious part of her feared what he might think, feared he'd see her as weak for even considering the gods' ultimatum.

"It doesn't matter," she said finally, trying to step around him.

Thorwulf didn't move, his hand coming up to gently grip her arm. "It matters to me," he said, his voice softer now. "Astrid, I've stood beside you through every trial. I've seen your strength, your resilience. But you don't have to carry this alone."

His words, the quiet sincerity in them, cracked something inside her. She met his gaze, and saw the truth in his dark eyes. He meant every word.

"They want me to choose," she said finally. "You or Frostfjord. One must fall for the other to rise."

Thorwulf's expression darkened. He released her arm, stepping back as he ran a hand through his dark hair. "Those gods are bastards," he muttered, his voice low and bitter.

Astrid let out a breathless laugh, the sound tinged with despair. "You're not wrong."

For a long moment, they stood there, the wind swirling

around them, carrying with it the faint howl of a wolf in the distance. Finally, Thorwulf spoke again, his voice quiet but resolute. "The gods don't deserve your loyalty," he said. "They don't deserve your sacrifices."

She looked at him, her brow furrowed. "What makes you so sure?"

He hesitated, his gaze dropping to the ground. When he spoke again, his voice was tinged with a pain she hadn't heard from him before. "Because I've seen what blind loyalty does. What it costs."

Astrid tilted her head, curiosity flickering in her chest despite the heaviness of the moment. "What do you mean?"

Thorwulf let out a slow breath, his gaze distant. "My father," he said, the words clipped and heavy. "He wasn't the man everyone thought he was. The great warrior, the proud leader of our family. He was a liar. A coward."

Astrid's heart ached at the bitterness in his tone. "What happened?" she asked softly.

Thorwulf's shoulders tensed. "When I was a boy, Ironcrag came for us. A feud over land, over pride, who knows. My father swore he'd defend our home, our people. But when the raiders came, he was the first to flee. Left my mother and me behind to fend for ourselves." He paused. "She didn't survive."

Astrid's breath hitched as she saw the raw pain in his expression. "Thorwulf, I'm so sorry," she said. And she meant it.

He shook his head, a bitter laugh escaping him. "I spent years hating him, hating the gods for letting him live while she was taken. But I realized something. The gods don't care about us, Astrid. They care about their games, their balance, their chaos. We're just pawns to them."

She stepped closer, her hand hesitating before resting gently on his arm. "You're not a pawn," she said firmly. "And neither am I."

Thorwulf met her gaze, his dark eyes searching hers. "Then don't let them break you," he said, his voice soft but filled with conviction. "Don't let them take what matters to you."

Astrid's heart ached at the weight of his words, the vulnerability in his gaze. She nodded, swallowing hard as she gripped his arm. "I won't," she said quietly.

As they resumed their descent, the wind howled louder, the wolf's cry echoing once more through the mountains. The gods may have set the pieces in motion, but Astrid was determined to play by her own rules. For Thorwulf, for Frostfjord, and for herself.

29

WHISPERS OF REBELLION

The Frostfjord wind howled against the walls of the longhouse, but inside, the air was thick with unease. Astrid sat at the wooden table in her family's home, staring at the worn map of Bjornhold spread before her. The inked lines of the four territories – Frostfjord, Solfjord, Seastone, and Ironcrag – seemed to blur under her scrutiny. Each border carried its own weight of history, of grudges, of spilled blood. But now, for the first time in centuries, those lines might shift.

A knock at the door startled her from her thoughts. Thorwulf entered, his broad shoulders brushing against the frame. Snow clung to his dark hair and fur-lined cloak, his cheeks flushed from the cold.

"You've got a visitor," he said, his voice low. "From Seastone."

Astrid's heart skipped a beat. Seastone? She hadn't expected to hear from the coastal clan, not after the raid and the lingering tensions with the Jarls. Rising from her seat, she followed Thorwulf to the main room, where a woman stood near the hearth, her sea-blue cloak shimmering in the firelight.

Freya's sister, Ingrid.

Ingrid was striking, with long golden hair braided intricately down her back and piercing green eyes that missed nothing. Though her frame was smaller than Freya's, she carried herself with the same confidence that spoke of years spent surviving the political undercurrents of Seastone. Her expression was calm, but her gaze held a spark of urgency.

"Astrid," Ingrid said, inclining her head in greeting. "It's good to see you alive."

Astrid crossed her arms, her gaze steady. "Alive and defying the gods, apparently. What brings Seastone to Frostfjord?"

Ingrid's lips quirked into a faint smile. "The same thing that brought Solfjord to us. Change."

Astrid's stomach tightened, her pulse quickening. "Solfjord?"

"They've sent word," Ingrid continued, stepping closer. "Both Seastone and Solfjord are beginning to see the truth. The Jarls' rule is not divine, and the gods' games are not sacred. Your defiance has stirred something, Astrid. A spark that could become a fire."

Thorwulf leaned against the wall, his dark eyes narrowing. "And what does Seastone want with this... fire?"

Ingrid met his gaze without flinching. "We want to unite the clans. To end the Reckoning, to challenge the Jarls and their stranglehold on Bjornhold. You proved that defiance is possible. Now it's time to prove that it can lead to something greater."

Astrid's breath caught. She'd spent so long fighting for survival, for Frostfjord, that the idea of rebellion on this scale felt impossible. Yet the conviction in Ingrid's voice, the sheer boldness of her words, struck a chord deep within her.

"And Solfjord?" she asked, her voice quieter now. "They've always cared more about their gold than their honor."

Ingrid's smile turned sharper. "True. But even gold loses its luster when the gods demand too much. Solfjord's Jarl is tired of the Reckoning, of sacrificing their strongest for a game they can never win. They're willing to meet."

Astrid exchanged a glance with Thorwulf, his brow furrowed in thought. "A meeting," she said slowly. "Where?"

"On neutral ground," Ingrid replied. "The northern cliffs near Skarn. If we can bring Seastone, Solfjord, and Frostfjord together, the Jarls will lose their grip."

Thorwulf straightened, his voice tinged with skepticism. "And Ironcrag?"

Ingrid's smile faded. "Ironcrag will never join. Hakon's thirst for vengeance has blinded them. They'll fight to keep the old ways."

"Then they'll be a threat to us all," Thorwulf said darkly.

Astrid's mind raced. A meeting with Seastone and Solfjord could be the beginning of something monumental, or it could spell disaster. The Jarls were powerful, their influence rooted deeply in every clan. Challenging them would mean risking everything: their homes, their people, their lives.

But as she thought of Frostfjord's ruined village, of the lives lost to Hakon's raid, of the Valkyrie's warning and the gods' games, a new determination burned in her chest.

"When?" she asked, her voice steady.

Ingrid's green eyes gleamed. "Three nights from now. I'll guide you there."

Thorwulf stepped closer, his hand brushing Astrid's arm in a quiet gesture of support. "This is dangerous," he said softly. "The Jarls will see this as treason."

Astrid met his gaze, her resolve hardening. "Then let them. If we don't fight for something better, we'll be fighting for survival forever."

~

That night, as the wind howled outside the longhouse, Astrid sat alone by the dying fire. The flames cast shadows on the walls, and the map of Bjornhold lay before her once more. She traced the borders of Seastone and Solfjord with her fingers, imagining what it would take to unite them, to stand against the Jarls and the gods themselves.

Thorwulf sat down beside her, his presence a quiet comfort. "You're ready for this," he said, his voice low.

Astrid looked at him, the weight of the coming days pressing on her. "I don't know if anyone can be ready for what's coming."

He reached for her hand, his touch warm against her cold skin. "You're not alone, Astrid. Whatever happens, I'm with you."

For the first time in days, a faint smile touched her lips. "Thank you," she whispered.

The fire's glow flickered across Astrid's face, her expression a storm of conflicting emotions. She stared at the map of Bjornhold, her fingers tracing the jagged lines of Frostfjord's borders as if the answers to her fears could be found in the inked parchment. The idea of rebellion, of uniting the clans against the Jarls, burned like a spark in her chest, but with it came an overwhelming weight. If they failed, the consequences wouldn't just fall on her. They'd fall on her people.

Thorwulf's presence beside her was steadying. He didn't speak, but his quiet support was palpable. His hand rested lightly on her shoulder, grounding her as her thoughts swirled like the winter winds outside.

"I never wanted this," Astrid said softly, breaking the silence. Her voice trembled slightly, but her gaze remained fixed on the map. "To lead, to decide the fate of so many. I just wanted to survive the Reckoning. To save my sister."

Thorwulf shifted closer, his dark eyes fixed on her profile. "Sometimes the gods, or whatever forces are out there, choose leaders, even when they don't want to be chosen," he said. "You didn't ask for this, Astrid, but you're here. And these people need you."

She let out a bitter laugh, shaking her head. "What if I fail? What if this rebellion brings more death, more destruction? I can't drag Frostfjord into another war."

Thorwulf's grip on her shoulder tightened slightly, his voice firm. "You won't fail. You're stronger than you think, Astrid. You've faced the gods and lived. You've faced Ragnar, Hakon, and even your own people's doubt. You've already done the impossible."

She turned to him then, her blue eyes filled with a vulnerability she rarely showed. "But at what cost? Every decision I've made has left someone else bleeding, someone else suffering. How can I ask people to fight for a cause that might destroy them?"

Thorwulf's expression softened, and he reached for her hand, his calloused fingers warm against hers. "Because they believe in you," he said simply. "They see what you've done, what you've survived. You're not forcing them to fight, Astrid. You're giving them hope."

The word hung between them, fragile yet powerful. Hope. It was something Frostfjord had been stripped of for so long, something she hadn't realized she was carrying until now. The idea of rebellion wasn't just about defying the Jarls, it was about giving her people a reason to believe in a future where they weren't just pawns in the gods' games.

Astrid looked down at their joined hands. Thorwulf's faith in her was unwavering, and she wasn't sure she deserved it. But she knew she couldn't bear to let him, or her people down.

"I'm scared," she admitted, her voice barely above a whisper. It was the first time she'd allowed herself to say it aloud, the first time she'd let someone see the cracks in her armor.

Thorwulf leaned closer, his dark eyes searching hers. "Good," he said, a faint smile tugging at his lips. "Fear means you care. It means you'll fight that much harder to protect what matters."

His words stirred something in her, a flicker of courage that she hadn't felt in days. She straightened slightly, her gaze returning to the map. The jagged borders of Bjornhold no longer looked like insurmountable barriers. They looked more like possibilities.

"I can't do this alone," she said finally, her voice stronger now. "If Solfjord and Seastone are truly willing to stand with us, we'll need to plan carefully. The Jarls will see this as treason. They'll come for us."

Thorwulf nodded, his expression serious. "Then we make sure we're ready. We fortify Frostfjord, rally the villages, and make alliances where we can. This isn't just your fight, Astrid. It's all of ours."

She looked at him, her heart swelling with gratitude. "Thank you, Thorwulf," she said quietly. "For standing by me. For believing in me."

His gaze softened, and for a moment, the weight of their struggles seemed to fade. "Always," he said, the word carrying more weight than she'd expected.

The sound of footsteps interrupted the moment, and Astrid turned to see her father, Sigurd, entering the longhouse. His face was etched with lines of exhaustion, but his eyes held a quiet strength.

"I heard about the meeting," Sigurd said, his voice low. "Solfjord and Seastone aligning with Frostfjord... it's risky."

Astrid straightened, meeting her father's gaze. "It's our best chance," she said. "If we don't stand together, the Jarls will crush us one by one."

Sigurd studied her for a long moment, his expression unreadable. Finally, he nodded. "Your mother would be proud," he said, his voice softer now. "She always said you had a fire in you. I didn't see it then, but I see it now."

The words caught Astrid off guard, and she felt a lump rise in her throat. She nodded, unable to speak, and Sigurd placed a hand on her shoulder before retreating to his room.

As the door closed behind him, Astrid turned back to the map, her resolve solidifying. The path ahead was treacherous, but for the first time, she felt like she could see the way forward. She wasn't just fighting for survival anymore, she was fighting for something greater.

Thorwulf's voice broke the silence. "So," he said, his tone light. "Are you ready to lead a rebellion?"

Astrid smirked, the fire in her chest burning brighter. "Let's see if the Jarls are ready for us."

The two of them exchanged a determined glance, the weight of the moment hanging heavy in the air. Outside, the wind howled, carrying with it the whispers of change.

The journey to Solfjord was grueling, marked by endless stretches of snow-covered plains and wind that felt like icy blades against their skin. Astrid and Thorwulf traveled alongside Ingrid, their small group cloaked against the elements, moving swiftly but cautiously. The landscape shifted as they neared Solfjord's borders, the barren Frostfjord terrain giving way to Solfjord's rolling hills and fertile valleys. Even in the dead of winter, the wealth of the clan was apparent. Their lands were dotted with large, well-kept farms, and the fortified village gates loomed tall against the horizon.

The air was tense as they approached the gates. The Solfjord guards, clad in polished armor and armed with finely crafted spears, eyed them warily. Ingrid stepped forward, speaking in calm but firm tones, and after a few moments of deliberation, the gates creaked open.

Inside, Solfjord's wealth was even more evident. Longhouses

with intricately carved beams lined the streets, and merchants bustled about despite the cold, their goods protected under heavy furs. The aroma of roasted meats and spiced ale wafted through the air, a stark contrast to the sparse rations of Frostfjord. Astrid felt a pang of resentment at the disparity but forced herself to focus on the task at hand.

In the grand hall, the warmth of roaring hearths and the glow of golden tapestries did little to ease Astrid's nerves. The leaders of Solfjord sat at a long table, their expressions a mix of curiosity and skepticism. At the head of the table sat Harvik, a man of middle years with sharp features and an even sharper gaze. His fur-lined cloak and ornate arm rings spoke of his power in this clan, and his piercing blue eyes fixed on Astrid as she entered.

"So," Harvik said, his voice carrying easily through the hall. "The famed oathsworn of Frostfjord graces us with her presence. Tell me, Astrid, why should Solfjord risk its prosperity for your rebellion?"

Astrid stepped forward, her chin held high. "Because your prosperity won't last," she said, her voice steady despite the weight of a dozen scrutinizing gazes. "The Jarls' games have bled every clan dry. You may have gold now, but how long until the gods demand more? How long until the Reckoning takes one of your heirs? You know as well as I do that their rule is unsustainable."

Murmurs rippled through the room, but Harvik's expression remained impassive. "Bold words," he said. "But words alone won't convince me. If you want Solfjord's allegiance, you'll need to prove your strength. A leader who cannot fight for her cause is no leader at all."

Astrid's heart quickened, but she didn't flinch. "What do you propose?"

Harvik's gaze flicked to a man seated further down the table.

He was a towering warrior with broad shoulders and a scar running across his cheek. "Sven will be your opponent," the Jarl said. "Defeat him, and Solfjord will consider your alliance."

Thorwulf tensed beside her, his hand instinctively moving toward his axe. "This isn't necessary," he said, his voice low and dangerous. "Astrid's already proven her worth."

Harvik raised an eyebrow. "Has she? Perhaps to Frostfjord, but not to Solfjord. We value strength, and we need to know that the leader of this rebellion has what it takes to win."

Astrid placed a hand on Thorwulf's arm, stopping him. She met Harvik's gaze with unwavering determination. "I'll fight."

The hall erupted into cheers and jeers as the tables were pushed aside, clearing space for the duel. Astrid removed her cloak, revealing the leather armor beneath, and unsheathed her sword. Across from her, Sven rose to his feet, his size as intimidating as his reputation. He wielded a massive axe, its blade glinting in the firelight.

The room fell silent as the two combatants faced each other, the air thick with tension. Harvik raised a hand. "Begin."

Sven charged first, his axe swinging in a deadly arc. Astrid sidestepped just in time, the wind of the blow brushing her cheek. She countered with a quick slash, her blade glancing off his armor. He was fast for his size, and each swing of his axe was devastatingly precise. But Astrid had faced worse. She had faced gods.

She ducked under another swing, using her smaller frame to her advantage as she moved in close. Her sword struck his side, drawing a shallow cut, and she danced away before he could retaliate. The crowd roared, some shouting encouragement, others hurling insults.

Sven growled, his movements becoming more aggressive. He feinted left, then swung right, and Astrid barely managed to block the blow. The impact reverberated through her arms, but she gritted her teeth and held her ground. Sweat slicked her brow despite the cold, and her breaths came fast and heavy.

Thorwulf's voice cut through the chaos. "Stay light on your feet, Astrid! He's trying to tire you out!"

She adjusted her stance, her focus sharpening. Sven lunged again, and this time she didn't retreat. Instead, she sidestepped and brought her sword down on his exposed wrist. The axe fell from his hand, clattering to the ground, and before he could recover, she pressed the blade to his throat.

The hall went silent.

Sven froze, his chest heaving as he stared at her with a mix of anger and respect. Astrid's voice was steady, but there was steel in it as she spoke. "Yield."

Sven's jaw tightened, but after a moment, he nodded. "I yield."

Astrid lowered her sword, her heart pounding as the crowd erupted into cheers and applause. Harvik rose from his seat, a faint smile tugging at his lips. "Well fought," he said. "You've earned my respect, Astrid of Frostfjord. Solfjord will stand with you."

Relief washed over her, but it was tempered by the knowledge that this was only the beginning. As the hall filled with the sound of celebration, she caught Thorwulf's eye. He nodded, a faint smile on his lips, and she felt a flicker of hope.

They were one step closer to rebellion. But the gods and the Jarls would not let them rise without a fight.

The applause was deafening, echoing through the grand hall as Astrid sheathed her sword and turned toward Thorwulf. He stood at the edge of the cleared space, his expression a mix of relief and something more guarded. She could see the tension in his jaw, the way his hands were clenched at his sides as though he were holding himself back.

"You didn't have to do that," he said quietly as she

approached, his voice low enough that only she could hear. His tone wasn't harsh, but there was a sharpness beneath it, an edge of frustration that sent a flicker of irritation through her.

Astrid raised an eyebrow, crossing her arms over her chest. "Didn't I? You heard Harvik. Words wouldn't have been enough."

Thorwulf shook his head, his dark eyes narrowing. "You could've let me fight for you. You've been through enough, Astrid. You didn't need to prove anything to them."

The fire of victory that had burned in her chest only moments ago cooled slightly. She stepped closer, lowering her voice to match his. "This isn't about you protecting me, Thorwulf. I'm not some shieldmaiden in need of saving. I'm leading this rebellion, and I'll do what needs to be done."

For a moment, he looked like he wanted to argue. But instead, he exhaled sharply and ran a hand through his dark hair. "I know you're capable, Astrid. That's not the point."

"Then what is?" she demanded, her frustration bubbling to the surface. "Because from where I'm standing, it sounds like you think I should step aside and let someone else take the risks."

Thorwulf's gaze hardened, and he stepped closer, his voice dropping to a near growl. "That's not what I think, and you know it. I just..." He broke off as he struggled to find the words. "I don't want to lose you."

The weight of his confession hung between them, raw and vulnerable, but it only added fuel to Astrid's simmering anger. She softened slightly, but she refused to let him off the hook entirely. "And you think that means holding me back? That protecting me is more important than trusting me?"

Thorwulf opened his mouth to respond, but before he could, Ingrid's voice cut through the tension. "You two might want to save the lover's quarrel for later," she said, her tone dry but amused. "Harvik's watching."

Astrid turned sharply, realizing that the Jarl and his council were still seated at the long table, their gazes fixed on her and Thorwulf. Harvik's expression was inscrutable, but the faint smirk tugging at his lips made Astrid's blood boil. She straightened, lifting her chin as she turned back to Thorwulf.

"This isn't about us," she said firmly, her voice barely above a whisper. "This is about Bjornhold. About Frostfjord. And if you can't accept that, then maybe you shouldn't be here."

The words came out harsher than she intended, and she saw the flicker of hurt in Thorwulf's eyes before he masked it. He nodded once, stepping back and crossing his arms over his broad chest. "Fine," he said quietly, his tone carefully neutral. "Do what you have to do."

Astrid watched him retreat toward the edge of the hall, the space between them feeling wider than it ever had. She wanted to call after him, to explain that her words came from a place of frustration, not doubt. But the moment passed, and she turned back to Harvik, forcing herself to focus.

The Jarl rose from his seat, his hands spread in a gesture of magnanimity. "You've proven yourself, Astrid," he said, his voice carrying easily through the hall. "Solfjord will stand with Frostfjord in this rebellion. But I hope you understand the risks you've taken today. The Jarls will not take kindly to this alliance."

Astrid met his gaze, her shoulders squared. "Let them come," she said, her voice steady. "We'll be ready."

Harvik nodded, his expression thoughtful. "I hope so, for all our sakes."

As the hall erupted into conversation, Astrid felt a pang of guilt as she glanced toward Thorwulf. He stood apart from the crowd, his face unreadable as he spoke quietly with one of

Solfjord's warriors. She knew he wasn't truly angry with her. At least, not in the way she'd feared. But the tension between them felt like a bruise that hadn't yet healed.

Ingrid appeared at her side, her green eyes flicking between Astrid and Thorwulf. "He'll get over it," she said lightly. "Men like him don't stay mad for long, especially not when they care as much as he clearly does."

Astrid frowned, her gaze lingering on Thorwulf. "It's not about him staying mad," she said. "It's about him understanding. I need him to trust that I can do this without him trying to shield me from everything."

Ingrid smiled faintly, her tone turning serious. "He does trust you, Astrid. But trust doesn't erase fear. And from what I can see, he's terrified of losing you."

Astrid let out a slow breath. She knew Ingrid was right, but that didn't make the tension any easier to bear. "I don't want to fight with him," she admitted quietly. "Not when we're about to face so much more."

"Then make it right," Ingrid said simply. "Before the gods or the Jarls have a chance to tear you apart."

Astrid nodded, her resolve hardening. The rebellion was bigger than her or Thorwulf, but she couldn't deny that their bond was a cornerstone of her strength. As the evening wore on, she resolved to find him, to bridge the gap that had formed between them before it grew into something unfixable.

The road ahead was treacherous, but Astrid knew she couldn't walk it alone. And she didn't want to.

30

THE SIEGE OF FROSTFJORD

The news arrived with the dawn. A lone rider, frost clinging to his beard and desperation etched into his face, galloped into the heart of Frostfjord just as the sun breached the jagged peaks on the horizon. Astrid and Thorwulf were among the first to meet him as he dismounted in the village square, his trembling hands clutching a sealed scroll bearing the crest of the Jarls.

"The council has declared Frostfjord an enemy of Bjornhold," the rider said, his voice hoarse and cracking from the bitter cold. "An army marches from Ironcrag as we speak. They'll be at your gates within three days."

The villagers who had gathered around them broke into panicked murmurs, their voices rising like the howl of the winter wind. Mothers clutched their children, and the men exchanged grim looks. Astrid's stomach tightened, and she glanced at Thorwulf, whose expression was as unreadable as ever.

"Three days," Astrid repeated, her voice steady despite the chaos around her. "That's not much time."

"It's enough," Thorwulf said firmly. His hand brushed hers briefly, a silent reassurance. "We'll make it enough."

The great hall of Frostfjord buzzed with frantic energy as Astrid and the village leaders gathered to plan their defense. The map of Bjornhold was spread across the long table, its inked borders and markers suddenly feeling far more real. Jorik, Astrid's uncle, stood at the edge of the group, his lips pressed into a thin line. Though his treachery had been exposed, he remained a reluctant ally, but his survival now tied to the fate of the village.

"They'll come from the east," Thorwulf said, tracing a path on the map with his finger. "The Ironcrag forces will take the main pass through the mountains. It's the fastest route, but it's also narrow. If we can hold them there, we can slow their advance."

"And if we can't?" Jorik asked, his tone cutting. "Ironcrag's warriors are ruthless. Frostfjord can't match their numbers."

Astrid met his gaze, her voice hard. "We don't have to match them. We just have to outthink them."

She turned to Ingrid, who stood nearby with her arms crossed, her sea-blue cloak shimmering in the firelight. "Seastone will honor its alliance?" Astrid asked.

Ingrid nodded. "Our warriors are already on their way. But it'll take time for them to arrive. You'll have to hold the pass until then."

Astrid nodded, her mind racing. "We'll use the terrain to our advantage," she said, her voice firm as she addressed the room. "We'll set traps in the pass, force them to fight on our terms. The cliffs are steep. If we can bottleneck their forces, we can hold them off long enough for reinforcements to arrive."

Jorik let out a humorless laugh, shaking his head. "You make it sound so simple," he muttered.

"It's not," Astrid shot back, her blue eyes blazing. "But it's our only chance. Unless you have a better idea, Uncle?"

Jorik fell silent, his expression sour. Thorwulf stepped closer to Astrid, his voice low but filled with quiet support. "You're right. The pass is our best option. We'll need to mobilize the villagers, everyone who can fight or build. If we work together, we can make this place a fortress."

As the day wore on, the village transformed into a hive of activity. Men and women worked side by side, sharpening weapons, fortifying the wooden palisades, and gathering supplies. Astrid moved among them, offering guidance where she could and reassurance where it was needed. Though fear lingered in the air, so too did a sense of purpose, and a determination to protect their home, no matter the cost.

Thorwulf was everywhere at once, his commanding presence galvanizing the villagers. He led the warriors in drills, teaching them to fight as a unit rather than as individuals, and his booming voice carried over the sound of hammers and saws.

"You're doing good work," Astrid said as she approached him during a brief lull. The sun was sinking lower in the sky, casting long shadows across the village.

Thorwulf turned to her, his face streaked with dirt and sweat. Despite the exhaustion etched into his features, he managed a faint smile. "We'll be ready," he said. "But Astrid, this is going to get bloody. Are you sure?"

"I'm sure," she interrupted, her voice steady. "This is our home. If we don't fight for it, no one will."

His gaze softened, and for a moment, the chaos around them seemed to fade. "You're stronger than you know," he said quietly.

Astrid didn't look away. "So are you."

That night, as the village prepared for the coming storm, Astrid climbed the watchtower overlooking the pass. The wind was biting, carrying with it the scent of snow and the promise of battle. She stared out at the darkened horizon, her thoughts churning.

Thorwulf joined her a few moments later. He didn't speak at

first, but simply stood beside her as they both gazed into the distance.

"They're coming," Astrid said finally.

"They'll regret it," Thorwulf replied, his tone fierce.

She turned to him. "What if we fail?"

Thorwulf looked at her then, his dark eyes filled with unwavering determination. "We won't," he said simply. "Because we're fighting for something bigger than ourselves. Something worth dying for."

Astrid nodded, feeling her resolve hardening further. The Jarls might have declared Frostfjord an enemy, but they hadn't counted on the strength of its people, or the fire that burned in Astrid's heart.

The wind howled around them, carrying with it the echoes of the battle to come.

The night was cold and moonless, a shroud of darkness blanketing the mountains as Astrid gathered her raiding party at the edge of Frostfjord. The plan was simple but dangerous: strike at Ironcrag's supply lines before their army reached the village. Without food, fuel, and ammunition, their forces would falter in the unforgiving winter terrain.

Astrid's breath formed clouds in the icy air as she scanned the faces of her companions – Ingrid, Leif, and a handful of Frostfjord's best hunters and warriors. Each of them carried weapons and packs of kindling soaked in oil, their expressions a mixture of determination and grim resolve.

"We move quickly and quietly," Astrid said, her voice low but firm. "We hit their supply wagons, destroy what we can, and retreat before they know what's happened. No unnecessary risks."

Leif shifted his weight, his bow slung over his shoulder. "And if they catch us?" he asked, his tone laced with unease.

Astrid met his gaze, her blue eyes hard. "They won't," she said. "We'll be ghosts in the snow."

Ingrid smirked, adjusting the dagger at her belt. "Let's hope the gods are feeling merciful tonight."

Astrid didn't respond. She wasn't counting on mercy. Not from the gods, not from anyone.

Thorwulf stood atop the village's outer wall, his eyes scanning the horizon as he barked orders to the villagers below. The defenses were nearly complete. Spiked barricades lined the narrow paths leading into the village, and hidden pits had been dug and camouflaged with branches and snow. The watchtower had been reinforced, its archers armed with fresh quivers of arrows, and the smithy glowed with the heat of freshly forged weapons.

"Make sure those barricades are secure," Thorwulf called down to a group of workers struggling to haul a log into place. "If they breach the wall, that'll be our last line of defense."

He turned to one of the elders, a wiry man named Olaf, who had taken on the role of organizing the non-combatants. "Are the stores ready?" Thorwulf asked.

Olaf nodded, his face lined with worry. "We've stockpiled what we can. Enough food and water for a week, maybe two. But if this drags on..."

"It won't," Thorwulf interrupted, his voice firm. "We'll end this quickly."

But even as he spoke, a sliver of doubt crept into his mind. He knew the odds. They all did. Ironcrag's warriors were seasoned and ruthless, and Frostfjord's defenses, while ingenious, were hastily constructed. They were relying on Astrid's raid to tip the scales.

Thorwulf's heart ached at the thought of her out there in the dark, risking her life to protect their home. He trusted her, he always would, but the thought of losing her was a weight he couldn't shake. Pushing the fear aside, he focused on the task at hand. The village needed him to be strong, and he wouldn't let them down.

Astrid's group moved like shadows through the snow, their footsteps muffled by the thick drifts. The mountains loomed around them, their jagged peaks silhouetted against the starless sky. The air was so cold it burned their lungs, and every breath felt like a struggle against the elements.

When they finally spotted the caravan, Astrid signaled for the group to stop. They crouched behind a ridge, peering down at the line of wagons and the small contingent of guards accompanying them. The wagons were laden with crates and barrels, their wooden frames creaking under the weight of supplies.

Astrid turned to Ingrid, her voice barely a whisper. "Two guards by the lead wagon, another two at the rear. Leif, take the ones at the back. Ingrid, you're with me."

Leif nodded, his expression grim but resolute. He nocked an arrow, his movements silent as he crept toward the rear of the caravan. Ingrid unsheathed her dagger, a wicked grin flashing across her face as she followed Astrid down the ridge.

They struck swiftly and without mercy. Leif's arrows found their marks with deadly precision, the guards at the rear collapsing into the snow before they could raise the alarm. Astrid and Ingrid took out the two at the front, their blades flashing in the moonlight. The remaining guards scrambled for their weapons, but the Frostfjord raiders overwhelmed them, cutting them down with brutal efficiency.

"Light the wagons," Astrid ordered, her voice sharp. "Quickly!"

The raiders moved with practiced ease, dousing the wagons

in oil and setting them ablaze. The flames roared to life, their heat a welcome reprieve from the bitter cold. Astrid stood back, her sword in hand as she scanned the area for any sign of reinforcements. The firelight reflected in her eyes, a flicker of triumph breaking through her usual stoicism.

But the victory was short-lived. A horn sounded in the distance, its mournful wail cutting through the night. Astrid's stomach dropped as she realized reinforcements were closer than they'd anticipated.

"We need to move!" she shouted, her voice carrying over the crackling flames. "Now!"

The raiders scattered, disappearing into the shadows as the sound of approaching horses grew louder. Astrid stayed behind long enough to ensure the last wagon was fully engulfed before retreating into the mountains, her heart pounding in her chest.

~

Thorwulf was pacing the village square when Astrid and her group returned, their cloaks singed and their faces streaked with soot. Relief flashed across his features as he hurried to meet her, his hands gripping her shoulders as he looked her over.

"You're alive," he said, his voice low but filled with emotion.

Astrid nodded, exhaustion etched into her face. "We hit the caravan," she said. "Their supplies are gone, but they know we're onto them."

Thorwulf's expression darkened. "Then they'll come for us even harder."

"Let them," Astrid said, her voice fierce despite her weariness. "We're ready."

As the villagers gathered around, cheering their return, Thorwulf pulled Astrid aside, his gaze searching hers. "You did good," he said quietly. "But don't ever scare me like that again."

She smirked, a flicker of humor breaking through her exhaustion. "I'll do my best."

Thorwulf shook his head, a faint smile tugging at his lips. "You're impossible."

"And you're stuck with me," she shot back, the warmth in her tone softening the words.

The moment passed quickly, the weight of the coming battle settling over them once more. But for now, they had bought themselves a sliver of hope. And sometimes, that was enough.

31

BETRAYAL UNVEILED

The night was eerily quiet, the kind of silence that set Astrid's teeth on edge. She stood on the wall overlooking Frostfjord's outer defenses, her eyes scanning the horizon for any sign of the Ironcrag army. The snowfall had stopped, leaving the landscape bathed in the pale light of the moon. It should have been peaceful, but something felt off. There was a heaviness in the air that she couldn't shake.

Thorwulf approached from behind, his presence as solid and comforting as ever. "No sign of movement," he said, his breath visible in the frigid air. "Maybe the raid on their supplies slowed them down."

"Maybe," Astrid replied, though doubt lingered in her voice. Her instincts told her otherwise. Ironcrag's warriors were relentless, and their hunger for vengeance wouldn't be easily sated.

As they descended from the wall, a shout echoed through the village. Astrid and Thorwulf exchanged a glance before rushing toward the commotion. Villagers were gathering near the gate, their murmurs growing louder with each passing moment. When Astrid pushed through the crowd, she froze.

The massive wooden gates of Frostfjord stood wide open.

Snow tracked through the gap, footprints leading into the darkness beyond. Astrid's stomach twisted as she scanned the scene. Someone had betrayed them. There was no other explanation. Her mind raced, piecing together the implications. Whoever had opened the gates had invited death into their midst.

Thorwulf's voice broke through her thoughts. "Astrid," he said, his tone grim. He was kneeling near the gate, holding up a small, broken pendant. It bore the crest of Frostfjord's chieftain.

Jorik.

Astrid caught her breath as the pieces fell into place. Her uncle had been distant and sullen since the rebellion began, his loyalty to the old ways and his fear of the Jarls' wrath always evident. But this? Opening the gates to Ironcrag was beyond treachery. His actions were was unforgivable.

"Where is he?" Astrid demanded, her voice sharp as a blade.

A young boy stepped forward hesitantly, his eyes wide with fear. "I... I saw him heading toward the longhouse," he stammered.

Without a word, Astrid turned and marched toward the longhouse, her footsteps crunching in the snow. Thorwulf followed close behind, his hand resting on the hilt of his axe. The villagers trailed after them, their whispers carrying on the wind.

The longhouse was dimly lit, the fire in the hearth casting flickering shadows on the walls. Jorik stood near the center of the room, his face pale but defiant. He didn't flinch as Astrid burst through the door, her fury like a storm barely contained.

"You opened the gates," she said, her voice low and dangerous. It was a statement rather than a question.

Jorik straightened. "I did what I had to do," he said, his tone defiant. "You've brought this upon us, Astrid. Your rebellion, your defiance of the Jarls has doomed us all. I had to protect Frostfjord."

"By handing us over to Ironcrag?" Astrid spat, her eyes blazing. "You didn't protect anyone, Jorik. You've doomed us."

Jorik's gaze flickered, a hint of guilt breaking through his resolve. "The Jarls would have spared us if you hadn't dragged Frostfjord into your madness," he said. "They promised."

"They promised nothing!" Astrid snapped, stepping closer. "You think Ironcrag would have spared us? You think the Jarls wouldn't have punished us anyway? You're a fool, Jorik. A coward."

Thorwulf moved to her side, his presence a steadying force. "Astrid," he said quietly, his voice a warning.

But she wasn't done. Her hands shook with rage as she stared down her uncle, the man who had not only betrayed her but also the people he was supposed to protect. "You didn't just betray me," she said, her voice trembling with emotion. "You betrayed your clan. Your family. Everyone who trusted you."

Jorik's defiance crumbled under her gaze. He looked away, his shoulders slumping. "I didn't want this," he murmured. "I only wanted to save us."

Astrid's heart ached with the weight of his words, but she couldn't afford to let emotion cloud her judgment. This was about more than his betrayal, it was about what it meant for Frostfjord. If she let him live, it would signal weakness, a fracture in their unity. And they couldn't afford that now.

"I trusted you," she said, her voice barely above a whisper. "But trust is earned, and you've squandered it."

Jorik looked up, his eyes filled with something that might have been regret. Or fear. "Astrid, please..."

The blade of her sword glinted in the firelight as she drew it, her movements slow and deliberate. The room seemed to hold its breath as she stepped closer, her gaze locked on his.

"You've made your choice," she said, her voice steady now. "And now I'll make mine."

Jorik's eyes widened as she raised the sword. "Astrid!"

The blade came down in a swift, clean arc. The longhouse fell silent, the crackle of the fire the only sound as Jorik crumpled to the ground. Astrid stood over him, her chest heaving, her sword dripping crimson onto the wooden floor.

Thorwulf stepped forward, placing a hand on her shoulder. "You did what you had to do," he said quietly.

Astrid nodded, though her hands still shook. She turned to face the villagers who had gathered outside the longhouse, their faces pale in the torchlight. "Let this be a lesson," she said, her voice carrying over the crowd. "Frostfjord will not tolerate betrayal. We fight together, or we fall together."

The crowd murmured their agreement, their fear giving way to a newfound respect. Astrid had proven her authority, but the cost weighed heavily on her shoulders.

As the villagers dispersed, Thorwulf stayed by her side, his presence a quiet comfort. "You're stronger than you know," he said, his voice low.

Astrid looked up at him, her eyes filled with a mixture of pain and determination. "I just hope it's enough."

The snow continued to fall outside, blanketing Frostfjord in an eerie silence. But Astrid knew the peace wouldn't last. The enemy was still coming, and the true battle was only just beginning.

~

The longhouse was empty now, its silence heavy in the wake of Jorik's execution. Astrid stood near the hearth, staring into the fire as if the dancing flames could burn away the weight of what she'd just done. Her sword lay on the table, wiped clean of blood but still gleaming in the firelight, a reminder of the line she had crossed.

Thorwulf lingered in the shadows near the doorway, his dark eyes fixed on her. He didn't speak right away, letting the quiet stretch between them. When he finally stepped closer, his footsteps soft against the wooden floor, Astrid didn't turn to face him.

"It never gets easier," Thorwulf said quietly, his voice a low rumble. "Taking a life."

Astrid's fingers tightened around the edge of the table, her knuckles white. "It shouldn't," she replied, her voice barely above a whisper. "If it ever does, that's when you've truly lost yourself."

Thorwulf nodded, though she couldn't see it. He moved closer, standing beside her as the firelight cast shadows across his strong features. "You did what had to be done," he said. "Jorik's betrayal would've torn the village apart. Frostfjord needed to see that you're willing to make the hard choices."

Astrid finally looked at him, her blue eyes shimmering with unshed tears. "And what about me?" she asked, her voice trembling. "What does it say about me that I could kill my own uncle? That I didn't hesitate?"

Thorwulf's gaze softened, and he reached out, brushing a stray strand of hair from her face. "It says that you're a leader," he said gently. "A warrior. You're doing what no one else has the strength to do, Astrid. And that's why they follow you."

His words struck a chord deep within her, but they didn't erase the ache in her chest. She turned back to the fire, her shoulders slumping. "The stakes keep getting higher," she murmured. "Every decision feels like another nail in the coffin for me, for Frostfjord. I don't know how much more I can take."

Thorwulf stepped closer, his hand resting lightly on her arm.

"You don't have to carry this alone," he said. "I'm here, Astrid. I always will be."

She looked up at him, her heart pounding as she met his gaze. There was an intensity, a certainty in his eyes that gave her strength. For a moment, the weight of the world seemed to fade, leaving only the two of them standing in the quiet glow of the fire.

"Thorwulf," she began, but he cut her off, his voice soft but steady.

"I need to say this," he said. "Before the next battle, before the next storm, before we lose another moment. Astrid, I don't just follow you because you're a great leader. I follow you because I believe in you. Because I..." He hesitated, his usual confidence faltering for the first time. "Because I love you."

Astrid's breath caught in her throat, her eyes widening as his words sank in. Before she could respond, he reached into his belt pouch and pulled out a small silver ring. It was simple but beautiful, engraved with a pattern of intertwining runes.

"This belonged to my mother," he said, his voice barely above a whisper. "She gave it to me before she died, told me to give it to the woman I wanted to spend my life with. And Astrid, I can't imagine anyone else by my side."

Her heart felt like it might burst as he held out the ring, his dark eyes searching hers. "I know the world is falling apart around us," he said. "I know we might not make it through this war. But if we do, I want to spend whatever time we have left with you. Will you be my betrothed?"

Astrid stared at him, her mind racing. She wanted to say yes. More than anything, she wanted to say yes. But the fear lingered, the voice in the back of her mind that reminded her how uncertain their future was, how much they still had to fight for.

"Thorwulf," she began, her voice trembling. "I... I don't know if I can."

"You don't have to decide now," he interrupted gently, stepping closer. "I just needed you to know how I feel. No matter what happens, Astrid, you have my heart. Whether you take this ring or not."

Tears pricked at her eyes, and she reached out, her fingers brushing against the cool silver of the ring. "You're impossible," she said softly, a faint smile tugging at her lips.

"And you're stubborn," he replied, unable to stop a grin breaking through his serious expression. "Which is why we're perfect for each other."

Astrid laughed despite herself, the sound bittersweet but genuine. She closed her hand over his, holding the ring tightly between them. "I'll think about it," she said, her voice barely above a whisper.

Thorwulf nodded, his gaze filled with understanding. "That's all I ask."

For the first time in what felt like days, the weight on Astrid's chest lightened. The fire crackled softly beside them, and for a moment, the world outside the longhouse faded away.

32

THE VALKYRIE RETURNS

The night was restless, the air heavy with tension after the execution of Jorik. Frostfjord's villagers retreated to their homes, their whispered conversations muffled by the thick walls of their longhouses. The flickering light of torches cast eerie shadows on the snow-covered ground, making the village seem even more isolated in the vast wilderness.

Astrid sat alone on the steps of the chieftain's hall, her thoughts spiraling as she stared into the darkness beyond the village gates. Thorwulf had tried to stay by her side, but she had insisted on solitude, the weight of her uncle's betrayal still pressing heavily on her chest. She pulled her cloak tighter around her shoulders, the biting wind cutting through even the thick fur lining.

The stars above were brilliant, unyielding pinpricks of light against the vast, infinite black. Astrid let her gaze drift upward, seeking some kind of comfort, or at least clarity, in their cold beauty. But none came. The gods felt distant, silent, as though they were watching her with disapproval from their celestial halls.

Her fingers absently traced the runes engraved on the hilt of her sword. Every decision she made seemed to cut deeper into her soul, leaving her raw and questioning everything she thought she knew.

A sudden gust of wind swept through the village, extinguishing the torches along the main path. The world plunged into darkness, save for the silvery light of the moon. Astrid stiffened, her hand instinctively going to her sword. The silence that followed was unnatural, and her breath misted in the freezing air as the temperature seemed to drop even further.

"You walk a dangerous path, Astrid of Frostfjord."

The voice was low and haunting, a melodic yet chilling tone that seemed to echo from everywhere and nowhere at once. Astrid shot to her feet, her sword drawn, her heart pounding in her chest.

Out of the shadows, the Valkyrie appeared.

She was as otherworldly as Astrid remembered. Taller than any mortal woman, her raven-black hair cascading in waves down her back. Her armor shimmered like liquid silver, each plate etched with intricate runes that seemed to shift and writhe in the moonlight. Her eyes, sharp and piercing, glowed faintly like embers, and the massive wings folded against her back shimmered with an iridescent sheen.

"You again," Astrid said, her voice steady despite the chill that ran down her spine. "What do you want?"

The Valkyrie tilted her head, her expression unreadable. "You defied the gods once," she said. "Do you think they will allow you to do so again?"

"I don't answer to the gods," Astrid replied, her voice firm. "They've taken enough from us. They've taken our families, our homes, our lives. I won't let them take anything more."

The Valkyrie's lips curved into a faint, enigmatic smile. "Brave words. But bravery alone will not save you from what lies ahead."

She stepped closer, her movements unnaturally graceful, as though she were gliding across the snow rather than walking. Astrid stood her ground, though every instinct in her body screamed at her to run.

"You seek to unite the clans," the Valkyrie said. "To challenge the Jarls and the gods themselves. But do you understand the price of such defiance?"

Astrid lifted her chin, her blue eyes blazing. "If the price is my life, so be it. I've made peace with that."

The Valkyrie laughed softly, the sound both beautiful and unsettling. "Your life is not the price, Astrid. It is the lives of those you love. Thorwulf. Leif. Your people. They will suffer for your choices. And when the gods are done, you will be left standing alone in the ruins of Frostfjord."

The words struck Astrid like a physical blow, her breath catching in her throat. She thought of Thorwulf's dark eyes, his unwavering loyalty. Of Leif's quiet support, even when his jealousy threatened to break through. Of the villagers who had followed her, trusted her, even as the odds mounted against them.

"Is that a threat?" she asked, her voice trembling but defiant.

"It is a warning," the Valkyrie said, her tone colder now. "You have been given a gift, Astrid. A chance to bend fate. But every choice you make ripples through the tapestry of destiny. The gods watch, and they do not forgive easily."

Astrid's grip on her sword faltered for the briefest moment before she steadied herself. "If the gods think they can break me, they're wrong. I'll fight them. I'll fight anyone who stands in the way of a better future for my people."

The Valkyrie's expression softened, a flicker of something almost like pity crossing her features. "You are bold, Astrid. And boldness can change the course of history. But remember this, every fire needs kindling. And every rebellion leaves ashes."

With that, she extended her hand, palm open, and a vision flared in Astrid's mind. Bjornhold in flames. Frostfjord's longhouses reduced to smoldering ruins. Thorwulf's lifeless body cradled in her arms, his blood staining the snow. The cries of the dying echoed in her ears, the scent of smoke and death overwhelming her senses.

Astrid gasped, staggering back as the vision faded. The Valkyrie's eyes glowed brighter, her wings unfurling with a sound like distant thunder. "The choice is yours, Astrid," she said. "Continue on this path, and you may yet achieve greatness. But greatness always comes at a cost."

Before Astrid could respond, the Valkyrie spread her wings and leapt into the sky, vanishing into the night like a shadow swallowed by the wind. The torches flickered back to life, their flames casting long, trembling shadows across the snow.

Astrid sank to her knees, her sword falling from her hand. Her chest heaved as she struggled to catch her breath, the Valkyrie's words ringing in her ears.

The stakes had never felt higher. And for the first time, doubt began to creep into the edges of her resolve.

The fire in the longhouse had burned low by the time Astrid found her way back, her thoughts a tangled web of doubt and fear. The Valkyrie's warning still echoed in her mind, her vision of Bjornhold in flames and Thorwulf's lifeless body haunting her with every step. She felt the weight of the world pressing down on her shoulders, threatening to crush her.

Thorwulf was waiting for her. He sat by the hearth, sharpening his axe with slow, deliberate strokes. The moment she stepped inside, his gaze lifted, his dark eyes filled with concern. He set the axe aside and rose to meet her, his expression softening as he took in her pale face and trembling hands.

"You've been gone a long time," he said gently. "What happened?"

Astrid hesitated, her fingers gripping the edges of her cloak as if it could shield her from the storm inside her. She didn't want to speak of the Valkyrie, didn't want to put her fears into words and make them real. But Thorwulf's steady presence, his quiet strength, drew the truth from her.

"She came to me again," Astrid said finally, her voice barely above a whisper. "The Valkyrie. She warned me that my path will lead to great loss. That I'll lose everything and everyone if I keep defying the gods."

Thorwulf stepped closer, his hands brushing her arms in a gesture of comfort. "The gods don't control you, Astrid. They don't decide who you are or what you fight for."

Her lips trembled as she met his gaze, her blue eyes shimmering with unshed tears. "What if they're right?" she asked, her voice cracking. "What if I'm becoming something I don't recognize. What if I become something monstrous? I killed Jorik, Thorwulf. My own uncle. And I didn't even hesitate. What kind of person does that make me?"

Thorwulf's hands cupped her face, his thumbs brushing away the tears that spilled down her cheeks. "It makes you someone who loves your people enough to make the hard choices," he said firmly. "Someone who's willing to do whatever it takes to protect them. That doesn't make you a monster, Astrid. It makes you a leader."

She let out a shaky breath, her hands resting lightly on his chest. "But what if I lose myself along the way? What if I lose you?"

"You won't," he said, his voice soft but filled with conviction. "I won't let that happen."

Astrid closed her eyes, leaning into his touch as a single tear slipped down her cheek. For so long, she had carried the burden of leadership alone, refusing to let anyone see the cracks in her armor. But with Thorwulf, she didn't have to pretend. She could let the weight of her fears fall away, if only for a moment.

"I'm so tired," she whispered. "Of fighting. Of doubting. Of wondering if I'm doing the right thing."

Thorwulf pulled her into his arms, holding her tightly as if he could shield her from the world. "You're not alone, Astrid," he murmured. "You never have to be alone."

They stood there for what felt like an eternity, the silence between them filled with unspoken words and shared understanding. When Astrid finally pulled back, her gaze met his, and something in the air shifted. The firelight cast a warm glow over his face, highlighting the sharp lines of his jaw and the softness in his eyes.

"Stay with me tonight," she said, her voice trembling but steady.

Thorwulf searched her face, his own expression softening. "Are you sure?" he asked, his voice low.

Astrid nodded, her fingers curling into the fabric of his tunic. "I don't want to be alone. Not tonight."

Thorwulf cupped her face again, his thumb brushing against her cheek as he leaned in. Their lips met in a kiss that was both tender and desperate, a silent promise to hold on to each other no matter what the future held. Astrid's hands slid up to his shoulders, her fingers threading through his dark hair as the kiss deepened.

When they finally pulled apart, their breaths mingling in the space between them, Thorwulf rested his forehead against hers. "I'll stay," he said softly. "For as long as you'll have me."

Astrid's heart swelled, and for the first time in what felt like ages, the ache in her chest eased. She took his hand, leading him toward the corner of the longhouse where a simple bed was tucked against the wall. The furs were warm and inviting, a sanctuary from the cold that seeped through the wooden walls.

As they lay down together, Astrid curled into Thorwulf's side, her head resting on his chest. His arms wrapped around her, holding her close as his steady heartbeat lulled her into a sense of calm. The world outside the longhouse faded away, leaving only the quiet intimacy of the moment.

33

GATHERING STORM

The wind howled through the narrow pass as Astrid and Thorwulf made their way toward the hidden glen where the meeting was to take place. The mountains loomed like ancient sentinels, their jagged peaks shrouded in mist. Snow swirled in the air, carried by biting gusts that seemed intent on driving them back. The landscape was both beautiful and treacherous, a fitting backdrop for the perilous alliance they sought to forge.

Thorwulf adjusted his cloak, his sharp eyes scanning the path ahead. "Do you trust them?" he asked, his voice low enough to be carried away by the wind.

Astrid pulled her hood tighter around her face, her breath visible in the icy air. "Trust is a luxury we can't afford," she said. "But if we're going to stand a chance against the Jarls, we need their swords."

Thorwulf nodded, though his expression remained wary. "Let's hope they see it the same way."

The hidden glen lay beyond a cluster of ancient pines, their snow-laden branches forming a natural barrier. As they approached, Astrid spotted the faint flicker of torchlight through the trees. Her heart quickened, a mixture of anticipation and unease knotting in her chest. This was the moment that could decide the fate of Bjornhold.

The glen was unlike anything Astrid had seen before. Sheltered from the worst of the storm, it was a quiet sanctuary, its frozen ground blanketed in pristine snow. In the center stood a massive stone monolith, weathered by time but still imposing. Carved into its surface were the symbols of the old gods, their jagged runes faintly glowing in the torchlight. It was said to be a place of ancient power, where alliances had been forged and broken for centuries.

Representatives from the clans were already gathered, their cloaks dusted with snow and their faces set in grim determination. Ingrid of Seastone stood near the monolith, her sea-blue cloak a stark contrast against the white landscape. Beside her was Harvik of Solfjord, a broad-shouldered man with a braided beard and an air of quiet authority. A handful of warriors flanked them, their hands never straying far from their weapons.

As Astrid and Thorwulf stepped into the glen, all eyes turned toward them. The tension was palpable, the air heavy with unspoken words.

"You're late," Ingrid said, though there was no malice in her tone. She stepped forward, her sharp gaze taking in Astrid's windburned face and Thorwulf's stoic expression. "I was beginning to think you'd lost your way."

"Not yet," Astrid replied, a faint smirk tugging at her lips. "Though the storm did its best to stop us."

Harvik crossed his arms, his voice rumbling like distant thunder. "You called this meeting, Astrid of Frostfjord. I hope you have more to offer than clever words."

Astrid stepped closer to the monolith, her chin held high. "I called this meeting because the Jarls have turned Bjornhold into a battlefield. They've pitted us against each other for centuries, all in the name of appeasing the gods. But the gods didn't bleed in the Reckoning. We did."

A murmur rippled through the gathered warriors, their expressions shifting as her words sank in.

"The Jarls have declared Frostfjord an enemy of Bjornhold," Astrid continued. "They've sent Ironcrag's armies to destroy us. But this isn't just about Frostfjord. It's about all of us. If we don't stand together, the Jarls will crush us one by one."

"And you think you can unite us?" Harvik asked, his tone skeptical. "You, who defied the gods and survived the Reckoning? Some would call that arrogance."

"Maybe it is," Astrid admitted, her blue eyes blazing. "But it's also hope. Hope that we can be more than pawns in the Jarls' games. Hope that we can build a future where the clans stand together, not apart."

Ingrid stepped forward, her sharp features softening. "She's right," she said, her voice carrying over the crowd. "The Jarls thrive on our division. They fear what we could become if we united. That's why they sent their armies against Frostfjord. Because they know Astrid has the strength to lead us."

Harvik's gaze flicked between Ingrid and Astrid, his expression unreadable. After a long pause, he nodded. "If Seastone stands with Frostfjord, so will Solfjord. But this alliance won't be built on words alone. We need a plan."

Astrid glanced at Thorwulf, who stepped forward, his presence commanding. "The Jarls are fortified on Skarn," he said. "If we're going to challenge them, we'll need to strike at their stronghold. But we can't march on Skarn divided. We need every clan, every warrior."

Harvik frowned. "And what of Ironcrag? Their armies won't sit idly by while we march on the Jarls."

Thorwulf voice was firm. "Ironcrag is a problem we'll have to face. But if we strike quickly and decisively, we can cut the head off the snake before it bites."

The gathered warriors exchanged uneasy glances, the weight of the task ahead settling over them. Astrid stepped forward, her voice firm.

"I'm not asking for blind faith," she said. "I'm asking for a chance. A chance to show the Jarls that their time is over. A chance to prove that Bjornhold belongs to its people, not its tyrants."

For a moment, the glen was silent, the only sound the distant howl of the wind. Then Ingrid raised her sword, the steel catching the torchlight.

"Seastone stands with Frostfjord," she said, her voice ringing out.

Harvik followed suit, and his axe gleamed as he raised it high. "And so does Solfjord."

One by one, the warriors raised their weapons, their voices joining in a chorus of unity. Astrid's chest swelled with a mixture of pride and determination. For the first time, it felt like the tides were turning.

But as she met Thorwulf's gaze, she saw the worry in his eyes. The battle ahead would be unlike anything they'd faced before. And the gods would not let their defiance go unanswered.

As the final echo of raised weapons and voices faded into the stillness of the glen, Astrid let out a breath she hadn't realized she was holding. For a fleeting moment, she felt the faintest stirrings of hope, like a fragile ember glowing in the cold darkness of doubt. The clans were united, their leaders pledging their strength to the cause. But unity didn't guarantee survival.

The glen emptied slowly as warriors returned to their camps, leaving Astrid and Thorwulf lingering near the ancient monolith. The runes etched into its weathered surface seemed to pulse faintly in the firelight, as if the gods themselves were watching. Astrid shivered, pulling her cloak tighter around her shoulders.

Thorwulf stepped beside her, his presence as steadying as the mountains that surrounded them. "You did it," he said, his voice low. "You brought them together."

Astrid turned to him, her eyes searching his face. "For now," she said. "But this alliance is held together by threads, not steel. One wrong move, one failure, and it could all unravel."

Thorwulf studied her for a moment, his gaze soft but unreadable. "You're carrying too much," he said quietly. "You don't have to bear this weight alone."

She shook her head, a faint smile tugging at her lips. "You've said that before."

"And I'll keep saying it until you believe me," he replied, stepping closer. "Astrid, you've been leading this fight with fire in your heart and steel in your spine, but even warriors need someone to lean on."

His words touched something deep within her, a vulnerable part of her heart she rarely let herself acknowledge. She looked away, her gaze falling to the snow-covered ground. "What if leaning on someone makes me weak?" she whispered.

Thorwulf reached out, tilting her chin up so she was forced to meet his eyes. "It doesn't," he said firmly. "It makes you human."

The intensity in his gaze made her feel, for a moment, that the world around them had faded. The looming rebellion, the gods' wrath, the weight of her choices. All of it melted away under the warmth of his presence.

"Thorwulf," she began, her voice trembling. "What if what we have doesn't survive what's coming?"

He hesitated, the question hanging between them like a blade poised to strike. When he finally spoke, his voice was softer, tinged with a vulnerability she rarely saw in him. "I think about that every day," he admitted. "Every time we go into battle, every time you step into danger, I wonder if it'll be the last time I see you. And it terrifies me."

Astrid's breath hitched, her heart pounding in her chest. She hadn't expected him to admit that, hadn't realized how deeply he felt the same fear that gnawed at her.

"But if there's one thing I know," he continued, his hand brushing against hers, "it's that what we have is worth fighting for. Even if the odds are stacked against us. Even if the gods themselves try to tear us apart."

Astrid's lips parted, a lump rising in her throat. She wanted to believe him, wanted to hold on to the strength in his words. But the fear lingered, a shadow she couldn't shake.

"Do you think they'll let us have this?" she asked. "The Jarls, the gods, do you think they'll let us be happy?"

Thorwulf's dark eyes hardened. "They don't get to decide that," he said. "We do."

His words were a promise, a declaration, and they sparked a fierce, unrelenting determination within her. She stepped closer, her hand finding his, their fingers intertwining.

"Then we fight," she said softly. "For this. For us."

Thorwulf smiled, the tension in his features softening. "Always."

The moment stretched between them, the cold air swirling around them as the firelight danced on their faces. Then, without warning, Thorwulf leaned down, his lips brushing against hers in a kiss that was both tender and filled with the weight of unspoken fears and unyielding hope. Astrid melted into him, her arms wrapping around his neck as the world narrowed to just the two of them.

When they finally pulled apart, their foreheads resting against each other, Thorwulf's voice was barely more than a whisper. "No matter what happens, Astrid, you'll always have me."

Tears prickled at the corners of her eyes, but she blinked them away, her resolve hardening. "And you'll always have me," she replied, her voice steady despite the storm raging in her heart.

As they turned to leave the glen, their hands still clasped tightly, Astrid couldn't help but glance back at the monolith. The runes seemed to glow brighter, their light almost taunting. She knew the gods were watching, their judgment looming over her like a storm cloud.

But for now, she had Thorwulf. And for now, that was enough.

34

THE FINAL TRIAL

The storm clouds above Skarn churned like a restless sea, their heavy darkness pressing down on the courtyard where the fate of Bjornhold would be decided. The biting wind howled through the assembled crowd, carrying with it whispers of unease and disbelief. Warriors and villagers alike had come from every corner of the clans to witness this moment. The stone walls of the Jarls' stronghold rose high around them, their carved runes seeming to glow faintly in the stormlight, as though the gods themselves were watching.

Astrid stood at the center of the courtyard, her breath visible in the frigid air, her heart pounding a relentless rhythm in her chest. Her sword was steady in her hand, but the weight of the moment pressed heavily on her shoulders. This was more than a battle. It was a test of her worth, her resolve, and her vision for a united Bjornhold. The Jarls, their cold and imperious gazes fixed on her, sat on their high dais like judges in a trial where the verdict had already been decided.

"Astrid of Frostfjord," Jarl Sten intoned, his voice carrying over the crowd like the roll of thunder. "You have defied the gods, incited rebellion, and dared to challenge the authority of this council. Today, you will prove whether you are worthy to lead, or whether your ambitions will be your undoing."

Astrid met his gaze, unflinching. "I don't fight for myself," she said, her voice ringing out clear and strong despite the wind. "I fight for Bjornhold. For the clans. For a future where we're not bound by the Jarls' decrees or the gods' whims."

A murmur rippled through the crowd, a mixture of admiration and doubt. Thorwulf stood at the edge of the ring, his dark eyes fixed on her, his jaw tight. She could feel his unspoken plea, the tension in his stance as if willing her to reconsider, to let someone else bear the burden of this fight. But Astrid knew this was her battle to face.

Jarl Sten's lips curled into a cold smile. "Then let us see if you are as strong as your words."

He raised his hand, and from the far end of the courtyard, three figures stepped forward.

The Ironcrag champion led the way, his massive frame casting a shadow that seemed to stretch across the entire courtyard. He was a mountain of muscle and scars, his face twisted into a grimace of contempt. In his hands, he held a war hammer so massive it seemed impossible for any mortal man to wield. The spiked head gleamed menacingly, a testament to the destruction it could unleash.

Behind him came the Seastone warrior, her movements quick and fluid like a serpent. Her twin daggers gleamed like shards of ice, and her narrowed eyes scanned Astrid with predatory intent. Her cloak, a deep navy blue trimmed with silver, fluttered in the wind like the waves of the sea she called home.

The final opponent was the Solfjord champion, a towering man clad in golden-hued armor that caught the faint light like a beacon. His spear was long and ornate, the blade at its tip etched with runes that shimmered faintly. He exuded an air of confidence, his gaze steady and unyielding.

The crowd hushed as the three champions took their places. The tension was a living thing, thick and suffocating, as Astrid stepped forward to face them.

The Ironcrag warrior wasted no time. With a roar that echoed like an avalanche, he charged, his war hammer arcing through the air with terrifying speed. The sheer force of his attack was enough to make the ground tremble, but Astrid was ready. She sidestepped at the last moment, the hammer slamming into the stone where she had been standing and sending shards flying.

Astrid didn't wait for him to recover. She darted in, her sword slicing toward his exposed flank. The blade bit deep, and the Ironcrag warrior let out a grunt of pain, but he didn't falter. He swung again, forcing Astrid to leap back to avoid being crushed.

Their clash was brutal, the courtyard echoing with the sound of steel on steel and the warrior's guttural roars. Astrid's movements were swift and precise, her smaller size allowing her to outmaneuver his powerful but sluggish strikes. Each time he swung, she countered, her blade finding its mark again and again. Blood stained the snow beneath their feet, but the Ironcrag warrior refused to yield.

It wasn't until Astrid feinted to the left, drawing him off balance, that she saw her opening. With a swift, upward slash, she struck the strap holding his hammer, sending the weapon tumbling to the ground. Before he could react, her blade was at his throat.

"Yield," she commanded, her voice cold and steady.

The Ironcrag warrior glared at her, his chest heaving, before finally nodding. "I yield," he growled, stepping back.

The crowd erupted into a mix of cheers and gasps, the first trial won.

The Seastone warrior was next, her daggers flashing as she lunged at Astrid with a speed that was almost impossible to follow. The clash of blades was a blur, the two women circling each other in a deadly dance. The Seastone warrior's strikes were quick and precise, her movements almost graceful as she sought to exploit any opening in Astrid's defense.

Astrid gritted her teeth, her muscles burning as she parried strike after strike. She could feel the Seastone warrior's smirk, her confidence growing with each passing moment. But Astrid was patient, biding her time. When the Seastone warrior overextended, Astrid struck, her sword slicing through the leather of her opponent's gauntlet and sending one of the daggers clattering to the ground.

The Seastone warrior cursed, her remaining dagger slicing toward Astrid's throat. Astrid ducked, her blade driving forward in a powerful thrust that sent her opponent sprawling. She pressed the tip of her sword against the warrior's chest, her eyes blazing.

"Yield," she said.

The Seastone warrior glared at her, her pride wounded, but she finally nodded. "I yield."

Astrid stepped back, her chest heaving as the crowd roared once more.

The Solfjord champion was last, his spear spinning in his hands as he advanced with measured precision. His strikes were calculated, each one designed to push Astrid back, to wear her down. Thorwulf's warning rang in her ears: "Watch his footwork."

Astrid moved with him, her sword deflecting the spear's thrusts and arcs. The battle was a test of endurance as much as skill, the clash of steel against steel ringing out like a song of war. She could feel the strain in her arms, the ache in her legs, but she refused to falter.

The Solfjord champion pressed his advantage, his spear grazing her shoulder and drawing blood. Astrid bit back a cry of pain, her focus narrowing to the weapon in his hands. She needed to disarm him, to find a way past his reach.

In a desperate move, she feinted to the right, drawing his spear in that direction, then pivoted and lunged forward. Her sword struck the haft of the spear, snapping it in two. The Solfjord champion stumbled, his weapon reduced to a splintered shaft, and Astrid drove him to the ground.

"Yield," she demanded, her blade at his throat.

The Solfjord champion hesitated, his pride warring with the reality of his defeat. Finally, he nodded. "I yield."

Astrid rose to her feet, her sword dripping blood, her breath coming in ragged gasps. The courtyard erupted into chaos, the crowd's roar deafening as the Jarls exchanged dark looks on their dais. Thorwulf pushed through the throng to her side, his hand steadying her as she swayed on her feet.

"You did it," he murmured, his voice filled with a mix of pride and awe.

Astrid nodded, her gaze fixed on the Jarls. But as she met their cold, unyielding eyes, she knew this wasn't over. The gods weren't done with her yet.

Astrid staggered back, her chest heaving as the shattered spear clattered to the ground at her feet. The Solfjord champion's blood smeared the snow, crimson streaks against a blanket of white. She wiped the back of her hand across her brow, smearing dirt and sweat as she turned her gaze to the dais.

The Jarls sat stone-faced, their eyes cold and calculating. They made no move to acknowledge her victory. The crowd was still roaring, but Astrid barely heard it over the pounding of her heart. Her body ached, each breath a sharp reminder of the punishment she had endured.

"Astrid!" Thorwulf's voice cut through the cacophony as he pushed through the crowd, his expression etched with worry. His eyes flicked over her bloodied shoulder and the shallow gash on her thigh. "You're hurt."

"I'm fine," she said, though her voice was strained, and her legs trembled beneath her. "It's not over yet."

The Ironcrag warrior was subdued. The Seastone warrior yielded. And the Solfjord champion, his pride broken, had retreated to his knees. But the air around her still thrummed with menace, the weight of something unfinished pressing down on the courtyard.

The Jarls rose from their seats, their cloaks billowing in the icy wind. Jarl Sten stepped forward, his gaze heavy as it fell on her. "You fight well, Astrid of Frostfjord," he said, his tone devoid of warmth. "But the gods demand more."

Astrid's breath hitched. "You named your champions," she said, her voice raw but defiant. "I defeated them. What more do you want?"

Jarl Sten's smile was thin, cruel. "The gods are not yet satisfied," he said. "If you would defy them, if you would challenge their will, you must prove yourself worthy to lead."

Astrid's heart sank as three more figures emerged from the shadows at the far end of the courtyard. These were not champions, they were beasts.

The first was a hulking bear, its fur matted with ice and its breath steaming in the cold air. Its eyes glowed an unnatural yellow, and its claws raked the ground as it snarled. The second was a massive wolf, its gray coat streaked with silver, its fangs bared in a menacing grin. The third was a monstrous creature that seemed to be a twisted amalgamation of man and beast, its muscular form bristling with spikes and its face contorted in a permanent snarl.

Astrid's stomach turned, but she forced herself to stand tall. The gods weren't content with testing her skill against warriors. They wanted her blood.

Thorwulf grabbed her arm, his voice a low, urgent whisper. "This is madness, Astrid. You're already injured. You can't fight them alone."

She turned to him, her blue eyes blazing. "I have to," she said. "If I don't, everything we've fought for will mean nothing."

Before he could argue, the beasts charged.

The bear came first, a wall of fur and fury that barreled toward her with terrifying speed. Astrid rolled to the side just as its massive paw swiped the air where she had stood, the force of the blow cracking the frozen ground. She came up swinging, her blade slicing through its flank, but the creature barely flinched. It roared, the sound shaking the very walls of the stronghold, and turned on her with a ferocity that left her scrambling to stay ahead of its strikes.

Astrid ducked and weaved, each movement a desperate attempt to stay alive. Her sword flashed, striking the bear's side again and again, but it wasn't until she drove her blade deep into its chest, straight through the heart, that the beast finally fell. It collapsed to the ground with a thunderous crash, its glowing eyes dimming as its body went still.

Astrid barely had time to catch her breath before the wolf was upon her. It moved like a shadow, its fangs snapping inches from her throat as she stumbled back. The crowd gasped as she fell, the wolf pouncing on her with lethal intent. Astrid thrust her sword upward, the blade piercing its chest just as its jaws closed on her shoulder.

Pain exploded through her, but she gritted her teeth and

shoved the beast off her, blood pouring from the wound. The wolf collapsed, its body twitching as the life drained from it.

The final creature was the worst. Its monstrous form towered over her, and its glowing red eyes fixed on her like a predator sizing up its prey. It moved with unnatural speed, its claws slicing through the air as it lunged at her. Astrid raised her sword to block, but the force of the blow sent her crashing to the ground, her weapon skidding out of reach.

Thorwulf shouted her name, his voice a raw cry of anguish, but he was held back by the Jarls' guards. Astrid struggled to her feet, her vision swimming as the creature advanced on her. Her body screamed in protest, every muscle burning, but she refused to yield.

She spotted a fallen spear. It was one of the Solfjord champion's broken weapons, lying nearby. With a desperate burst of energy, she lunged for it, her fingers closing around the shaft just as the creature leapt at her. She rolled onto her back, raising the spear, and the creature impaled itself on the jagged tip.

It howled, a sound that was both animalistic and eerily human, before collapsing on top of her. Astrid shoved its lifeless body aside, her chest heaving as she struggled to rise.

The courtyard was silent, the crowd stunned into stillness. Astrid stood amidst the carnage, bloodied and broken but unbowed. She raised her sword, its blade glinting in the faint light, and turned to face the Jarls.

"I have proven myself," she said, her voice strong despite the pain that lanced through her with every breath. "No more trials. No more games. Bjornhold belongs to its people, not the gods."

Jarl Sten's expression was unreadable, but a faint flicker of reluctant and grudging respect crossed his face. "You have fought well, Astrid of Frostfjord," he said. "But the gods are not so easily defied."

Astrid didn't flinch, her gaze unwavering. She had faced death and emerged victorious. Whatever came next, she was ready.

35

A DIVIDED BJORNHOLD

The fire in the hearth crackled softly, casting flickering shadows across the wooden walls of the Frostfjord longhouse. The scent of herbs and burning pine filled the air, mingling with the metallic tang of blood. Astrid lay on a bed of furs, her body wrapped in bandages that bore the faint stain of her wounds. Her face was pale, her breathing shallow but steady.

Thorwulf sat beside her, his broad shoulders hunched as he soaked a cloth in a bowl of steaming water. His usually strong, calloused hands moved with surprising gentleness, carefully dabbing at the gash along her collarbone. Despite the warmth of the fire, his jaw was tight, his eyes dark with worry.

"You shouldn't be awake," Thorwulf muttered, his voice gruff but tender. "The healer said you need rest."

Astrid cracked one eye open, her lips twitching in a faint smile despite the pain that radiated through her body. "Hard to rest when it feels like I've been trampled by a mammoth," she murmured.

Thorwulf huffed a laugh, though it lacked his usual warmth. "That's because you practically were," he said. He wrung out the cloth and pressed it gently to her wound, his touch soothing even as it stung. "You pushed yourself too far, Astrid. You should have let me..."

"No," she interrupted, her voice firmer now. She winced as she shifted slightly, her fingers gripping the edge of the fur beneath her. "This was my fight, Thorwulf. I couldn't let anyone else carry that weight."

Thorwulf didn't argue. Instead, he sat back, his hands resting on his knees as he looked at her. “You keep saying that,” he said quietly. “But do you ever stop to think about the people who want to carry it with you?”

Astrid's gaze softened, but before she could reply, the door to the longhouse creaked open. Leif stepped inside, his face drawn with fatigue. His eyes darted between Astrid and Thorwulf, his expression unreadable.

“The clans are restless,” he said, his voice low. “Word of your victory has spread, but so has the Jarls' defiance. Solfjord and Seastone are preparing for war. Ironcrag is fortifying their borders.”

Astrid sighed, her head falling back against the furs. “So much for unity,” she muttered.

Leif crossed his arms, his posture stiff. “You knew this wouldn't be easy,” he said. “The Jarls won't give up their power without a fight. And the clans... they're looking to you for answers, Astrid. If you falter now...”

“I won't falter,” she snapped, though her voice was strained. She forced herself to sit up, ignoring the pain that flared through her side. “I didn't go through all of this to watch Bjornhold tear itself apart.”

Thorwulf reached out, his hand on her shoulder, steadying her. “You're still healing,” he said, his tone firm but gentle. “You can't lead if you push yourself to the grave.”

Astrid looked at him, her eyes searching his face. "And what do you suggest?" she asked softly.

Thorwulf hesitated, his gaze flicking to Leif before returning to her. "We need to buy time," he said. "Send envoys to the clans. Remind them what's at stake. If we can convince them to hold back their swords for just a little while longer, we might be able to broker peace."

Leif snorted, his expression skeptical. "And what makes you think the Jarls will allow that? They'll use the delay to strengthen their grip."

"Then we make sure they don't have the chance," Thorwulf shot back, his voice hardening. "We focus on Frostfjord, and on rebuilding and fortifying. If the Jarls want a war, they'll find us ready."

Astrid closed her eyes for a moment, the weight of their words pressing down on her. Her body ached, her wounds a constant reminder of how much she had already sacrificed. But she couldn't afford to waver. Not now.

When she opened her eyes, there was a flicker of determination in their depths. "Send the envoys," she said, her voice steady despite the pain. "And start fortifying the village. If the Jarls want a fight, we'll give them one, but not on their terms."

Leif nodded, though his expression remained tense. "I'll see to it."

As he turned to leave, Astrid called out to him. "Leif." He paused, glancing back at her. "Thank you," she said, her voice softer now. "For everything."

Leif hesitated, his gaze lingering on her for a moment longer than necessary, before he nodded and stepped out into the cold.

The village of Frostfjord was a somber sight. The scars of the recent raid were everywhere – in the charred timbers, crumbled walls, and the lingering stench of smoke. Villagers moved through the streets with purpose, their faces grim as they worked to rebuild what had been lost. Children carried bundles of firewood, their small hands red from the cold, while elders mended fishing nets and repaired tools.

Astrid watched from the window of the longhouse, her heart heavy. These were her people, and they had suffered because of her. Because of her defiance. The weight of their struggles pressed down on her, each broken home a reminder of the cost of leadership.

Thorwulf appeared at her side, his presence steadying. "You can't save them all, Astrid," he said gently. "But you can lead them."

She turned to him, her eyes searching his face. "And if I lead them into ruin?" she asked, her voice barely more than a whisper.

"You won't," he said firmly. He reached out, his hand brushing against hers. "You've already shown them what it means to fight for something bigger than themselves. They believe in you, Astrid. And so do I."

For a moment, she let herself lean into him, drawing strength from his unwavering support. The world outside the longhouse was a storm, but in Thorwulf's arms, she found a fleeting moment of calm.

~

The soft glow of the fire flickered across the longhouse, illuminating the faint lines of exhaustion etched into Astrid's face. Outside, the sound of hammers striking wood echoed through the village as the people of Frostfjord worked tirelessly to rebuild. Astrid stood at the window, her arms crossed tightly over her chest as she stared out at the desolation that once was her home.

Thorwulf approached her from behind, his footsteps deliberately heavy to avoid startling her. His broad frame cast a shadow beside hers as he stopped, his dark eyes studying her profile.

"They're resilient," he said, nodding toward the villagers. "But they can't endure this forever."

Astrid didn't turn to him, her gaze fixed on the scene outside. "They shouldn't have to," she said quietly. "If the Jarls would see reason, if they would just step aside."

"That's not how this works," Thorwulf interrupted, his voice firm but calm. "You've seen how they rule, Astrid. They won't step down willingly."

"And what do you suggest?" she snapped, finally turning to face him. Her tone was sharp, but there was a flicker of vulnerability in her eyes. "Do you think I don't know that? Do you think I haven't thought about the cost of all of this?"

Thorwulf met her gaze, his expression steady. "I think you're too focused on the fight," he said. "You're leading with a sword when you should be leading with your words."

Astrid's brow furrowed, confusion mingling with frustration. "Diplomacy?" she asked, disbelief lacing her voice. "You think diplomacy will fix this? The Jarls declared war on us, Thorwulf. They sent raiders to burn our village, to kill our people. Do you honestly think words will stop them?"

Thorwulf stepped closer, his tone softening but losing none of its conviction. "Not the Jarls," he said. "But the clans. You've already united some of them, Astrid. Solfjord and Seastone believe in you because of what you stand for. But if you keep pushing for war, if you keep fighting every battle as though it's your last, you'll lose them."

Astrid's lips pressed into a thin line, her shoulders stiffening. "And what happens when diplomacy fails?" she asked. "What happens when the Jarls use my patience against me and slaughter us all while we wait for peace that will never come?"

Thorwulf's expression darkened, his frustration evident. "Do you think I want to sit idly by while the Jarls tear Bjornhold apart?" he asked, his voice rising slightly. "Do you think it's easy for me to watch you throw yourself into battle after battle, knowing how much it's costing you? Costing all of us?"

Astrid flinched, his words striking a chord she wasn't ready to confront. She looked away, trying to rein in her emotions.

Thorwulf sighed, his hand lifting to rest on her arm. "I'm not saying you shouldn't fight," he said, his voice gentler now. "I'm saying you don't have to fight alone. And you don't have to fight every battle with steel."

Astrid turned back to him, her blue eyes searching his face for a long moment. "I don't know how to do this any other way," she admitted, her voice barely more than a whisper.

Thorwulf smiled faintly, his thumb brushing against her arm. "Then let me help you," he said. "Let me be the one to remind you that there's more to leadership than strength. Sometimes, it's about knowing when to fight, and when to listen."

The words hung between them, heavy with unspoken truths. Astrid wanted to argue, to tell him that war was the only language the Jarls understood. But deep down, she knew he was right. The clans were fragile, their alliances tenuous. Another misstep could shatter everything she'd worked for.

Her shoulders sagged slightly, the weight of the conversation pressing down on her. "Fine," she said at last, her tone begrudging but sincere. "We'll send envoys. We'll try diplomacy. But if the Jarls show even the slightest hint of treachery..."

Thorwulf nodded, his expression softening. "We'll be ready."

For a moment, they stood in silence, the crackling of the fire the only sound between them. Then Astrid sighed, her gaze dropping to the floor. "I don't know if I can do this," she admitted. "Not without losing who I am."

Thorwulf stepped closer, his hand lifting to cup her cheek. "You won't lose yourself," he said firmly. "Because I won't let you."

Astrid looked up at him, her heart twisting at the sincerity in his eyes. She wanted to believe him, to trust that she could walk this path without being consumed by it. But the shadows of doubt lingered, a constant reminder of the cost of leadership.

"Thank you," she said softly, her voice thick with emotion.

by it. But the shadows of doubt lingered, a constant reminder of the cost of leadership.

Thorwulf hesitated, his gaze searching hers before he spoke again. "When this is over," he said softly, "when the Jarls are dealt with and the clans are safe... will you let me stand by your side? Not just as an ally, but as your soulmate?"

Astrid heard the vulnerability in his voice and she loved him more for it. Thorwulf had become more than a companion, more than a partner in battle. He had become her anchor in the storm.

"I..." She stopped, her throat constricting as a whirlwind of emotions surged within her. "Thorwulf, you know how much you mean to me. Of course I will. But only when this is done. And I... I don't even know if we'll survive this."

Thorwulf's smile was faint but understanding. "I'm not asking you for a ceremony tomorrow, Astrid," he said. "I'm asking you to commit to me. To our future. To believe that there's something waiting for us beyond this war."

Her gaze softened, a flicker of hope breaking through the storm of doubt. "I want to believe that," she admitted. "I want to believe in a future where we're not constantly fighting."

"Then hold on to that," Thorwulf said, his voice steady.

"Hold on to the thought of us, and of Frostfjord, Bjornhold, all of it being at peace."

Astrid nodded, her hand reaching up to cover his where it rested on her cheek. "I'll hold on," she said softly. "But right now, we need to focus on the fight ahead."

Thorwulf smiled, leaning down to press a gentle kiss to her forehead. "Then we fight," he said. "And when it's over, we build the future we deserve."

36

THE UPRISING

The wind howled through the mountain passes, carrying with it the acrid tang of smoke and the distant clamor of steel on steel. Astrid stood at the crest of the ridge, the jagged peaks of Bjornhold's unforgiving landscape rising behind her. Below, the Jarl-controlled fortress of Skarsgard loomed, its stone walls weathered but unyielding, its battlements bristling with armed guards.

The rebel clans had gathered in secret under the cover of darkness, their banners hidden but their resolve burning like wildfire. Astrid turned to face the warriors assembled behind her. Their faces were a patchwork of determination and fear, their armor a mix of scavenged iron and boiled leather. Each of them bore the scars of a life lived under the tyranny of the Jarls.

Thorwulf stepped to her side, his axe resting casually on his shoulder, though the tension in his posture betrayed his readiness for battle. His dark eyes scanned the gathered clansmen, his presence a pillar of unshakable strength.

Astrid raised her voice, the wind threatening to snatch her words away. "Today, we end their rule," she called, her tone sharp as the edge of her blade. "Today, we fight not just for

Frostfjord, but for all of Bjornhold. The Jarls think they are untouchable, that their power is eternal. We will show them that they are wrong."

The warriors murmured their assent, the weight of her words settling heavily upon them. Thorwulf stepped forward, his voice a low growl that carried over the howling wind. "They've taken everything from us. They've taken our homes, our kin, our freedom. They've ruled through fear, but fear will not win this battle. Strength will. Unity will."

Astrid's gaze swept over the crowd, catching familiar faces. Freya's younger brother, standing tall with his spear; Leif, his face a mask of grim determination as he adjusted the straps of his shield; the warriors of Solfjord and Seastone, their grudges set aside in the face of a common enemy.

"We attack at dawn," she said, her voice steady despite the fire burning in her veins. "We take Skarsgard, and from there, we take back Bjornhold."

The first rays of sunlight crept over the horizon, painting the fortress in hues of gold and crimson. Astrid crouched low among the rocks, her breath fogging in the frigid air. She could feel the tension thrumming through her, every muscle coiled tight as a bowstring.

"Are you ready for this?" Thorwulf whispered, his voice close to her ear.

She glanced at him, her lips curling into a wry smile. "I've been ready for this my entire life."

A signal horn echoed through the mountains, its mournful note carrying far and wide. The warriors surged forward like an unstoppable tide, their war cries splitting the dawn. Astrid led the charge, her sword flashing as she descended upon the enemy with the ferocity of a storm.

The defenders on the walls scrambled to respond, their shouts mingling with the clash of weapons and the dull thud of arrows striking shields. Astrid's blade bit into flesh and steel alike, her movements precise and unrelenting. She felt the heat of battle coursing through her, a primal rhythm that drowned out all fear.

Thorwulf was a whirlwind at her side, his axe carving through the enemy ranks with brutal efficiency. Together, they fought as if they were two halves of the same whole, their movements synchronized in a deadly dance.

At the gate, Leif and his squad worked furiously to breach the heavy wooden doors. They set fire to the tar-soaked beams, the flames licking hungrily at the wood as the defenders poured water from the battlements in a desperate attempt to quench them.

"Hold the line!" Astrid shouted, her voice cutting through the chaos. She threw herself into the fray, cutting down a spear-wielding guard who threatened to overtake Leif. The two shared a brief nod before returning to the battle.

The gate finally gave way with a deafening crack, the charred wood splintering under the combined weight of the battering ram and the relentless fire. The rebels surged forward, pouring into the fortress like a flood breaking through a dam.

Inside the walls, the fighting was fierce. The narrow corridors turned into killing grounds, every corner a potential ambush. Astrid led a group toward the central keep, her sword flashing as she cut through the defenders who tried to block their path. The air was thick with the scent of blood and smoke, the cries of the wounded mingling with the clash of steel.

Thorwulf stayed close, his presence a constant reassurance. At one point, he shielded her from an archer's arrow, his own axe flying through the air to silence the threat. Astrid shot him a fleeting glance, a mixture of gratitude and love.

As they neared the keep, the Jarls' personal guard emerged. They were a unit of heavily armored warriors who fought with brutal precision. The rebels faltered, their morale wavering in the face of the elite force.

"Stand your ground!" Astrid shouted, her voice rising above the din. She threw herself into the fight, her blade clashing against the guards' shields. Thorwulf was at her side, his axe splitting armor and bone with terrifying ease.

The battle raged on, the courtyard slick with blood and littered with the fallen. Astrid's arms burned with fatigue, her breaths coming in ragged gasps, but she refused to yield. This was a fight for freedom, not just survival.

Finally, the last of the guards fell, their bodies crumpling to the ground in a heap of broken steel and shattered pride. The rebels pushed forward, storming the keep as the defenders retreated deeper into the fortress.

At the heart of the keep, Astrid confronted one of the Jarls' lieutenants, a cold-eyed man with a scar that ran from his temple to his jaw. He sneered at her, his sword raised in defiance.

"You think you can defeat us?" he spat. "The Jarls are eternal. You are nothing."

Astrid's voice was steady and cold. "The Jarls are finished. Bjornhold belongs to its people now."

Their blades clashed, the force of the impact reverberating up her arm. The fight was brutal, each strike met with equal ferocity. But Astrid was faster, her movements honed by years of survival and struggle. She drove her sword through the man's chest, his sneer fading as he crumpled to the ground.

As the rebels secured the keep, a cheer rose from their ranks. It was the sound of victory, of hope. Astrid stood in the center of it all, her sword still in hand, her breath heavy but her resolve unbroken.

Thorwulf approached her, his face streaked with blood and soot but his eyes alight with pride. "You did it," he said, his voice low but filled with emotion. "We did it."

Astrid looked at him, a faint smile tugging at her lips despite the weight of exhaustion pressing down on her. "This is only the beginning," she said. "The Jarls won't stop here. Neither can we."

Thorwulf nodded, his hand resting on her shoulder. "Then we'll fight. Together."

~

The victory within the fortress was only the first step, but the toll it had already taken was staggering. Astrid stood in the keep's shadowed hall, the taste of iron heavy in her mouth as she surveyed the aftermath of the battle. Bodies, both friend and foe, lay strewn across the stone floors. The air was thick with the acrid stench of blood and sweat, the moans of the injured cutting through the low murmur of victory.

Thorwulf's voice broke through her thoughts as he strode toward her, his axe still slick with blood. His tunic was torn, a gash along his shoulder seeping crimson, but his focus remained unshaken. "The outer walls are secure," he said, his voice low but commanding. "But we've lost too many already. We need to regroup."

Astrid nodded, though the weight of the losses bore heavily on her. "How many?" she asked, her throat dry.

Thorwulf hesitated before he answered. "Eighteen dead. Another dozen wounded, some... badly."

Astrid's stomach churned, but she forced herself to hold his gaze. "And the enemy?"

"Nearly wiped out," Thorwulf replied, though his voice lacked any satisfaction. "But they fought harder than expected. If this is the resistance we're facing at one fortress, imagine what's waiting for us at the next."

The enormity of their rebellion loomed before Astrid like an unscalable mountain. This was just the beginning, and already, the cost was staggering.

"We press on," she said, her voice firmer than she felt. "We can't let their sacrifices be in vain."

Thorwulf studied her for a moment, his dark eyes searching hers. "You don't have to carry this alone, Astrid," he said quietly. "We'll find a way through this. Together."

Before she could respond, a shout echoed from the courtyard below. Both Astrid and Thorwulf turned, their weapons instinctively at the ready as they moved toward the sound. Outside, a small group of warriors huddled around one of the wounded, a young man from Frostfjord clutching at a wound on his leg as blood pooled beneath him.

"He's losing too much," one of the warriors muttered, panic lacing his voice.

"Move," Astrid commanded, pushing through the crowd. She dropped to her knees beside the boy, her hands immediately moving to press against the wound. His face was pale, his breaths shallow.

"You're going to be fine," she said, her voice steady despite the chaos around her. "Stay with me."

Thorwulf knelt beside her, pulling a strip of cloth from his belt and tying it tightly above the wound to stem the bleeding. The boy whimpered, his eyes glassy with pain.

"Thorwulf, get the healer," Astrid said, her tone sharp.

"No time," Thorwulf replied, his voice grim. "It's up to us."

Astrid didn't hesitate. With practiced precision, she worked to clean and bind the wound, her hands steady even as her mind screamed with doubt. The boy's breathing slowed, his eyes fluttering closed.

"Don't you dare give up," she whispered fiercely. "Not now. Not after all we've fought for."

Minutes stretched into an eternity, but finally, the boy's

breathing evened out. Astrid sat back, her hands trembling as the adrenaline began to fade.

"You saved him," Thorwulf said quietly, his voice filled with admiration.

Astrid shook her head, her gaze distant. "Not all of them," she murmured. Her eyes drifted to the bodies being carried out of the fortress, each one a reminder of the lives she couldn't save.

And as night fell, the rebel camp settled into an uneasy quiet. Fires flickered in the darkness, their light casting long shadows on the fortress walls. The air was thick with the scent of smoke and blood, a grim reminder of the day's events.

Astrid sat alone near one of the fires, her sword resting across her lap as she stared into the flames. The weight of leadership pressed down on her like an iron chain, each loss another link in the unyielding burden she bore.

Thorwulf approached, his steps soft on the stone. He lowered himself beside her, his presence a comforting anchor in the storm of her thoughts.

"You can't save them all, Astrid," he said gently, echoing the words he had spoken before. "No one can."

"I should be able to," she replied, her voice barely above a whisper. She turned to look at him, her eyes glistening with unshed tears. "They're counting on me. And I'm failing them."

Thorwulf reached out, his hand covering hers where it rested on her sword. "You're not failing them," he said firmly. "You're giving them hope. You're giving them a chance to fight for something better."

Astrid held his gaze, the sincerity in his eyes cutting through the fog of doubt. "And if I lead them to their deaths?" she asked. "What then?"

Thorwulf's grip tightened, his voice steady. "Then you'll have led them with honor. With courage. You've already done more for these people than the Jarls ever have. That's what matters."

For a moment, the weight lifted, the storm in her mind quieting under the warmth of his words. She leaned into him, her head resting against his shoulder as the fire crackled softly before them.

"We're not finished yet," she said, her voice resolute. "The Jarls think they can crush us, but they don't understand what they've unleashed. We'll make them see."

Thorwulf smiled faintly, his arm wrapping around her shoulders. "I never doubted it," he said. "Not for a second."

37

SKARN IN FLAMES

The sharp tang of ash hung heavy in the air, mingling with the coppery scent of blood. Skarn, the sacred island, was no longer a place of reverence and legend. Its once-majestic ruins, carved with the stories of gods and heroes, were now shrouded in fire and smoke, a battlefield littered with the bodies of the fallen.

Astrid lifted her chin, breathing the air. The distant roar of battle was a cacophony of chaos and clashing steel, underpinned by the cries of the wounded, and the bellowed commands of warriors. Beside her, Thorwulf's axe gleamed in the flickering firelight, its blade stained with the blood of their enemies.

"This is it," Thorwulf said, his voice low and steady despite the storm of violence around them. His dark eyes met hers, his expression unreadable but resolute. "The Jarls will throw everything they have at us now."

Astrid nodded, the weight of the moment pressing down on her like the mountains of Frostfjord. She took a step forward, her boots crunching against the shattered remains of an ancient mosaic beneath her feet. The image of a Valkyrie, her spear raised in triumph, seemed almost mocking now.

"Stay close," she said, her voice firm despite the tremor of fear that crept into her chest. "We finish this together."

Thorwulf gave a sharp nod, his presence beside her a steadying force. They moved as one, their steps purposeful as they pushed deeper into the heart of Skarn. Around them, their allies from Solfjord and Seastone clashed with the Jarls' elite forces of warriors clad in blackened armor, their movements precise and deadly.

Astrid's sword met the blade of one of the elite guards, the clash of steel reverberating through her bones. The guard's strength was overwhelming, but Astrid had learned to fight smarter, not harder. She shifted her weight, allowing his momentum to carry him off balance before driving her blade into the gap between his armor. The man crumpled, his lifeblood staining the sacred ground.

"Behind you!" Thorwulf's shout cut through the din, and Astrid spun just in time to block an incoming strike. The force of the blow jarred her arm, but she held firm, countering with a swift slash that found its mark. Her attacker fell, and she turned to find Thorwulf cutting down another foe with a feral roar.

The two moved like a storm, their strikes coordinated and relentless. Thorwulf's raw power complemented Astrid's agility, their partnership honed through weeks of battle. But for every enemy they felled, more seemed to rise, the Jarls' forces pouring from the ruins like an unending tide.

"We're being overrun!" Leif's voice rose above the chaos, and Astrid turned to see him fending off three guards at once. Blood streaked his face, and his movements were growing sluggish.

Astrid surged forward, her blade a blur as she joined the fray. Together, she and Leif dispatched the attackers, but not without cost. Leif staggered, clutching a wound on his side as blood seeped through his fingers.

"Get to the rear lines," Astrid ordered, her voice sharp with urgency. "We need you alive."

Leif hesitated, his pride warring with his pain, but a look from Astrid silenced his protests. With a grim nod, he retreated, leaving Astrid and Thorwulf to face the onslaught.

The fighting grew more desperate as they neared the inner sanctum, the sacred heart of Skarn where the Jarls had made their stand. The ruins around them were a maze of crumbling pillars and shadowed alcoves, every corner a potential ambush. Firelight danced across the walls, casting eerie shadows that seemed almost alive.

As they reached the final approach, a horn sounded a deep, mournful note that sent a chill down Astrid's spine. From the shadows emerged the Jarls' champions, a trio of warriors unlike any they had faced before. Clad in ceremonial armor etched with runes, their faces were obscured by helmets shaped like snarling beasts.

"Astrid of Frostfjord!" one of them called, his voice echoing across the battlefield. "You have defied the gods and the Jarls. Your rebellion ends here."

Astrid stepped forward, her sword raised as she met the man's gaze. "It ends when we say it ends," she said, her voice steady despite the tremor of fear that rippled through her.

The champions charged, their movements impossibly fast for warriors clad in heavy armor. Astrid barely had time to block the first strike, the force of it driving her back a step. Thorwulf was at her side in an instant, his axe meeting the blade of another champion with a resounding crash.

The battle was brutal and unrelenting, each clash of steel a test of their resolve. Astrid's arms burned with exhaustion, her breaths coming in ragged gasps as she fought to keep up with the champions' relentless assault. But she refused to yield, her determination burning brighter than the fires around them.

Thorwulf fought like a man possessed, his strikes ferocious and unyielding. He took a hit to the shoulder, blood staining his tunic, but he didn't falter. His axe found its mark, shattering the helm of one of the champions and sending him crumpling to the ground.

Astrid faced the final champion, her blade moving with a precision born of desperation. Their swords met in a flurry of strikes, the clash of steel ringing out like a bell. Finally, she saw her opening and drove her blade into the gap beneath his arm. The man fell, his lifeless body collapsing at her feet.

The battlefield fell silent, the flames crackling in the oppressive stillness. Astrid and Thorwulf stood amidst the carnage, their bodies battered but unbroken. Around them, their allies cheered, the sound a triumphant roar that echoed through the ruins.

But Astrid couldn't celebrate. Her gaze turned toward the sanctum ahead, where the Jarls waited. This was far from over.

Thorwulf stepped to her side, his hand resting lightly on her shoulder. "We're almost there," he said, his voice low but steady. "One final push."

Astrid nodded, her resolve hardening.

The fires of Skarn burned low, the battlefield settling into an uneasy quiet as the sounds of clashing steel and dying cries faded into memory. Astrid stood at the edge of the ruins, her gaze fixed on the sanctum that loomed before them. Her chest heaved with the effort of breathing, every muscle in her body aching from the relentless fight. The blood staining her hands and armor felt heavier than it ever had before, not just from the weight of the battle, but from the decisions that lay ahead.

Thorwulf stood beside her, his axe still in hand, though his posture had relaxed slightly. The firelight danced across his face, casting shadows over the sharp angles of his jaw and the exhaustion etched into his features. His shoulder was still bleeding from the earlier blow, but he didn't seem to notice. Or perhaps he simply didn't care.

"You're quiet," he said, his voice breaking the silence between them.

"I'm thinking," she replied, her tone distant.

Thorwulf shifted to face her fully, his dark eyes searching hers. "About what?"

She hesitated, the words caught in her throat. How could she explain the storm raging within her? The vision she'd seen in the Norn's Well, the weight of the rebellion, the uncertainty of what came next. And now... this. Her free hand drifted almost unconsciously to her stomach, the faintest gesture, but one that held a thousand unspoken truths.

"I'm thinking about what happens after this," she said finally, her voice quieter than she intended. "If there even is an after."

Thorwulf frowned, his gaze softening as he stepped closer. "There will be," he said firmly. "Because we're going to make sure of it."

Astrid turned to him, her eyes locking with his. "And what if we don't?" she asked. "What if we win this battle, but lose everything else?"

Thorwulf's expression darkened, the intensity in his eyes unwavering. "We fight because we have to," he said. "Because if we don't, we'll lose everything anyway. The Jarls won't stop until they've crushed every last bit of resistance. But you... you've given these people hope, Astrid. You've given me hope."

Her breath caught at the raw emotion in his voice, the way his words seemed to cut straight through her defenses. She wanted to believe him, to cling to the strength he offered, but the weight of her vision, with the flames, and the awful choice, refused to release its hold on her.

"Thorwulf," she began, her voice faltering. "There's something I need to tell you."

He tilted his head slightly, his expression shifting to one of concern. "What is it?"

She hesitated, her hand pressing lightly against her abdomen as if to shield the secret that lay within. The realization had come to her in the quiet moments between battles, the absence of her moon cycle a silent revelation she hadn't dared to confront until now.

"I..." She took a deep breath, the words heavy on her tongue. "I think I'm carrying your child."

The admission hung in the air between them, the weight of it settling over them like a shroud. Thorwulf's eyes widened, his lips parting as if to speak, but no words came. For a moment, the world seemed to still, the distant crackle of flames and the murmurs of the survivors fading into nothingness.

"Are you sure?" he asked finally, his voice barely more than a whisper.

Astrid nodded, her gaze dropping to the ground. "I missed my moon cycle," she said. "And I've felt... different. I didn't want to believe it, not in the middle of all this, but I can't ignore it anymore."

Thorwulf stepped closer, his hand reaching out to cup her cheek. "Astrid," he said, his voice filled with a mixture of awe and worry. "This changes everything."

She looked up at him, her eyes brimming with uncertainty. "Does it?" she asked. "We're in the middle of a war, Thorwulf. The Jarls won't care that I'm pregnant. If anything, it'll make me a bigger target."

"Then we protect you," he said without hesitation. "We protect both of you."

Astrid's emotions threatened to overwhelm her. She wanted to believe him, to let herself hope for a future where their child could grow up in a world free of the Jarls' tyranny. But the vision of Bjornhold in flames lingered in her mind, a haunting reminder of the cost of her rebellion.

"We can't think about that now," she said, her voice steady despite the storm inside her. "We have to focus on the fight ahead. The sanctum is just beyond those ruins, and the Jarls are waiting for us."

Thorwulf's hand dropped to her shoulder, his grip firm and reassuring. "Then we fight," he said. "But we fight knowing what we're fighting for."

Astrid nodded, a flicker of determination igniting in her chest. She turned toward the sanctum, her resolve hardening.

"Let's finish this," she said, her voice strong and clear.

Thorwulf smiled faintly, his axe resting against his shoulder as he fell into step beside her. Together, they moved toward the ruins, the fires of Skarn lighting their path as they prepared to face the final battle.

38

THE SACRIFICE

The fires on Skarn burned brighter now, licking the darkened sky with fingers of molten orange and gold, casting long shadows over the ruined sanctum. Smoke hung heavy in the air, choking and clinging to Astrid's skin as if it wanted to drag her down. The cries of the dying and the sharp clang of steel were a symphony of chaos, a cacophony she couldn't escape no matter how far she ran, or how hard she fought.

Thorwulf was a steady presence beside her, the heat of him a beacon in the nightmare unfolding around them. His axe was an extension of his arm, cleaving through the Jarls' elite with brutal precision. They moved as one, her sword finding openings that his brute force created, their rhythm as natural as breathing. This was what they had become. A unit, a single force in a world determined to break them apart.

But Skarn wasn't just breaking. It was crumbling, collapsing under the weight of centuries of divine wrath. The ground split in jagged lines, flames erupting from fissures as if the gods themselves were punishing them for their defiance. The sanctum stood in the distance, the last obstacle between them and the Jarls.

Astrid stole a glance at Thorwulf as they pressed forward, his face slick with sweat and blood. His jaw was tight, his dark eyes scanning the battlefield with laser focus. She wanted to tell him to stop, to rest, but she knew it was futile. Thorwulf wasn't the type to falter. Not when they were this close.

"We're almost there," he shouted over the din of battle, his voice hoarse but commanding. "Stay with me."

"I'm not going anywhere," she shot back, her breath hitching as her sword collided with another opponent's blade. The force rattled through her arms, but she twisted her wrist and drove her sword into the man's unprotected side. He crumpled, but the victory tasted like ash.

They pushed forward, inch by agonizing inch, through a tide of unrelenting enemies. The Jarls' elite were merciless, their blackened armor reflecting the firelight, their movements sharp and deliberate. Astrid's arms burned, her muscles screaming with every swing, but she refused to stop. Not when they were so close to ending this.

And then, as if summoned by her determination, the leader of the Jarls' elite forces stepped forward. He was a mountain of a man, clad in ceremonial armor engraved with runes that seemed to glow faintly in the firelight. In his hands, he held a warhammer that pulsed with power, its head crackling with what looked like lightning.

"Astrid of Frostfjord," he bellowed, his voice cutting through the chaos like a blade. "You think you can defy the gods? You are but a mortal. Today, you pay the price for your arrogance."

Astrid's heart pounded in her chest, but she raised her sword, her grip steady despite the tremor in her limbs. "I don't bow to tyrants," she spat, her voice fierce and unwavering.

The man's lips curled into a sneer before he charged, his hammer swinging in a deadly arc. Astrid barely managed to dodge, the ground where the hammer struck erupting in a spray of dirt and stone. She countered, her blade slicing toward his exposed flank, but he was faster than she anticipated, deflecting her strike with ease.

The fight was brutal. The man's blows were like thunder, each one forcing Astrid to retreat, her feet slipping on blood-slicked ground. She was fast, her agility keeping her just out of reach, but she couldn't keep this up forever.

Thorwulf's roar cut through the haze as he joined the fight, his axe colliding with the warhammer in a shower of sparks. Together, they pressed the attack, their movements a flurry of coordinated strikes. But the man was relentless, his power seemingly endless, and Astrid felt her strength waning with every second.

And then she saw the hammer arcing toward her, too fast, too sudden. She braced herself for the impact, for the pain that would surely follow.

But it never came.

Thorwulf was there, his body colliding with hers as he shoved her aside. The hammer struck him instead, the sickening crunch of bone and metal reverberating through the battlefield. Astrid hit the ground, her sword slipping from her grasp as she watched Thorwulf stagger, blood pouring from his mouth.

"No," she whispered, her voice breaking as she scrambled to her feet. "No, no, no!"

Thorwulf turned toward her, his steps faltering as he collapsed to his knees. The warhammer clattered to the ground beside him, its wielder already slain by Thorwulf's final, desperate strike.

Astrid was at his side in an instant, her hands trembling as she cradled his broken body. Blood stained his tunic, the wound gaping and unforgiving, but his eyes found hers, dark and steady even in the face of death.

"You're okay," she said, her voice frantic as tears streamed down her face. "You're going to be okay. We'll get you to a healer. Just... just stay with me."

Thorwulf smiled faintly, his hand reaching up to brush her cheek. "You always were a terrible liar," he murmured, his voice weak but laced with affection.

"Don't do this," Astrid begged, her sobs choking her words. "Don't you dare leave me, Thorwulf."

His grip on her hand tightened for a brief moment, his gaze softening. "You're stronger than this," he said. "Stronger than me. You'll finish this, Astrid. You'll win."

She shook her head, her heart breaking with every word he spoke. "Not without you," she whispered. "I can't do this without you."

"You can," he said firmly, though his voice was barely more than a whisper. "You will. For Bjornhold. For our child."

His words shattered her, the weight of them almost too much to bear. "I love you," she said, her voice breaking as she leaned closer, her forehead resting against his.

"And I love you," he whispered. "Always."

His eyes closed, his hand falling limp in hers. The world seemed to stop, the fires of Skarn flickering as if even the gods mourned his passing. Astrid's scream tore through the silence, a raw, anguished sound that shook the battlefield.

She held him for what felt like an eternity, her tears soaking into his bloodied tunic. But the battle wasn't over. The sanctum still stood, the Jarls still held their power. And Thorwulf's sacrifice would mean nothing if she didn't see this through.

With trembling hands, she laid him down gently, her fingers brushing over his bloodstained cheek one last time. Then she stood, her sword gleaming in the firelight as she turned toward the sanctum. This battle would end here.

The fires of Skarn smoldered in the distance, casting shadows over the ruins. The battlefield was silent now, save for the low groans of the wounded and the occasional crackle of fire as it consumed what was left of the sanctum. The air was thick with the scent of smoke and blood, clinging to Astrid's skin, her hair, her very soul.

She knelt beside Thorwulf's lifeless body, her hand resting on his bloodstained chest. His axe lay beside him, the weapon that had felled so many enemies now still, its blade dulled by ash and grime. Astrid's fingers trembled as she brushed a strand of dark hair from his face, her heart aching with every beat. She didn't cry anymore. There were simply no tears left. Just an unbearable hollow ache that threatened to consume her.

Around her, the remnants of her army stood silently, their gazes averted, their weapons lowered. The Jarls' forces had been defeated, their banners trampled into the dirt, their power shattered. Skarn belonged to Astrid now, but it felt like a hollow victory. She had won the war, but she had lost the man who had made the fight worth enduring.

"Astrid," Leif's voice broke through the silence, soft and cautious. He stood a few paces away, his face streaked with dirt and exhaustion. "We need you. The others... they're looking to you for what comes next."

She didn't answer, her gaze fixed on Thorwulf's face. He looked almost peaceful, as though he were merely sleeping, but the blood soaking his tunic told a different story. Her hand drifted to her stomach, where a new life grew. A life she hadn't even known to dream of until now. How was she supposed to lead a people, to rebuild a broken Bjornhold, when the weight of grief threatened to crush her?

The world around her seemed to dim, the edges of her vision blurring as a chill swept over the battlefield. The flames flickered and dimmed, the air growing heavy with an unnatural stillness. Astrid's breath hitched as a figure emerged from the shadows, her presence otherworldly and undeniable.

The Valkyrie.

Her armor gleamed like polished silver, etched with runes that seemed to pulse with an inner light. Her wings, black as midnight, arched high above her, their feathers shifting like smoke. Her eyes burned with an intensity that pierced through Astrid, her gaze both judgmental and curious.

"You fought well," the Valkyrie said, her voice resonating like the toll of a distant bell. "The gods have watched, and they have seen your strength."

Astrid rose slowly, her legs unsteady as she faced the divine figure. She tightened her grip on Thorwulf's axe, her knuckles white. "What do you want?" she asked, her voice hoarse but steady.

The Valkyrie's lips curved into the faintest hint of a smile. "You have defied the gods and proven your worth, mortal. And so, I offer you a choice."

Astrid's breath caught, her heart pounding in her chest. "A choice?"

The Valkyrie inclined her head, her gaze flickering to Thorwulf's body. "Your love's sacrifice has earned him a place among the honored dead. His soul awaits in the halls of Valhalla, where the brave and the fallen feast for eternity. You may join him, Astrid of Frostfjord. Leave this mortal realm behind and find peace in the afterlife."

The words hung in the air, heavy with promise and temptation. Astrid's gaze fell to Thorwulf, her heart aching at the thought of being with him again, of leaving behind the pain and struggle of this world to rest in his arms. But then her hand drifted to her stomach once more, her fingers brushing against the faint curve there.

"And if I don't?" she asked, her voice barely more than a whisper.

The Valkyrie's expression grew solemn. "If you choose to remain, your path will not be easy. The gods are not kind to those who defy their will. You will face trials beyond imagining, and your life will be one of sacrifice and hardship. But you will protect the legacy he left behind." Her gaze dropped pointedly to Astrid's stomach. "The choice is yours."

Astrid closed her eyes, the weight of the decision pressing down on her like a physical force. She thought of Thorwulf, of his smile, his laugh, the way he had always looked at her as though she were the only thing that mattered. She thought of the child growing within her, a piece of him that would live on, that would carry his strength and courage into the future.

"I can't leave," she said finally, her voice trembling but resolute. "Not yet. Not while there's still so much to do. Thorwulf's sacrifice has to mean something. Our child... they need me."

The Valkyrie studied her for a long moment, her expression unreadable. Then she nodded, a flicker of approval in her gaze. "So be it. But know this, Astrid of Frostfjord: the gods do not forget. Your defiance will have consequences."

Astrid lifted her chin, her resolve solidifying. "Let them come," she said. "I'll face whatever they throw at me. For Thorwulf. For our child. For Bjornhold."

The Valkyrie's wings unfurled, her form dissolving into a swirl of smoke and light that disappeared into the night. The battlefield was silent once more, the air heavy with the weight of what had just transpired.

Astrid knelt beside Thorwulf one last time, her hand resting gently on his chest. "I'll keep fighting," she whispered, her voice breaking. "For both of us."

She rose to her feet, her gaze turning toward her waiting people. They needed a leader now more than ever. And though her heart was shattered, though the grief threatened to consume her, she would lead them. She would build a world where her child could grow up free, where Thorwulf's sacrifice would never be forgotten.

With Thorwulf's axe in her hand and a fire burning in her heart, Astrid turned toward the future. The gods may have demanded blood, but she would give them something far greater: a legacy.

39

VICTORY AND LOSS

The echoes of war clung to the air, a haunting reminder of the cost of victory. The ruins of Skarn were eerily silent now, the fires reduced to smoldering embers that cast a faint orange glow across the broken battlefield. Astrid stood at the center of it all, the weight of triumph pressing heavy on her shoulders. Around her, the remaining warriors of the clans murmured quietly, their eyes filled with a mixture of awe, grief, and exhaustion.

Astrid griped Thorwulf's axe, the familiar weight a comfort and a curse. The weapon was stained with the blood of their enemies, a testament to the countless lives it had claimed in their pursuit of freedom. But every swing, every success, had come at a price.

Thorwulf's absence was a gaping wound, one that no amount of cheering or victory songs could fill.

"Astrid of Frostfjord!" a voice called, breaking through the hushed silence.

She turned slowly, her gaze landing on Leif, who stood atop a makeshift platform of stone and rubble. His face was streaked with soot and blood, but his voice carried strength as he addressed the gathered clans.

"Today, we stand victorious!" Leif declared, his voice rising with each word. "The Jarls have been defeated, their tyranny broken. And it is because of her. Astrid, our shield, our sword, and our leader."

The crowd erupted into cheers, the sound echoing off the jagged cliffs that bordered the ruins. Astrid felt their eyes on her, their gratitude and admiration palpable, but it didn't ease the ache in her chest. She raised her hand in acknowledgment, the motion stiff and mechanical.

Leif stepped down, approaching her with a cautious smile. "They need this," he said softly. "They need you."

"I know," Astrid replied, her voice hoarse. She looked out over the crowd, her people, and forced herself to meet their gazes. "But it doesn't feel like a win."

Leif's expression softened, his usual sharp tongue absent in the face of her grief. "It never does," he said quietly. "Not when it costs so much."

Astrid nodded, the weight of his words settling over her like a shroud. Her gaze drifted to the horizon, where the sea met the sky in a blur of gray and gold. Somewhere beyond those waters, Thorwulf's soul rested in Valhalla, feasting among the honored dead. The thought was both a comfort and a torment.

"Your child will know what he gave for this," Leif said, his voice steady. "We'll make sure of it."

Astrid placed a hand on her stomach, her heart twisting with the duality of joy and sorrow. Thorwulf's sacrifice had given them this moment, this fragile chance at rebuilding Bjornhold. But the thought of raising their child without him, of never seeing his face light up at the sight of their family, was a pain she couldn't put into words.

"Come," Leif said, gesturing toward the crowd. "They're waiting for you."

Astrid hesitated, her feet feeling as though they were rooted to the ground. But then she straightened, drawing on the strength that Thorwulf had always seen in her. She stepped forward, the axe heavy in her hand, and addressed the gathered clans.

"We have won," she began, her voice carrying over the crowd. "But this is only the beginning. Bjornhold is ours now, and it is up to us to decide what we make of it. We cannot go back to the ways of the Jarls, to the greed and the tyranny that nearly destroyed us. We must be better."

The crowd murmured in agreement, their expressions solemn. Astrid continued, her gaze sweeping over the faces of those who had fought and bled beside her.

"We will honor those we lost," she said, her voice breaking slightly. "And we will carry their memories with us as we rebuild. This land belongs to us now, and we will protect it for them, and for those who come after us."

The cheers were quieter this time, more subdued, but they carried a deeper weight. Astrid nodded once, signaling to Leif that she was finished. As the crowd began to disperse, she turned back toward the ruins, her heart heavy.

She found herself wandering to the edge of the battlefield, where the remnants of their camp still stood. The tent she and Thorwulf had shared was there, its canvas scorched and torn but still standing. She stepped inside, the familiar scent of leather and steel washing over her like a wave.

Astrid sank to her knees, the weight of the day finally catching up to her. She placed Thorwulf's axe on the ground beside her, her fingers tracing the worn handle. "I hope you're watching," she whispered, her voice trembling. "Because I'm going to make sure your sacrifice wasn't in vain."

The tears came then, silent and unrelenting, as she allowed herself to grieve the man she had loved, the man who had fought beside her until the very end. She stayed there until the sun dipped below the horizon, her heart heavy but resolute.

When she finally rose, the axe in her hand and the weight of her grief tucked away in the corners of her mind, she knew one thing for certain: Thorwulf's legacy would live on. In their child. In Bjornhold. And in her.

~

The pyre was built with care, the wood stacked high and laced with herbs to send Thorwulf's spirit to the gods with honor. The clans gathered in solemn silence, a circle of warriors, elders, and children standing shoulder to shoulder under the slate-gray sky. The wind was a mournful wail through the jagged cliffs, carrying with it the faint scent of salt from the distant sea. Astrid stood at the edge of the pyre, her cloak pulled tightly around her, the bitter chill of the mountain air sinking into her bones.

Thorwulf's body rested atop the wood, his arms crossed over his chest, his axe laid beside him. A warrior's farewell. He looked almost at peace, as though he might wake at any moment and flash her that crooked grin she'd grown to love. But she knew better. Thorwulf was gone, and all that remained was the shell of the man who had given everything for Bjornhold.

Astrid's fingers curled around the hilt of his second axe, the one she had taken as her own. Its weight was unfamiliar in her hand, a reminder that Thorwulf would no longer be there to wield it. She swallowed hard, forcing down the grief that threatened to consume her, and took a step forward.

"Thorwulf of Frostfjord," she began, her voice steady despite the tremor in her chest. "A warrior, a leader, a man who gave his life so that we could stand here today, free. He fought with honor, with courage, and with a heart that never wavered."

The crowd murmured in agreement, their faces etched with

sorrow. Leif stood nearby, his arms crossed tightly over his chest, his expression unreadable. Members of Solfjord and Seastone stood alongside them, their presence a testament to the alliances Thorwulf had helped forge.

Astrid continued, her gaze never leaving Thorwulf's still form. "He was more than a warrior. He was a friend, a protector, and the love of my life. His sacrifice will not be forgotten. Not by me, not by any of us."

Her voice cracked on the last word, but she pressed on, drawing strength from the weight of her grief. "We will honor him by building the Bjornhold he dreamed of. A land where the strong protect the weak, where clans stand together, not divided. That is his legacy."

She stepped back, the tears she had fought so hard to hold back slipping down her cheeks. Leif stepped forward then, his expression softening as he placed a hand on her shoulder. For once, he said nothing, his presence a quiet reassurance.

An elder stepped forward, a torch in hand, the flame flickering in the cold wind. He turned to Astrid, his gaze heavy with meaning. "It is your right," he said, offering her the torch.

Astrid hesitated, her hand trembling as she reached for it. The weight of the moment pressed down on her, the finality of it stealing the breath from her lungs. She stepped closer to the pyre, the warmth of the fire licking at her skin, and held the torch aloft.

"For Thorwulf," she whispered, her voice carrying over the silent crowd. "May the gods welcome him with open arms."

With a deep breath, she touched the flame to the wood, the dry timber catching immediately. The fire spread quickly, engulfing the herbs and kindling, the flames rising high into the sky. Astrid stepped back, her gaze fixed on the pyre as the heat washed over her, her tears falling freely now.

The crowd began to chant, a low, mournful hymn that rose

and fell like the waves of the sea. The sound wrapped around Astrid, a collective expression of grief and reverence. She closed her eyes, the image of Thorwulf's face burned into her mind, and whispered a silent prayer.

"Watch over us," she said. "Watch over me. And know that I will protect what you've given me. Our child will know who you were."

The flames roared higher, the smoke curling into the sky like a beacon. Astrid stayed until the fire burned low, the warmth giving way to the biting chill of the night. When the last embers faded, she turned to the crowd, her expression hardened with resolve.

"We move forward," she said, her voice steady. "For Thorwulf. For all of them."

The clans nodded, their faces solemn but resolute. As they began to disperse, Astrid lingered by the remains of the pyre, the smell of ash and charred wood heavy in the air. She placed a hand on her stomach, her heart aching with both grief and hope.

"I'll keep us safe," she whispered. "I promise."

The wind carried her words away, the cliffs echoing with their weight. And as the first stars appeared in the sky, Astrid turned and walked toward the future, Thorwulf's axe heavy in her hand and his memory burning brightly in her heart.

40

THE NEW ORDER

The hall was a far cry from the Jarls' grand sanctum on Skarn, but its simplicity suited Astrid's vision for Bjornhold's future. Built from sturdy timber hewn from Frostfjord's icy forests, the gathering hall stood as a testament to resilience and renewal. The long tables were lined with representatives from each of the clans, their faces reflecting a mix of curiosity, wariness, and thinly veiled dissent. Outside, the wind howled across the cliffs, carrying with it the salt of the sea and the promise of an uncertain future.

Astrid sat at the head of the central table, her cloak of thick gray wolf fur draped over her shoulders. Thorwulf's axe rested against her chair, its presence both a comfort and a reminder of the price that had been paid to bring them all here. Beneath the heavy fabric of her tunic, her rounded belly pressed against the table's edge, a quiet symbol of the legacy she carried. Six months along now, the child was a constant, grounding presence, even as the weight of leadership pressed down on her.

"Let us begin," she said, her voice steady as it carried across the room. The murmurs of conversation quieted, all eyes turning to her.

Leif, seated to her right, leaned forward, his expression guarded. He had grown quieter in the months following Thorwulf's death, his sharp tongue tempered by the gravity of the rebellion and its aftermath. He gave her a small nod, an unspoken assurance that she wasn't alone.

Astrid's gaze swept the room, taking in the faces of Solfjord's wealthy merchants, Seastone's shrewd sailors, Ironcrag's hardened warriors, and her own Frostfjord's resilient leaders. They were here, together, but the cracks in their unity were already beginning to show.

"We stand here today because we chose to fight for a different Bjornhold," Astrid began. "The Reckoning is over. The Jarls are defeated. But the battle we face now is far greater. How to rebuild a fractured land."

Her words hung in the air, met with a ripple of agreement from some and stony silence from others. An elder from Ironcrag, his beard streaked with silver, crossed his arms over his chest. "And what does this new Bjornhold look like, Astrid of Frostfjord? A land where warriors no longer test their worth? Where the gods themselves are defied?"

Astrid met his gaze unflinchingly. "A land where no child is sent to die for the gods' amusement," she replied. "Where clans are not pitted against each other in bloodsport. We will honor the gods in ways that do not demand sacrifice. The Reckoning is abolished, effective immediately."

The hall erupted into noise. Some voices were raised in support, others in anger. A merchant from Solfjord stood, his face flushed. "And who decides this?" he demanded. "You? Frostfjord has gained much in this rebellion, but the rest of us have paid just as dearly. What makes you the one to dictate the future?"

"I am not dictating anything," Astrid said firmly, rising to her feet. The room quieted as her presence commanded attention. "This council is not about one clan's rule over another. From this day forward, Bjornhold will be governed by all of us, equally. Each clan will have a voice. No single leader. No single ruler."

A ripple of shock ran through the room, the very idea a sharp departure from the centuries of rule under the Jarls. Some faces softened with intrigue, while others hardened with distrust.

"You expect Ironcrag to share power with the likes of Seastone?" the elder from Ironcrag scoffed. "Their 'cleverness' is nothing more than trickery."

"And you expect Frostfjord to relinquish the strength we fought so hard to gain?" another voice chimed in, this time from her own clan. "We bled for this victory, Astrid. For you. And now we are to hand it away?"

Astrid took a deep breath, steadying herself before speaking. "We bled because the old ways tore us apart. If we continue down that path, nothing will change. The Jarls' tyranny is gone, but if we let greed and mistrust replace it, we will fall into the same cycle. This is our chance to build something better for our children."

The mention of children seemed to resonate, murmurs rippling through the room as her hand instinctively brushed against her belly. She pressed on. "This council is a beginning, not an end. Every clan will have a seat, and decisions will be made together. If you want to protect your people, then work with us."

Leif stood then, his voice cutting through the tension. "Astrid's right. We didn't fight for one clan to rule another, we fought for all of Bjornhold. And if you think she's giving up Frostfjord's strength, you don't know her."

A few chuckles broke the tension, but the unease lingered. Astrid scanned the room, noting the subtle shifts in posture, the whispers exchanged behind cupped hands. The elder from Ironcrag leaned back in his chair, his expression unreadable.

"This council is fragile," he said after a long pause. "The bonds between our clans are weaker than you'd like to believe, Astrid. Your vision may hold for now, but storms come quickly in Bjornhold."

"They do," Astrid agreed, her gaze steady. "But we're stronger together than apart. And I'd rather face the storm united than see us torn apart again."

The elder grunted, neither agreeing nor opposing, and Astrid took it as a small victory. As the council began to discuss the details of the new order, like seats, decisions, and trade, Astrid's mind wandered briefly to Thorwulf. He would have loved this, she thought. The chaos, the defiance, the hope.

The meeting stretched into the night, and when it was over, Astrid stood on the steps of the hall, watching as the representatives returned to their camps. The air was sharp with frost, the stars scattered across the sky like shards of ice.

Leif joined her, his breath visible in the cold. "You think it'll hold?" he asked, his voice low.

"I don't know," Astrid admitted, her hand resting on her stomach. "But it has to. For them."

Leif followed her gaze to the distant fires of the camps, his expression thoughtful. "They'll test you," he said. "All of them. You know that, right?"

"They can try," Astrid said, her voice firm. "But I'll fight for this. For him, for Bjornhold, for all of it."

~

The transition to rebuilding was as harsh and relentless as the winds that swept through Bjornhold. Beneath the jagged mountains and rolling plains, the clans worked tirelessly to forge the new world Astrid had envisioned. The scars of war were everywhere. In the charred remains of fortresses, the broken blades scattered across battlefields, and the faces of those who had lost family. But there was also resilience, a flicker of hope in the midst of the chaos.

Astrid stood at the edge of Frostfjord's central village, watching as wooden beams were raised into place for a new hall. The air was alive with the sound of hammers and saws, mingled with the hum of voices. Seastone's carpenters worked alongside Frostfjord's hunters, while Solfjord's merchants bartered supplies in exchange for labor. It was a fragile harmony, but a step forward.

The village itself was changing, taking on a new shape under Astrid's leadership. The once-scattered longhouses were being rebuilt closer together, forming a communal square at the heart of Frostfjord. Astrid had insisted on the design, envisioning a place where all could gather and where decisions would be made openly, and no one would hold power in the shadows.

Near the edge of the square, Astrid's own home had been restored. It was modest compared to the chieftain's quarters she could have claimed, but that suited her just fine. Inside, her father and sister awaited her return, their presence a quiet comfort amidst the weight of her responsibilities.

Her father, Sigurd, had taken on a new energy since Thorwulf's death. While he still bore the grief of losing his wife years earlier, helping Astrid seemed to give him purpose. He spent his days repairing fishing nets, mentoring younger men in the village, and keeping an eye on her growing belly with a mix of pride and worry.

Her sister, Solveig, had also found her place in the new Frostfjord. Though her legs would never carry her into battle, her sharp mind and steady hands had earned her respect among the villagers. She often worked late into the night, carving intricate designs into the beams of the new hall. Her work was a reminder that beauty could rise from the ashes of war.

As Astrid approached her home, Solveig waved her over, her face lighting up with a smile. “You’ve been on your feet too long today,” she chided, though her tone was teasing. “Come sit before the little one decides to protest.”

Astrid smiled faintly, placing a hand on her belly. “The little one has been protesting all day,” she admitted, settling onto a bench beside her sister. “But there’s too much to do.”

Solveig handed her a carved piece of wood, its edges smooth and polished. “I’ve been working on this for the cradle,” she said. “It’s not finished yet, but...”

“It’s perfect,” Astrid interrupted, her voice soft. She traced the lines of the carving, a design that resembled the waves of the sea and the mountains of Frostfjord. “Thank you, Solveig.”

She shrugged, a faint blush creeping up her neck. “It’s the least I can do.”

Their father appeared then, carrying a basket of freshly caught fish. “You’re still working,” he said, his tone more scolding than Solveig’s. “You need rest, Astrid.”

“I need answers more,” Astrid replied, though her voice lacked the sharpness it once held. She glanced toward the square, where the new council hall was beginning to take shape. “The clans are uneasy. Some think the changes are too fast. Others think they’re too slow.”

Sigurd set the basket down and joined her on the bench. “Change was never going to be easy,” he said. “But you’re doing what needs to be done. That’s all anyone can ask.”

Astrid nodded, though doubt gnawed at her. The council’s formation had been a victory, but it was far from secure. Seastone and Solfjord were eager to embrace the new system, seeing opportunity in unity. Ironcrag, however, was less convinced, its leaders wary of relinquishing the strength they had wielded for generations.

"They'll come around," Solveig said, as though reading her thoughts. "They have to. The alternative is chaos, and no one wants that. Not after what we've been through."

Astrid wasn't so sure. The traditions of Bjornhold ran deep, and there were those who clung to the old ways with a ferocity that rivaled the fiercest storm. But she couldn't let that deter her. The future of her child, and of Bjornhold, depended on her resolve.

As the evening wore on, Astrid made her way to the square, where a gathering of clan representatives awaited her. They stood around a fire pit, their faces illuminated by the flickering flames. The air was thick with tension, but also with possibility.

"The new hall will be completed within the week," Astrid announced, her voice steady despite her fatigue. "It will serve as a place for all clans to meet, to make decisions together."

"And who will enforce those decisions?" asked an elder from Ironcrag, his tone skeptical. "What happens when one clan defies the council?"

"We will hold each other accountable," Astrid replied. "Through dialogue, through compromise. The days of one clan ruling over the others are gone. We all rise, or we all fall."

The elder frowned, but another voice spoke up. It was a young woman from Seastone. "I believe in this," she said. "I've seen what we can accomplish when we work together. Frostfjord stood against the Jarls, and we all followed. Now it's time for us to lead."

Murmurs of agreement rippled through the crowd, though the elder remained silent. Astrid met his gaze, her own unflinching. "The clans united to defeat the Jarls," she said. "That was just the beginning. If we want Bjornhold to thrive, we must keep that unity alive."

As the meeting continued, Astrid felt a flicker of hope. The road ahead was long, and the challenges were many, but she was no longer walking it alone. The clans were learning to trust one another, to build a future that honored their differences while embracing their common ground.

And as the stars emerged in the night sky, Astrid allowed herself a moment of quiet. She placed a hand on her belly, her heart aching with the loss of Thorwulf but filled with determination.

"For you," she whispered. "For all of us."

41

THE RUNE NECKLACE

Astrid traced the rough lines of the runes carved into the smooth, weathered wood of the necklace. The light from the hearth flickered across her fingers, casting dancing shadows on the walls of her small, sturdy longhouse. She sat in the quiet, the only sound the faint crackle of flames and the muted roar of the sea beyond the cliffs. Her belly, swollen and heavy with the weight of new life, pressed against the fabric of her tunic. Each movement of the child within her was a sharp reminder of everything she had gained and lost.

The necklace had been tucked away in a wooden chest for months, forgotten in the chaos of rebellion, rebuilding, and grief. But tonight, as she sifted through the remnants of a life that no longer existed, her fingers had closed around the familiar shape. Its presence felt heavier than she remembered, as though the runes themselves bore the weight of the past.

Leif had given it to her the day she volunteered for the Reckoning. She had dismissed it then, brushing aside the meaning behind his gift, but now, as she sat in the quiet glow of her hearth, the memory of that moment washed over her with startling clarity.

"I made it for you," he'd said, holding out the necklace with a mixture of pride and desperation. The carved runes had been a prayer for her survival, a plea to the gods to spare her life. She had scoffed at the gesture, her focus solely on protecting her sister. But now, the memory of his face, so open, so full of fear, stabbed at her chest.

Astrid ran her thumb over the central rune, its edges smoothed by time and wear. She recognized it now: Algiz, the symbol of protection. Her lips twisted into a bitter smile. Protection. The irony of it was not lost on her. How many had been lost along the way? How many sacrifices had been made for the fragile peace she now fought so hard to protect?

Her father's voice broke the silence. "You've been sitting there for hours."

She glanced up to see Sigurd leaning against the doorway, his broad frame silhouetted against the dim light. His face was lined with age and grief, but there was a softness in his eyes that hadn't been there before. He had changed, just as they all had, the weight of leadership forcing them to become something more than what they once were.

"I didn't realize how late it was," Astrid admitted, her voice low. She held up the necklace, the runes catching the firelight. "Do you remember this?"

Sigurd stepped closer, his gaze falling to the necklace in her hand. He nodded slowly. "Leif's work. I remember. He carved it for you before you left for the Reckoning."

"It feels like a lifetime ago," she said, her thumb tracing the lines of the runes once more. "I thought it was just a silly trinket then. But now..."

She didn't finish the thought, letting the silence fill the space between them. Sigurd pulled up a stool and sat across from her, his weathered hands clasped in front of him. "Things always look different when you've walked through the fire," he said. "What seemed small before... it has a way of growing in meaning."

Astrid nodded, the weight of his words settling over her. She looked down at the necklace again, her mind drifting to Thorwulf. He had never seen it, never asked about it. He had understood her in a way few others had, but there had always been parts of her – small, hidden pieces – that even he hadn't reached.

"Do you think the gods are still watching us?" she asked suddenly, the question tumbling from her lips before she could stop it.

Sigurd tilted his head, considering her words. "I think they always have been," he said. "But whether they approve of what we've done... that's another question entirely."

Astrid's hand moved instinctively to her belly, the child within her kicking in response. "I don't know if I care anymore," she said softly. "I used to believe they held all the power. But now, I wonder if it's us who hold the power to shape our fate."

Sigurd's eyes softened, and he reached out to place a hand over hers. "You've already shaped it, Astrid. You've done what no one else could. The clans are rebuilding because of you."

"And because of Thorwulf," she added, her voice barely above a whisper. "I couldn't have done this without him."

Her father didn't argue, his silence an acknowledgment of the truth in her words. They sat like that for a while, the fire crackling between them, the weight of their shared loss hanging in the air.

When Sigurd finally stood, he placed a hand on her shoulder, his grip firm but comforting. "Get some rest," he said. "The council meets tomorrow, and they'll be looking to you for answers."

Astrid nodded, watching as he left the room. She turned the necklace over in her hands once more before slipping it over her head. The carved wood rested against her chest, its warmth a small comfort against the cold.

As she lay back on her bed, the fire casting shadows across the walls, she closed her eyes and let herself drift. For the first time in weeks, her dreams weren't filled with battle or loss. Instead, she saw a future. One where her child ran through the square of Frostfjord, where the clans stood together in peace.

And in the distance, she thought she heard Thorwulf's voice, a soft whisper carried on the wind: *You're stronger than you know.*

The early morning light seeped through the cracks in the wooden shutters, painting the room in soft hues of gold and amber. The fire in the hearth had dwindled to embers, its warmth barely reaching the corners of the room. Astrid stirred on the worn fur blankets, the weight of her pregnancy making her movements slow and deliberate. Her hand instinctively rested on her swollen belly, and as she sat up, the rune-carved necklace shifted against her chest.

The knock at the door was light but firm. Before she could answer, it creaked open, revealing Leif. He stood hesitantly, his frame filling the doorway. His hair was longer than she remembered, tied back in a leather cord, and there was a nervous energy in the way his hands lingered at his sides.

"You're up early," she said, her voice soft but steady.

"I figured you might need someone to walk with you to the square," he replied, stepping inside and shutting the door against the chill. His eyes flicked briefly to the necklace around her neck before meeting hers. "You've been overworking yourself again."

Astrid gave a small, wry smile, shifting to stand. "I'm fine, Leif. The council doesn't leave much room for rest."

"You don't have to carry it all alone," he said, his tone more insistent this time. He stepped closer, his presence grounding and familiar. "You never did, Astrid. You just never let anyone help you."

Her smile faded, replaced by a flicker of guilt. She turned away, her hand brushing the edge of the table. "I couldn't afford to let anyone in," she admitted quietly. "Not when everything was so fragile."

Leif's voice softened. "It's not fragile anymore. The clans are rebuilding, thanks to you. And you've lost so much. Thorwulf..."

His name hung between them, a heavy presence that neither dared to disturb for too long. Leif exhaled slowly, his eyes dropping to the floor. "I just don't want you to lose yourself in all this."

She turned back to him, her gaze steady. "I'm trying, Leif. It's just... hard to know where to start."

Leif reached out then, his hand brushing against her shoulder. "Start here," he said simply. "With the people who've always stood by you."

Astrid nodded. There was a warmth in Leif's touch, a reminder that not everything in her life had been lost. Perhaps, in time, she could rebuild more than just the village. Perhaps she could rebuild the bonds she had neglected, the ones that had never truly broken, despite everything.

Before she could reply, a sharp, unfamiliar pain ripped through her, doubling her over. Her hand flew to her belly, her breath coming in short gasps.

"Astrid?" Leif's voice was panicked, his hands steadying her. "What's wrong?"

"The baby," she gasped, clutching his arm. "It's time."

Leif didn't hesitate. He called for Sigurd, his voice echoing through the quiet morning. Within moments, her father was at her side, his face pale but determined as he helped Leif guide her to the bed. The room became a flurry of movement, her father's steady voice a lifeline as Leif fetched water and cloths.

The hours stretched into what felt like an eternity. The pain was relentless, but Astrid bore it with the same resilience that had carried her through every battle. Sigurd stayed by her side, his weathered hands never letting go of hers. Leif moved with surprising calm, his earlier nervousness replaced by a quiet determination.

When the cries of the newborn finally filled the room, Astrid's exhaustion melted into overwhelming relief. Sigurd handed her the baby, his eyes misted with emotion. Astrid cradled the tiny, wriggling boy against her chest, tears streaming down her face as she looked down at him.

He had Thorwulf's dark hair, his strong features softened by the innocence of infancy. Astrid pressed a trembling kiss to his forehead, her heart breaking and mending all at once.

"Wulf," she whispered, her voice thick with emotion. "His name is Wulf."

Leif, standing at the edge of the room, smiled faintly. "It suits him," he said softly, his voice carrying a mixture of pride and the quiet acceptance of his place in her life, whatever that might be.

Astrid looked up at her father, who nodded, his own tears glistening in the firelight. "Thorwulf would be proud," Sigurd said, his voice steady but filled with unspoken grief.

The weight of the moment settled over them all. For the first time in what felt like forever, Astrid allowed herself to feel hope. As Wulf nestled against her, his tiny hand grasping her finger, she felt a sense of purpose more profound than anything she had known.

She had lost so much, but in this small, fragile life, she saw a future worth fighting for. With Leif's quiet support and her father's unwavering strength, Astrid knew she wasn't alone. Together, they would rebuild Bjornhold, not just for the clans, but for Wulf, and for the legacy Thorwulf had left behind.

The wind outside howled through the cliffs, carrying with it the promise of a new dawn.

42

THE FLAME ENDURES

The wind whipped across the cliffs of Frostfjord, carrying with it the briny tang of the sea. Waves crashed against the jagged rocks far below, their relentless rhythm echoing the beating of Astrid's heart. She stood at the edge, her boots firmly planted on the frosted ground, her long braid tangled by the breeze. The air was sharp and cold, but she barely felt it. The warmth of the tiny bundle in her arms anchored her against the chill.

Wulf stirred, his small, delicate fingers curling against the soft wool of the blanket she had wrapped him in. Astrid's hand gently smoothed the dark tuft of hair on his head, a bittersweet ache blooming in her chest. He looked so much like Thorwulf, and yet, there was a piece of her in him too. He was a blend of their love, their strength, their sacrifice.

The village behind her hummed with the sounds of rebuilding. The clang of hammers, the murmur of voices, and the occasional laughter of children carried on the wind. Frostfjord had endured, battered but unbroken. Its people had risen from the ashes of war, piecing their lives back together with the determination that had always defined them.

Astrid tilted her head to the sky, her breath misting in the frigid air. Above, the clouds parted, revealing a pale sun that cast its golden light over the sea. She thought of Thorwulf, of the life they had dreamed of building together. The pain of his loss was still fresh, an open wound that throbbed with every heartbeat. But standing here, with their son in her arms and the promise of a new Bjornhold taking shape behind her, she felt a flicker of something she hadn't allowed herself to feel in weeks.

Hope.

"You'll be proud of him," she murmured, her voice nearly lost to the wind. "I'll make sure of it."

Wulf's small, sleepy face turned toward her at the sound of her voice, and a soft smile tugged at her lips. She pressed a kiss to his forehead, her tears falling unbidden onto the blanket. "He'll grow up in a better Bjornhold," she said, her words firm despite the lump in her throat. "A Bjornhold where no one has to fight to prove their worth. Where no one has to lose what I lost."

The sound of footsteps drew her attention, and she turned to see her father, Sigurd, approaching. His broad shoulders seemed less weighed down than before, and there was a softness in his weathered face that she hadn't seen in years. He stopped a few paces away, his gaze falling to the baby in her arms.

"Wulf looks strong," he said, his voice warm and steady. "Just like his mother."

Astrid smiled faintly, shifting Wulf slightly to ease the ache in her arms. "He'll need to be. There's still so much to rebuild."

Sigurd nodded, his gaze drifting out over the sea. "But you've given them something to believe in," he said. "That's more than most can say."

She followed his gaze, her mind turning to the clans that had banded together under her leadership. Solfjord, Seastone, even parts of Ironcrag. Each had played a part in overthrowing the Jarls, and each had a stake in the future they were building. It wasn't perfect. There were still those who resisted the changes, who clung to the old ways with a stubbornness born of fear. But the flames of rebellion had ignited an unyielding desire for a better tomorrow.

"Do you think they'll remember?" she asked, her voice barely above a whisper. "Everything we sacrificed to get here?"

Sigurd's hand rested gently on her shoulder, grounding her. "They'll remember," he said. "Because you won't let them forget."

Astrid glanced back at the village, her eyes lingering on the new council hall rising in the center of the square. It was a symbol of everything they had fought for. It was a place where every voice could be heard, where decisions would be made not by the whims of a few but by the will of many.

As she turned her gaze back to the horizon, a sudden gust of wind caught the edge of her cloak, sending it billowing behind her like wings. She held Wulf closer, his tiny warmth against her chest a reminder of the future she was fighting for. The sun dipped lower, casting long shadows across the cliffs, but its light remained, stubborn and unyielding.

"We'll endure," she said softly, the words more for herself than anyone else. "Just like the flame."

Sigurd nodded, his expression one of quiet pride. "You've always been the strongest of us," he said. "And now, so is he."

Astrid smiled, a genuine, aching smile that felt like the first crack of light after a long, dark storm. She reached up to touch the rune-carved necklace around her neck, the familiar weight of it grounding her in the present while tying her to the past. Wulf stirred again, his small hand clutching at the edge of her cloak, and she kissed his forehead once more.

The wind grew quieter, as if the very earth was holding its breath. Astrid stood still, her gaze fixed on the horizon, where the sea shimmered with the last golden rays of sunlight. She could feel Wulf's gentle breath against her chest, a steady rhythm that tethered her to this moment. Her lips curved into a soft, bittersweet smile, but before she could move, a faint voice, like the rustling of ancient leaves, echoed in her mind.

"The frost may break, but the flame endures."

The words sent a shiver down her spine, though the wind was no longer bitter. It was warm now, carrying with it the faint scent of salt and pine, and she knew at once who had spoken. The Valkyrie. The same ethereal presence who had stood by her side in her darkest moments, who had watched her with eyes that saw too much and revealed too little.

Astrid closed her eyes, the weight of the words settling over her like a heavy cloak. The frost, the harsh trials, the losses, the betrayals would fade, she realized. But the flame, the hope, the resilience, the unity would burn on. She felt it in her core, a fire that could not be extinguished, not even by the gods themselves.

When she opened her eyes again, the sun had slipped beneath the horizon, painting the sky in hues of indigo and crimson. Stars began to pierce the growing darkness, tiny flames that mirrored the one within her. She pressed a kiss to Wulf's forehead, his small body warm against hers, and she whispered to him, "You are my flame now, little one. And I will protect you with everything I have."

Behind her, the village of Frostfjord stirred to life in the quiet evening. The faint glow of lanterns and hearths spilled through the windows of longhouses, their light flickering like stars fallen to earth. She turned back toward the village, her heart swelling with pride and determination. These were her people. They had faced unimaginable trials, and still, they stood.

Sigurd emerged from one of the houses, his broad shoulders silhouetted by the warm light. He raised a hand in greeting, and Astrid nodded in return, her steps steady as she approached. She passed familiar faces, each etched with the same resilience and hope that mirrored her own. Some smiled, others bowed their heads in silent respect. All of them were rebuilding, just as she was.

But as she walked, the Valkyrie's voice lingered in her mind, a reminder that the road ahead would not be easy. There would be challenges, dissent, perhaps even more sacrifices. Yet, for the first time in what felt like years, Astrid did not feel afraid.

The frost may break. The flame endures.

Astrid lifted her head, her stride confident as she entered the heart of the village. There was work to be done, alliances to strengthen, and a world to rebuild. And she would face it all, not as a warrior consumed by battle, but as a mother, a leader, and a protector of the flame that burned within her and her people.

Tomorrow would bring new trials, but tonight, beneath the watchful gaze of the stars, Astrid allowed herself a moment of peace. She cradled Wulf closer, her smile soft but unwavering, ready for whatever came next.

Because the flame endured. And so would she.

For Wulf. For Thorwulf. For all of them.

Printed in Dunstable, United Kingdom

66230443R00184